# The Migrant

## LUCIAN LEONTE

Versantae

www.lucianleonte.net

Published by Versantae
First edition August 2016
www.versantae.com

ISBN: 978-0-9801456-1-8

Printed in the USA
Also available as e-book

The Migrant

# 1

They wheeled down another car length to first in line before the customs scanner. Brett glanced in the interior viewer and flew his hand over his bristled hair, then looked at Susan, who turned her wary eyes at him. In the raised backseat, Tara kept gazing out the window, her fluffy dress hardly in contrast with the all-beige car interior. With the vehicle in the scanner released, he fixated on the nearing barrier as their car was wheeled in.

"You drove all the way from the FSA?" the live officer asked in a barely rhotic tongue.

The drive-in instructions petered out and his head and shoulders glittered over the dashboard, as he looked past Brett somewhere between the bounds of the graph.

"We flew into Baires and drove down," Brett answered, "but actually—"

"No visa comes up," the officer cut in. "Please check that it's casting with your IDs."

"Actually, officer, they couldn't process our application anywhere," Brett said, taut against the back of his seat. "We'd like to apply for immigration."

The officer refocused on him, then panned slowly over the inside of the car where Susan and Tara gazed his way.

"On the exceptional clause," Brett added.

The officer edged back. "Please switch back into auto-drive, sir. We don't issue visas at the border customs."

"It just can't be done from the outside—"

"I'm sorry, sir!"

"We only ask—"

"Sir! Switch back into auto or the grapple will damage your car. Now!"

"We only ask for someone to listen to us!" Brett roared back at the holograph, which went out, then he swung his head to search through the monolithic glass wall beside the vehicle lane. "Please! For one minute!"—he raised his hand, as the gateway's restraining buffers closed in.

The buffers paused at arm's length. He looked at Susan. She stayed solemn, breathing through her slightly open mouth. Beyond her reddened cheeks, the glass wall on the other side of the lane mirrored the same grays of concrete and stainless metal trusses.

"Daddy, we finished the road trip?" Tara asked. Then again.

The buffers retreated and folded back down into the pavement, and the car graph glittered up in the thick air.

"Switch into auto to go to the blinking port," the officer prompted. "Remain in the car."

They drove through the scan and around the end of the glass wall to between the two armored vehicles that flanked the blinking parking space. Stiff against the headrest, Brett clenched his jaws and felt his close shave down. Susan opened her window a palm wide. Fresh air gushed in over her hair bun, still chilly despite the late, sunny morning. She zipped up her top and lifted the window to just a sliver opening, as they both kept looking out the narrow frame of view between the building and the bulky front of the military vehicle. Hedging the immaculate lawn, the shrubs swayed in the relentless wind. A patrol car drove by, then lifted off and zoomed out to the skies beyond.

As she turned back in, he flicked his finger down the middle of his chest, to which she shook her head and unzipped her top back down, when the building doors slid open. Tall and clone-like, the two officers ushered them to the front room inside the building, scanned them for eyeset corneas, and stepped out to stand beside the open door.

In the otherwise bare room, Tara reached for the flag-printed physical cards on the side shelf. Susan brought her to stand next to her and Brett as hurried steps squeaked closer in the hallway. A third officer walked in, seemingly wearing an eyeset.

"Brett Falco and… Susan Connelly?" He stopped inside the door in his gray boots and uniform and glanced them up and down. "You're not about to perish. What's there to explain?"

"Officer." Brett crossed his hands below the waist. "We believe in merit and responsibility, and that's why, as a family, we're here today," he said to the officer's growing frown. "We share your roots, we're highly trained professionals, all fit, and eager to contribute to—"

"Hold it, hold it!"—the officer flipped his hand up. "All of that might be true, but there's nothing I can do for you," he said and halted at the jarring sound of Tara dropping the card holder. He turned to her frozen, big eyes, while Susan squatted in front of him to whisk the scattered cards off the floor and slip them back in the holder.

She smiled a "sorry" while rising and dusted her hand off on her cream jeans, with the girl glued to her thigh.

"All we ask for is that someone looks at our record," Brett said, and nipped the personal set off his wristband to hold it out. "On merit and an exceptional fit. In an exceptional country."

With an open-mouthed smirk, the officer turned his head between the two of them. "Look, I'm sorry you had to come all this way, but you do know our zero-immigration policy. Now—"

"There's the exceptional clause."

"That has been used… twice. All right?" he tipped his hand at him, saying. "Now, you're welcome to visit, but you need a visa from a physical consulate," he added, turning to leave. "Try Baires."

"We have," Susan said. "Couldn't even book an appointment."

He looked at her and walked out through the open door.

"Our great-grandparents just missed the boat, you know?" Brett called as the officer nodded at the two junior ranks and walked away. "Honestly officer! How often do you get people like us here?" He stepped into the doorway. "Like us!"

The officer didn't turn. "I'm not here to make a judgment."

"Then let us see someone who does, please! That's all we ask!"

He stopped and turned halfway, but held his words. Next to Brett, Susan thinned her lips in another smile, the plastic holder in one hand and Tara toying with a tricolored card on her other side. Flanking them, the two ranks looked at him too.

"Just for the chance to apply, officer," she said.

He walked on. "Keep your IDs on. I'll check back with you."

He returned after a long twenty minutes. He strode over the large national emblem on the hallway floor and to the same spot inside the room and exhaled curt. "You." He pointed his finger at Brett, ever reading off his eyeset. "You will surrender the handgun in the car and pick it up from here upon leaving. You have to register every one of your monetary assets," he added, switching his finger between them both, then refocused on them. "You have one week on a cross-border worker pass. There's a Foreign Office presence in Ayland, in case you want to spend your time on that." He raised his finger to hold Brett off. "That's one week. Be back by twelve noon next Friday when your registration keys expire, or you'll be picked up." He nodded to the officer who'd come to his side and stepped back. "Now, they'll match your bios and set your keys. Welcome to the Commons."

———

With the customs compound shrinking in the rear viewer, Brett sped up. He gulped half of his water bottle then gripped the steering wheel with both hands and rammed his back against the seat. "Yooowzaaa!"

Susan yahooed along and swiveled her seat to Tara to tickle her into the long laughter that followed. She turned forward again and, as they wound down, untied her hair and waved it loose over her shoulders. "Missed the boat…"

They burst anew, Brett turning his glee between her and the road. "Told you babe, the way to do it."

"Yah. Buffing your car in some bad-luck-stricken place in the middle of nowhere." She looked out. "Gosh, that Tencun was scary. We're so flying on the way back."

"We're not flying anywhere back," he spelled out. "We're here Suse. We're in!"

"You're unbelievable."

He stretched his arm back to Tara for another tickle. "And you're officially my best investment." He grinned, then shrugged at Susan's scolding look. "Did she drop it by herself?"

"Yes."

"Gee…"

The freeway felt silky smooth and, with the shifting tailwind, it made for a noiseless drive. The side hedge flowed by, trimmed to a uniform, endless channel, bowing wide through the nearly flat steppe. Only the occasional crossing flyers reminded them that they were moving fast.

He peeked with her at the hillock out her window as the

sunlight beamed off the rounded glass structure.

"Is that one of those buildings? Gosh, I still can't believe it." She turned to him. "How old were you on that trip with your parents?"

"Like eight."

"Amazing," she murmured into the window. "Thirty years later and what a world."

He kept to the empty lane ahead. "It was already screwed up good."

The auto-drive flashed on as available. He called it up, but the car asked for the road code instead.

"Daddy, what is screwed?" Tara said.

Susan swiveled around to her and turned the plush duck's imaging on to cast a story.

He glanced in the viewer as the child lay lower in the caving seat, then at Susan as she turned forward. "She's growing on me this little girl," he muttered.

She paused, before settling in her seat. "She better."

He unzipped his sweater and pulled it down his shoulders, swapping hands on the steering wheel, to which the car weaved outside the lane. He unzipped his padded vest too, while she queried her set for the road code on the new key.

Once he could let go of the wheel, he removed the sweater and leaned sideways to jolt the vest down his arms. "Did you see that guy's face when he had me unload it?"

She heaved to help him dislodge the vest from between his back and the seat. "I thought they'd make more of a fuss."

"Nah. They know what's out there." He felt the strips of padding all around its inside, pushed the two jutting, shiny bars back into their strips and thumbed them sealed. He then heaved the vest to below the rear seats and massaged his shoulders, watching the first car show up ahead. "First thing tomorrow, I'll rent a safe box."

"Don't we wait to see what they say?"

He frowned over. "Suse—"

"Shh. She fell asleep."

He raised the speed to yellow and put his sweater back on, then checked out the nearing car to the whizzing of the motors now coming through. "We get going early."

"Yup. I'm crashing early anyway."

He tugged the stubborn sweater down his back. "Shall we share a suite?"

"Uhh... let's wait a bit."

"No, it's just that it's more expensive here."

She glanced at him as he struggled. "Here, let me do it"—she reached over, but he sat back.

"It's fine."

The barren land rumpled into a cluster of low hills and the traffic picked up some, as the first urban sight peeked over the shallow ridges. A dozen mini-zeps sailed about. Scattered with the patches of shrubs, the glass claddings sparkled in the low northerly sun behind the car, then changed into flimsy shapes and frames against it as the freeway weaved wide around the hillside. A couple of nearer buildings passed by unassuming, in smooth, wind-daring bodies of restrained styling and details, and then a last top twinkled off in the rear viewer as the hills morphed back into the frigid steppe.

He slid his seat back and stretched out. Head hanging over her shoulder, Susan snored lightly. He reclined her seat, then gulped more water and poured some in his cupped palm to wet his face. A ball of tumbleweed rolled across into the side hedge and the wind hissed up. The car showed the charge at a quarter-full and enough to get to Ayland, just over an hour away.

———

The quince ale frothy on his lips, Clarens let the pint down and kept his eyes on the scene across the barroom. The reeling man stumbled on another chair and dived. He wobbled on his feet while being helped to rise, red-faced atop his rather sharp business wear.

"Didn't he get in at the same time we did?"

Lynden and his two other colleagues turned their heads one by one to the scene. "Yes he did…"

"That's one fast undoing," Clarens said, watching the man being walked to the front doors, when their new colleague walked in.

"So far," Lynden said to the mean guffaws going off, which couldn't make the locale any noisier.

The newcomer made it through. "Hey, got the message late. Congrats Clarens!"

"Just shut up and get your beer," one colleague quipped.

"What message?" Clarens said and turned to Lynden.

Lynden peeked away and exhaled. "Guy, how many more wins do you need before we throw you a party?"

"Yeah! Go Clarens!"

Amid the cheers, Lynden downed a third of his beer then raised the stein high in the air and stood on his stool's footrests. Looking over the barroom, he yelled three times louder. "If you think this place is roaring, wait till all our lawyers come home!"

"Hahaha!"

He sat back down, his brawny chest quaking under the fine jersey, and landed a hard pat on Clarens's back as he leaned close. "Guy, you're brilliant, shine on. These dudes would take any chance to get wasted anyway." As Clarens dimpled, he winked and drank up with him, then rolled his lips in and out with a tut. "By the way, you *are* coming to the Dome next month. Can't miss this year"—he stuck his finger out.

"Oh, your ten-year anniversary…"

"Hey, Gwyn made friends with this hot legs at skiing last week—"

"Lyn! I'm coming. For you guys."

The new drinks arrived just as the sober voice called to

Clarens from behind. On his last step through the standing crowd, Talbot brought his large hand forward and spared a smile. "Congratulations!"

"Hi Tal!" He shook his hand. "Not a big deal, really."

"Listen, I want to hear about it," Tal said, his thick brows ever stuck in a frown. "Come by my office on Tuesday. Three o'clock?" He released Clarens's hand and looked at Lynden, who rushed to sip from his full-headed lager. "Lynden! Ever holding on to your jug."

"Hi Tal." Lynden wiped the foam off the tip of his nose. "I thought it was a job requirement."

"Haha! I don't do hops. Should've learned that by now," Tal said, and patted Clarens. "I'm taking a table, have some work to do." He then turned and shook more hands left and right as he walked away, his balding head a palm above all others.

Lynden watched him go. "The ultimate loner, isn't he? You go out downtown, you see Talbot sitting with his bourbon and pricking that huge finger through his stats," he griped, just loud enough. "He'd fire me tomorrow if it weren't for you."

"Come on." Clarens brought his glass to his mouth and eased a smile. "There's Gwyn's father too."

Lynden chortled, his face ruddy again below his back-combed, light-brown hair. He knocked Clarens's pint to a spill, then held his stein out and cheered for him one more time with everyone in the group. Clarens dropped his head and complied to raise his pint too. He rolled his eyes high through the roaring as he drank, his gaze sweeping the period ceiling's flat, angular soffits all the way to the clerestory straight above. Outside, lights sparkled off the higher glass cladding that spanned over the building. Beyond the shell, the top of the high-rise dipped into the late sunrays ablaze.

"Clarens?"

He lowered his head. "Heslin..."

9

"Not hard to spot you in here!" she cheered. The rich pink lipstick around her beaming smile and the azure eyes pinning the fair oval of her face removed her from the clatter around. The thistle jacket didn't help either.

"I bet." He recovered and put a foot down to rise for the light hug. "How are you?"

"I'm great! Hi there, Lynden."

Just turning from another round of laughs, Lynden jerked his head back. "Heslin! As sizzling as ever."

She laughed. "Well, so what's happening? I'm walking in and you people seem all too happy."

He wried his face and poked his thumb at Clarens. "Won big again." As Clarens dismissed it, he shuffled sprightly on his stool and fixated Heslin while gesturing with both hands. "Guy cheats on wife. Wife slams car into his, injures both him and girlfriend. Wife walks, with kids and assets. Guy's stuck in wheelchair for good, girlfriend's stuck with homecare bills."

"Wow! That's a vintage movie."

"That's what I'm saying!" Through the laughs, he sipped and stuck his hand out. "And there's Clarens in front of the jury," he went on to mimic him. "Looks up the walls, holds two fingers on his chin… and talks about action and reaction in a closed system." He shrugged and flipped his palm up. "I mean, if I were that wife I'd have freaked out!" he burst, and so did Heslin again. As Clarens held off his smile and shook his head, he threw his arm around his shoulders. "This guy's a genius!"

"All right, and Lyn's way too sober right now."

"Well"—Heslin held two fingers on her chin and looked up. "A genius would never see the need for compliments and such pampering," she mused, and glimpsed at Clarens. "I'm with Lynden." She fluttered her blond curls around as they laughed and raised her hand toward the front doors, then swung back. "Got to go, girls night out," she said, and opened her arms to Clarens. "Anyway, congratulations!"

He leaned over for the bye hug, her dry lavender scent coming through.

She took her arms to Lynden and turned away, but paused to smile at Clarens over her shoulder. "We should catch up sometime. I'd like to hear who cheated and who slammed who really."

He chuckled, idling his hand over his drink on the counter. "Sure. I might just share that information."

"Excellent. Lunch? Tuesday?"

"Uhh... yes. Lunch Tuesday."

She beamed one last time, then, as striking they had come, her curls vanished into the crowd.

Lynden turned to the bar counter too. "Looks like someone's not coming alone to the Dome after all," he said and drank.

Clarens lifted his pint and slanted his head at him, slowly.

"Guy, it's Friday night! It's a happening place!"

He rolled his lips in with the tart flavor. "I didn't know you can actually cheat."

Loud and stirred, two younger colleagues broke through. "Hey Clarens, weren't they going when she slammed into them?"

More people tuned in as Clarens rose to the chat. He soon found himself inside the buoyant bunch, taking questions and rubbing shoulders with them. He smiled and blanked at the younger, unfamiliar faces, as he did at the legal slang and gibes being tossed around, but let himself into the course of the blather nonetheless.

When he returned to the bar his seat was taken, but Lynden was still there, turned to his own, rowdy conversation, his undershirt rucking over his lower back as he bowed with the guffaws. He reached for his lager, when he saw Clarens and swiveled around.

"Dude, I didn't mean for you to be a role model there."

"I hope not," Clarens said. "Imagine the poor kids."

Lynden choked, spilling his beer. "What, now you're funny too?"

"Perhaps." Looking up the back bar, Clarens slipped his hands in his pockets. "Things have a tendency to happen all at the same time."

Lynden stared at him. "Nah, you're my guy."

He finished his drink while Clarens continued panning the encapsulated exhibits.

"Hey, Lyn, what do you think of Heslin? I mean, really."

Burping under his breath, Lynden knocked his stein down. "You know I always thought she's a super girl. With a bit of pampering." As Clarens hummed, he graphed up his ringset in his palm. "And it's beyond me how you two can't make it work," he added, then mocked a deep frown and drawled. "Ale, or bour-baaaun?"

# 2

With his back against the elevator's fabric lining, Clarens watched the doors open and then the warning lights flash anew. He thrust forward through the closing doors and walked out onto the plush office floor.

From inside the redwood enclave, the receptionist glanced over and kept working his fingers through the wide graph below. "Lunch better downtown?"

Clarens inhaled and slipped his hand over his flat abdomen. "No question." He smiled back, then checked his set. "So, to whom do I owe this?"

"Uhh... You'll just have to see them. Since you take interesting cases only."

He left and walked down the humming aisle to his office, where he left the door open and stepped to the window. The sun had cleared the corner of the neighboring high-rise, but he overrode the presets and turned the glazing tint lighter. He stared out over the shell towards the open-air boulevard. A block back in under the shell's glass cladding, the restaurant frontage peeked through at the base of the footer building. A wisp of air touched his cheek with the gust hurling a palm outside. He turned around and sat, then brought up his graph over the silken desk. As he read through the appointment briefing, new mail arrived, from Heslin. "Could do dinner too, if necessary." He smiled and typed in. "Seems necessary. Saturday?"

He rotated his chair slowly toward the side wall. The brighter light made for crisp lines along the projecting Doric pillars. Overlapping the last pillar, the edge of the open door looked especially sharp, like a white-laser frame with a hollow inside, except for the floating knob, which shone like a second sun within its own domain, when his appointment showed up beside it.

The young woman held the dressed-up little girl's hand close, her lips pinched in a smile, as their male companion stopped in the doorway behind them. They looked staged.

Clarens rose as the receptionist disappeared and brought his hand forth. "Please come in. I'm Clarens Mann." Through the introduction, he bent to greet the child also, to which she only lowered her eyes under her bangs and kept close to her mother's beige trousers. He stepped back around the desk to his chair. "So. You like our wind chill better."

They chuckled short, then Brett waited for Susan to settle Tara on her lap, his back straight in his chair. His close shave and parted black hair looked impeccable. "Thank you for seeing us in person on such short notice," he said, with hardly a trace of accent. "No one would even do immigration, so thank you"—he nodded again, his wide eyes just as cogent, only reddened around the lids a little.

"Sure. You should know, however, that we only had one case before, and that was within our practice of civil law," Clarens said, toggling between the two of them, then peered at the appointment briefing. "But what did they tell you at the Foreign Office exactly?"

Brett and Susan looked at each other, with Brett speaking on. "Not much. They were polite, but dismissed us right off." He flexed his hands open and stilled. "We know all this might seem unusual but, it shouldn't. We're a most eligible family and we want to be part of the best system on earth. We're big believers. And we're your own, you guys"—he passed a smile—"and like… left out in that populist place the Alliance has become, which you don't need me to tell you about, but we did take a public stand for the Rights with Responsibilities charter, against the tax vote, against the faith vote, against the…"

His brows creased slowly as his steady voice carried on. Clarens watched him quiet, only nudging his chin up and down every now and then. He, too, glanced at Susan when Brett turned his head to her again, with a renewed statement. Above the open neck of her shirt, her hair weaved sheen dark into a low bun, just as classic smart. From below, the girl's big hazel eyes kept fixating him.

They turned back to him at the same time, Brett's hand still out. "We pretty much made you a declaration of love and we're not even given a chance." He smiled, briefly. "I mean, yes, it's the law. But if we look at the principles of this exceptional affinity clause, we meet every one of them."

Clarens sat back. "You do realize there are millions of people out there who could make this claim."

"And how many come over all the way, burning bridges behind? How many like us?"

Through the poised silence, he raised his gaze to the wall behind them. "What you're up against is that, as you know, the cornerstone of our Constitution is the right to self-preservation," he said and looked back down, as the girl stretched her neck around under her mother's chin to examine the blank wall too. "You may visit, trade, get help, but you may not plant yourself in." He shrugged and looked at Brett.

"That's just how they said it," Susan cut in on a soft voice.

"What else did they say? Anything specific?"

"Uhh… No." Her eyes met with Brett's. "Just at the end, we crossed words a bit with that older gentleman there and he said some wronging would always occur…"

"With an incongruous part in a contained system," Brett spelled out to complete the sentence, and shook his head. "We're not from the Tan-tans, for god's sake."

Clarens dismissed it too and stilled, just like the three blurry faces now in the corner of his eye. With the door closed and out of the way the end pillar looked as crisp as the others, especially since the sun had shifted west, nearly over the boulevard tip of the shell. He blinked and looked higher up the side wall as the girl appeared to turn her face and follow his line of sight again. He glanced at her.

"Sorry, she's a watcher," Susan said, and reseated Tara on her lap, while the girl remained arrested by the fishing skiff lithographs hanging farther aside. "Big on water stuff. We're good now."

"Should that matter, by the way?" Brett asked Clarens. "You know, that we're a family and all."

"Not in the Commons," Clarens smiled, saying, "unless it was a reunion." He recomposed and swiveled back to his graph. "The only thing we could try is to petition our senator. He could make a recommendation to the Foreign Office, who could work with the judiciary to make a judgment. Unless they call it an ASG."

"An ASG…"

"An act of self-gratification, which is a misdemeanor for a public official. I know, ironic," he added as Brett gasped a smile, and then he faced them both. "Chances are this will be an expensive waste of your time, even for a visa extension. I'm sorry to be so frank."

"We appreciate it," Brett nodded. "We want to do it." He snipped a set off his wristband and pushed the flat bead across the desk. "Everything's in here, with some personal stuff if it helps."

"Anything supportive, but time's short," Clarens said, tapping his hands on his armrests.

He stepped with them to the door, where Brett turned for the handshake and asked for a bank recommendation. A physical bank.

"I do know of one, in fact. Sargent Bank, on the west side

of the shell."

He smiled again and let them leave first, taken over by his assistant. However understated, their immaculate wear drew his second glance, before he turned to walk the opposite way down the aisle.

A moment later, Lynden caught up with him from behind. "Hey, who was that? Some actress or something?"

"Nooo…" Clarens kept walking. "Office day?"

"Yeah, some crap. Swimming tonight? Super," Lynden said, straying to a different aisle, and pivoted around to walk backward. "How was lunch?" He grinned, then, as Clarens cast a slight smirk, he raised his hand above the floor's islands and humming.

The rose-mallow oval was empty, with just the lighting bow flashing by in the mirrored water surface in the middle. A few white petals dotted the rest area's benches and pavement around the mini pond's retaining brim.

Past the second meeting room, Talbot's office door stayed a sliver open. Clarens knocked once and entered.

At his desk, Talbot frowned at his graph a moment longer, then raised his head. "Clarens!" He felt his back as he rose to pick up his café takeout and trudged around the desk with it to the side table.

Clarens turned to the window bounding the curved side of the room. "I never knew you could see Mount Palachi from here."

Talbot shut the door. "What, you want my office now?" He let him chuckle and returned to his chair, then flicked his hand at the plush armchairs in front of the desk for him to sit too. "Listen. Good work on that last case, but I'm going to save us time here." He shrank his graph to the side of the desk and cleared his throat. "I've known you for… over eight years now. You're my best attorney, people respect you, they respected your father. Isn't it time we move higher from here?"

Clarens swayed his head. "Tal, you know…"

"I know, you don't want to manage people and all that, but hey, there's your challenge. And this one keeps on going."

"I know, but I'm not sure I'd even be able to do it. You know," he smiled to say, "once they figured it was all about my graying hair."

"Well, I'll never let that secret out." Talbot spared a smile under his piercing brown eyes, then leaned forward and lowered his voice a notch. "But frankly, do you want to rub your mind against affidavits and subpoenas for the rest of your life?" He leaned back and swiveled his chair sideways to make room for crossing his legs. Past the edge of the desk, his foot tipped large up in the air. "We're growing. I need to move to the real estate and leave the civil to you and Fred. Won't step over you." To Clarens looking back at him, he bobbed his head. "Think how far this could go, how much could be made."

"That shouldn't be the issue."

"Your choice. But even philosophically, isn't there the motivation to leave a stake behind? And I won't go there, though I will leave you with this…" He brought his elbows to the armrests and steepled his fingers as he looked out the window, a new frown shading his face. "If I learned anything, it's that life gives if you want to take and takes away if you don't." He turned to him. "This is an opportunity. I can't keep it open-ended. Not even for you, Clarens."

Clarens sighed and looked out, in turn. He anchored his gaze on the flat side of the adjacent high-rise, against the fast moving, dispersing clouds. "I'm grateful to be here, Tal. I don't see myself working anywhere else. It's just that..." He switched back to him. "Let me sort out a few things first. I have three cases, one just in."

"How long would it take?"

"I don't know, a month."

"You can have a month."

"But… I'm not saying anything."

"You're not saying anything."

Talbot uncrossed his legs and thumped his feet on the floor. "What's the new case?" He heaved and braced his hands on his knees to rise, then joined him and lumbered toward the door as he listened to the case details. He slowed to a stop. "So what are you thinking?"

"Petition the senator. Exceptional affinity."

He let his head down, brows higher.

"I know. They're keen," Clarens shrugged. "And it's kind of interesting."

Feeling his lower back, Talbot clenched his teeth wide and groaned. "Who said sex was good for everything?" As Clarens snorted a smirk, he patted him on the shoulder and moved on. "I'd cross-check everything. Can they pay?"

"Apparently that's not an issue."

"We should charge times one point five. We put our name on the line." He stopped beside the door. "You mind that?"

Clarens wavered. "No…" Hand on the doorknob, he looked at him and eased a smile. "Did you just step over me?"

"Ha!" Talbot brightened up and pointed to his feet. "Can you blame me?"

---

Peeping through the foot-wide opening, Brett reached one more time inside the safe deposit box to push the black handbag all the way back. He closed the door and watched the pinhead light change to red with the barely audible click, and then the door number brighten up. Fifty-two. He wedged his fingertips into the fine joint between the flush doors but couldn't claw onto any edge. He turned and checked his newly authenticated Commons visitor account while walking back to the bank lobby, which was as quiet. Beyond, a few shadows moved through the frozen water tails and rounded stones of the riverbed-styled feature wall. At the small courtesy counter, the attendant looked up as he stepped closer.

"Boy, this exchange rate really hurts," he quipped, to her forced smile. "One other question," he added and pointed to the outside, then at the mapping in his palm. "Which one's the larger jewelry outlet in here?"

"In Jefferson? Uhh..." She craned her head to stare at the pulsating locations and blushed slightly as she ran her hair back around her ear with two fingers.

He smiled. "I love your staffed outlets, you may say."

"Sorry? Oh!" She giggled and switched her finger to the graph. "I know these two. This one's a bit high-end, though."


Breezeless and dry, the air outdoors was no different from inside, other than for the light street clatter rolling in wide echoes between the back-set buildings. Much alike the couple of pedestrian levels that cascaded down as building-heeding canopies and shot over in high, slender passageways to the other side of the street every here and there. He paused his eyeset map and stopped to look straight up. Faraway, the glass-clad ceiling was still glittering in full sunlight. He smiled and closed his eyes for a few long seconds.

He brought his sight down and moved on, then crossed to the fast belt in the middle of the street and stood behind the side row of readers. Left and right, the buildings' ground stories slid by in mostly the same ochre stone and flush glass panes, while the occasional ads for wellness programs and energy investments glistened over in matching tones. He couldn't miss the jewelry outlet, though. The gems sparkled in the narrow, story-high hologram and then real exhibits staged the front window right there at the sidewalk, brazen behind the mere millimeters of glazing. He hissed under his breath and walked in.

The attendant soon broke away from the other clients and came forward, crisp in his linen overshirt. "Is this for an appointment, sir?"

Brett glanced around. "Actually, do you purchase physical here?"

"You mean scrap? No, we don't, I'm afraid."

"No, bars."

The attendant took a little longer. "No sir, I'm sorry, we don't." He then confirmed that the larger outlet for marked jewelry was in Friedman shell, across the boulevard.

Walking away, Brett blinked at the floor to relay his set back to his eyes, when the attendant added.

"Are you visiting sir?"

"Oh, this? It's just mapping…"

The attendant smiled, a little long again. "You could try the pawn stores. There's one at the south end."

Back on the fast belt, Brett swapped the several segments between the crossing streets until he reached the south tip of the shell. He hopped onto the long escalator that zoomed down to the lower street. It looked cozier here under the prevailing artificial lights and with the shell's echoes fading behind. He only spotted the store at the second pass. Filling the narrow gap between a snack station and a gateway to the parking garage, it looked indistinct, including its small, textual display: "Vit's Collectibles." Once he passed the entry threshold, the fruity scent spurt an unpretentious welcome, while the sound of a sports broadcast came through from somewhere in the rear. He stepped that way between the freestanding showcases and lumps of wood furniture, when a muffled greeting came through from aside.

Showing his head above a showcase, the man held his jewelry glasses lower down his nose and pasted on a smile.

"Sorry, I thought someone was back there," Brett said, changing direction.

21

The man ducked again. "No, I just watch the checkered flag."

"Car racing?"

"Yes.

"Love racing."

He glanced over as Brett stopped before the case. "Where are you from?"

"The FSA."

"Ah, the motherland!" He stood up and grinned, which made his cheeks look even fuller between his ashen hair locks. "I'm Vitaly. What can I do for you?"

"Actually," Brett said, passing his hand at Vitaly's glasses, "you buy jewelry, right?"

"You foreigners... Depends. What do you have?"

"Platinum. In a bar." At Vitaly's mute look, he held his thumb and index a few centimeters apart, then reached inside his jacket for the bar and tweezed it out of its plastic sleeve.

Vitaly picked it slowly from his hand and flipped it over then pushed his glasses back up his nose to examine the commemorative marking. "2134-2209. Seventy-five years of prosperity," he mumbled.

"It's the national mint. Or I have it uni-denominated."

"No, this would be your better bet. In case you people split again," he chuckled. "No offense," he added quickly and switched back to the white metal. "Let's see, if this was three hundred pure, I could do..." Mumbling on, he beamed up his set and began punching his puffy fingers through the crowded graph. "Four thousand two hundred and eighty," he said loud, and turned to Brett.

"*Four* thousand?"

"We don't do bullion much"—he shrugged and clacked the bar onto the glass top. "And anything over a hundred grams needs registration and all that." As Brett fixated on the bar, he swayed to his felt work mat. "Four point three tops. You can buy it back within a day, if you want to ask around," he muttered over the minute disassembled parts.

To Brett's nod, he rose again and walked to the back of the store. His short, plump figure, the orange shirt and matching mini-clip in his dangling neck-long hair, they all looked at home among the framed pictures, trinkets, and gadgets lining the wall shelves. He returned with the small assaying device and placed it in front of him on the case top, then carefully clamped the bar in and stoop over to watch the readings. "Splendid."

Brett turned to his set and watched the transaction amount populate his new account, when the broadcast commentary livened up. He walked after Vitaly, who rushed around the armoires at the rear of the store to the vivid display. The race was idle, as several cars seemed to have been terminally damaged in a crash that was being reconstructed and analyzed.

"What do you expect?"—Vitaly threw his hand at the flying debris in the graph. "They take a kid from a completely different motor class, completely different racing school, completely different mentality."

To Brett's good-bye, he held his hand up, cheeks merry with his smile once again.

Out of the store, Brett checked again on his cleared balance tag and then flicked to the portfolio alert beside it. The Great Concord ten-year notes were off by two hundred basis points and the growth index had plunged five percent on the day. The broad markets were mixed or slightly lower and, except for the new detonation in Vritain and the larger drop of the uni, the news was ordinary.

"Boyz, boyz..." He soured his lips, then palmed the graph and walked into the snack station. The dispensers steamed of fresh bakery and hearty flavors from the orders of the handful of shoppers down the arcade. He cued his set and called Susan as he strolled from one bay to another. "Hey, I got the money... Yup, just paid that too. Shall we eat out tonight?... Awesome." He canceled the flashing lasagna order and walked to the beverages aisle instead. The beer rack listed the most popular brands, with the indigenous ones mixed in. Ten minutes of fine reading later, he settled for a pack of double-pilsner.

The escalator accelerated through the wide opening in the street floor, back to the main level, with the changing views revealing the true scale of the shell. The stony buildings huddled tight together down the small near street, under the stories-high envelope of metal rods and glass that webbed over them until out of sight. Beyond the corniced rooftops, two high-rises thrust through it and higher to the sky. Most buildings jutted only a few stories above the shell and others stayed entirely under it, as hanging towers or stumps for the overgrowing, supple cover, which touched down along the glimpsed outside boulevard. All climatized and staged with people and vehicles going their ways, and peculiar trees and slivers of burgundy awnings, it was a real-size architectural gallery.

From the whirring fast belt, he swept over the ritzy frontage back toward the main street. A flower outlet zoomed by on the upper level. He walked off at the belts' crossing and wandered over. Beside the outlet's display, he slowed to look at the real bouquets inside the small window as the vendor's smiley face shined up.

"It's for someone in the business, so something different perhaps," he told her once inside the showroom.

He was presented with a miniature, pink rosebush. The clear pot balanced on a single point of its half-oval weighty base, while the flat top was entirely closed off, other than the orifice for the stem. The glass was voltaic and the pot was self-conditioning through a hardly visible condenser coil, while the soil inside was transparent too in the finely granular material. Roots to petals, the engineered plant was entirely exposed. "It should stay like this for years," the vendor said. "Blooms every month."

Back on the escalator, he laid the plant's carry case over the beer pack in one bag and pinged the car. It looked like he could use the next garage hub, around the street corner. Three levels under, he let the car roll toward the hoister, but then steered to the empty self-drive exit instead, and through the outbound tunnels to the open air and the expressway thereafter. He blinked off his eyeset's corneas and joggled them in his palm, then tossed them in the console. He turned up the vintage riff and grasped the steering wheel again as he joined the fast flow northwest, into the enduring sun.

# 3

With Tara directing a puppet show in his lap, Brett looked at Susan as she returned to the suite's main room.

"They still don't know," she said.

"They still don't know? It's Thursday two p.m.!"

"Don't they know that?"—she stared back. "Just don't have me call next time."

She sat on the bed and stretched her gown down. He grabbed the spirited dolls and laid them back on the sofa as he rose, to Tara's surprise, then grasped his neck and ambled down the hallway.

"Mommy, can I play by myself?" she upped her feeble tone on the second try, which pulled Susan out of her thoughts.

"Yes, sweetheart, just for a bit."

"But you said it's not good to play by myself."

"Only at the crèche, sweetie," Susan said, then, as Brett turned around, she picked her up in her arms and silenced the dolls. "Huggy hug. We'll make up for a lot of hugs. Two years' worth of hugs…"

He ambled back while she pivoted slowly in place with the mellowed child over her shoulder. She scowled at him on another circle turn. He returned to measuring his steps toward the window.

"Daddy, are we going on a road trip?"

He looked out, before turning. "No Tara. We're not going on any road trip."

Twenty minutes later, Susan took a call in Tara's bedroom. Through the open door, he watched her pause from stacking clothes.

"Oh that's wonderful!" he heard her say, and sprang from the sofa to step closer. "We will... That shouldn't be an issue," she added, then came out, beaming. "We've got the extension!"

He snapped her off her feet for a roaring spin. He let her down to fix her gown as they tapered their jubilation. "How long?"

"One month. We need to go pick up the new keys. They're getting them now."

"Perfect!" He waited for her to hug Tara over the dolls' new stage on the bed corner.

"Oh, yeah, there's this additional fee."

"How much?"

"Twenty-four hundred."

"What? Just like that?"

She glanced over on her way to the closet. "What, we won't pay?"

"Freakin' lawyers—"

"Brett..." She stepped inside the closet. "I thought you liked him."

He braced his hands on his waist, shaking his head, then muttered the figure again under his breath. "You know, I should check out the other pawn store. Can you just go by yourself?"

She craned her head back out and stilled, hair stuck in the sweater and masking her cheeks. "What if they need you?"

"For what, to hand me a tiny pin?"

She went back in the closet. "This is petty."

"How is it petty? I need to sell another bar, don't I?" He turned in the hallway. "Take the car if you want."

She rushed by.

He exhaled and walked slowly after her to the bathroom. He rested his hand high on the door frame and looked at her slanting in the mirror to brush her hair. "I'm coming, all right?" He shrugged and glanced away. "You know me, I hate waste. I got thrown off."

"Waste? You said we'd do anything it takes."

"Wrong word"—he rolled his eyes. "But we don't own the gold mine, do we? I mean, of all people, I thought you'd appreciate keeping the tabs here."

She stopped brushing and switched to him. "That was a long time ago, Brett."

"I know, I'm sorry."

She gathered the hairs inside the sink in small, circular runs with her finger. "You know, that's not even the point." She dropped the knot in the wall aperture and turned to him, circling her finger between them. "The point is that we still come second. Just like you couldn't get over a losing trade on Christmas Eve, just like you conferenced with your clients every day in Praia, just like you fretted about your speeding ticket on our first anniversary date in three years—"

"Theeere it is." He swept over the ceiling again.

She held her words as Tara showed up in the doorway, a doll in one hand and holding her crotch restless with the other hand. She picked her up and whispered the other way to his face. "You so went on and on about how things would be different here. And a week into it you let me go it alone because of some stupid fee?" she said, brows creasing up above her gleaming jade eyes.

Shortly, she cheered by out of the bathroom with Tara. "And we can get fresh fruits too!" she said to the hopping girl, then changed course to reach for the rosebush pot on the side table, turned to him, and pressed it against his abdomen. "And here. Regift it to me when you're ready to keep promises."

As she let go of it, he scrambled to catch the falling pot,

which did hit the edge of the table. He exhaled. "Go ahead, be yourself."

She didn't look back and just took Tara to her bedroom, where she rushed to dress her up.

He turned his frown out the window, running his finger slowly around the rim of the pot in his hand. He paused to feel the small nick over, then the rim back around, before he walked out the suite door.

———

Clarens jogged his chair back to reach for the satchel next to the leg of the desk. The white case was in there, under the pleated sweater. He rolled his chair back to the desk slowly to continue reading.

The receptionist showed up in the corner of the graph. "Ms. Connelly is here and she's asking if you're in and if she can have a word."

Clarens kept to his work. "Did you give them their registrations?"

"Actually, can she pick up his too? Since they're married. I'm still waiting for that cross-check, though."

He brought his hands behind his neck and let his air out of his bulging cheeks. "Days would be too boring otherwise," he muttered, to the receptionist's chuckling. "Just take an affidavit. And yes, she can have a word."

He reached for the water bottle and stepped to the window. He leaned close and rested his head against the glass to sight the far view to the left, inching backward until he pricked his back on the bronze fern sculpture in the room's corner. He flattened his cheek against the glass once more. The mountain chain emerged, only beginning to climb into the opposite frame of the window. He sipped again, when the receptionist knocked on the open door and let Susan and her daughter in.

"Hi, Mr. Mann," Susan came forward saying as Clarens

stepped off the rattling sculpture base. "I just wanted to thank you in person for the visas."

"Sure, you're welcome"—he returned the smile. "As I said, this was the easy part."

"Still, we're so grateful." She looked down at the floor and hesitated, to which he pointed to the chairs and sat too. "And also," she resumed, her hands together in her lap, "I wanted to reiterate how much Brett and I appreciate you taking our case. Staying here would be like… a cherished dream come true."

"Well, we always do our best," he said, while she let the girl climb quiet from her own chair to her lap instead. "But, if you don't mind me asking, do you have an alternate plan?"

"No. I mean, nothing comes close. We'd rather go back, although…" She slowed her words. "I don't know." She looked aside, her neckline fair between the tightly clipped hair and the auburn, collarless sweater.

He broke the silence and reached for his satchel. "I've never been to the FSA. Is it difficult over there?"

"For us it is. We're more like the self-made kind and feel sort of… uprooted." She met his eyes and smiled. "Which is strange because when I'd go riding on Sundays, I'd feel that it was where I totally belong."

"Riding?"

"Horseback riding. At this ranch up in Kewan. Low hills overlooking the crops, beautiful setting," she added, waving her hand along the desk, as he stilled with the bag in his hand. "Oh, silly me, I'm keeping you."

"No, it's interesting. Tell me more on the way," he said, and rose along with her. "So, is this far from the city?"

"About an hour on the back roads. Unless Brett's driving," she smiled over the shoulder, and carried the eye-rubbing girl out the door.

Once she grabbed her tote from inside the reception enclave, she continued from where she'd left off, and then in a lower voice in the elevator, as eyes turned at her foreign references and aura.

Downstairs, the building lobby bustled with people crossing the floor. They stepped away from the elevators core and to the less animated area beside the exit to the garage hub.

"One trip I'll have to do sometime," he said as she pulled the stroller stick out of her tote.

"Hope we'll still be around," she quipped, "'cause you'll need a few tips."

He chuckled. "I hope so too." He moved on, pointing to the garage.

She clicked the featherweight stroller into bright off-whites and reds. "Actually…" She heaved the girl in, a pack of pears slipping out of the tilting tote. "We're taking a taxi."

"Ah, which way?"—he halted, as she crouched to slip the pears back in.

"We're in the northwest, off that boulevard…"

"Hume?"

"Yes!"

"Well, I'm passing by there."

She shoved the tote under the stroller seat and smiled. "That's too kind, really, but we'll take a taxi," she said, and checked on her daughter, who had already sunk her cheek into the side air-pad. She looked back at him. "Well…"


The thick floor slabs dropped by quietly through the hoistway then the stream of cars stayed just as steady through the merging tunnels. Clarens glanced out here and there at the flashing junctions, otherwise keeping his head down over his work. When he slid his seat a tad farther back he checked over his shoulder and smiled at Susan in the backseat. Apart from that, the drive remained silent all the way to daylight.

"Is this peak hour?" Susan said.

He raised his head to look out the windshield. "Yes. A little heavier today."

"Amazing…"

"Why is that?"

"Don't know. I'm used to things flying at me and over."

He chuckled quietly at the interior viewer. "Did you commute to work?"

"Every day. Sometimes I'd do the supplies too."

"Ah." He glanced back. "I'm sorry, what was it that you did?"

"I owned my own flower outlet. Downtown."

"Right. Impressive."

"Would that count? For the petition."

"Perhaps," he pondered, over another mail read. "Was it inherited, a start-up?"

"I bought it, on a loan." She looked out her window. "Brett helped me with that. He worked at the bank back then. That's how we met, actually."

"Excellent." He bobbed a smile in the viewer and shrank down his graph as they changed lanes towards the ramp. "Here's Hume…"

He glanced at her one more time, but she kept looking out. The girl had drifted into her cushioning arm, sound asleep. They slowed down some on the boulevard, where the few aging storefronts caught his eye along the first couple of blocks, before they veered on the crossing street for the hotel.

"Mr. Mann?" She looked at him. "For the petition… Brett and I, we actually don't have a formal marriage license. I mean, we never got it transcribed."

"Well, is it recorded somewhere?"

"Yes, at the chapel." She arched her brows and nodded. "We've been together for a long time and can prove it."

He waited for the car to make the drop-off turn. "Would you call it home partners? You'd only need to change the affidavit."

Lips tight, she creased her eyebrows and jiggled her head up and down. "We will," she said, a frail shrillness in her voice, and looked out.

He turned to look at her directly. "Are you all right?"

"I'm sorry. I just hope everything will work out... Oh, I'm so lame." She smiled, blinking rapidly, and turned to grab her tote.

He nodded back at her hand wave through the closing door and then glimpsed the red and white stroller in the small hotel entryway as he drove back out.

The boulevard was not as busy going in the opposite direction, and he could speed down the few blocks to the next overpass. He merged on and slowed hard to land in the small intersection. Several narrow streets thereafter, he pulled into a side spot, swung his seat around, and took his jacket and shirt off. He reached inside the satchel for the casual sweater and zipped it on then reached in again for the white case and laid it before him on the backseat. He grabbed a food bar from the console and stared at the case while chewing on. A minute later he stepped out with the case, crossed the street, and walked toward the lively building entrance a few doors down.

The large, bright classroom buzzed with young faces and chatter. He nodded his way through to one of the few stations left, a little before the teacher stepped in front of the class to greet them with a clap of the hands.

"Today we'll try the last technique in the classic series. The pencil," he said loud. "As usual, we'll watch the demo and then you'll pick your image and start making those beautiful drawings," he added over the renewed twitter.

Motionless in his chair, Clarens watched the sketch come alive under the large, anonymous hand across the front wall. He switched to his station's display to flip through the collections of fruit platters, suborbital shuttles, and Tuscan squares, then picked the purple pencil from his case. He fixated on the sample image and idled his hand over the blank sheet of paper, then brought the pencil to the upper third of the left side and drew the thin line of the horizon.

By the time the teacher stopped by, the sheet abounded with color.

"We love those outdoors!"

Clarens eased a smile and sat back from the drawing board. "If only I knew what you're saying."

The teacher kept a straight face. "What do you mean? You always pick the landscapes." His graying red sideburns brushed the air as he turned to the drawing. "Is this… heaven?"

Clarens leaned his head back and chuckled. "I appreciate the uplift."

"Everyone does. That's why I'm still here after eight years"—the teacher winked. "You still don't know what I'm saying…"

"Is it *not* about heaven?"

He braced his hand on the board and pitched his head towards him. "Now, do you really believe in that?" As Clarens chuckled again, he turned to the board, laid a blank sheet over the drawing, and began selecting pencils from the case. "But since you asked for something closer to our prosaic reality…" he mumbled, glancing the foothills on display, "pick the colors you want, put them all aside, then pick the same palette again, only half as tinted." He leaned over the sheet and sketched fast in long, uninterrupted lines, then the pencils clacked in his hand as he filled the shapes with color. "Hatching it all in the same direction should help too…"

At his side, Clarens watched closely. "I see what you're saying."

"You do!" the teacher jested, then straightened up and put the pencils down. "In four months you'll draw just like that. Or I won't see you in my class anymore."

"I'll remember that."

He smiled back and stepped around the board. "Clarens, right? I did like your colors."

As he moved on to somewhere at the rear of the room, more titters cracked through the background shuffle. Clarens laid a new sheet over the board and flattened it under his palm. The horizon, the long hills rolling away, the far mountains pinning the sky, the sparse shrubs, rocks, and bushes spreading life into the foreground, they were all there some twenty minutes later. The lines were just as timid, but the new colors and strokes made for a leaping difference. He picked another sheet and this time he brought the horizon higher and left the mountains out. One's sight didn't have any more peaks or obstacles to climb to, and just swept from atop the hills to the all-encompassing plateau farther out. He tried the new dynamic over from different heights until past the end of the class, when most stations around him were deserted. He gathered the pencils and curled the drawings into a tight roll, bouncing it on his shoulder as he strolled out.

He had just turned onto the overpass when a call came through, from his sister. He paused typing and looked at her, returning her rushed greeting.

"I'm good! You know, busy busy"—she pulled a smile. "Actually, I need to ask you… Can you go to Mom's Saturday instead? We'd like to take the kids to this show."

"This Saturday? I'm sorry, I have something."

"Really?" she almost shrilled. "They're dying to go now. Can you move it to earlier?"

"No, that wouldn't work." He paused at her loud sigh. "Can just one of you go perhaps?"

"It's three kids Clarens," she dropped her tone, then looked away. "Anyway, you wouldn't understand."

He inhaled and glanced out.

She sighed again. "I'll just have to book that nurse I guess. All right, 'bye."

"Wait, not on a Saturday. Hello…?"

He firmed his lips and looked ahead. The lane merged into the eastbound flow of cars on the expressway, then split and curved along the myriad of exit and ramps while zooming between the downtown's shells. By the time he exited to the

East Sector the streetlights had come on against the reddened, scant clouds. With the next turn the red dulled down, framed by the brighter street fronts, then the car wheeled quietly to its home spot inside the building's garage. He walked by the waiting elevator cabin to take the stairs instead, and trod in smooth, heel-rising steps two floors up, then around the courtyard glazing to his apartment door.

He dropped his day clothes on the vestibule's loveseat and stepped through the open living area to the first room inside the closed quarters, and in here, to the stack of drawings on the credenza. He slipped the satchel onto the lower shelf, sprawled the new drawings on the floor, and added his picks to the stack, then folded the rest in the side crate and walked back to the open area. Around the kitchen island, the counter margin glowed thin, removed from the luster of the paneled-wall storage behind it. Next to the nearly full tea mug on a tray, a grape stalk loomed over a bitten slice of bread with peanut butter. He tapped the refrigerator light on but left the door closed, then turned to stare out over the island instead. He closed his eyes and remained still, before slowly extending his arm toward where the back of the nearest tall chair had been. He didn't touch it, for another minute, with his open hand out and his brows beginning to squirm. He leaned forward, and his hand scraped down the sleek back of the chair, then on the chairs to the side as he fell. Eyes open, he kept grasping higher through the air and tried to rise, lurching awkward between the overturned chairs, until he found the edge of the counter to pull himself up and anchored his elbow on it. He stayed crippled over the surface, breathing heavily, as the sweat beaded on his forehead. He stood up slowly, lifted the chairs, and wiped his loaded brows. The back wall shined on, the refrigerator light had dimmed down. He reached in for another grape cluster and put it next to the leftovers on the tray, along with two thick slices of blue cheese and a half glass of red wine, and stepped to the lounge in the middle of the room.

When the second comedy show ended, he let the idle graph shrink down and remained flat on the couch, then dimmed the lights further. In the corner by the window, the heliconia cast a jagged shadow across the wall, sharp against the now prevailing outside light that flooded in.

The time flashed midnight at the bottom of the graph, and the Friday reminder shimmered up: "hair, car vac, bed sheets." He lay still for another minute then thrust himself up and took his sweater off, went around the low table, and braced his palms on the floor to start doing push-ups. The rhythm dropped in the upper teens, but he did manage another dozen, then rolled over under the soft-white ceiling alcove. He rose and added "lavender" to the reminder while heading to the closed side of the apartment.

# 4

**B**rett pulled down the lat bar and held it below his chin then let it snap back and gushed as the weights thumped the floor strut. He lay back in the machine's seat, chest pounding, and checked the time. A couple more people had showed up, but the gym remained mostly empty this early on Saturday morning. Loud to his ears again, the rhythmical cello tune sounded just as hollow. He sprang up and grabbed his towel, then watched himself in the nearing wall mirrors as he walked to the locker room. The veins ran thick up his lean biceps to under the shirt, and then out over his reddened neck.

Chilly to walk against, the breeze seesawed through the open passageway on the way back to the hotel. The clouds dispersed as the sun tore through. Upstairs, he strode out of the elevator and onto the deadened corridor floor. He stopped in front of Susan's room and leaned close to the door. Nothing came through. He hesitated, then stepped aside to his room. Minutes later he left again, tweaking his new sweater straight and gulping the last bite of muffin. He checked his pockets and whisked his hand left and right over his temples' hairline as he prompted the elevator for the garage level.

Sargent Bank's lobby was open and staffed. He headed straight to his safe deposit box and brought up the registration on his set, but he was denied access. Passing the set over the physical scan made no difference. He stared at the access prompt, then at the safe, before rushing to the lobby.

He called for assistance while approaching the counter, to which the attendant raised her head with a brisk greeting.

"You can't open the safe…" she repeated confused after him, pushing her hair around her ear with two fingers. She was the same young woman who had initiated his safe box a few days earlier. As he lowered his tone and elaborated, she leaned closer over the counter to examine the access prompt in his hand. "Oh, your personal device won't work here I'm afraid."

"But it works everywhere."

"This is a seven-digit zone." She smiled and raised her eyes at him, when a blush passed over her face and she pulled back. "You could use the original enabler, or a seven-digit device," she continued, then skimmed through her graph below. "But I can override it for you…"

"Great! Thank god you're here."

She rushed another smile. "Anyone could do it really."

"No, I meant that you people do weekends nowadays."

"Oh." She pushed her hair back around her ear and stared into the graph. She edged back, to the droning of her chair's actuators, then refocused and brought two fingers over her lips. "So I need your physical access key and ID key. And you'll need a new passphrase, I'm afraid," she added as Brett ejected the tiny pins out of his set.

With the reset completed, he returned to the safe box. Under the plain black polymer, the bar stacks were all in place. He lowered the first stack by two and dropped the bars in his chest pocket. Back in the lobby, he handed over the borrowed key-enabler, nodded a smile, and turned to the sheen of the front doors.

He stepped on and off the fast belt segments down the main street blocks. The few hums and echoes unraveled around him nowhere nearly as fast, with the sidewalks still slack. The upper street frontage had perked up, the contrast sharp between the shaded sides and the tall facades and the strips of glass within. In the abundant sunlight and shelter, they appeared destined to ever look this way.

The airy morning carried through to the very end of the shell, then ebbed into the lower level's artificial lighting, as he reached the pawn store. Feebly audible from deep inside, the broadcast sounded more like a newscast this time. He advanced past the island of showcases in the entryway to the middle of the floor.

"I was just thinking about you," Vitaly said from up on a stepladder, dragging a statuette in place on the wall shelf. He blasted air over the exhibits, as Brett moved closer, then switched his miniature cleaner to vacuuming and waggled it around. "Tensana... Isn't that near where you're from?"

"No, that's in Concord, by the border. I'm from the Alliance. Why?"

He pitched his head toward the back of the store. "They're unhappy with the federal elections," he said, and laid an unsure foot on the floor, then turned his paunch around. "They're holding a referendum for secession."

"What? Nah, they're beyond hope."

"Haha... What is it like in the Alliance?"

"In the Alliance"—Brett sighed, reaching inside his chest pocket—"the left is creeping in, and the phonies buy into the goodwill schemes all over again."

Vitaly snickered and turned his head, locks swinging, to scan the shelves. "For fifty, I had a shuttle to heaven here..." He chuckled and palmed his shirt down, then tapped the low showcase between them. "What can I do for you, sir?"

"Brett."

"Brett. Vit," he nodded, and looked at the bullion bars in Brett's hand. "Two more? So I did overpay..." He nipped a bar out of its plastic sleeve and peered at the mint marking. "All right, here's what I can do. I can either pay you now a price you won't like, or the old price when I find a collector," he said and clacked the bar down, then switched to Brett and

40

pinched his lips while waiting. "Or, if you had another one, I could list all four on the rares."

The newscast beeped in the background, just as the store's voice privacy warning chinked off, to which he raised his hand at the ceiling corner. "Enjoy!" he shouted that way, then dropped his hand back on the case top. "Loves his lunch. Where were we?"

"Rares?"

"Yes, one kilo minimum. For defense, energy start-ups. Pays a little better, I think." He shifted his weight and deployed his graph over the showcase, then mumbled on with the query, his belly bulging over the metal edge.

Brett raised his eyes to the wall exhibits above the stepladder. Two bronze horses galloped side by side off the flat base of the antiquated statuette. They looked almost like an integral part of the vintage physical hologram of the rings of Saturn hanging just behind. He lingered over the bronze pair and swayed away, searching over the sandstone floor print, and called Susan. She didn't pick up. "Hey, can you at least tell me where you are?" he muttered in her mail. "Can't do this here."

"Comes to 4,185 each," Vitaly spoke up. "In two days."

Brett turned around and nodded, then again to the mention of a half a point commission fee. He glimpsed his milky-blue eyes as he handed him the second bar. "Amazing. A kilo bought you a house not long ago."

"Still does. Two hours north of here," Vitaly said and chuckled as he lumbered away toward the rear of the store. He returned with the assayer, then wheezed on while stooping over to check the numbers. "Well Brett, you certainly travel in style. Touring our little country?"

"Yeah. Sticking to Ayland for now."

"You're a city guy…"

Brett skipped through his Commons account. "Uhh… it's just awesome, this mega glass, walk everywhere without getting jumped…"

"We have our spots."

He puffed. "You travel outside? Or you're a news guy."

Chuckling, Vitaly swept the case top for the transparent sleeves. "I do, I do"—he quivered his chubby shoulders. "Oh, I do…" He stilled to slip the bars in, then flipped his graph closer and sent the money over. "Splendid."

He grabbed the stepladder and walked with him to the framed paintings section at the front of the store, dwelling on more current events and the uneven advancement of the human species. Set to continue, he sighed his words as he climbed the steps, but turned his head with a grimace when a group of teens rushed in.

———

Susan and Tara were not in. Only by midafternoon did he hear their voices out in the corridor, then the soft clunk of the closing door. He watched the game on low a little longer before going over.

Susan was pulling Tara's pajama shirt over her head, and they both turned to look at him through the open bedroom door. Tara hopped to him in the main room, then giggled in his arms. "Can I touch the ceiling?"

He lifted her all the way up, then held her lower in one arm and looked at Susan. "Where did you guys go?"

She glanced at him while folding the comforter over. "We had brunch and then we checked out the spas. And then we got lost."

"What? How?"

"She just… Anyway, my fault. They found her quickly."

"Who did?"

"They called emergency."

Boggled, he switched to the girl.

She picked the shirt on his shoulder quietly, then suddenly speared her finger at the wooden tray on the table.

"Scrunchies!" She twirled around, her hair whipping his face, to also show him the large, boat-shaped scrunchie tying her braid.

Susan stepped closer with the tray. "Orange, purple"—she stroked the fanciful scrunchies under Tara's smile, then the one on her braid—"and pink!" She gently pulled the scrunchie off, her eyes shunning Brett's, and let her fly it over to place it next to the other two in the tray.

He lowered Tara to the floor and watched Susan follow her back to the bedroom. "Hey…" He held his hands out.

"In your room…"


Minutes later, he turned down the volume on the game and dropped his feet off the side of the coffee table as she walked in his room. She removed his sweater from the armchair and sat, then stared at the gridiron over the bed.

He turned to it too. "It's the Rockets. They made the semis!"

She hummed quiet.

With the ball out of bounds, he looked at her again. "How could you not call me?" he said, to which she only shrugged. "Anyway, I got the money."

"Good. We have to redo that affidavit also."

"Oh yeah, the affidavit…"

She propped her chin in her fist and looked aside, then sniffled.

He sighed and moved closer to sit on the sofa armrest instead, and grabbed her hanging hand. "Suse, it's gonna be okay." He rocked her hand lightly until she turned, eyes glowing.

"How is it going to be okay? He repeated that chances are very small."

"I know but, we'll make it happen." He tightened his grasp and smiled. "We're petitioning the freakin' senator!"

She threw a scolding glance over and stood up to reach for a paper tissue.

"Just making the point," he added, and stood up too. "Hey, about the other day. I'm sorry I let you go on your own."

She blew her nose and stepped to the window. "That's fine, I overreacted... I sort of created this silly image in my mind that things would change overnight." She huffed lightly. "Can you believe I now long for the fights we used to have before you moved to Orion?"

He rested his hands on his waist and measured her figure in the soft sunrays. "I know, it's just... You know how it's been with everything." He peeked at the nearly-scoring drop punt as she crumpled the tissue and turned. He held his hands out. "But I'll change back. We're just getting started baby."

"We are?"

He stepped close, grabbed the tissue ball from her hand, and lobbed it toward the waste receptacle. He turned back to catch her passing smile. "Let's eat out tonight," he said. "We could go early and hang out a little."

"We could..."

"Would you like that?"

"I'd like that," she said and sniffled anew, as he laid his hands on her waist. She brought her arms to his shoulders as they touched foreheads and kissed. "It's been too long..." she murmured in between.

"I kept on saying..."

He slipped his hands down her hips as she held his head to press his lips on. They drifted toward the sofa and knocked the coffee table over as they lay down.

He pushed himself up slightly and brought his graph on while peeking at the game, then pushed himself higher over her. "Wanted to pause it but haven't keyed this in yet." He rose to sitting and scanned the floor. "Where's that freakin' key..."

She turned back flat and looked at the ceiling as he raised

the overturned table to search the other side of the floor. She bent one knee up and ran her hair off her face. "You should let it play. I'm actually sort of tired," she said, and felt her abdomen over before strapping her jeans back tight.

"That's it, I'm done."

"No, really. I need a nap too." She stood up and straightened her shirt around her waist.

He let his arms hang down and, his mouth half open, watched her step around the sofa and to the door.

She grasped the handle, barely turning her cheek to him. "I'm just tired. I might sleep through the evening."

———

The waiter cleared the plates and salad bowls with hardly any clatter. He let his hands work just as fast to gather the silverware as he slanted his head at Heslin. "As for desserts, we have the raspberry mousse, lemon meringue tart, crème caramel..."

"I'll have the lemon"—she tapped her pale hand on the table. The diamonds-on-gold bracelet and ring looked like they simply belonged there.

He turned to Clarens to take his pick too, then flipped his hand up to point to the bottle. "More wine, madam?"

She swiftly pushed her empty glass towards him and beamed as Clarens craned his head to peek over.

"Ah, missed that one."

"Haha! Excellent wine, by the way," she told the waiter, who finished pouring and landed the bottle midway between the candle and water carafe.

"Yes, fabulous cru. I'll be back with the desserts," he said, and hustled away in front of his wood-veneered mini-buffet.

She chuckled softly.

Clarens held his smile. "I don't know if I could do it every day."

"Oh, I could sooo do it. Just bring a couple more restaurants to this town!"—she beamed and grabbed her glass.

He grabbed his too. "Remember that place in Nantibes where they'd refill until you tipped them not to?"

Nearly choking on the wine, she put the glass down and cleared her throat. She blinked off her tears and smiled. "Tipping is kind of fun, though. I mean, that whole vacation was." She twinkled over to meet his eyes as she sipped anew.

He bobbed his head and wandered his gaze higher over the etched-glass divider behind her. The ceiling pane was also laced with the elongated silver grid, oriented along the main lines of the techno design. Back on the floor, the mini-buffet turned past the vocal corner table and rolled closer on the short aisle by the window row.

"But I'm thinking north this year. Get my dose of swanky-cranky old world," she continued, as the waiter slipped the dessert plate in front of her. "Like this for a whole week."

The waiter laid a small pack of dry lavender beside her plate and wisped a smile at Clarens. "And the mousse for you, sir."

She turned her head as he left but stopped short of calling him back and looked down at the clear pack instead. She looked at Clarens and eased her grin. "I can't believe you." She opened the pack and poured the small petals in her hand, then rubbed them between her palms until the last one fell shriveled on the table. Hands walled around her lemon tart, she leaned over to inhale, then spooned a first piece and relished it. "And you? Off to anywhere?"

"I guess I'm overdue but... By the way, I have some clients from the north. From the Alliance."

"Oh. So they fly you there?"

On hearing the case details, she stilled her full spoon in the air to roll a laugh.

"It's all ideological," he continued, "which makes for a nice challenge."

46

She picked her glass and sighed. "Some things never change."

He eased a smile. "Well, you should hear the guy talk. He sure had enough," he said, and pushed his empty dessert cup away. "They asked for a bank, and I mentioned yours actually."

"Thanks! Don't wait for the tip!"

They laughed. Sitting back, he watched her savor the last piece, then the fine necklace rise inside her open blouse as she drank up. He switched his finger between the empty bottle and the venues across the street outside. She looked out and mused, then wondered if she would rather laze and watch a show somewhere, to which he suggested his place.

"Your place is fine," she said, reaching in her purse, and slipped a smile. "I'd want to check what else happened there anyway."

He chuckled, head down, and paid the bill, glancing over as she ran the moisturizer on her lips. "Your heliconia is still there."

"Is it?" Rolling her lips in, she flicked a curl back from her cheek. "Tsk, tsk… Mr. Perfect."


He took the detour through the quieter, south midtown. The road curved wide as it climbed the terraced hillside. As it reached the ridge, the row of town houses on the outer side gapped abruptly.

He pulled over into the layby and pivoted the car toward the open view. "Remember this?"

"Vaguely…"

The two-story metal-clad buildings filled the area immediately below. Dark and bulky. The ones scattered beyond carried the technology-age sight all the way to the mushrooming lights atop the next hillside out, where the zeps flit about and the city thrived once again. Compact wind turbines and equipment housings shaped the rooftops against the twilight, while large signage embossed the nearby muted parapets.

"Our second date, I think."

She turned and poked his chest lightly with her finger. "I can't believe your memory is better than mine."

"I just drive by every now and then." He swept his hand over the dashboard. "Doesn't this feel so… present?"

She left her hand lie on his armrest and looked out. "I thought this would be cleaned up by now." She laughed and brushed against his shoulder. "So-rry! But if you asked me, I'd like an apartment in that tower over there."

He followed her finger to the slick new high-rise in the corner of the windshield, then returned to the view below. "Imagine this back then. Nothing else around, just a few roads and the winds lashing over, and cars driving in and out these plants, people checking in their digital stations, crowding out to lunch in that glass corner, or on that overpass tube there, and watching the drones bring the next building up, and wondering if all this was going to take hold…"

She tapped his arm.

"What's a hundred years…"

She tapped him again. "I like it when they go home."

He let a smile out and nodded at the outside. "By the way, they sell them by the quarter floor. Since you're looking."

"Yeah. Let me get my tools tuned up."

They chuckled, then he set for home and looked in the rear viewer as the car backed up slowly. "I think it would be pretty cool. Even for a bank manager."

She leaned close, her curls amber on her shoulder. "This bank manager *is* pretty cool. But she takes fun over cool. And she takes fine living over cool," she said quietly, and raised her chin. "That's not to say she's not open to other possibilities."

"She must be rather wise then," he murmured back.

"It's about time that's being acknowledged…"

Her lips glistened in the streetlight as he stopped the car.

She grasped his jacket as they kissed, rising closer in her seat with his hand sliding over her waist. She eased back and looked at his lips. "Can we go chill now?"

# 5

Lynden threw his arm over the floating lane divider and blew water out of his mouth. "I'm done!"

Clarens flip-turned against the end wall of the pool and resurfaced. "I'll do another lap." He thrust under to just above the bottom of the pool and kept breast stroking his way forward. The sunrays swept toothless over the blue, linear pattern, and only some distant thumps still told of the outside. He went up and broke through to fill his lungs, then stroked a couple of times on the surface before diving back under.

Near the end of the twenty-five meters return, he let the last air bubbles out and closed his eyes as he weaved to the above.

"Man comes from fish after all!" Lynden grinned as he scuffled his hair under the hooded towel.

Clarens swam to the ladder and climbed next to him on the pool coping. "By the way, for the lake party—can I switch to a premium suite? It's Heslin."

Tilting over, Lynden lifted his towel off his ear. "Say what? The last part..." As Clarens smiled, he jabbed him lightly in the torso and widened his grin. "You sure can!"

They turned the corner of the pool deck to walk back to the shower rooms. Swimmers crawled slow laps in just about every lane all the way to the far side of the hall where, out the panoramic glazing, the flow of cars snaked through the woven ramps of the city belt.

"Is she still downtown?" he asked.

"Yes, two blocks down."

"Sweet. Can use the garage."

"Tsk…" Clarens exhaled. "How's Gwyn and the kids?"

"Oh, super." Flopping along in his slippers with short, sideways steps, Lynden tossed his towel onto the other shoulder. "They're with my in-laws. Gwyn is coming to the city for dinner."

"You people are discouraging."

"Wanna come? We're getting a drink beforehand," he said, as they turned into the men's quarters. "You know she'd love to see you."

A step behind, Clarens split to his locker. "Thanks, but I need to check back in. Say hi though."

"You check back in? Guy, don't get married to it," Lynden chuckled and slipped his swim shorts down to the floor, then treaded his feet out of them. His pink, fatty back quivered as he hopped to the shower booth, where he extended his arms sideways to the translucent surround and reveled in the water jets. "Did you know these do thirty liters a minute? I'm having one installed at home!" he yelled, tapping the controls, while Clarens stepped to his booth across the aisle. "Hey, you should try this!" he added and bent all the way down, resting the top of his head against the wall base. "Dude, for once!"

———

One or two indistinct voices came through from the idle office floor, but he didn't run into anyone on the way to his room. Outside, the facing high-rise splattered yellow over the clear dusk, while a same-hued quarter moon seemed to have landed atop it, as if part of the vertex design. He kept the lights low and sat down, then spread his graph over the desk. He leaned back and pivoted his chair slowly, two fingers over the chin.

51

He set his sight on Brett and Susan's file case, sat up, and flipped it open, then cast their thumbnail set through his own device. The neat array of objects gridded up the desk.

All personal records checked as originals, and even the neighbors' references were biomarked. He cross-read through the statements and curricula vitae, then turned to the "other supporting documents" object beside them. A new array of mostly visual contents lay over. He skipped through: "Brett & dad speedway '87," "Brett '94 division playoff," "Brett on FastStats 3/11." He paused and opened the title. In the graphic setting, Brett was one of three participants in what appeared to be a business cast, looking as trim as on the day he had sat before the desk in this office. The debate about the feasible yield for a new city debt offering pitched him against the two government officials and quickly escalated into controversy, before the moderator steered it elsewhere. The next title read like his appearance on the same casting but on a different date, and then a large group of Tara's titles rolled through. He glimpsed the first few on fast viewing, slowing with the changing scenes. They were all recent, with a one-year timestamp or newer, and most featured the narrow, well-cared-for backyard of a suburban house. The sandstone foot path wound around the flower bush island and to the gazebo in the back; the neat lawn stretched across the middle between the thick, flowered hedging that lined the fencing on both sides of the yard. Other than Brett and Susan, the clips showed the same three or four adults on the named occasions, such as Tara's party for turning three years old. One of them turned out to be Susan's father and the other were the neighbors.

The few Susan-labeled contents squared up the array. She looked stunning and terribly young in "Susan's 21yo beauty pageant," although that could barely befit the sixteen years in between. On her turn to answer the setting-wide question, she held her hands together low over her satin suit, then smiled nervously in the brief aftermath as the presenter cheered. "Susan horseback riding club" opened up with several people, she among them, trotting their horses in line on a wide country trail with what appeared to be stables in the background. The action cut ahead a few times before an entirely different scene flashed in, with Susan alone. It could have been late fall and the same building glimpsed on and off through the row of young poplars in the distance. Susan cantered her quarter around the open field and smiled the first time she rode by. Her loose hair seemed longer, or the fluttering rendered it that way. When she made the far turn on the third round she cued the horse into galloping back, shrieking as they thumped by at full speed with chunks of moist soil flying about. She slowed it down shortly and turned it around, then let it walk back and zipped down her turtleneck below her beaming face.

The stilled contours dissolved into the main array as the last clip ended. Cheek against his fist, Clarens tipped his fingers onto the desk and strayed further through the miscellaneous contents. Half an hour later, he zoomed into the satellite view of their dwelling, although the clear-weather feed was days old. Encroached by snow-laden branches, the backyard looked quite different, including the gazebo, whitened all the way up the side screens. The snow looked untouched throughout the yard, other than for two tire tracks and some footsteps in front of the average row house. He glided down the quiet street and over the several small intersections until reaching the traffic on the crossing avenue, then followed the thickening lanes toward the city center. Susan's "Nursery and Gifts" outlet checked out as a two-story filler building in what could have been the historical downtown, several crowded blocks away from Brett's physical business location in a new-age office tower. He leaped high over it to the surrounding country of giant white swells and thin, cutting black lines, then much higher, and remained suspended over the glowing blue.

He rose and stepped to the window. The moon had left the building top and now glimmered through the smoky patch moving in. The shell's lights thrived about the glass cladding refractions, all the way out to the boulevard, which streamed the red and white dots across his shirt's reflection in between. He went back to his desk, shrank the graph down, and began typing. "Dear Senator:…"

———

"Sorry, I'm keeping you from closing."

Vitaly snapped the platinum bar off the assayer slot just as the puny chink went off twice in the ceiling corner behind. "There's my closing bell."

Brett looked up the transaction, too. "Long hours…"

"Oh, no. I take my siesta in the back room," Vitaly said, feeling his belly down, then poked his chin at the ceiling. "The one place they let me be." He chuckled, his mango shirt trembling on his shoulders, and touched knuckles with Brett. "And we want you here in Ayland till that last dime."

"You sure do!" Turning away, Brett paused and glanced at the outside. "By the way, would you recommend a bar nearby? Like, happening…"

"Happening?"

"Yeah, but not kids' stuff."

"Uhh… I know *of* one, but it might not be what you want," Vitaly said, weighing the bar in his palm as he headed toward the back room. "The Revox." He swung his head around and quipped over his shoulder, "Not my kind of drink. Over in Friedman."

He rinsed hard a second time and bared his teeth in the mirror. He tossed the tooth cleaner, patted his face dry, and walked out of the restroom to the eatery lobby and to the sidewalk. He called Susan. "Yeah, it's me…" He held his words, then shook his head and deleted the message as he turned the corner.

The mapping kept him on the lower level for two more blocks, till he reached the busy underpass toward the adjacent shell. He gripped the handrail as the long belt picked up more speed while, outside the clear tubing, the walls turned plain past a couple of spas and the underpass went soulless. Another sequence of ads shone up along the middle bay, now with travel settings from an all-too-familiar country in the other hemisphere, one from his own state included. He snorted to himself and leaned his head back in the warm draft.

Friedman shell looked like a no-different part of town. Ochre stone and tall, round-cornered glazing lining the streets, with mostly stainless metal in the rare deviations from the compact and flush forms, all under the high glass cladding that spanned between the higher buildings. Only a little quieter, given the after-hours time, until he got closer to the target. He palmed his set and stepped off the belt, then turned the corner behind a middle-aged couple into the narrow side lane. They disappeared inside the first door, which let out a thick waft of clatter before sliding back closed. It was one out of many bars that marked the suddenly lively sidewalk, with the Revox near the other end.

He slowed down across from the rather swank entrance and glanced around. Two finely garmented women walked in, and so did an older, snug-looking man, followed by another single one, all vanishing beyond the electrically suspended fog screen. He turned his head to the giggles behind him and saw the three more women crossing over. One of them rushed through the screen in front of the others, leaving her forearm visible outside the matte-white surface to hook her finger at her friends, who renewed their giggles and disappeared inside too.

He followed the patch of fragrance inside the screen and

then onto the conveyer that led down the curved, funneling lobby. The noise level increased in just the opposite ways, and abruptly once more as he landed on the platform inside the actual venue. Prompted by more laughter closing in from behind, he stepped out of the way and looked over the cozy, irregularly formed space, before treading the few steps down. A subdued dance vibe stroked through the zesty feel, although the half-full place looked more like a restaurant, with low booths and tables along the two crescent-shaped floor levels, which lay staggered to engage each other, and abundant accent lighting all around. Real wood burned in the feature fireplace, flush-glazed within the wall across the room. He spotted a standing bar on the lower floor beside the platform and walked that way, but, as no one else seemed to pick up drinks there, he changed course for an empty table.

Most parties were of two and three people, and curiously watchful, as if waiting for a missing other, unless the no-eyesets etiquette no longer applied. His beer arrived quickly and he sipped often, glimpsing around in between. Behind him, another lone sipper looked down in his palm. He grabbed his glass and walked over.

"Hi there!" he smiled and nodded at the opposite chair, as the business-suited man barely raised his balding head. "You mind company? All straight," he tipped his hand up.

The man bumped a shrug and returned to scrutinizing his graph, then flicked the graph smaller over the standalone, pen-styled set next to his empty glass as Brett sat. He looked late fifties, and tall, the way he lay slanted in his chair with his legs crossed, one shoe sticking out large from under the table.

Brett bent forward. "I'm Brett by the way."

"What?"

"Brett!"

"T!" The man gave a slight nod, then switched his frown away to sweep over the room.

The music had picked up some, and more people landed

onto the entry platform. The same well-dressed types, forty and over. No stage or dance floor could be seen anywhere, however, even from here on the raised level, other than the open area in front of the bar. Behind it, the curtain-like ribbed panels remained still, floor to ceiling, in deep carmine.

Brett drank and tapped the glass down. "Do people dance here, like later?"

"Sometimes. If someone gets wasted."

He chuckled as T glanced over.

"Where are you from?"

"The FSA."

"Huh. Enjoying it?"

"Oh, it's awesome. Smart, clean..."

"Huh..." He wiggled his glass and looked in it before tossing the remaining drop in his mouth. "What does a sex joint look like over there?"

Brett chuckled again but, with T keeping sober, he petered out and circled his finger above the table. "Is this a...?"

Pursing his lips, T stared at him, then let a chuckle out too. He pulled his feet in abruptly to sit the other way and stretched his mini-graph to the new angle. As Brett pointed to his glass for another round, he agreed to a straight Willett.

Brett gulped down his beer and peered at the order in his other hand. "Why would it say I have two bids?"

T waited until the newcomers had cleared his chair to sit at the table behind him, then leaned in closer. "Because you received two bids in legal tender," he laid out. "And I'll let you get that drink then." He twitched a smile and returned to riffling through his own display. "You're a married man Brett?"

"What?" Broadening his smile, Brett looked around. "Actually, I am. Technically. You?"

"Me? Do I look like a married man?"

"I don't know," he laughed over the ever louder music. "You guys seem to do it a little differently here."

"Maybe. Enjoying that part too? Technically..."

"Haha! No, but, you know... Life gives only if you're willing to take, doesn't it?"

T raised his head to bolt him from under the thick eyebrows once more and hummed.

Zooming up to the table, the server uncovered the two drinks. They swapped their old glasses and sipped in unison, looking out over the buzzing floor.

T stooped closer over his set and turned to himself. Brett glimpsed his hand too, where a third bid was waiting. He looked it up. The forty-six-year-old woman looked younger than her stated age, and rather attractive. He entered the guest's gallery and wandered about, as the deeper dance vibes stroked through.

He left the rosy faces behind and entered his investments room. Most titles ticked on slowly with the overnight markets, except the ones on the Eastern exchange which were picking up, though also deep in red. He frowned and checked the string of positions piercing his hedge band, then his clients' accounts. In the side slot, a small equity title had just turned burning red with the renewed plunge. He cursed to himself and queried his contacts, then scrambled to type in. "Need that return favor... 38574mcx, all solid." He toggled between the falling bid and the idle typer until the response lit up, then longer until his pal gathered his crowd. He pushed the title back up along them and then exited last for a small loss. "Justice done, superman. Off the hook?" his pal returned and went off with a soldier's salute flyover. He passed a smile and switched back to frowning through the reds and rolling his hedges out.

"Getting rich there Brett?"

"Uhh... got a fourth one at one sixty."

"Beautiful."

"You?"

T kept reading, head beaming in the down lights. "I've got

neither hair nor an exotic address."

Brett laughed and grabbed his pint. "What do you do, T?"

"What?" T shouted, despite the question being asked equally loud, and let Brett repeat it. "A bunch of things, real estate. And you?"

"Financials. Asset management and stuff."

"Financials... So you do have a plan here." Finally raising his eyes, he cracked a smile and swallowed most of his bourbon, ice cubes rolling on his upper lip. "Lucrative?"

"Yeah, before the govie's cut."

He puffed expressionless and finished off his drink. "I'll get the next round."

With all the seating taken, standing newcomers had engulfed the bar, ever glancing around, while the flames in the fireplace burned higher and keener still. Brett glimpsed his last bidder in the indicated direction and then looked back around just as slowly, over T's poking shoe. "Hey, T. What would be a decent bid, you think?"

T glanced him down. "Two hundred. Tax free."

"No," Brett chuckled. "For me to make."

"Just say hi. Unless she's thirty and got the wrong door," T added, then suddenly uncrossed his legs. "Having said that... my two hundred got me in. Probably because we're at the same table." He dropped his pen in his chest pocket, then felt his back as he rose and held his half fist out. "Brett... maybe I'll see you again. You save me money." He twitched his smile and left.

Brett grabbed his pilsner and watched him tread tall through the jutting chairs and down the steps to the lower floor where he slowed among the crowd. A woman joined him shortly. She tossed her fluffy hair back as they appeared to laugh and then walked with him toward the exit.

"Hi there!"

Brett turned to the two women smiling beside his table. Bending over slightly, the nearest one pointed at the empty chairs, which he let them take. They turned to their own sets and their talk across the opposite corner of the table, rolling shoulders lightly with the music, or with whatever could make it through the chatter. He looked out and pinned the pint between his thumb and middle fingers, rotating it in slow quarter turns on the table.

"Excuse me, are you Brett?" the same woman shouted, and thinned her lips in another fine smile. Her green clip earring glistened from under her dark hair, which then weaved down her sleeveless black top to just below her shoulder.

"Uhh... yep."

She looked just about his age as she beamed. "Are you really from the Alliance?"

At his confirmation, they both giggled, then she leaned back toward him. "So you guys really speak the same language!" she asked, loud again.

"Yes, we do. Well..." he leaned over a tad too, "we think it's more like you guys speak the same language."

"Hahaha! I always wanted to go. Can you still rent gas cars?"

"You know, I don't even know. But you could definitely get a ride I'd think."

As she and her friend burst anew, he glanced at her and then lowered his eyes to his pint. He stopped turning it and rose. "Actually, I have to wish you an awesome night out," he said, and pointed inside his hand, before palming the bidding hologram off.

"Oh ... To you too!"

He walked to the base floor and waded through the tony crowd to the side exit. The outside air was faint and quiet, until the service alley butted back into the front lane. It looked as merry as it had two hours earlier and then some, with small groups huddling outside of just about every bar door down to the main street.

He turned the new corner and crossed to the westbound

belt. The echoes soon faded behind, except for a lone guffaw or two from elsewhere beyond the muted buildings, as he traced the way back to the underpass between the shells. He kept taut by the rail, scouring the tunnel ahead. The droning of the street belts and cleaners was all the life left under Jefferson's clad, then that waned into the tap of his footsteps inside the D-12 section of the garage.

# 6

Heslin waved her hand high, although her smile was impossible to miss even from this far down the block. Clarens waved back and smiled with his approaching steps. She wore heels and a bright purple shirt under her wrinkleless suit and stood tall against the corner spa.

He coiled his hand gently around her waist as they kissed. "Whatever couldn't wait till tonight looks pretty compelling to me."

"Mmm… Lawyer talk." She grabbed his hand. "C'mon, we'll get lunch after. Let me show you this."

They jumped on the fast belt, then switched streets to the bridge over the expressway. Midway through the square tube, she left her vivid talk hanging and swayed over to the glazing, pulling him along. She beamed and pointed to the new tower sided by cranes in the open sky of northeast downtown. "Funny, we were just saying. The other Saturday…?"

"In that one? Slick it is."

She tittered and stamped her feet rapidly in place, then cuddled her arm around his as they glided over the last lane and started descending to the other side of the bridge.

Off the belt, they crossed through the busy hub toward the gateway to the new addition, then her heels rapped louder with the clearing floor.

Except for the odors of new furnishings and the intermittent tools whirring behind the temporary walls, the building lobby looked immaculate. Embedded in the topping of the wood-like monolithic floor, golden strands ran along the wood fibers and gathered up in an uneven yarn to lead the way. They followed the suggestive footpath to the portal of the elevators' battery, then out again on the fourteenth floor. The nearly street-wide corridor was flanked with smaller stone portals for the private doorways. A crew was unloading boxes off their vehicle at the other end. Heslin rushed ahead and turned inside the second portal.

"Excited?"she burbled, punching the code in her hand.

"If I could speak."

He followed her through the wide door inside the rectangular, patio-like foyer. The flat ceiling glowed a soft white as of daylight, while two sconce lights warmed the granite walls left and right with a yellow tint. A finely leafed shrub rose tortuously from the round cutout in the floor in one corner.

"Two bistro chairs there."

"Ah..."

They crossed to the symmetrical opening in front, then her heels' rap died off as they went through the door-lined hallway and out to what looked like the apartment's main room. From one side to the other of the double-height space, the curved glazing overlooked most of the downtown and the far south city beyond.

He slipped his hands in his pockets, strolling to the window, and smirked lightly over the shoulder.

She laughed loud. "Isn't this gorgeous? You've got to see the bedroom." She sprang up the open stairs to the mezzanine and looked down over the top rail. "C'mon!"

He treaded up the U-shaped stairs slowly. "Doesn't this cost a fortune?"

"It does but... I passed enough."

He panned around from the top landing, then turned after her and crossed the floor toward the sculptural wooden coil that spiraled up the end of the freestanding wall. The low wall rose in one step to the ceiling before turning sideways to cross their way with an opening within, where the walnut coil unwound into a tame, flat band, recessed in the wall surface at just below eye level. It led them inside the walled quarters and to the bedroom, where it merged into the floor-to-ceiling horizontal striping of the same walnut with threads of gold in between.

With two pirouettes and a "ta-da," she landed on the edge of the super-sized bed, then pointed to the lapped opening in the adjacent wall to mention the lavish tub and sauna.

He sighed and swiveled around, as she hopped in front of him toward the far window.

"I think you can see your apartment from here," she said, spotting the tiny building front out east.

He peered out with her. "So... you would just lower your scope and wave good night."

As her laughing tapered off, she turned to him and felt the front of his jacket. "I was thinking more like a tiny nightgown and calling you over."

They kissed while she slipped his jacket off and stepped backward toward the staged bed.

"Hes, what if anyone..."

"I have an exclusive showing." She turned around with him and pushed him on the bed. "For you."

She left her purple shirt on and lay over him to kiss again, then they rolled together to the middle of the bed. They held hands as she kneeled over him, watching each other through her loosened blond curls.

When she dropped next to him, she rested her hand on her chest and smiled, then felt her ear and turned onto her other side to take the short call. Rolling back next to him, she ran her fingertip over his cheek. "So what do you think of it?"

"It's great, but..."

"I could bring in some scrap sheet metal if you'd like."

They both laughed, as she propped her head higher over him. "There's an office room on the other side, by the way."

"Oh, yeah?..." He turned and looked into her eyes. "We need to get going."


Back on the bridge belt, she fixed his collar and grinned, then turned her head away to call her assistant back. Beside her fluttering hair, he watched the deli island slide by, bright and busy, and then the sidewalk crowding up with lunch takers, bench after bench, over the bridge's apex. Out on the other side, Friedman shell had all but vanished against the sun. He squinted higher and stretched his chest slowly in the snug jacket.

"Bummer!"—she turned his way. "I can't make the lake party. Bank retreat in Norpen..." As he tilted his head back with a sigh, she pecked him on the cheek. "I'll make it up to you," she added, and slipped her hand under his arm as they stepped off the conveyor belt, then looked at the bridge behind them. "Is Lynden still doing residential, by the way? I could give him the deal, so he won't get all mad."

He chuckled. "He is. I'll ask."

She let go and went ahead of him inside the freeze-less deli then hustled down the short aisle, tipping her finger from one dispenser to another.

"Isn't this something!"

He turned his head to the ad she was pointing at, over the aisle's end. The colorful settings of traditional, small downtowns morphed into one another and then into a classic, two-dimensional map. It was a travel ad for the Free States Alliance.

"Oh yeah..." He sent his order off and glimpsed the ad again, as the itinerary line expanded into a row of rugged cars pulling over in front of a quaint, wood-sided inn, before the next ad shined over.

She grabbed her bag and stepped back to him. "Let's do it. I'll pay for it," she said into his ear, "with whatever I save on the agent's fee."

He picked up his panini and nudged at the hovering graph. "And you won't scream 'tacky, invertebrate people'?"

"I won't scream 'tacky invertebrate people.'" She leaned her head back with a smile as they walked out and looked up the ad on her set. "Nonrefundable, end of August… That's plenty."

When they turned the corner on the main street, she split and rushed to the belt. "Nine? Oh wait, half past?"—she beamed above her stellar shirt, and mimicked drawing in the air. "Mr. Renaissance!"

———

Rolling close behind Tara, Brett lifted her from under her arms and slowed through the looped end of the skating lane. He praised her and let her gently back down on her roller skates. She went on to circle the white rubber turnaround and cheered at Susan, who, next to the school guide, watched from meters away in the open foyer.

"That was a long run, sweetheart!" Susan cheered back, as Brett came to a stop at the curb.

"It runs all around to the back fence. Pretty awesome," he said to the guide, and slipped between the foam panels to sit on the bench.

"So let me know if you'd like to register her," the guide said, turning to Susan, "when you're ready. We can't hold the spot with two months left, however," she added, as Susan looked at Brett.

"We actually—"

"We're ready. Looks great!" he said, and heaved his second boot off, then shouted at Tara. He slipped his shoes on to sprint after her as she rolled back out onto the yard-bound lane. He snatched her flat under one arm to her whines and giggles and brought her back.

"She knows what she wants!"—the guide smiled. She switched to her graph. "Now, I need the deposit, and your IDs on... Thank you. And you'll update me on that by mid-February you said."

Pads and helmet off and back in her shoes, Tara sprang to Susan. Brett tidied up the gear and then followed them inside the foyer.

The guide sent the preschool package over, then bent to the child. "Welcome to District One Preschool!"

Tara queried her with a serious face then turned to Brett and Susan too, as they all laughed.

As the guide walked off, they crossed the empty foyer in the opposite direction, toward the entry doors. Susan swept around and over the shining, wide skylight. "Wow... I so don't miss the barbed wire."

He glanced over as the doors beeped open. "Finally!"

She slipped a smile back and stepped out, then held her hair off her face and crouched to Tara against the rushing breeze. She pulled the peachy scrunchie off the girl's loosened braid and laced her fingers through her hair then slipped the scrunchie back up on a tidy, low ponytail. She rose next to him and watched her hop onto the sunny plaza in front of the building. "Stay close!"

They strolled behind her by the flowerbeds that lined the pavement all the way to the street sidewalk ahead. Susan bent to the low bush and held a flowered stalk still to look at it up close. She slid her hands back in her spring coat's pockets and strolled on with a slow pirouette to look around. "By the way, did you get the lawyer's message?"

"Oh, that's right,"—he rushed to check his set. "I couldn't hear it back there..."

"You won't believe it. He invited us to some party at a lake resort. This weekend," she said, and chuckled as he frowned.

Brows rising, he bobbed his head as he listened in.

She grabbed Tara as they turned onto the sidewalk. "It's free. And she'll have kids to play with."

He pinged the car out of its spot farther down on the park side. "Nice. Or he's just prepping us for more fees." To her rolling her head away, he added quickly, "In any case, we should start looking at houses. I actually gathered a few listings…" He browsed through them, then raised his head and looked over the waiting car's roof at the park entrance in the corner of the next intersection. "Let's walk in for a bit. She can just roam in there."

Past the limestone portal, a row of flat-branching trees flanked the entrance on both sides and to the stone-paved roundabout. Several alleys spiked out into the park, from which they picked the one that looked like it ran by a wide open lawn. Susan put her sunshades on and stopped in the new wind tantrum to zip Tara's sweater all the way up then let her spring ahead.

"So I also looked at townhouses," he said, browsing on, "with a little yard or patio. Still three bedrooms, the sunroom, ten-year warranty—"

"We said yard."

"Small yard."

"You said patio."

"Suse, for starters."

"I can't live somewhere with a patio."

He slowed and turned to her. "Between shipping things over, getting set up, starting a business, networking around," he spelled out, "between all that we'll have our hands full."

"It can come out of my share. And it's not you getting your hands full, right?"

He griped and glanced over the rustling shrubs as she stared on from behind the oval shades. He shook his head and walked again. "I won't remove myself to some stupid house in the burbs. When I do it, I'll do it in style."

"And till then, what? You'll get your own place again?"

To his silence, she flicked her hair off her cheek and looked away. He looked over the pavement ahead. The gray, long-cut stones crossed the alley in irregular rows, yet at the same oblique angle every time, made more apparent by the thin brownish joints in between. It all looked like a protruding section of a large rock formation underneath.

"Why are we here, Brett? Why are we here if we don't get anywhere?"

"There it is..."

He slipped his hands in his pockets too and turned to the hedging on his side.

Her steps lagged behind, and she whooshed her coat abruptly. "Where is Tara?" she said, swiveling all around as he turned to her. "Tara!... Tara!"

They hustled back, peeking through the bushes and sweeping over the lawn, until they reached the small footpath that had split off the alley.

"Stay here," he said, and rushed in the new direction.

The narrow path bowed on the outside of the nearly solid hedge until it cut into a patch of flag trees, where it split again. He stopped and yelled for Tara one more time, then ran down the new footpath until it tapered off into the free-range shrubs. He peeked through and under, then ran back to the split-off and on down the old path. It switched to bowing the other way, and it eventually brought him back to the alley, farther up from where they had turned around. To the side, an elderly bystander held his startled terrier close and replied that he hadn't seen the child. Brett spared a nod and raced away to close the loop, but Susan was not there anymore. He spotted her across the lawn, as she saw him, and they rushed toward each other. With her shades off, her eyebrows creased up in the middle of her forehead and her eyes' green grew wider than the grass field behind.

"Nothing?"—her voice pitched high. "We just couldn't fix

that darn tracker, could we!"

"Is this the time?" He scowled, then searched over the lawn once more. "We would have seen her in front of us… Just stay here!" he said, and took off in the opposite direction. "Tara!"

He ran down the alley back toward the park entrance, slowing before a few curious faces on the way, although none of them affirmed having seen the girl. He slowed down in the roundabout, heart throbbing, then dashed out to the sidewalk and scoured the crossing streets too, without spotting her. He flicked through the park mapping while striding back when Susan called.

"I'm calling emergency."

"Let me do another round. She's somewhere."

"Listen to me!" Her lower lip quivered as she let her head into the viewer. "If something happened to her I'm not staying! You understand?"

"Calm down, we'll find her. Susan!"

As she hung up he switched back to the mapping and rushed down the adjacent alley. Between the running and the shouting he kept turning heads his way, until all that was left was the chirping of the birds in the empty park. He slowed his stamping steps to catch his breath and took his jacket off then propped his hands on his waist and looked back and forth. A distant shriek came through the shivering leaves. He stilled, pointed that way.

"That can't be…"

Before the bushy backdrop on the other side of the lawn, a little girl appeared to yank her foot out of the hand of a crawling man and ran back into the brush, the bright tie jouncing on her dark ponytail. Brett raced across the lawn and waded through the tortuous branches after them. "Tara!" He fended off another branch snapping at his face and tore his shirt while hurling by the next one but, with neither Tara nor the man in sight, he paused for a new shriek to pierce through.

He thrust that way and slalomed through the remaining thickets until he reached the open patch where, on the other side, she crawled inside the hedge and the head-shaved man reached for her. His snicker cut out as Brett lunged to him from behind and fell him flat, face sinking in the groomed soil under the hedge. Up on his knees, Brett turned him over but held his fist over his scrunching eyes as the little girl, who wasn't Tara, came out of the hedge and froze.

"Daddy?"

"Oh... I'm sorry," Brett mumbled, as the man blinked at him. "I'm very sorry. It was a mistake," he added and rose, then snatched his jacket and rushed back through the brush.

"What the hell... Hey!"

With the yelling fading behind, he ran back across the lawn and to what looked like the same birch-lined alley, then checked the map and changed course back toward the inner park, renewing his shouts for Tara.

Susan sighed in his ear. "They've found her. They're bringing her over."

"Is she okay?"

"Yeah. She was watching the geese by the pond."

He slowed and dusted off with the back of his hand. His shirt's torn flap winged in the air above his hip. He shoved it in his pants and zipped his jacket on neat. His hands smelled like pine. He kept rubbing them over, although they were still sticky by the time he came upon the rocky alley again.

Tara was already there, with Susan and the park ranger. They saw him approaching too. He knelt on one leg and held his arms out for her to come quietly to him. He ruffled the top of her head, walked her back, and shook his head at Susan. "By the pond, huh?"

She rolled her eyes. They turned to thank the ranger, an actual police officer, who seemed to be listening in to a call but nodded at them.

"Not a problem," he said, eventually shaking Brett's

extended hand. "You should get that tracker updated, however." He let his hand down and looked at him again. "Would you mind waiting here for a minute?"

He took a few steps away, talking in on a low voice. A minute later he raised his hand at the open vehicle that showed through the alley bend.

"Oh great," Brett murmured.

In the passenger seat, the shaved man held his daughter on his lap. He pointed toward them as the vehicle stopped, then brought one leg out and lowered the brown-haired girl to standing on the ground. His cheek showed red around a small bandage.

Susan looked at Brett, who turned his hand out at him. "Hey man, I said I'm sorry…"

"'Hey man I'm sorry'?" the man returned, head forward, and stepped toward him. "You jump on my back from the woods and you're sorry?" he flared, as the other officer threw his arm in between, then he confirmed filing charges. "I don't need to worry about locos in my park," he yelled at Brett, with a last push forward. "I'm here every day, pal!"

Brett snorted and looked away, as the officer asked them both to cast IDs.

"Wait, sir"—Susan came forward—"we really are sorry. Is this your daughter?"

The man glanced over, still fuming.

"Because what happened is that our daughter got lost," she continued, bringing Tara in front of her, "and we just freaked out."

"How's that my problem?"

"It's not, of course." She advanced to an arm's length before him, under the officer's watch. "But you obviously love your daughter just as much and, see… my husband here is a driven man and…" She went on, her voice low, leaning her head and tangled hair to brush down her shoulder, as Brett changed his weight and resigned to glowering at the mossy

72

spot aside.

When she turned back around, the man looked at him, then at Tara, then at his own daughter holding his hand. "Well... perhaps I would have," he said, feeling his bandage over, and glanced at Brett, who pressed his lips and nodded a new apology. He let his hand down and turned to the waiting officer. "Who said there's no entertainment in our park?" he added to everyone's relief, before he and his daughter walked back to the vehicle.

Tara rubbed her eyes. Brett lifted her high to sit her down on his neck and grabbed her ankles as they started walking back toward the park entry.

"A driven man...?" he said.

Susan didn't turn her head, either. "Maybe you should have him file. Or straight with the senator's office."

Beyond the fluttering leaves, the entry portal remained out of sight. He picked up the pace.

She blew out a breath. "What was that, training day? Gosh..."

"She wore a red ribbon, okay?"

"Yah. Tara's is peach. And it's a scrunchie."

He glared over, then filled his lungs and exhaled. Tara's foot dangled over his chest as he let go briefly to unzip his jacket. Susan made room for a jogger to go by, then her footsteps dropped behind.

When they reached the portal Tara begged to get down, with newfound energy, and Susan walked her onto the street sidewalk. He stretched and pressed his lower back with his knuckles. At the prickle in his waist, he glimpsed the torn shirt, now tainted with a red smudge.

"You know... I don't feel like going to that party really."

She glanced back from a few steps ahead. "Very mature Brett."

He moved on and pinged the car.

"Don't you think it's important? You of all people, who

73

lectures me on networking?"

He snorted. "Why don't you go then?"

She stopped. "Me?" She looked at him walk by. "Perhaps I will then."

"Good."

"For Tara."

"For Tara."

With a new group of joggers gone behind, the sidewalk went quiet again.

"And what do I say?"

"Don't know. That I'm sick or something."

# 7

He stayed a step behind as Susan helped her daughter up the stairs to the second floor veranda. Guffaws pitched higher through the muffled chatter, which grew loud as they walked unnoticed into the large, crowded room. The terrace doors were wide open toward the lake, and a raw tune of drums and vocals stirred the air over the shrills of the children chasing one another through the groups of standing adults.

"Clarens, finally!"

"Hi Gwyn. Sorry, I had to pass by my mother's."

"Is she okay?" she said, touching cheeks with him, then extended her hand and greeted Susan with an affectionate smile. "Too bad your husband couldn't make it."

"Yeah, he got this cold when he walked out of the gym," Susan replied, bringing Tara forward, "but thank you for having us."

"Absolutely!" Lynden showed up saying, and rested his elbow on Clarens's shoulder, looking at her. "Actually, you could just stay in the Commons as far as we're concerned."

Gwyn rolled her eyes with a smile over his chortling. "My husband Lynden…" She bent to cheer Tara with a few words and then grabbed her hand to lead her and Susan toward the jolting boat bouncer.

Susan glanced back and fluttered her fingers at Clarens, her diamond stud earring glinting through, then she weaved away in her fit black jeans and loose, silky top, her lush hair jouncing over.

With a hard pat on his back, Lynden turned him his way, then threw cheers left and right on their way to the fridge. He took two beers out and guzzled half of his as they turned to the hockey chatter of the three male friends standing by.

They manned up to making bets on the season's top scorer, to which he burped his say. "Boy, that guy's a sniper. I put my twenty on him."

"Sure, I can use another twenty," the bet taker quipped. "You Clarens?"

"Uhh… I haven't really followed this year."

"As opposed to last year."

"Hahaha!"

"Yah, better talk to Clarens about lunar triathlon. He's planning on migrating there," Lynden yapped, to everyone's renewed laughter, then turned away pointing to the holoset across the room. "I'll move it up!"

The others looked at Clarens. "Seriously, you're into that?"

"Well, it's sort of interesting, isn't it?" he said, unable to stifle his smile.

"Maybe. After five minutes I'm snoozing, to be honest," the one beside him said, and flew his hand up and down slowly. "Waeeooooun, waeeooooun…"

"It depends," Clarens said, chuckling too. "But when they switch to the leader view and there's no commentary, no sound, just the breathing, and you're just sailing over those craters it's like… you're there"—he stilled his beer bottle before him and smiled, as the three stayed quiet. "Then you get this four-limb powersuit vaulting over all of a sudden and it lands in a blaze of dust ahead of you and you're… here." He pulled his hand back and sipped. "I think that's quite entertaining."

"The moon migrant…"

"Hahaha!"

The music died down and someone dinged what sounded like metal on glassware until everyone was silenced. It was

Gwyn's father. He straightened up in his stiff, old-fashioned shirt and cleared his throat, then spoke in a firm voice with Gwyn and Lynden at his side. "Ten years ago yesterday, my daughter married this one here on a heartbeat. I gave them two years. Year after year they proved me wrong, and that he's the best husband money can buy." As everyone laughed, he turned to them both, arms out. "And I love them!"

Through the cheers, Gwyn hugged him and raised her hand to start her own anniversary speech. She then praised the friendship of the ones present and their annual gathering tradition. "Let's keep at it right here, year after year!" She turned to Lynden for their public kiss, then both laughed boisterous at the flying remarks. "And we have someone new with us," she added and craned her head around to spot Susan. "Her name is Susan and she's from the Free States, so make her feel at home!"

Susan smiled with a light blush at the turning faces and then drank as people began mingling again. By the time Clarens made his way through, she was flanked by two men and swiveling her head from one's chat to the other's. They wore calf-length baggies and hanging-sleeve shirts like just about everyone else, only made brighter by their tan. She leaned her head back to laugh at a new joke, to which Clarens stopped walking their way and brought his drink to his mouth, but only to choke at the patting on his back.

"Lost already? Boss…" Lynden winked and downed his beer. As Clarens shook his head and let a smile out, he poked his finger at his own chest. "You won't forget about this dude here, will you?"

"It's nothing certain. And Tal would keep the realty part for himself."

"What? He'll be on my tail every day?"

Clarens drank and looked at him. "You want me to take the job or not?"

Lynden burst, then rose on his toes to look over the talking heads across the room. "I'll be back."

"By the way, did you call Heslin about the apartment?"

"Yes. She was happy with the fee!"—he grinned over his shoulder.

Shortly, the large graph glittered higher before the back wall and the sound volume went up, which turned everyone to the fly-through feeds of the hockey arena. The pregame livecast retreated some to the background to make room for a newsflash, which started with a country tag for the Great Concord of Egalitarian States clearing over the skies of its Tensana province below. Views of flag-waving, chanting crowds mixed with ones of military vehicles lining city streets, while the side tag flashed with the state-of-emergency declaration. A bloody-faced man was rushed on a stretcher toward dazzling ambulance lights and then a busy freeway rolled out in an endless straight line before an orbital feed came through to show the border with the Free States Alliance to the north. The news switched red again to the world financial markets and then to home views of people sunbathing in camping armchairs and skating on a flattened glacier under a "Participation Day" holiday banner, when someone near the graph dashed the news object off as the players came out for the warm-up.

Susan wasn't in the same spot anymore, but he glimpsed her through the less crowded area behind him. She smiled scant in return at the people pursing lips at her on her way to the children's play zone, where the bouncer rocked and wobbled ever wilder. When he pulled out of the next conversation and glanced over again, she had taken Tara aside to tidy her hair, then she held her hand and walked with her behind the chatting moms and toward the entrance.

He rushed over. "Susan! Everything all right?"

She turned in the doorway. "Oh! Yes. I'm sorry, a little late for us here with the trip and all," she said, fondling Tara over her bangs.

"Must be." Clarens smiled at the girl, awkwardly stroking her head too, then looked back at Susan. "You do remember the way back…"

"Yes." She drew her finger through the air. "It's down, then straight, then up three levels, then left, no, second left…"

"You know, I think I'm calling it a day too. I got up at six."

"You're sure?"

He spotted Gwyn in the women-only group opposite from the sportscast. They were just as gay, however, and saying an early good night took only a side hug and not much explaining. He walked back and out on the veranda.

Helping Tara down the stairs, Susan turned to the rushing of his steps. "I didn't know there would be this many people."

"Yes, they have friends," he said, slowing beside them. "A lot of them are family, in fact."

She sighed a smile. "We never made the time for either, I guess." She fanned her shirt out a few times as they reached the ground pavement. "Perhaps I overdressed a little."

"You looked fine. I mean, look at me," he added quickly, picking at his loose blue slacks, which also revealed the strapped-on leather sandals. He smiled. "We'll get our chance tomorrow."

She chuckled, as they strolled at the girl's pace down the open passageway. It felt just as warm as upstairs, other than for the dainty breeze coming through the gray, aged-wood trellis. Traces of sand creaked on the flagstones under their feet as the party clatter ebbed behind, then dulled into the beat and spirits of another gathering on the way to their suite, in the opposite wing of the hotel compound.

Inside, he retreated to his unit and caught up with his mail, but met the two of them again some twenty minutes later in the common kitchen. In her polka-dot pajamas, Tara rose on her toes to place the milk cup on the counter for Susan's refill.

"Sorry, just getting some tea," he said, crossing through.

"Oh, sure." Susan made room for him at the dispenser,

then turned to Tara and had her say good night to him before leaving, which she eventually mumbled, with Susan's word-by-word help, including his name.

They laughed as she rolled her eyes at her, as Susan lifted her up to her chest, rocking her gently on the way to the door. She returned his good night, then swung her head again over her shoulder. "Oh, maybe I'll have a tea too."

From out on the terrace, he heard her footsteps back in the kitchen a few minutes later through the open doors. His cup warm in his palm, he glanced over when she stepped out. "Quite a view at this time of the day."

She wowed flabbergasted beside him.

In the late dusk, the glass clad of the gigantic dome spread shades of purple over the lake and against the dark sky beyond. The very apex soaked in red still, from where the circular nervures changed to deeper indigos one by one, till too far and subtle to be deciphered with the naked eye. With a fleet of zeps hovering over, the growing thread of lights twinkled along the outer shore and closer around, mirroring off the lake and off the glazing above. Meanwhile, the same warm breeze feathered the air, just enough to bring on the distant music vibes.

He sipped. "Tomorrow night they'll put on a lights show, for the holiday."

"A lights show?"—she smiled, stepping to the armchairs. "Gosh, I didn't see this being so huge when we drove in."

He spaced the next armchair apart and sat too. "It's harder to grasp in full sunlight. I forgot how that works to be honest."

"You come here often?"

"For a long time, rather. They've been doing their anniversary every year."

She wowed again, quiet, and brought the steaming cup to her mouth, her sight lower, to somewhere above the handrail.

He took another sip.

She rotated her head away. "Is that a lightning bug?"

He followed the flashing-red, minuscule light, too. "Yes it is. They brought some in for the decor."

"They did? There's another…"

The second light flashed on from a fixed spot farther on the planter until the first one reached it and then twinkled about until they were too hard to distinguish apart.

"Remarkably effective, isn't it?" he said slowly, leaning her way to watch.

She chuckled. "They'll have plenty of decor around here soon."

"They prey, in fact. This species. Probably easier to control." He pulled back as she hummed and tried her tea anew.

"I remember them as green when I was a kid." She lay back, her hair satin under the terrace lamp post. "We would sit on the porch after dinner waiting for them to come out and then we would chase them down the lawn till we couldn't see our footsteps anymore. Just a bit of moonlight above the tall black oaks, if that. And the deafening noise from the pond." She swayed her smile to him. "I was fascinated."

Propped on his elbow, he stared at her. "So… this was the house in the country."

Her eyes gleamed larger. "You saw the clips! Yes, my parents' house down south in Natoba, about an hour from the border." She looked out over the railing, silent again.

The outer shoreline sparkled on, while the party overtones had tuned out.

"And you? Grew up in the city?" she said.

"Yes. We did have a backyard," he smiled to add. "And the small greenhouse, of course. My mother loves gardening."

"Oh, really?"

"She was always in there. Before the Alzheimer's…"

He rested his head back on the chair. The crescent moon hung bright in the clear outside the hazy dome skin. Sirius and Rigel flickered in and out of a fast-moving patch.

She grasped her armrests to rise. "Well, I can so fall asleep watching this."

"I know. Well… have a good night."

"You too." She smiled back, stepping around the chair. "You're a night person, huh?"

"I don't know. Just a bad habit."

She chuckled softly then stopped, her silhouette against the terrace light. "Thanks again for doing this for us."

"Absolutely. I'm happy to." He looked back out as she left, but only to swing his head around again. "Susan…"

She turned halfway and waited through his pause.

"Area G-one tomorrow."

She flashed her hand open before slipping through the doorway.

———

He was early, but the raked sand was already printed with sinuous chair-wheel tracks going toward the front of the beach lot, near the water. He walked down the deck and grabbed a chair from the storage rack, then nodded good morning to the other newcomers and steered the chair to midway down the narrow lot. He slipped out of his sandals, looking out. A few sloops staked out the lake with whites and yellows. The line of near floaters jounced up and down with the regular, small waves, which then tapered off dovish over the flat shore. He kept watching them from under his sun cap while lying back in the chair, then closed his eyes and let the sounds take over.

He heard himself snore and cracked his eyes open. It was more than an hour later and voices flitted around. Outside the dome, a lone cloud looked like it was misting a few drops along. He brought his hands behind his neck to stretch.

"Guy!"

He turned.

Lynden grinned under his dark shades as he and his friend

they had chatted with the previous night marched closer, sand dusting up behind their slippers. "Not much rest last night?"—he snickered spry.

Reaching for his own shades, Clarens suppressed his smile. "You're sick."

"I can't believe you missed the game. Again!" He patted him on the shoulder as he turned to chortle with his friend.

They both carried a small scratch pad hanging on a bright nylon necklace over their sleeveless shirts. The other man grabbed his and looked it over. "So Clarens, here's your chance... To reach escape velocity," he added for another laugh with Lynden, then straightened up. "Here's your chance. Lawyers, or the rest of the world?" He nudged his head at Lynden. "They're short a few people."

Clarens reset his sun cap down. "I appreciate the thought, but why me?"

"Because everybody wants you, genius," Lynden said.

"No closing arguments on my team"—the other stuck his hand out. "Just grab that pole and ram it. C'mon, what is it going to be?"

Clarens chuckled along. "Can I just pass this time?"

"No way."

He paused, looking between the two of them. At the rear end of the beach lot, Susan strolled on the wood decking, holding Tara's hand. She wore shorts and a white tank top, while her straw hat matched the girl's. She stopped to look over the seated guests, then moved her tote to the other shoulder and strolled closer.

"And there's our rest of the world," the team captain muttered, for he and Lynden had also turned that way. "All right, I guess we'll let you ask. Noon rock-off!" he added, as Clarens took his shades off and waved his hand high at Susan. She didn't see him, though.

He waved again as the two men left, but she had slowed amid the bystanders in front of the open bar and didn't reemerge. He dropped his cap on the chair and headed that way.

"Clarens! You're just getting here?"

Lying back in her beach chair, Gwyn lifted her large shades just enough to squint at him.

"Gwyn! Mornin'!" He stepped toward her. "No, I've been out there in front."

"Oh, I guess it paid off to sneak out so early," she quipped and let her shades back down, a tad lighter, then tapped the armrest of the empty chair next to her. "Come catch up a little."

"Sure." He pointed to the bar. "Do you want a drink?"

"Yes, let me order. What would you like?" She darkened her shades again as he sat and then appeared to blink behind them with each slight nudge of her head. "Bear with me, I just got these replicas." She felt his forearm. "Lynden wanted me to be cool." She tilted her head to him and smiled. "So happy about you and Heslin, by the way. You know that she and I stayed close all the way through."

The small bar kiosk was now entirely obscured by the groups in front of it, but the drinks arrived within minutes and Gwyn kept the questions going between cold sips and people watching. Just about all the guests seemed to have made it in and, on the other side of the straw divider, the next beach lot looked just as crowded under the slow-fluttering fishtail flags and the preteen shrieks flying about.

Clarens raised his half-full cup before his eye. The condensation had beaded up, and the new burst of the sun dazzled through the pulpless mango inside.

"But we should get together all four of us soon," Gwyn continued. "Kenton's for dinner?"

"I'm sure she'd love that."

"There you are you guys!" Susan said.

As he lowered his cup and turned to her, she raised her shades over her head and stopped with a large smile in front of Gwyn, who looked up too. She was alone, her hat flapping out of the tote on her shoulder, a strawed drink in her hand.

Through the three-way greetings, Gwyn pointed to the empty chairs lying around. "Grab one. My kids are just going to bounce all day again."

"I know," Susan chuckled and looked out as Clarens dragged the nearest chair close. "I can't remember when Tara last played this much."

"You should bring her by. We have a wonderful playground on our street."

"Oh yeah? Thanks, we'd so love that." She put her drink in the chair's holder and sat. "You know, everyone's just so nice here at your party," she said in a lowered voice, as Clarens took his seat back between the two of them. "I mean…" she slowed again and pulled off her top to remain in her beach bra, just like Gwyn was. "It took me half an hour to get past the bar with everyone saying hello and such." She smiled at her.

"Well… thank you dear," Gwyn said, halted behind her shades. She drank. "It's the holiday, also."

A number of people around stood up, while farther out, others appeared to be heading toward the growing group by the water. Lynden showed up, his footsteps laboring through the sand. "It's time boys and girls!" A thread of sweat seeped from under his hairline and over the reddened forehead, while a wet spot came through his shirt, just below the broad chest. He stopped abruptly and pointed his finger at Susan, turning to Clarens. "Is she on?" As Clarens hemmed, he bristled, while Susan smiled at them both.

"It's this game they play every year," Clarens said to her, swinging his hand at the lake.

"Oh, I'm not a good swimmer actually." She uncrossed her legs and laid her hands on her lap as she shrugged.

Lynden stared at her. "You… are not… a swimmer?"

"You heard the girl Lynden," Gwyn prompted.

85

He twitched his head to Clarens. "All right. You!"—he pointed his finger at him. "You're with the rest of the world," he said, and marked off his scratch pad. "Sorry boss, I wish you could stay on my team."

"Don't worry, I won't remember it."

"Hahaha! On the barge in five!" he called over his shoulder and strutted away.

Gwyn brought her drink straw to her mouth and turned to Susan. "My husband can be nice too."

They all laughed, then Clarens stood up and removed his T-shirt. "Coming to watch?"

"Sure!" Susan dropped her cup back in the holder and rose, while Gwyn flapped her hand and nudged her chin at the children's water bouncer.

"I see it just about every day, dear," she said. "Tell him he better not call me to the rescue"—she smiled tightly, and brought her elbows high on the armrests as they left her behind.

They caught up with the last few people heading for the shore where the two large, solid-foam barges rubbed against each other with the synthetic waves. Several contestants were already climbing on from the chest-high water, while the watchers lined up on the narrow pier, a dozen meters away. Susan left to get Tara to have her watch the game too. When he climbed onto his barge, he spotted the girl reaching for the gulls at the outer end of the crowded pier and then Susan bringing her back to find a place behind the guardrail. He waved in return just as the yells intensified with the start of the game, then he reeled on the rubber grooves to join his teammates along the middle line of the barge. Arms wrapped around the inflatable battering pole, they rocked it back and forth and sideways into the arms of the people on the other barge, as the two teams tried to down each other into the water. The first few fell off within minutes, then the laughs and mocking cheers kept flying with every new splash until the last men standing, him among them, struggled to regain their breath and footing through a momentary truce. They roared with a new thrust, when a high-pitched scream speared through from elsewhere. Jolting with the pushback, he looked out over his pole-grappling arm as the cheering from the crowd on the pier waned and the screaming came through clear.

"Tara!"

With a few people following her, Susan raced to the outer end of the pier. He let go and slipped as he sprang off the barge for a side dive, but recovered under the surface and kept breast stroking through the deepening water. He broke to the above only to see a frantic Susan kneel and point down the second to last stilt, then he filled his lungs and dived again. Tara's bright purple scrunchie glimmered in the gauzy sunrays, against the darker lake bottom under the pier. He stroked down and seized her under his arm, then clasped the metal stilt to thrust himself up and kicked his way higher to the surface.

"Tara!" Utterly distressed, Susan lifted the inert girl from his extended arms and kept calling her name as she laid her on the pier deck. She scrabbled her hands over her for a moment, then pumped her chest bone a few times before bending to blow air in her mouth but, to the collective sigh of relief of the ones gathered around, Tara coughed water out on her face. Between tears and joy, Susan turned her on the side to spew it all out, then she rose with her in her arms, cheek to cheek, and nodded a weary smile at the remaining few who hadn't already turned to the restarting game.

Clarens waved his finger at his teammates calling him back on the barge, then he reached for the higher bar on the guardrail to pull himself out of the water. "That's one pretty boat"—he bobbed his head at Tara's scrunchie, to which she coughed anew over Susan's shoulder.

Susan turned around to him. "Isn't it? We have three

of them." She smiled and laced her fingers through Tara's gleaming hair as he landed with a smooth jump. She wept. "She'd just gaze at those waves." She crumpled and wiped her cheeks.

"She must have slipped off. They turned them up for the game"—he pointed toward the climactic barge fight as they walked down the pier.

"I'm so sorry, I spoiled your thing."

"No, no." He kept looking out, ruffling his hair, then smiled at her. "It was a pretty good exit I thought."

The middle of the pier was overcrowded with the players who had climbed on from the water, now all boisterous and rooting for their own still in the contest. Plodding her way through in front of him, she turned and leaned her head away from Tara's on her other shoulder. "I think we'll check with the medical room, just in case."

With another cough, the child pushed against Susan's chest to pivot her head toward him. Under her lowered lids, her murky eyes made her face look even paler, as they were able to move again.

"Or we could leave today, I have work to do anyway," he said. As Susan slanted her head back at him, he tipped his earlobe and slowed behind her through the new roaring.

———

Someone had stepped to the end of the bench press and held his hands under the barbell. Brett peeked at him over his crimpled forehead and lifted the bar strenuously four more times, the last of which he bulged his cheeks and swayed the barbell sideways on the way up, where the man helped him place it on the supports.

"Good stuff!"

Brett rose to sitting. "Thanks," he exhaled, and glanced over.

The forty-something man bent his bare, sinewy arms to rest his hands on his waist. "From the hotel too?" he tossed his chin at the windows saying, and grinned at Brett's nod. "Something to lift in every town."

Brett looked at him, then stood up and threw his towel on his shoulder. "You've got it wrong, pal." He walked to the side aisle and turned toward the gym's locker room. "A fuckin' break here please," he muttered, eyes rolling at the ceiling.

He slowed inside the closing doors to listen in to his set but, other than the market alerts, he had no new mail. In the shower, he braced his hands against the wall and let his head back with the front jet flooding his face. It looked like a cloud moved past the sun as the matted skylight above suddenly lit up. Another cloud never moved in.

A patch of stale air sneaked out as he entered his hotel room. He turned the air controls up, dropped his shoulder bag on the floor, and sank into the armchair. There were two bites left in the ham roll on the coffee table, plus a discolored celery leaf. The fallen beer can had dripped in an amorphous spot over half of the tray. He rose and ambled to the closet, then returned with a garment cover and circled the lounging area to discard the snack remains and other beer cans in the makeshift bag. When the Orion Clearway call came through, he frowned and picked up, voice only.

"Mr. Falco, I'm sorry to disturb you on a Sunday morning."

"Afternoon here."

"Oh, yes. Briefly sir, when can we have an update on your adviser status?"

"Did you not read my message?"

"Yes but, clients are getting uneasy with the... limited availability. In light of the current events. Several opted out."

"Well, their loss. I need the two extra weeks."

"Two weeks. Just confirming. Thank you, sir."

He hung up, then lay back in the chair and tapped the armrest slowly, gaze on the ceiling. A minute into it he turned his palm up and thumbed the room display on. He sank his cheek into his fist while browsing through, until he reached an adult source. He turned the sound low and sized up the hologram in front of the wall, then rose and stepped to the refrigerator to take a beer out. He stood motionless and watched the fleshy tones, only lifting his can to sip some every so often. He browsed again and settled for a qualifier football game, but shortly brought his financial source on instead, tapped the can down on the table, and began fiddling with the numeric objects across the room.

He twitched with the new chime inside his ear, a broad note from his stepbrothers about their father's upcoming retirement bash, which he deleted through the first sentence. He tried to refocus on the display but turned it off and rose. Out the window, the streets below the hotel looked dormant. In the far left corner, cars ran sparsely over the long shadows that now crossed the boulevard. He called up Susan's name, then hesitated over the call prompt. He turned to walk to the closet, where he changed shirts and jeans and slipped into a new pair of shoes, then watched himself rinsing his mouth in front of the bathroom's mirrored wall. The two jackets of choice hung quiet in the entryway's side closet. He slowly swung the door closed and, an instant later, he struck it lightning fast. His fist went through it and, as he tried to pull it out the splintered hole, the door came off, unhinged. He grabbed the first jacket, pitched the door against the frame, and left.

———

Outside the windshield's hue, the road climbed up the rocky hillside. A few turns higher, the top of the dome arched over the bald ridge on the right once more, in ethereal sparkles and whites, although its sheer size could hardly tell that they had long left it behind.

"So who won, by the way?" Susan said.

"The rest of the world." Clarens smiled back. "This time."

She chuckled softly and turned to Tara who snored in the back seat. "Sweetie… One boo-boo after another," she murmured, then faced forward again. "You must be a really good swimmer, the way you dove there."

He shrugged. "I'm actually better under. It's my weekly splash."

"I wish I could do that."

They steered onto the freeway ramp, then he let his head back with the speed. "You do horseback riding, you said."

"Yeah… Haven't had time for it lately. With the trip preparations and stuff." She looked out her window. "Who knows what Ronan's doing now. My horse"—she glanced over. "We had to sell him. It was like selling family."

"I can imagine. I wish I could do that."

She sniffed short, but widened her eyes as he nodded straight-faced to her. "Riding? Have you tried?"

"No, I've never had the chance. When young enough."

"When young enough…?"

Low brush sprinkled the side of the hillock, then the freeway unwound to a straight band crossing the steppe out. Car rooftops shone along it in the distance, dotting the way to beyond the blurring lines. The surface felt flawless and only the slight hiss cued to the outside winds, leaving Tara's snoring to fill the cabin alone.

"There's this road that crosses over the hills," he said, and pointed to her side of the windshield, where the gray-purple row of hills continued rolling along. "It's slower, but there's a village to see up there if you'd like."

"Oh yeah?"

"Well, artisan farms, restored. They have greenhouses from the early 2100s."

"Sounds great." She slanted her head closer and raised her brows. "We call that green rush rash, by the way."

The exit came up within minutes and then he brought his hands to the steering wheel for the narrowing, unfurnished road. It soon started winding tightly up the hills, while the wind settled down in the shelter of the terrain and of the few trees braving the ever arid grounds. In the interior viewer, Tara yawned and rubbed her cracked-open eyes as Susan swiveled around to her, then she asked for food.

The slopes greened up past the top ridge, then, two knolls farther, the first greenhouse flashed a light dot from across the valley ahead. A few yellows and reds spotted through the shrubs as the road bottomed out, just in time for the refinished, period road sign: "Chesterhills, founded 2107."

They pulled into the small parking lot by the village hall. The shed-like metal building looked freshly painted, all in a maroon-red, except the single, gray front door and the glass canopy above it. A group of people strolled by on the crushed-stone walkway, toward the cars in the shade of the old beech trees surrounding the lot. Atop the pole next to the building, the national flag hovered with the tentative wind, while some of the benches below still bathed in the late sun.

"This is neat!"

"Isn't it?"

He toured the small green around the building, while Susan and Tara sat out on a bench to snack. The hall was closed but, having come back in a full circle, he stopped to read the plate on the pedestal by the front door, then squinted under his hand at the hills out west, on the other side of the road. Tara stamped the ground next to him, jolting him, and tilted her head back with a smile, then leaped farther down the walkway as Susan walked closer from behind him.

She ran back to them with a small, flowered stalk in her hand. "Mommy, what is this?"

"Hmm... I don't know sweetie, some paintbrush. Perhaps Mr. Mann knows."

He pulled his head back from the orange, odorless tip that

Tara stuck under his chin. "Uhh... not entirely sure on this subspecies," he muttered, a smile in the corner of his mouth, then chuckled along with Susan while Tara took off again. He pointed out that way. "A little tour?"

The walkway left the village green to merge with the sidewalk along the main road, which they followed briefly to the first corner and turned onto a quiet side road, where Susan let the girl hop ahead once more. A row of mature thujas lined the pristine, white-marked pavement on both sides. Past the first stretch, a small farmhouse showed up on the right, in spotless paintwork and unweathered copper spouts and gutters. The restored gas-powered tractor beamed green and yellow from the driveway to further liven the setting.

"People are still farming..."

"For fun perhaps," he replied, and looked with her back toward the road, which began coasting and then curved to cut into the hill slope, opening a wide view over the valley on the left.

A greenhouse glared over from the bald strip on the hillside across, and another from within the brush padding the lower versant as they stopped to spot the remaining few.

"Some are still rusting away, since the first settlement," he said, and passed his extended hand over the view. "Imagine... Sheep on that parcel there, Mount Palachi always out there, motor noises here back and forth." He turned and took a few hurried steps down the road, craning his head higher. "There was another one just here, if still empty..."

Arms crossed over her chest, she strolled after him. "So you always stop here?"

"Just once, but stayed in the car. Rainy day."

Around a large, embedded boulder, the unkempt driveway split off the road to wind around more boulders and shrubs up the flattening hillside. Amber stalks of grass lined the cracked pavement and spiked through it in two parallel rows spaced to about a car track. As they followed it in, a dull metal rooftop peeked through the whispering tree crowns.

Like the other, the farmhouse was simply a round mansard roof over an elongated ground-level shed, only smaller. A whitish paint coat had all but disappeared to reveal the moss-stained, corroded panels, while several punctures spattered the roof itself. When Tara ran ahead into the driveway turnaround a hawk flew over her from the top of the barn, prompting her quick return.

"It's gone. Just stay close to Mommy," Susan said, stroking her back. "What, you're cold?" She reached with her other hand for the sweater inside her tote, which slid down her arm and fell on the ground. "Oh my, I keep on doing this!"—she laughed short, as the water bottle and Tara's prescription drink rolled out and another bird swooshed silent over the house. She squatted with him to pick up the scattered contents. "When was the last time you scouted abandoned farms," she went on, "with an overseas client, checking the tarmac cracks for lip moisturizer?" She raised her head and smiled, just as he did.

"You know, I don't even remember."

The greenhouse behind the farmhouse had most of the glass cladding knocked out, to the benefit of the outgrowing shrubs, yet he moved closer to wonder at the exposed girts, purlins, struts, and their time-defying bolted connectors. They completed the tour around the barn to end up back in the L-shaped courtyard, which was enveloped by the long shadow of the house. Tara bounced ahead over the remaining strips of sunlight that crossed the driveway on the way out. The lines flickered with the stronger breeze scuffing through.

"This was interesting. You could almost see that tree crawling out of the frame," Susan said, crossing her arms again.

"Right." He smiled. "That always seems to happen when you put the new and old together."

"What do you mean?"

"Just... how they reveal themselves more clearly that way."

"Yeah, maybe." She looked at him, lips thinned in her quiet smile. "You seem to prefer the old."

He chuckled and looked ahead. "We don't get much of it here, remember? But it does give you this sense of time, and grounding." He turned his head. "And you?"

"Don't know, either one. I don't mind the new." She turned too. "I grew up in a wooden house." She laughed softly, but grasped her upper arms with the new spell in the air.

"You're cold."

"No, just for a bit there."

"Here, take this," he said, slowing to take off his jacket. "I insist. Just a liability issue."

She chuckled and pushed her arm through the sleeves as he held the collar and her tote, then turned and zipped up. She glanced up at him for an instant before they kissed. She pulled back. "I'm sorry, I don't know why I did that."

"No, I'm... sorry too."

They turned and walked again, only more steady.

A couple of greenhouses lit a soft orange from the south side of the valley, the tractor had not moved, then the main road looked just as quiet. Only one other car was left in the lot, while the large lantern had turned on above the hall's door.

Once the road climbed over the last ridge north the wind firmed up, against the distant whirring of the car, and the winged, impetuous shapes of the remaining trees made it seem more so that way. Dry brush rolled over the lower grounds, with the road unwinding to an almost straight line once more, toward the lights of Ayland.

95

# 8

The soft flooring padded his steps through the stillness of the empty corridor. He slowed as Susan's suite door came into view, cracked open, and walked by to his own door. Before he could swing it closed behind him, Susan was out.

"Brett?"

He glanced over his shoulder and walked farther in.

"Where have you been?" she asked.

"Since when are you interested?"

"Wonderful…"

He threw his jacket on the chair and turned. "What about you? You weren't supposed to be back till tonight."

She leaned against the wall in the entryway in her lounge pants. "We had to cut it a day short." She waited for him to ball the soiled napkin from the table and lob it in the wall disposal. "I didn't hear you coming back last night," she continued, when someone stopped behind her in the half-open entry door.

"Excuse me, miss. Sir, would you like the spare room during the door replacement?"

"No, I'll just step out. If we can have a few minutes."

"Sure. Very good, sir," the hotel staffer said, and left.

"You have a spare room?"

"You heard him."

"What replacement is that?"

"Okay, anything else?"

"Yes, actually." She returned his stare. "The application got denied."

Paused, he only let his hand back down. Her hair covered her cheek as she looked aside and squeezed her lips. He turned around. "Fuck!... C'mon, let's go to your room."

Tara was sleeping. Susan closed her bedroom door gently before climbing into her own ruffled bed in the main room and locked her hands over her knees.

On the sofa, Brett bent forward. "So what did he say?"

"Not much. We've been denied." She shrugged and kept her eyes on her tipping thumbs. "That the senator sympathized and all that but they can't make exceptions."

"Just like that."

"Yep. And that we could get another month on the visas."

"Bullshit!"

"Shh…" She frowned, and lay against the headboard to reach for a tissue. "Oh, Clarens mentioned this option of living outside the border and applying for a multiple-entry program. You know, like in that place we went through."

"Tencun?"

"Yeah."

"He told you to live in Tencun?" he whispered loud. "He's got some nerve, this slick."

"He's just trying to help, Brett. He went through every single thing we gave him to put it all together, you know?"

"Yeah. For eight thousand." He rested his elbows on his legs, head sunk between his shoulders. Susan's and Tara's dusty sneakers lay on an empty grocery container under the table. Beside them, her open travel case was mostly packed still, and the carrier display blinked the time, four hours lagged.

She shuffled slowly in bed. "It's got some better areas, apparently."

He raised his head. "Are you kidding? I'd rather go back."

"So we go back now?"

He glared over, then stood up and stepped around the

sofa. "I can't believe they denied it. They have the most eligible people, financially, professionally, culturally fuckin' identical…"

"Brett!" she whispered loud. "What do we do?"

He fixed on her. "We go there first thing tomorrow. He has to try again."

"To try what?"

"He has to try again!"

"Shh!"

"He needs to find something."

"I'm not going there to say how much I love the Commons and all that all over again and make a fool of myself."

"You will."

"I don't think so."

He stepped closer, braced his hands on the edge of the bed, and leaned to her. "You want to go back to old sweet Kewan then."

She wiped her nose and returned to staring out. "I shouldn't have listened to you."

"Boy, was I waiting for that one!"—he thrust himself back to standing. "You actually want to. And to get your store back too? And hose down the urine on the back door every morning, and roll up the filthy shutters, unless someone's holding your ass at knifepoint already."

"All right Brett."

"At least all those friends will call in no matter what. And we'll be sure to go see your father on the semiannual visit," he muttered on, unfazed, and wavered his hand. "For about forty-five, tops, before you two start arguing all the way to the gate. Just so that we'll have some steam to blow on the way back in case they finished working on the bridge."

Behind the bedroom door, Tara mumbled indistinctly. Susan shook her head but stayed numb.

He clenched his jaws and looked out too. "We committed to this."

Without an answer, he watched her pick up another tissue.

"I am committed," she murmured. "For Tara. She's all I have at this point."

"Oh, oh…"

"You know, why don't you go check on your new door."

————

"G'night, Clarens."

"G'night, Tal."

Talbot stopped behind the glazing and took a step backward to show his head in the open office door again. "Decided yet?"

"Uhh… not yet," Clarens said, temple resting on three fingers over the desk. "I know, it's ticking." He smiled as Talbot nodded to move on. "Hey Tal, have a second?"

Talbot backed up again. "One."

"All right." Sitting higher, Clarens panned over the wall and back down to him. "Same entity. Two precedents make no precedent."

"Whoa… What area?"

"Immigration."

"Oh, that thing. What's the second precedent to?"

"Asylum."

Talbot nudged his head forward.

"Well, I'm also turning the tables on them. Here's the Constitution," Clarens added, bending to the text object in his graph. "'Any act of self-gratification by a public servant, whether to a tangible end or to fulfill his or her personal legacy or faithful beliefs, shall be deemed a criminal offense," he read, then slowed to spell out louder, "'as well as sanctioned, within our bounds and prerogatives, as an ill to free societies elsewhere.'" To Talbot's puff, he tipped his chin at the other side of the desk. "You should see the guy in this material."

"It's a stretch."

"Probably." He eased back in the chair. "There just isn't much to get a grip on."

Talbot tapped his hand twice on the door frame before leaving. "Just don't rewrite that little old book, will you?"

Half an hour later Clarens gazed up the wall one last time, then rose abruptly and walked out too. He nodded more good nights to the few on the office floor, then kept searching through the midair on the way to the elevators, and to the empty garage platform thereafter. He remained still beside the arriving car, until footsteps squeaked close from elsewhere, then he sat in and let the car follow the path out and to the expressway, seemingly always behind the same blue car out in front.

Heslin called, just as he exited to the small streets near home. He cleared his voice and whisked his ruffled hair back over his temple before picking up. "Hey! How was it?"

"Hey! Great, met some cool people," she said, beaming from her own driver seat. "You know, energy and defense execs down there. Nothing like your trip, I hear!"

"What, why's that?"—he widened his smile.

She laughed. "Nothing. Gwyn called me. She mentioned you brought your client to the party, and that she turned heads backward."

"Haha! Yes, it was quite funny. Did she mention dinner?"

"Oh, yes! Next weekend?"

"Get started on the anniversary speech," he quipped, to her leaning her head back with another laugh. His car slowed before the building garage. "So, you're coming over?" he added.

"I'll call you," she said, and looked aside to read aloud the trip-time estimate. She pondered over it and turned quickly. "Hey, do you think it was a little odd to show up with her?"

"Hes… She's a married woman with a child. Her husband just couldn't make it."

"And who would know that? She's a stunning young

woman, with a child, who stayed in our suite," she firmed her tone, saying. "What does that make me look like?"

He smiled. "You're not serious."

"C'mon Clarens, you've never been a hypocrite."

He exhaled, as the car came to a stop inside the garage. "Wait, my sister keeps calling…"

In the new call, his sister scowled between the padded shoulders of her sports vest. "You're doing court this late?"

"No, I—"

"Why did we say we'd pick up the urgents? For me to just hang in here?"

He rested his head on his knuckles. "I picked up. What is it?"

Her brows unknitted some. "Mom had a situation. The nurse called and said that she was hitting her and tossing things off the shelves." She opened up a side feed with two medical staff next to a bedded patient in what looked like the interior of an ambulance in motion.

He let his arm slip off the door mold.

"Can you go?" she asked. "We have hockey."

"Sure."

"Ping me when she wakes."

As the call went blank over the dashboard, he stared at the parking number plate beyond, then higher over the frieze of leaves in the concrete wall's bas-reliefs. The elevator doors slid open and his neighbor walked out onto the garage floor. Once she pasted a return smile outside his window, the aging woman minced on in her white and purple ankle boots, to lead her impeccably groomed chow down the parking row.

He switched back to Heslin, who jarred her eyes between him and the road, with the low townscape fast unfolding by her cheek. "All right… We had that empty suite and at the last minute I thought to do a nice thing and invite them along," he said, and waved one hand. "These people have lived in a hotel for a month now. You do develop some empathy for that."

"Oh, that's why you two left early."

He waited for her to glimpse in again. "I can't believe you said that. Her daughter got sick."

"She was not sick."

"She was fatigued after almost drowning."

"That is not sick."

"Hes... Why?"

She exhaled. "I just think it's ridiculous and that you should recognize it."

"What's ridiculous? That she turned heads? Or that you simply presume it didn't make you look good?"

She edged forward to meet his eyes, her tone that much firmer. "People do care about image, Clarens. It's called reality. But we shouldn't go there."

She thrust back in her seat and shook her head.

He looked back up the tall frieze. "You know, you're right. That might take the fun out of it."

"What's that supposed to mean?"

He stayed quiet. Three parking spots down, the neighbor petted her dog in its front seat harness one last time, then let the door slide down and stepped around her car. Her wobbling blond curls looked strikingly youthful from behind.

"Clarens, what's that supposed to mean?"

"Perhaps that... my definition of reality doesn't come close to yours," he said slowly, as the silence and lighter hue returned with the garage doors butting back closed.

As he turned his head, she pinned his eyes with her stern gaze. "You know we can't do this forever."

"I know. But let's talk later," he added, when she raised her hand and looked out, pinching her sheen-pink lips and eyes gleaming. She let her chin down to swallow and turned to him again. "We could have had it all. Instead, it just amazes me how someone supposedly brilliant gets wasted in such... purposeless decadence."

"Hes, that's your view—"

"My view? Of course. Yours got derailed again. By a needy pair of tits. Excuse me, empathy. Just!" she shrilled as he opened his mouth, her eyebrows twitching without aim. "Don't call me."

Unhurried, the minuscule light sailed over the southern suburbs and into the twinkling city skyline, as another one moved in through the emerging stars past the window's muntin. Midway through the new descent, Clarens looked over his shoulder at the waiting area, where a couple with two young teens walked closer and took seats. The man grabbed the boy to reseat him next to the girl in the middle. The woman reached out to them both, then crossed her hands on her lap and turned to the idle hospital foyer. Back outside, the distant aircraft had already disappeared, and no other flew by within the next several minutes. He swung around with the visitor service call and headed to the specified inlet. The medical staffer nodded in the doorway and led him inside the core foyer and around the glacier wall to the elevators. Two stories up, they turned into a new hall, a bowing, door-laden corridor, and passed by half a dozen of the recessed doorways before stopping.

"The doctor will be here in a minute," the staffer said and entered the room.

A second staffer nodded back and continued shelving linens in the small, rose-scented entryway. The room's perimeter soffit diffused a soothing, warm light around the sole fixture in the center of the ceiling, above the pastels-clad bed. Raised with the bed's upward tilting half, his mother frowned at the geography program in the large hologram glinting across the room in midair. Her plain, round-collared shirt lay unevenly to one side, unlike her brilliant-white hair which was combed back neatly and away from the wrinkles in the corners of her eyes. She didn't seem to see him step closer.

"Mom?" He bent forward and laid his hand on the edge of the bed. "Mom."

She turned and looked long at him, then at the doctor who had just approached from behind. She kept frowning as she turned to the program again. He watched her until he felt a hand on his shoulder, then he rose and blinked his moistened eyelids before turning to the doctor, who nudged her head toward the door.

"It will come back to her. She just had a fit," she said, holding the door open, then let it close quietly behind them and looked at him from under her arching eyebrows. "But she's nearing a late-moderate stage. Home care could get expensive."

"Right…"

She pressed her lips, fixating him an instant longer. "Sleep on it. We'll call you if there's anything," she added, then hustled away.

He watched her blur down the corridor's bow and disappear inside another side recess. He twitched and moved out of the way for a wheel-chaired patient and a staffer to pass through from behind, who then took a little longer to leave the corridor empty again. He turned to the dew-green door and paused, then drifted toward the elevators.

Crossing out the hospital doors, he raised his gaze off the pavement. Although the wind had all but ceased, the air felt much cooler. He exhaled slowly before calling his sister.

"Wait," she prompted and quelled the shrieks behind her. "You're out already? Why didn't you put me on?" Once he went through the details, she toned it down, until he mentioned the facility care.

"But nothing can make it home, the things she's been around forever," he countered. "It's her anchor in this reality."

"Clarens, in this reality she doesn't remember where the bathroom is! And do you realize the cost of a second nurse, equipment and stuff?"

"I can cover it."

"Nonsense."

She swiveled to the backseats to yell over the children's renewed fighting, as he reached the street sidewalk and looked around. He followed the sidewalk to the right, where it ran beside the lawn in front of the building. She returned, shaking her head, then yanked the collar of her vest open and sighed loudly. "We should sell the house. The huge thing just stays there sucking up dues."

He searched over the lawn, out to the mulched knoll that bound the hospital grounds along the backdrop of lavish free-form cypresses. The smell of the freshly mowed grass weighed in the air. The virile green glimmered under the drops of condensation and the crisp lampposts that lined the diverging walkway.

"Perhaps your friend Lynden can do it and save us some," she added.

He wandered the new way. The grass balm only thickened. "Perhaps. I'll ask..." He looked up above the lights. "Hey, do you remember that time when we went to picnic in Kierwoods and Dad caught a hare with the fishing net?"

"What? Oh, just before he..."

"Yes."

"Somewhat. Why?"

"No reason. That was a fun day."

"It was. Goes fast, huh?" She paused over the tuned-out giggles. "You'll let me know then."


The fine click of the apartment door shut off the voices in the hallway. He hung his jacket and glimpsed in the narrow wardrobe mirror, then leaned closer and just stared, his eyes a palm away from the surface. The red vessels rooted over the gleaming, cloudy white, and encircled the irises' blues and greens, and the bronze around the dilated, very, very noisy black.

With the awakening lights, he stepped to the kitchen fountain for a glass of water, then ate the almond spread leftovers and picked grapes from the stalk as he returned around the island to the open floor. The downtown towers twinkled small between the two buildings across the street, and the northern extension peeked above the lower roofline aside in the same soft hues, other than for the flashes atop the new tower's cranes. From below, the pole lights beamed on. The heliconia stood large next to the bay glazing, one side awash in the outside light, the other wielding its shadow gradient across the wall into the dim room, layers of gauze webbing over and over.

# 9

Susan was there, wandering in the front roundabout, and looked over as he crossed into the park. She grabbed Tara and walked toward him, the tail of her ivory overcoat fluttering in the chilly gust and her hair gushing over her face when a few steps away.

"Hi…" she smiled coy. "Thanks for meeting us out here instead."

"Sure. Glad to get out of that shell for once," Clarens said, weighing his snack pack in his hand. He flapped his other hand at Tara, who turned against Susan's thigh while her musical pinwheel slowed to a quiet few notes.

Susan stroked her cheek. "We wanted a playground. And I did leave a message for Gwyn, but…" The few strands of hair covering her eyes couldn't quite hide the circles below. "We saw one in here, though. We could check it out."

"Good!" He raised his finger at the priority call coming in and turned to the side. "Tell them I'm not taking any new cases for another two weeks," he replied to his assistant, then returned to Susan, who wandered back toward the roundabout.

They crossed it to the larger alley spiking out into the park, where she let Tara walk ahead on her own and slipped her hands in her coat pockets.

He pressed his lips. "So, as I told Brett, the chances of an appeal are just as low."

"I know." She waited to pass a luncher on a side bench before continuing. "It's also that Brett and I are not all that sure about things anymore," she uttered slowly. "Between us."

"Oh... I'm sorry to hear that."

From under their feet, the stripes of long-cut stone crossed the alley in slanted, irregular rows, outgrowing one another. Two willows swelled up over the opening lawn, and Tara's pinwheel spawned colored figures in the lingering wind with the new segment of the nursery rhyme.

He glanced over. "I hope it has nothing to do with—"

"Oh no. We go back years." She turned to him abruptly. "We didn't lie or anything, about family and all."

"Of course."

She looked down the alley again and shook her head repeatedly. "It's just that he's so angry. He's so goddamn angry all the time!" she burst, shoulders quavering. She turned the other way and rushed her hand out of the pocket to wipe her cheek, as he stroked her back. Tara turned and watched her move on, then returned her gaze to the wheel high in her hand.

"Gosh, why am I telling you this?" Susan regained her voice, pulling out a tissue, and turned her head. "Sorry, none of the hotel staff were available," she quipped under the tearful eyes.

He chuckled.

"Ever been married?" she continued.

"No."

"Why? Because it's not trendy here?"—she slipped a smile. "If you don't mind me asking."

"People do marry, you've seen it. In fact, my sister has what you might call a successful marriage, right out of college. Stable, prolific... I feel like I've done it all."

They laughed again, and he leaned to the other side to take his assistant's new call. "Tell them that's just a rumor. Two weeks," he replied. "Lynden, Lynden..." he then muttered under his breath and turned back to her, as she beckoned Tara to change direction, toward what looked like the playground on the other side of the lawn.

She let her hands back in her pockets as they too ambled onto the soft lawn to follow the feeble musical sounds, between the crossing lunchers and their long-strawed drinks.


"I might not be made for it, but I so love this child." To his "hmm" she kept her sight ahead. "Gosh, why does it have to be so hard? You want to build something and... you can't have it."

He looked up with her as the field was immersed in the shadow of another passing cloud. "Well, like with everything, it's living up the highs and evading the lows."

"So that's what marriage is, you think?"

"I think that... it is an interesting trade-off between your freedom and your needs, including the one of attaining your intimate reflection in the surrounding world."

She slowed and smiled. "What? Interesting trade-off between what?" She chuckled softly as he returned the smile and shrugged, then walked on. "Interesting, interesting..."

Wings flapped the air as Tara chased the geese toward the pond by the playground. She then stopped well short of the water's edge to watch their landing splash.

"Ready to dive in?" Susan glanced at him, saying, when he twitched his head aside, hand over the ear again. "Oh, I'm keeping you with my silly things."

He let the call go unanswered. "No, I still have a minute. If you had more questions about options, or appealing..."

She shrugged. "I do but... I should take a few days." She looked around and met his eyes as they came to a stop. Surrounding her hair waves, the pond shimmered in the sunrays that broke through once again. "Thanks for coming. I feel better."

"You seem better."

"I do?"

"You do..."

They leaned closer and touched lips. Dry, although the bittersweet taste of her moisturizer was there.

She slipped her hand out of her pocket and laid it on his chest while he felt the satin coat over her waist. "What are we doing?"

"I'm not sure. But I couldn't stop thinking about it."

Her eyelashes combed the sliver of air between them. "I remember that first day in your office, when you leaned back in your chair and looked up like... beyond the wall somewhere."

His eyes dwelled on hers. "I remember when you came back... and talked about riding horses on your hills."

She looked back down at his lips. A new nursery rhyme played amid louder shrieks, and they turned their heads that way. A boy shot off the end of the slide with the pinwheel in his hand, followed by Tara and a handful of children, but was stopped by his guardian who returned the wheel to her. She left the playground to run with it toward Susan, on the verge of crying, with the other children in the new pursuit. Among the watching adults around, a man rushed to turn one of the little girls around and looked at Tara, then at Susan, who let her hand slide down Clarens's jacket.

"Hi there, how are you?" he said, and poked his chin at Tara. "Catchy toy."

"Oh, hi. Yeah"—Susan threw a half-smile over. She then reached for Tara as the other children were also steered back to the playground.

"You know him?" Clarens asked.

"Just from the park," she said, and knelt to Tara, who wriggled her lips quietly under her tear-flooded eyes. "Big huggy hug..." She snapped her pinwheel closed into a small stick and slipped it in her pocket, then lifted her in her arms and turned. "We'll be fine," she said, as he stepped with them back toward the pond. A tear crossed her cheek too, which she wiped swiftly. "We'll be fine."

Once they said good-bye, he hurried back over the lawn.

"Your lunch!" she shouted just loud enough from behind and nodded at his snack pack. "I ruined it again for you."

He muted his set and returned her frail smile. "Not you!" He tipped his earlobe with his finger, then he turned and walked on with the new sway of the wind.

———

The cheap, fruity scent had traveled all the way out to the street escalator. Brett crossed to the store and held his breath walking in, then idled in the middle of the floor while Vitaly dealt with the only other customer. When the word "Tensana" came through, he wandered to the rear of the store and peeked behind the tall showcase at the rolling newscast.

"Our permanent tourist!" Vitaly greeted from across the store. Resting his hands on the case top, he leered at him over his jewelry glasses. "Don't tell me…"

Stepping closer, Brett reached in his pocket. "Hey Vit. Yes, another bar please."

"Somebody had a good time the other night." Grinning, Vitaly swayed away to his antique tools cabinet and then plodded back in small steps with the assayer in his hand. He picked the platinum bar from Brett's hand and flipped it over. "Splendid… Now, is this going to be four thousand two hundred by itself?"

"Three hundred."

"Three hundred, I'm sorry. Although…" He raised his head from the assayer readings and brought up his graph. "I think the spot went down a bit, thanks to your countrymen," he said and glanced his leery smile over. As Brett frowned in puzzlement, he tipped on through the figures below. "You know, every time there's trouble somewhere, people flock to our warrants."

"But, this was a while ago."

He looked up at him again and bobbed his head toward the back of the store. "Today's news. Your province that wants to join Tensana, in the south… You're from the Alliance, right?"

"Yeah." Brett stared on, then switched his weight and shrugged. "I just didn't follow."

His laugh wobbling the tawny shirt over his chest, Vitaly tapped him on the shoulder. "Way to live Brett! Good for you! Ah… I could do young all over again," he added and put the assayer away, then bulged his belly over the lip of the counter anew. "So, forty-two hundred?"

Once they cleared the sale, he turned his nimble eyes to the rear of the store. "The qualifiers for the Sanzhou grand prix, live."

"Thanks but, got to go. Another time though."

"Another time it is!"

From the entry landing, Brett looked back and tipped his nose with his finger. "Hey, Vit! What's with the tropical thing?"

"It's not tropical," Vitaly shouted over, now out of sight behind the end row of showcases. "It's a fragrance from this little beach town I go to. North of Baires."

"Huh. Is it safe out there?"

"Depends. Hey, I need my gig too!"

His smile ebbing with his first steps down the sidewalk, Brett brought up the news in his palm. He skimmed through the headlines and latest reports while whizzing high above the floor on the escalator, then, just as absorbed, he walked off and away from the converging foot traffic on the main level. He stopped and paused his sight on the corner building, then on the punched facade across from it, then on the green pavilion in the middle of the street. He switched the news scan to voice only and hastened to the nearest beltway.

The doors hissed open, barely fast enough for him to rush through and into the hotel lobby.

"Can someone please send my car to the garage?" he said while nearing the service booth. "I didn't get my code right."

"Of course," the concierge said, showing his head past the back panel. "Uhh, Mr. Falco?" he then prompted him from behind. "We need to cover the last five days, sir. If you don't mind."

"Oh, right. How much was it again?" Brett said, returning to the counter, and browsed his messages for the bill. "Got it... Geez, we could have bought a house by now"—he raised his head with the smile.

"We still have the monthly rate available."

"Yeah, thanks, but we'll be looking into a rental, I think. There you go." He authorized the payment and turned away, looking over the shoulder for the confirmation.

"All good. I also sent you the new code, sir!"—the concierge pointed to the outside, though Brett no longer stopped.

Upstairs, he rapped Susan's door a second time before she slotted it open to frown at him.

"Can you slow down?" she whispered.

"Can you answer your calls?"—he glared back.

She exhaled and shook her head. "We've been out, she was a little difficult. What is it?"

"Did you see the news?"

"What news?"

"Can we just get in?"

She stepped back and crossed her arms as he slipped in.

"South Kewan's joining Tensana, for real," he rushed in a low voice. "We're in a state of emergency too."

"What?"

"There's our appeal!"

"Shh!"

He followed her into the bathroom and clicked the door

closed.

"Are you sure?"

"Yes I'm sure." He beamed, then held his hands out and looked at the ceiling. "Thank you South Kewan!"

She crossed her arms. "But… how does it make it different? They never give residency to refugees."

"It's in the context. It's just adding to our case." As she stayed silent, he dropped his hands. "I can't believe we're debating it. Can we call him now?"

"A little late, don't you think?"

"Yeah, maybe. First thing tomorrow." He grasped the doorknob as she turned to the mirror. "Okay baby?"

"Don't 'baby' me."

"Whatever."

In his room, he fizzed a beer can open on his way to the window, slowing briefly to sip. He stepped up close in the thin, cool draft before the glazing, which felt like firming up a tad with the wind gust that lashed the outside. Some streetlights were already on, with the thick overcast above. Far aside, the boulevard was streaming.

He put the can on the coffee table and brought up the markets on the room graph, when his set prompted a local call.

"Yes… Brett, right?"—the man's voice at the other end wavered. "We met in the park a few days ago. I was with my daughter, we cast IDs…"

"Yeah…"

"That was your wife and daughter, right?"

"Yeah," Brett returned, eyes jiggling over the blank call display. "What is this about?"

"Just 'cause you seemed all right and all, and I've been there myself so… None of my business, but just to let you know," the man went on. "I saw your wife out there with someone else. Kind of close." He waited for Brett, only his breathing coming through. "You're there?"

"Yeah. When?"

"Today. In the park."

"What did he look like?"

"I don't know, I didn't watch them or anything. Average, well dressed." He waited for another moment. "Well, that's all I had to say. Good luck to you."

"Yeah… Thanks."

Brett felt the ring-set over back and forth with his thumb, then he raised his head. He stepped back to the window but stopped short and leaned slowly against the wall, peering at the floor. He thrust forward and walked to the entry door, but turned around and drifted back to the spot against the wall, between the sofa and the now deep-violet window, his eyes ever scouring through the air.

# 10

Bowing into the light that beamed out the bathroom door, she slipped her second leg into her trousers and pulled them on under the shower robe, then tightened up and took the robe off. Brett stretched long, hands under the head, then bumped his pillow against the bed headboard and pushed himself higher. "This is a nice hotel actually," he said through a yawn, glancing around.

She turned and smiled. "Sorry, I woke you up."

"No, I've been watching for a while."

"Uh-uh…"

She clipped her bra on and reached for the pullover sweater on the chair.

"Busy Monday ahead?"

"Just meetings, chasing some contracts," she said, and showed her face again, a smile in the corner of her mouth. "Since I can't make money this way."

He snorted, then raised his brows. "You're sure we call it even?"

"Oh yeah."

As they laughed, she turned the windows shading a whit lighter and scouted the floor for her shoes, then hustled back to the bathroom.

He looked into the filtering light. It looked like a bright morning outside. "Hey, question for you," he said. "Suppose you didn't have to go to work. At all. How much would you want to have put aside to do that?"

"What?"

"You know, what would be your comfort zone?"

She laughed. "I don't know, three hundred kays?"

"Huh."

"Comfy, huh…"

"For sure." He turned to look into the bathroom door opening. "Suppose I gave you that money to marry me."

She took a few seconds to lean her head out the door, the brush in her hand tangled low in her hair. They looked at each other, then burst out laughing.

She disappeared back inside. "Already in love?"

"That too." He looked out again. "But suppose I wanted to stay here," he continued, "you know, like… immigrate. What would you say?"

She kept silent, other than clacking toiletries down, then reappeared. "You're serious?" Loose to below her shoulders, her chestnut hair looked lighter with the glossy finish. She moved out of the light and toward the bed in slow steps, a new smile in the corner of her mouth. "And I was worried that this barbarian was going to chop me up in tiny little pieces."

He bent his knee under the sheet as she bumped her thigh against him to sit on the side of the bed and feel his chest. The few wrinkles around her eyes faded into the dusk of the room as her fragrance surrounded his face. "Even a barbarian knows a piece of art," he muttered before she kissed him.

"You would know then that some art is priceless."

"Everything has a price."

"Not in this country"—she pricked his chest with her finger. She brought her feet on the floor and hustled around the bed. "It's been long tried before."

"We could make it perfect."

"Now, I thought this barbarian ain't no fool." She leered at him, slipping her jacket on. "But I can ask around if you want."

"No worries, just a thought."

"My advice to you… Forget the Revox. Get someone to love you." She tossed her hair back and shifted her body weight, slanting the other leg out, and braced her hand on her hip. "I'll see you around? Maybe?"

"You bet," Brett returned her smile. "Hope you net a comfy contract!" he added before she shut the door, then he turned to the balmy sunlight.

———

Gray silhouettes sailed side to side and lapped one another behind the translucent aisle wall. Along with the muffled voices. Which came through in fragments of recognizable sounds, while passing heads turned to look through the open door every now and then. His temple braced on three bowing fingers, Clarens twirled the vintage pen one more time on his desk, when Lynden showed up and he shifted his gaze to him.

"Guy, Gwyn told me about Heslin," Lynden said. "What happened? You're not telling anything."

He leaned back and exhaled. "Same old thing Lyn."

Lynden closed the door and sat on the desk corner, one leg hanging. "That sucks. I'm sorry dude."

"Don't be," Clarens said, and swiveled his chair to look away. "We really want different things."

"So this is it, huh?" Silent for a moment too, Lynden toned up. "You're one fussy son of a gun, you know that? But we'll fix ya up with something."

"Oh, just—"

"Dude!" He stood up. "Swimming tomorrow?"

"Sure."

"Super."

As he stepped to the door, Clarens swiveled back. "Lyn… Thanks. I was just in the middle of something."

"No problem, I understand, I understand…" Lynden

lingered in the open door and rapped a quick beat on the side glass. "By the way, do I still help her with the apartment?"

Clarens shrugged. "Of course."

"Cool. Just checking."

With Lynden gone, he swayed between facing the shored skiff lithography and the mum pillar in the room corner. He rose and fixed his jersey shirt around the waist, stared at the empty chair, then walked out in the aisle and headed toward the rose-mallow oval.

Jaw sagging, Talbot speared his long fingers through the graph objects over his desk. "I thought you'd never come," he said without raising his head, as Clarens stepped closer in.

"Hey Tal."

"This new language is very clever," he muttered, and poked his finger back in. "If only I had your kind of time at my hands."

Clarens held off his chuckle and stopped beside the guest chair in front of the desk. "I'm not sure that would do."

Talbot rolled his chair out and twitched a smile. "So."

"So... I couldn't decide. I'm sorry," Clarens said, searching over the glistening desk. "I didn't get a breather, and I didn't want to rush it either, and..." He raised his eyes. "You don't have to wait for me Tal."

Talbot steepled his fingers. "You still want to do this?"

Beyond his bald head, the east city lay crisp in the late-afternoon light.

"I just want to be sure that if I told you yes, I'd be entirely committed to it."

"How much more time would you need?"

"Well, one or two weeks, but as I said—"

"Two weeks. Once in a lifetime." He smiled anew under the inanimate eyebrows and rolled back in.

"I know Tal." Clarens pursed his lips. "I do appreciate it.

Tremendously."

He patted the back of chair and turned to leave.

"Is it that immigration case?" Talbot added.

"That also."

"Where are you at?"

"They just denied the appeal too, so… it looks like the most we could get is renewable entries."

"Huh. You win some, you lose some."

———

A whit apart, cars lined both sides of the narrow street in front of the learning center. Clarens drove to the underground garage, where the car could only find a space several levels down. By the time he made it to the classroom, the art teacher was standing in front of the full class, about to speak. A few faces turned as he stepped nimbly along the wall to the rear of the room, where he paused to scout for an empty station.

With a loud greeting, the teacher began pacing in front of the class and introduced himself. "Some of you know me from the elementary series. I'll be your instructor and art confidante for the next four sessions, should you be able to bear my remarks." He hardly allowed for the class's chuckles before continuing. "In this series we'll be combining two techniques every session…"

Clarens hunched and threaded through to the available station, laid his utensils case quietly on the board's shoulder, and sat still. He drifted his sight from the back of one head to another, some purple-haired, some tapered-haired, a few white and stooping forward, all directed to the same arresting point before them. With a new rumble of mirth filling the room, he picked up the words again. Today's mediums were ink and colored chalks. Once the vivid demonstration ran its course, he browsed the sample images, then over again, through the shuffle of everyone else turning to their blank sheets. He left the station's graph hollow and reached for the spindle-styled fountain pen inside the case, next to the fine paper texture.

When he sat back again, leafy tree crowns filled the upper corners of the sheet in rich black lines, while the view unfolded far over the hills in the middle. He smudged the first chalk over it, when he noticed the teacher was peeking over his shoulder.

"Pretty decisive there, Clarens."

Easing a smile, he leaned the other way. "Decisive…"

"Yes. Speedy drawing, clear view," the teacher said, and smiled back between his ever-kinkier sideburns, then he returned to the drawing. "You like your hills, don't you?"

Clarens shrugged. "They're easy."

"Nothing wrong with easy. Drawing is about how easily you can grasp your perception, right?" He peered closer. "Is that a house there? Boy, are you on a roll." He let Clarens chuckle quietly and moved on, but then he swung his stumpy ponytail around and pecked his finger at the side of the board. "Keep the far lines thin and simple. And don't ruin it with color," he added, staring out the glazed side of the room. "You're getting there."

A smile lasting on his face, Clarens watched him step to the next board, then bent to the upper corner of his drawing. The tree limbs swelled up line after line, and scarred over with crusts and knots, and branched up into thick offspring, to which the crown line all but disappeared behind the swarm of minute leaves with each screech of the nib. And then so looked the opposite corner. A tilting ground line ran across, just above the lower edge, with fine grass straws brushing the half-buried boulders around and up in the air over what looked like a valley ahead. On the slopes below, the shrubs topped off in firm, jagged outlines, their shaded sides hinted at with a few dots, which, at further thought, he multiplied in great numbers and made it seem that the sun was out there beaming indeed. Not much changed over the outer hills, now undoubtedly far, but the ridge in between did get a thick makeover of its own, with the pen nib lifting briefly to skip the thumb-sized house midway down.

Green after green, the colors came as easily. A tinge inside the foreground's unambivalent shapes brought them alive. A few more and the breeze rustled the leaves through, then the gravel ground under the feet. Purples and grays tinted the hillsides, hardly, but the blue chalk he held onto, rubbing it tightly against the ridgelines from the open sky above, and then from tree to tree and through the leaves in between, until the large color filling in the upper third of the sheet took on an unreferenced, ensnaring shape of its own.

"Blue... blue..."

He raised his head.

"Do you have another blue I can borrow?" the voice asked. Leaning over from the drawing station aside, the young man flicked his forehead. "Thought we had pastels today."

"Uhh... sure." Clarens held the chalk up. "Does this work?"

"Yes but... you're still using it?"

They both looked over Clarens's drawing. He pushed his lower lip up, then smiled as the young man let out a snort and reached over to hand him the chalk. "In fact, you can just keep it," he said, and stood up, gathered the other chalks in the case, then rolled up the drawing and threaded slowly through the stations toward the door.


The downtown towers climbed higher in the side of the windshield with the expressway humming on. He switched back to fixating on the winglet of the car in front, unfazed by the crossing roadways that zoomed in and over. He grabbed the steering to veer off course to the flashing exit, then called out the new destination and kept staring out through the splitting ramps and tunnels to Jefferson shell and to his office garage thereafter.

Upstairs, a threesome of colleagues were guffawing in front of the elevator when the doors opened and turned to him. "Clarens! Just in time for drinks."

"I wish"—he smiled, walking by. "I need to work on something."

"People! Whatever happened to working from your home tub sipping booze?"

"Haha! Dude, you've made it. Just give us a chance!" another said.

He let his head back to laugh along, walking backward. "Maybe later. Sam's, right?"

As the laughs cut off with the departing elevator, he crossed the empty reception area toward the main floor aisle. In his office, the lights brightened up over the low stack of cases on the desk. He bumped the chair out with his knee but didn't sit, resting on his fingertips on the glossy surface instead. On the top drawer of the period file cabinet, his father's name lustered in the fine embossment. He sat and picked the first case from the stack, removed the small set from inside it, and deployed his work graph.

Out on the floor some half hour later, the cleaner sounded like it made the turn onto the aisle. The flowered hedge striped the background of the paused hologram over his desk, trimmed neatly in greens, whites, and small blue dots from one side to the other. Susan knelt on the paved terrace in front of it. Driving Tara's hand and trowel inside a small pot, she arched her neck out, her hair bun faltering over and down to the collar of her paint-stained denim overshirt.

The whizzing sound faded in and out of the nearby rooms, louder each time, then suddenly ceased. Sunk in his chair, Clarens turned the graph off and swiveled the other way, then stared at the cleaning robot waiting poised in front of the open door.

# 11

"I mean, it took them only four days to deny it? Three actually. Or, no, two working days. Two fuckin' days to just flush the losers out"—Brett flicked his hand, looking over the tearoom's empty seating. "Efficient, I give them that," he griped on. "I mean, that self-gratification law works fuckin' wonders. But have the decency to let us hope a little for fuck's sake. Two fuckin' days…"

"If you swear one more time I'm going upstairs," Susan said, elbows braced on her chair's armrests.

Brett drank and looked the other way, glancing back at the staffer, who then refocused on cleaning the dispenser. He tapped the cup down on the coffee table and clasped his fist in his hand, then sank his head between his shoulders as he sat on the edge of the armchair. "How can they not give a crap?" he continued and tossed a grimace at the just arriving, colorful group who banged their powered luggage through the hotel doors and into the foyer. "They should want us. They should waive that original land bill for us."

"It's their law," Susan crossed, in the same low voice. "We tried to bend it, didn't work. Now what?"

"Hey, I'm for the law, but allow for some freakin' judgment."

"Yeah. When it suits you."

He glared at her and shook his head, then frowned over the table.

She stayed planted in her chair. "I'm considering Tencun."

He raised his head slowly.

"It's not much different from Kewan," she continued. "You get surveillance, gated private school, and come here whenever you want. And it's three times cheaper."

He stared her down. "Did we not drive through that place?" he lashed out. "I'd get a bungalow in the islands if I wanted that kind of life."

Moving on to the table next to theirs, the staffer peeked over and began running his handheld cleaner over the limestone top. Brett watched the few crumbs bounce off the cleaner's head and fall onto the tan sofa. "Are you changing that brush anytime soon," he prompted him, "or are you gonna smudge pastry and detergent over the whole place?"

Dazed, the staffer stepped back and away.

"Slobs freakin' everywhere I guess," Brett grumbled, as Susan squeezed her lips and turned her head to the foyer.

She exhaled long, then swung back to him, tight in her high-necked jersey. She lowered her eyes a tad. "I'm just not sure about going back. I don't see much good in that."

She grabbed her cup and stared into it between her hands, then sipped, hardly.

He meshed his fingers in his lap, thumbs rubbing slowly, and looked away. "You picked the right time."

She frowned slightly.

"Oh just… I know, okay?"

"You know what?"

He leaned over the table and spoke slowly in her face. "I know you've been messing around."

Her eyes gleamed up. She shook her head. "You're such a hypocrite. *You*'ve been messing around."

"Quick move. Was it good? Was it—"

"Over and over, for years."

"Bullshit. That was a one-timer, and we were separated."

"Some recent nights out come to mind," she carried on.

They edged back, eyes never dropping.

"We knew you can be a pain," he said, "but not a liar."

"There's nothing to lie about, you mean bully."

She turned her head and brought her hand under her nose. He sat back and looked out again. "Fuck this…"

Through the opening front doors, two children chased each other inside while the couple behind drove their luggage to the service scan. On the other side of the tearoom, the staffer tinkered silently with another leftover tray.

Susan put her cup on the table and checked her set, then pulled out a tissue for her nose.

He glanced at her again. "She's sleeping?"

Without answering, she whisked her hair back and swiped the corner of her eye with her coiled finger. She rested her hands on her knees before standing up, then stepped around the table, as he didn't budge, and stopped beside him. "Really, why pretend we're together?" she said, voice uneven, then tapped her steps away across the floor.

In the bright noon, green umbrellas overhung the glass parapets of the vivid upper-floor cafés. Farther above, the suspended passageway had lifted its side panels open, like a crystal bird about to escape the shell. As the street belt decelerated, Brett lowered his head and crossed to the sidewalk. Another row of umbrellas buffered the street corner venue, where shades-wearing customers were taking up tables for lunch. He made his way down the busy main street to Sargent Bank, where he slowed to peek in through the front glazing. The usual attendant sat at her desk behind the floating counter. He jolted his bag up his shoulder and walked in, then returned the attendant's prompt greeting and pointed to the safes' area aside.

"Let me know if you need assistance," she added, the smile intact on her face, and looked back down, her short hair brushing her cheeks. Her straight-cut teal suit just couldn't make her look anywhere past thirty.

As he passed by, the lobby doors slid open behind him and someone spoke loud. "Sorry, is there a Margret's Burger around here? It wouldn't map."

The attendant rose to the counter, pushing her hair behind her ear slowly. "There is a Marjorie's Deli, perhaps two blocks that way."

With the doors sliding back closed, Brett smiled over his shoulder. "Vegetarian?"

She chuckled and felt her jacket down behind her to sit. "Not really."

He swayed back toward the counter. "We've never gotten acquainted really. I'm Brett," he nodded.

"Sure. I'm Ethel, sir." She beamed a quick smile.

"I'm just here so often," he added, smiling on, then suddenly reached in his bag. "By the way, I thought of bringing this for you guys…" He carefully pulled out the glass flower pot with both hands, allowing the miniature rosebush to spring clear of the bag's slide, and placed it on the counter. "Just to thank you for being so helpful."

The pot swayed sideways a few times on its rounded bottom till resting upright in a single point on the polished basalt slab. The attendant gazed at it a moment longer. "I… don't know if we can accept this."

Street clatter filled the lobby anew as the front doors opened, then an elderly couple approached the counter slowly at the attendant's greeting. The sought-after investments adviser was still out for lunch, she explained, and pointed them to the side seating, then she turned back to Brett.

"Don't you take lunch?" he asked.

"Uhh… I do, a little later," she said, switching between the pot and her desk, and ran her hair off her temple with two fingers again.

He moved back, his hand leaving the edge of the counter. "Great day out there. We could grab a bite if you'd like." As she blushed, he nudged the bag strap higher on his shoulder. "Hey, you can pitch your awesome city to a tourist."

"I'm not sure I can, I'm sorry."

"No worries. But keep that"—he nodded at the pot, stepping away under the curious looks of the seated couple.

"I'll ask. It's beautiful! Thank you so much, sir."

"Brett."

He walked on to the safes' area, where he slowed to peruse the fine-gridded wall for his box number. He logged in and placed his palm over the box door, but the pinhead light stayed red. "Again?" He rapped the door, then started over, wiped his hand on his pants, and pressed it tightly over the door, which remained locked. He walked back to the lobby to ask Ethel for help.

"Let's see, you are inside the bank field…" She scouted her graph, then rose and walked side by side with him to the box, where she watched him repeat the access routine to no avail. "Strange. Can I see your hand?" She looked closer as he held his palm up and pointed at his thumb. "Is that a recent cut?"

"That? Yes."

"All right, let's try this."

She passed her palm flat above his, then worked on her ringset before having him try again, holding his thumb between her thin fingers to reposition it on the door. The light changed to green with the usual muted click. She stepped back nimble and brightened up in relief, when he held her hand on the way down.

"You're sure about lunch? On me now," he smiled.

This close she looked even younger, or the blushing under the round hazel eyes removed most signs of age from her face.

She glimpsed his eyes. "I can't risk my job. I just started…" She slipped her hand out of his with another step back. "I'm sorry. I'm very flattered."

He watched her hustle away and coil her hair around her

ear with her head down, then he turned and rested his fist against the box. He tapped the door open and dragged the inside bag to the edge of the opening, then reached in to feel the taped-over bar stacks between his fingers, pushing them aside one by one. He idled over the last one, pulled his empty hand out, and shoved the bag all the way back in.

A male attendant now sat at the desk below the counter, while across the lobby, a senior staffer led the elderly couple to the opening in the riverbed-like partition wall. She walked tall in her heels, with her blond curls wiggling rich as she turned beside the open door.

"We've just acquired a wonderful income pool actually," she told the couple, a large smile lighting her markedly fair complexion as she let them in, then she glanced around for a mere second while Brett crossed the lobby to head out.


By the time he reached the car, his tongue rubbed keen against his upper gums. He scrambled inside the console for the tooth stick, then let it tingle between the two molars till the stubborn steak fragment cleared out. He grinned in the seat viewer and examined his teeth, then kept looking in and felt the fine wrinkles in the corner of his eye.

He slid his seat back and brought his graph on in front of the steering wheel, only to frown as he flicked the portfolio objects around. Crimpling his brows deeper still, he tipped his finger through the top account, then waited for the call to chime a long few times before the voice came on, along with the Orion Clearway logo.

"Mr. Falco. We were about to call you—"

"We said two weeks," he crossed. "That was a large account."

"I know, but unfortunately—"

"So now what, I'm left with three junior accounts?"

"I believe that's the case, yes."

He smirked at the slow-shifting stars. "You know, I made you guys lots of money over the years, and now I'm gone for two months and you cut me out. I mean, forget fairness, this just isn't smart, is it?"

"I'm obviously not the one to—"

"Who is it? Charlie? Don? Put me through to Don."

"They're both offline for the day, but it was really the clients' choice. People are jittery right now," the speaker added.

"Jittery right now…" Brett murmured, eyes rolling up the windshield. "They just had to see it happen."

"I'm sorry? Mr. Falco?"

Between the rows of lights flooding the garage ceiling, the yellow one zagged along the aisles below to slowly stream away toward the hoister. He switched back and scurried his fingers through the graph. "Yeah, listen, have Don or Charlie take over everything. I'll need to focus on my own account for a while," he said. "By the way, I'll need to transfer it out, so take this for my verbal."

"Are you sure? I can have Don call you."

"No, no. It's just that I'm a little jittery about the times too."

He fisted off his ringset and pressed the back of his head against the headrest with a curse. He slid forward and powered up, then steered to the self-drive exit, screeching wheels into the aisle's turn before the tunnel.


At nearly the same warm twenty-one degrees as the indoors, the small plaza off Hume Boulevard was fully benched with sun-seeking faces of all ages, despite the inescapable breeze rushing through. A line of roller skaters split around him from behind, somehow threading through the group of two-wheeled youngsters who crossed his path, as he kept his pace steady toward the shaded passageway on the opposite side.

He only slowed inside the gym doors and glanced a "hi" to

the staffer, who then continued checking the wave machines in the front row. The place was its usual half empty, if that. He slipped his sports bag off his shoulder on the way to the locker room, when he saw the man who had asked him out two weeks earlier. The man glanced over too, while working his machine's controls.

"Hey!" Brett shouted, and frowned as the man instantly turned his head. "Sorry about the other day," he added just as loud, walking closer.

The man let his bulging arms down but remained speechless, as Brett didn't wait for an answer.

"You're free?"

"Free...?"

Brett bumped his chin to the side. "For the spar room."

———

Clarens waded through the terrace tables to the less buoyant, dark interior of the bistro and hastened to the full-service bar. He landed in the high leather chair and sent his order off, then kept his head down to continue browsing.

"Olive provolone melt, tomatoes... and the Pelegrino"— the bartender pushed the platter and capped glass closer across the cherry countertop.

Clarens switched his finger between pointing at his graph and at the lifestyle show playing in the holoset before the back bar. "Do you think I can watch this up there?"

The bartender glanced over the handful of lunchers on the floor and craned his head closer. "Lunars? Sure." He relayed Clarens's feed to the bar set and measured him with another glance before leaving.

Clarens stuck to the new display over his steaming meal and felt the counter for his silverware.

"Do we have a champion up there today?" someone pitched in from down the counter.

He looked at the man, who, bent over his lunch, nodded across the stretch of empty chairs. "Theoretically no, with three races left."

"True, eighteen points. Exciting this year, isn't it?" the man said, his voice just as flat. His nearly gray hair thinned above the temples, then brushed a little over the light-tan collar of his jacket as he grabbed his drink.

Clarens turned to the glinting broadcast. With dust dispersing high into the sheer sunrays, the flying cameras zoomed around the kilometer-long peloton of cyclists and then the main view advanced to the three leaders and stayed above them. They pedaled strenuously side by side and jounced the drum-wheeled bicycles off the smallest folds and bulges in the terrain to thrust up gliding and rest their legs. One of the three pulled ahead.

The man commented under his breath and, always absorbed, clinked his silverware neatly side by side in his empty platter. "If he can make the crater, he's through."

Clarens glanced over. "The crater..."

"The little one, after the straight. Where they take forever to climb out if they can't jump it."

He swallowed a bite as a personal call came through and turned the other way.

"So I actually like Brookdale the best," his sister said and then went on to describe the facility. "But go see it this week. They have only two units left."

He hemmed.

"Are you in a meeting?"

"No, not really." He brought the call image on and inadvertently in the bar display, but switched it promptly to his palm. "I stepped out for a bit."

She peered closer in and around him. "So did Lynden post the ad for the house yet?"

"Uhh... not yet. In fact I didn't tell him yet."

"You can't be serious."

"I just haven't decided. I didn't have the time."

"We *have* decided!"

He stooped lower and wavered.

She huffed and shook her head. "This is about Mom. And about me, by the way."

"I'm quite aware of that."

She hung up with a grimace. He stared into his palm, then pivoted back around and raised his gaze to the race. In their hulky, glittering suits, the cyclists heaved and leaped their spinning wheels higher for another bow over the black horizon.

"On a second thought, they must be sweating rivers in there," his fellow luncher said.

Clarens turned his head absent and watched him drink. The broadcast suddenly livened up when several riders collided on landing behind the leader, himself falling and skidding away in a cloud of dust, to which the man tapped his glass down with a soft interjection.

"Does that ruin it for you?" Clarens edged a brow up.

The man remained focused on the broadcast. "I don't really care who wins. I just like the whole... feel"—he passed his hand at the landscape in the main view. His hair tipped a little looser over his neck with his humping back, and the shifting graph light twinkled meager in his eyes, as he smiled over. "Like when you switch to the helmet and tune the voices out. That's pretty neat."

Clarens forked another oil-soaked tomato slice, slowly. The bartender passed by with a glass of beer, then ambled back, flipping the stem of an empty one around his fingers. The peloton had almost regrouped in a contiguous formation in the main feed, above the lower subgraph where the front racer's view rolled on unchanged through the mounds and sands. Clarens wiped his hands on his napkin, dropped the lumped cloth beside the half-full platter, and set one foot on the floor while thumbing off the pay, and then to his address book. He picked Susan's entry, cut the relay off, and squeezed his lips as the man peeked his way over his tulip glass. "Another call to make."

# 12

He pulled over in the street parking space and switched off. He looked at Susan. They leaned over the console and kissed.

"I feel like... nineteen," she whispered through smiling lips. "Since you called, I'd wonder in the mirror three times a day if I still knew dating."

"You do," Clarens said, and glanced at the rear seat. "Even while multitasking."

She feathered her hair fragrance over his face as she looked behind her seat at Tara, who snored soundly, cheek bulging against the side-rest. "This was so much fun."

As they touched lips once more, he left his hand caught between the seat and the thin jersey over her waist.

She arched slightly. "And if I went back, would you come see me?"

"I'd look forward to it. Why? You're leaning that way?"

"Don't know." She sat back and looked down the street. "My family is always there, I guess. And my best friend. But ... I'll have to drive around Tencun to be able to tell."

"Sure. Do you need me to come with you?"

"No, I'll probably have to go with him."

He watched her a moment longer. "Will you be all right?"

"Oh yeah. We're"—she puffed, slicing her hand flat through the air—"just business. I only want the best for Tara," she added, then exhaled, the fine silver necklace skipping lower down her open neck.

He looked out too. The car in front lit up and drove out of the parking space. A clear stretch lay ahead the entire way to the fanning intersection with the boulevard.

"If you want, I could help you stay. If that was your utmost consideration."

She turned her head to peer over the middle of the dashboard, then farther to him. Her gazing eyes encompassed everything around and beyond.

"I could vouch for you," he added.

"Vouch…?"

"As in… an engagement toward partnership. Technically."

She turned away abruptly. "This is crazy." She flicked a smile back at him. "We can't do that."

"We can. We only need to state the intention and that I'll be answering for all you do in the interim."

She opened her mouth a sliver but remained silent, eyes glowing wide, as he thinned his lips with a nod. "But, that's your life," she said slowly. "I mean, I won't say it hasn't crossed my mind but we…"

"It doesn't need to lead to anything." He shrugged. "And then we'd say it was me and they should let you stay. But you still have a few days to decide," he added, as she removed her eyes from his.

Behind her, a paper scrap made a loop outside the window, then he followed it as it was sucked down the same empty street without recourse to the sputtering wind, until her fingers touched his chin to turn his head back toward her.

"You're amazingly kind, you know that?"

"I was looking for more like… cool."

She chuckled softly. "That was a done deal," she murmured and brought her lips over his, and her infinitely scant chypre, and the smoothness of her weaving figure, for a little longer than a mere instant before slipping away. "Can't wait to know everything else. Either way…" She smiled, then turned and felt her forehead. "Gosh, is this for real?" She covered her sniffle with another chuckle then swiveled her seat around and hugged Tara to wake her up.

She bowed back in from the outside to fix her jacket and pick her up. "I'll call you." She smiled and walked off, then she glanced back through her wind-enthralled hair before turning at the side-street corner toward the hotel.

———

A faint thump made it through from somewhere beyond the dusky ceiling soffits. Brett tossed the sheet over and thrust out of bed then stepped to the bathroom and filled a glass of water. He stood behind her and drank up. "Sorry, thirsty."

Clipping her earring on, she glanced in the mirror, a crease in the corner of the mouth. "No kidding." She turned. "What's the size of that cash line anyway?"

"Three hundred kays. Negotiable."

"Hmm..." She flicked his bare abdomen with her finger. "Some package."

She swayed out to the main room to zip her sweater on. "Why don't you find someone to date you?"

Hanging his arms atop the bathroom door frame, he let his body loose. "I did but... he's wearing shorts," he said, to her laughter. "And I don't have much time."

She felt her gold-laced braid behind her neck, then stayed her slanted eyes on him. "Sorry, too chancy for me." She turned to the door and fluttered her fingers over. "I have your number though."

After she left, Brett dropped his arms and called off the room shades then scrunched his eyes and turned sideways in the white low sunlight flooding in. Hands on his waist, he panned over the posh furnishings and the wall reliefs surrounding the room in deep, up-staggered triple lines, just above the bronze inset frames of artwork of Ayland street views. He felt his abdomen down then began to swing his extended arms and stretch his upper body. He crouched and yanked the velvet bed cover away onto the floor, lay flat with his toes under the bed ledge, then started mouthing the sit-ups count with each breath. He heaved at forty and lay back flat until his chest slowed swelling. He yawned, rolled to the side, and tottered to the shower.

Out of the downtown the traffic lightened up, but he continued cruising in the first lane and checked another account. He tipped through the debt positions shaking his head and then began to reset the sell orders lower one by one, as the car steered to the Hume Boulevard exit.

A large group of tourists poured out of the hotel lobby. Luggage wheel tracks laced the floor as he walked by the service booth.

"Wow! Anyone left besides us?"

Checking the lockers' rack, the concierge returned the smile. "March is around the corner. But we're always busy in the city."

"Right. We'll keep the rooms a little longer by the way," Brett said, tapping the shelf, and moved on.

"Very good, sir. And you still want the new room for Ms. Connelly? On the fourth floor, starting tomorrow...?"

Halted, Brett looked past him. The aging tourists sailed up their coach escalator out the front glazing, hat after hat disappearing inside the high cabin. "Yeah, we'll take the new room." He turned and nodded terse, then walked away, glancing at the several tourists now waiting at the booth. "Sorry about that."

"Not a problem, dear. I had my Mondays," the nearest one said, a quiver to her voice, then giggled with the others behind him.

When he stopped inside his room, Susan was already standing in the doorway. He took his jacket off and grabbed the two empty beer cans from the nightstand. "You're wasting no time."

"Gosh, it must seem that way to you. Relatively speaking."

Their eyes pinged across the room as he tossed the cans in the disposal.

She closed the door and stepped in. "I waited for you yesterday."

"You said you couldn't make it."

"I said I was running late. Whatever." She leaned against the wall in the hallway, arms crossed over her chest.

He frowned. "What?"

"I have news."

"Oh yeah?"

She stayed still, only glancing at his eyes again. "Remember when we got Tara and swore to do anything for her?"

He bobbed, swinging his hand wide, and turned away.

"I can have her and me, and possibly you, stay," she added. "But not together."

He stopped and fixated her, until she looked down. He made a full turn and hooked his thumbs inside his jeans pockets. "Possibly?"

"As the father you'd get unlimited entries. And with a good record you'd get the residency, down the road."

He kept his sight on the far corner.

"Someone can vouch for me Brett," she uttered evenly from behind.

"And who is he?"

"How does that matter?"

"Who is he?"—he nudged his head over his shoulder.

"Clarens."

He turned and glared her down. "Is this a freakin' joke?"

She didn't budge, other than letting her breath out.

He shot up. "I paid the son of a bitch to screw my wife?"

"Stop it!"—she jumped backward to fend off the overturning armchair he kicked hard, the pillow rolling to her feet. "I'm not your wife! I've never been your wife!" she shrilled. "And he's doing us a huge favor!"

"Yeah." He rubbed the back of his hand over his mouth, searching the floor. "How huge?"

"You're such a jerk! It's all about your ego. You don't know a thing about who I am, really."

He stepped forward and lifted the armchair slowly. "You're right." He slammed the chair in place, to her jolt. "Not a thing." He knelt and straightened the broken leg, then grabbed the pillow from beside her foot and slapped it in the armchair, which caused the leg to pitch broken again. "Clarens Mann…" He snorted, kneeling once more. "What a fuckin' move, so to speak."

"We haven't done anything and don't even know if we will," she said, inching forward to reclaim her spot.

He kept examining the square wooden leg, which had splintered just under the joint with the front cross member, while continuing intact to form the curving armrest above.

She bent closer. "Thinking hat on please? This is for you too."

He stayed silent on his knees, tweaking the leg to wedge it in, until it came off entirely in his hand.

"I need some help here!" she burst. "I don't know if I can do this!"

He scoffed and straightened his back, fists on his squatting thighs. "What do you want me to do, huh?"

She turned her stare at the floor and swallowed. "Nothing. Just sign your consent to end the domestic union."

"What about the father thing?"

"You're the father. They're not required to know."

"Have you told him yet?"

"Not yet."

He looked around the room and exhaled. "I can do it under one condition."

She looked back at him.

"That you won't tell about the adoption," he added. "To anyone."

"But… I can't hold that from him."

"Then I can't do it."

"I can do it without your consent, you know."

"Go ahead."

"Oh my god, how does that matter to you now? It should only matter to me."

"Pffh. They can get a wood board pregnant here."

He stood up and glimpsed her tearful, distressed gaze. He clacked the chair leg on the coffee table, splinters tipping out sharp from the broken end.

Her shoulder crumpled against the wall, she looked down numb and let her tear run down her cheek.

She thrust her head back and whisked her hair off her face. "Fine, I won't tell. Until you get your status."

Her locks waved long over her shoulder and down to the Praia beach printing on her ruby tee. Beside, her shadow withered over the hallway wall.

He turned to the drinks dispenser. "Fine. Anything else?"

———

The blue stripe felt abrasive, even this deep under the tepid water. Clarens kicked downward to feel the stripe again, then continued breast stroking closely above the bottom of the pool. A passing shadow was instantly followed by a dull blow and then multiple kicks to his head and back. He thrust sideways and let the young pair of legs pedal up free, then rose to the surface too. Holding on to the lane divider, a tween boy ran his hand down his face and blinked rapidly as a woman summoned him from the pool deck. While the little girl gazed on from a step behind her, the boy on her other side leaped forward to splash into the next lane. The woman wailed and switched to Clarens with an apology, which he played down.

"Good dive," he said to the first offender, who held on to the floating divider to watch him with a jittery glance, then he stroked on to the pool ladder.

"Since when are you such a kid lover?" Lynden said, sucking water out of his ear.

"He just looked so startled."

He watched the woman walk away as Clarens stepped up on the coping. "Can you believe the waist on that woman after three kids?"

"All right Lyn."

"No, just look."

"I'm not going to look."

"Some genes, huh?" He threw his towel higher on his shoulder as they walked the opposite way, then his brows went up. "Hey, remember that time when we jumped from the mezzanine in the restaurant pool? At Gwyn's majors."

"At Gwyn's majors... Oh, that was a fun party." Clarens turned to him. "You pushed me."

"I dragged you! With that weird haircut of yours."

"I don't remember that."

"Yeah, right. You looked better when you got out of the pool."

His chortle slowing him down, he tapped Clarens on the forearm. "And then Gwyn's father"—he shrilled a laugh—"he's planted there when I climb out and his suit is like, soaked." He dropped his voice to mock the scolding through his teeth. "'Lynden... Let's call this your farewell bash.'"

"Hahaha!"

"Imagine he knew Gwyn and I had kicked it. He'd have choked me dead right there!"

They gasped with their laughter, swaying sideways on their feet, then slowly picked up walking.

Face still red, Lynden regained his voice. "You weren't there with anyone, were you?"

"I don't think so. Or, there was this girl, kind of."

"Kind of. That sounds about right."

Clarens smiled and looked out. "Twenty... four years. I've

never been back to that place."

"Neither I. Hey, that's an idea!"

Slippers flapping, they walked around the pool corner and toward the men's showers. In the shallow pool at the other end of the hall, the three children splashed and crawled under the watch of their mother.

"By the way," Clarens said, "remember Susan? My client."

"Duh… They let them stay?"

"No. So I'm thinking of helping them out."

As they walked through the shower room portal, Lynden stretched his neck back for a last look across the pool hall. "Like how?"

"Well, it's complicated but, essentially, I'm thinking I'll vouch for her. Till she gets the status."

He twirled his head back around and slowed down. "But she's married."

"It turns out they're home partners. And both want to end it."

He paused but, as Clarens pressed his lips together tight, he brightened and rocked him by the shoulder. "You're porking that hot mommy?"

Deflated, Clarens swung his head the other way. "And Lyn…" He crossed his lips with his finger. "Obviously."

"Hey"—Lynden pulled his chin back, hand pointing between his pectorals. He pushed his other arm around Clarens's neck. "You know, from all the kooky things you've done, this one just…" He grinned speechless, then turned heads in the room again as he pitched the crumpled towel toward the bench across the floor. "I want details! Don't leave without me!"

"I'm rushing, actually."

"Tomorrow, beers!" he yelled from inside the shower booth as the jets fizzed on. "Guy, is this one a *kind of*? 'Cause I'll bend backward in here!"

The coffee grinders hummed anew, then more people scuffled into the lounging area. Brett nudged his armchair closer to make room behind him, then pushed far out again and looked at Clarens across the table. "Is that all then?"

"I think so," Clarens said, and turned his head from him to Susan, then back to the affidavits spread floating over the small table. "We should just state it expressly that we've been free to consent to this and did so in truth and best faith."

"You got it," Brett said. He looked at Susan, who nodded her "yep" and kept to her cup between her hands.

Clarens leaned forward. "I do too," he said slowly, typing the addition in, and copied it to his office space. "And Brett, we should get your full biomark on this one too."

Brett hardly glanced the document. "I can do it now. I'm parked there anyway."

"Good. Someone's there until six."

He stood up, skidding his armchair back. "Well, you'll let me know then. Thanks again"—he held his hand forth, his clear eyes just as steady, as Clarens rose to the handshake. He said bye to Susan, then slalomed through the café seating and walked tall in the busy entryway until his hair bristles vanished out the doors.

Clarens raised his eyes to look at the mirrored light well in the opposite quadrant of the ceiling. With the new swish of the doors, the waft of ground beans tinted the bouncing daylight. He turned to Susan as she laid her hand over his.

"Thank you."

"Congratulations, you're a free woman." He smiled. "For the next two minutes at least."

She chuckled, then ran her bent finger under her watering eyes.

He gave her another moment. "We can still wait until you reenter."

"No, I can do it now." She tossed her hair back over the

white wooly sweater and pulled a brisk smile, then looked down at their still touching hands before raising her eyes to his. "I just have this strange feeling I can entirely trust you somehow," she said. "And then Tara can't wait with school. Ah"—she checked her time—"I have twenty minutes to pick her up."

"All right, let's mark this off," he said, and flipped the graph closer to bring up the new affidavit.

She cast her ID and consent over again, then gave him a light kiss, the mocha frail on her lips. She leaned back in the armchair and exhaled, looking up, then let her head roll to the side on the headrest. "Is that Sunshine Machine? I grew up with this song!"

"Really? They were big here." He tipped his chin higher and listened to the background tune. "That was my first live concert, in fact."

"You went to see Sunshine Machine?" She beamed. "I just can't imagine that for some reason."

He suppressed his smile and grabbed his tea. "I still have some scary photos, I think."

She laughed. "I'd love to see them." She kept her cheek resting on the cushioned chair back and reached for his hand. "I'd like us to take this slowly and give it the best chance. Partner."

"Agreed. Partner."

She rose to her feet. "See you Friday." She weaved in her black jeans through the tables and hardly slowed in front of the doors as newcomers gave way.

He sipped and stood up to watch her cross the street and hustle to the first cab in the drive lane. He remained standing after she drove off, raising his heels a whit above the floor with the new beat.

The standby call pulsated through, from a West Ayland realtor. He put his cup down and snapped his set back on his wristband then took the call and walked out. The realtor apologized for the intrusion and explained that he hadn't been able to reach Lynden yet. His own clients were holding off making their offer elsewhere as they had seen the just-listed house of Clarens's mother, herself out of reach.

"We'd like to offer ten percent over asking," he said. "Till tomorrow noon."


Barely missing the retracting doors, Brett stepped in. His feet apart and hand clasped over his wrist, he glanced at the deserted office floor as the elevator departed. Down on the garage platform, a handful of people were lined up at the call lane to board their arriving cars. He walked around the yellow line and to the self-drive aisle, which split several times, until his footsteps squeaked alone on the clear-sealed concrete slab. Ever frowning, he slowed in the middle of the new tier to let his car back out, then he sat in and felt the console for the water bottle, which remained tangled in the handles of the shopping bag, though. He looked down at it, grabbed the bag, and dashed it against the passenger door, then picked up the bottle and drank. Out the windshield, the light strip pulsed down the middle of the ceiling and toward the hoister, just as uniform as the queuing roof lights of the cars below. Albeit faster. He put the bottle down and checked the inside of the bag, where the wood glue bottle had leaked a small puddle. He snapped the cap back on tight and rubbed the glue stains thin between his palms, then grasped the steering wheel and sped down the side lane. Wheels screeching, he turned onto the almost empty aisle toward the self-drive exit. In the sharper three-quarter turn at the end, his left hand stuck to the steering wheel a split second too long. The front tires lost grip and all he could do was hit the brakes to lessen the impact of his car ramming into the rear of the sole car parked in the garage corner.

As the body shield deflated, he scrunched his eyes and slid

the door open, but paused to peek through the twisted-open rear door of the other car, where a couple scrambled to climb back onto their rear seats. The woman zipped up her shirt as the man poked his head against the car roof while appearing to hitch his pants on as the car alarm howled between the bare walls around.

"Stupid, stupid idea!" she said, when the alarm stopped and the man stepped out.

Feeling his neck and with his dress shirt bulging out of his trousers, the man cut off Brett's apology to grieve over the punched rear of his car. He tapped on the door, which droned in place without moving, then jogged it down to nearly closed and checked his set. "Your insurance wasn't on?"

"Oh, I have it"—Brett rushed to check his set too. "Just being updated…" He looked up at him. "Do you mind just settling this now? I'll cover everything."

Between the husky shoulders, the man deadpanned. "I need your insurance."

"What could this be?" Brett pointed at the car. "Five hundred, a thousand? I'll give you three thousand."

The man edged forward. "Listen guy!" he went off, when the woman stepped out of the car.

Her blond curls wobbled loose as she looked at the car's bashed rear, then at her partner, who held his hand out still toward Brett. "Can we just get this done?" She then pierced Brett with her bright blue glance. "Look, we're live"—she glanced higher. "And we couldn't take this kind of cash even if we wanted to."

Brett looked at her. "Do you work at the bank?"

She stared back. "What?"

He shook his head quickly, then turned to the security car that zoomed in, lights swirling around it. "Great…"

"Need the recording? Towing?" the operator said.

As the man hesitated, his partner pasted on a smile. "We'll know in a minute, thanks!"

They watched the car swivel into a side spot to wait, then Brett turned to the two of them. "I have physical unis, actually."

"Physical. This is not happening," the man looked away, saying.

"In platinum. You don't declare it up to thirty grams."

"But, that wouldn't do," she said.

"I'll give you a whole bar, three hundred grams. You can cut it, keep it, whatever. That's over four thousand market value." As the couple looked at each other, he nudged his head to the side. "You can check with the pawn store in the south shell."

"I know it," she murmured to her partner.

"And the report?" the man returned.

"I don't know, you parked next to an ice shelf or something." She kept her hands on her waist, elbows sharp in the silky blouse, and flicked her gaze at the upper wall. "Shall we wave too?"

He sighed long and turned to Brett, while she hustled back around the car. "All right, let's see it. Just keep it low," he rushed to add as Brett reached inside his jacket, then looked down at the bar in his palm. "How do we know it's real?"

"How do I know you won't make a claim?" Brett said, and flipped the bar with the markings up, then flashed it in the open before handing it to him. "In case you or I will need that."

Debris cracked under the front wheels as he backed up and drove away. He stayed his hands on the upper bow of the steering wheel as he reached the exit ramp. "Idiot. You're such an idiot…" he muttered, between the rattles coming through from the front of the car. He pulled over in the emergency parking just before the tunnel entry and stepped out to inspect the car all around. The hood warped up and over the corner of the windshield, one left-side light was shattered, the spoiler caved in and tipped down to the pavement. He grasped it from underneath and jigged it up clear of the surface, then pounded the corner of the hood down with both hands until another car drove up the ramp. He rubbed his hands off and looked out. Through the arched opening ahead, the tunnel flowed fast and steady. Still sticky, his hands had turned dark with the dust. He washed with the remaining water in the bottle and wheeled to the entry light, then boosted the car into the first lane and set it off. The panel warnings flashed on and the hood jarred closer to the windshield as cars sped by through the endless, tubular turns.

# 13

"A '94 Yuejin Skybird... You said you called live this morning?"

"Yes. Spoke with Kaj, or Gaj."

"Kaj," the serviceman said, tapping the stand, and looked out at Brett's car, which remained queued in the garage drop-off. He edged up in his actuated chair and felt his neck stubble. "The thing is that no one carries the print for this car. I can get the part made outside but it'll take two weeks, and it'll cost you," he continued. "Or I can have a source in Tencun make it in two days from an unlicensed print, but... perfect"—he tipped his thumb and forefinger together. He let Brett ponder for a moment. "It looks like the kind of car they'll carry, and I don't mean anything by that!" he added, rushing his hand forward, and snickered.

Brett smiled along. "Okay, great. I must have checked with every darn shop in Ayland for the past two days."

His snicker returning to wheezing, the serviceman worked his scheduler. "And they won't take insurance over there, so we'll need physical."

"That definitely works too. What kind?"

"Travel warrants. From any bank."

Brett grasped his chin. "I don't have that kind of account..." He mulled. "Bullion works? I could pay a little premium."

The serviceman looked at him impassive and wheezed on, then turned around to make a minutes-long call. He then confirmed with him the form of payment, of which eighty grams were required, and brought up a slow-turning array of rental cars over the stand for Brett to choose from. He stepped out of his chair mold and squeezed through the back door, but turned and wiggled his finger at the graph. "I still need a collision statement. Like an ice shelf rolled on you or something."

Sunk in his chair and frowning, Brett sent the statement over, then twiddled in and out of the blanks of his new Commons account. He switched to the sporty blue car that came to a swift stop in the pick-up lane. He rose and stepped outside, as the serviceman showed up too and struggled to sit in the car.

"You know how to set up the auto and all that?"

"I can figure it out."

"All right, let me just plug your ID in here…"

As he left, Brett took his place and swept his gaze over the black and blue interior and quiet dashboard, where a single "self" tag pulsed at the bottom of the windshield. He let the seat and viewers come into place and gently pressed his fingertips inside the steering wheel groove, though he still hit the headrest as the car thrust forward. He steered out of the garage grounds and onto the unkempt access street and tapped the power for the speed burst, but he still couldn't hear a whit of the outside.

The main road laid out just as smooth from the estranged comfort behind the shaded glass. He checked the bottom of the windshield for the growing speed band, which suddenly changed to red and chimed off. He peeked over the dashboard, which remained dark, while tilting his head with the wide turn through the roundabout. Before long, the chime went off once more, but the dashboard stayed devoid of any indicators. He slowed down and scoured the subdued controls, then reached for the rental's physical remote, fallen beside the passenger seat, to call up the command and then the music on. He settled for Analog's "Taverna Oblivion" and, brows arching, bobbed in disbelief at the leading guitars that tore through the surround, then he lay back and burst to the previous speed mark. A sole car zoomed by the opposite way and the suburban road stayed clear, with the immaculate, neo-traditional houses ranging by crisp in the three o'clock sun. He let out, then louder, with the throbbing tune.

When the chime sounded off again, the car's command, too, warned of the status of the upcoming roundabout. Sight out this time, he switched his fingers to the brakes as the side sign flashed by, albeit too late to make the updated speed limit. The last straight took him back to the city-bound avenue, although he broke with it and veered onto the freeway ramp. He kept the car in self-drive and checked for any restrictions ahead, then turned the volume higher and zoomed to the far left.

———

With a smile over his shoulder, Clarens swung the apartment door wide and stepped aside for Susan and Tara to follow him inside.

Susan craned her head to look past the vestibule corner as the windows turned lighter in the main room. "Wow, it's big! And neat!"

"I just don't have a lot of things."

"Well, that's a shocker. My hair's the only clutter in your car." She chuckled and walked onto the open floor to wonder at the view, then at the kitchen. In front of her, Tara stopped to gaze at the bare, glossy counters of the kitchen island, as he pulled out the first tall chair.

"I got this insert for her, if you need it."

"Oh my! Look Tara, you have your own chair sweetie." Susan wrapped her arm around her while feeling the padded chair with her other hand. "Nice, huh? What do we say?" She rocked her gently, though the girl kept mum and only glanced at Clarens.

"Where is Daddy?" she mumbled.

Susan stayed bent to her, hair weaving down long to one side. "Daddy needs to stay somewhere else, remember?" she said quietly. "But Clarens is just like Daddy, and he loves you just as much." She parted Tara's bangs off her forehead. "Remember when he took you to the jelly house? And to the aquarium to feed the penguins?" She kept stroking her. "So, do we say...?"

Long-faced, Tara uttered the "thank you" with her and raised her eyes to him, to which he responded with a bow, then she leaned on Susan for a hug.

He picked up the plate with unconsumed breakfast and shelved it in the fridge, then watched Susan step away with Tara back to the lounging area and stop next to the heliconia to look out the bay glazing.

The girl began exploring the floor around the couch, as Susan turned back to him.

He moved on and pointed behind him with his thumb. "You want to see the rooms?"

He led the way behind the privacy wall and to the bedrooms on the opposite side of the apartment. From the suite at the end, they returned and crossed the hallway to the middle room, where he stopped beside the open door. "And your bedroom..."

"This is great!" Walking around the room, Susan felt the satin of the built-in cabinetry along the side wall. She peeked inside the empty closet, then out the glazing overlooking the shared patio one story below. "I'm not going back out that door," she said, laughing with him, and then began measuring the floor for Tara's bed, to which he raised his hand and pointed down the hallway. She followed him to the new room by the apartment entry, and queried him with a smile as he ushered Tara in, who swung her ponytail as she looked around from the middle of the small floor.

He gestured at the credenza. "I didn't clear all my things yet."

Susan stepped that way. "Is that original artwork?"

"Noo.... Just a bunch of my absolute beginner drawings."

"Your drawings? You're kidding. You did this?"—she widened her smile. Turning to the stack of sheets, she uncovered the next drawing. "And this? Clarens, this is amazing!"

He chuckled. "By no means."

She leafed through, flipping the sheets up against the wall one by one and gazing at him in between. She paused over the new landscape drawing. "Where is this?"

"That's just... imaginary."

"Nice." Two sheets further, she slowed over the sketch of a nude woman. "This one too?" she quipped.

"That... was a model in class. I obviously wasn't into it."

She laughed softly and flipped the crude drawing over as Tara rose on her toes to peek over the edge of the credenza. He picked the next landscape drawing and laid it down on the floor for her.

"Gosh, you didn't tell me," Susan said, leafing on, and glanced at him from the corner of her eye. "Any other secrets?"

"Uhh... no. This was my big secret."

"Haha! Awesome secret to have."

She laid the sheets back down slowly, then tossed her hair around. "This is perfect." She squatted next to the girl and cheered with her. "When do we have to move in, by the way?"

"Well, the sooner you do it, the faster the trial gets rolling."

"Like tomorrow?" She grabbed her for a spin, then turned her rosy cheeks to him. "Can I borrow your car? If you don't check in today."

"Absolutely."

"You're sure?" She stepped up close for a fleeting kiss.

"You're soaking me in debt, Mr. Mann." She smiled, then swung back and grabbed Tara's hand. "C'mon sweetie, we can make a pie now!"

With the click of the closing door it was quiet again. He walked back to the workroom and joggled the drawings into a tight stack, then carried it to his bedroom's niche office. He returned, a smile still casting on his face, and gathered the art supplies, then the few winter jackets, leaving the closet and all drawers empty before calling the vacuum cleaner in. He unfolded the sofa bed and nudged it to the exact middle of the wall, then placed the sealed box of bird-themed linen beside it. He silenced the new work call and inched backward to look over the room till he rested against the credenza behind him, grasping the wood edge tight with both hands.

---

"Hey, look who's here! You gave up on your country?"

Brett let a smile out and walked closer.

Behind the showcase, Vitaly slipped off his stool to touch fists with him over the busy worktop felt, then let his jewelry glasses lower down his nose. "I like your choice with the ladies too." He grinned. "If I may."

"You do?"

"Worth every gram, even in uni-denomination," he added, to Brett easing a new smile, and edged forward. "By the way, we have the generic accounts, which only show a number in her tax file," he mock whispered, then bobbed his gleeful face and returned to the dismantled work parts. "Just saying. It seems like a shame to chop those bars in little pieces."

"Yeah," Brett muttered, reaching inside his jacket. "Where we need to go more generic, Vit, is with your own tax."

"Hahaha! Hey, I did my part. She came in again, I pretended I hadn't just seen her the other day. Now, how easy was that, even for an old fart?" Vitaly said and chuckled, glancing at

155

Brett's hand. "Some candy there for me too?"

Brett pulled the platinum bar out. "Actually, I need to cut eighty grams off this one if you could. I'm not kidding"—he smiled at his blank face.

"You're not kidding…"

"I'm not. You're charging me?"

Shaking his head, Vitaly swayed away with the bar. "No, I'm not charging you," he sighed. "I just don't see the logic. So that they cut it down in ten grammers?" he then shouted from the back room.

His fingertips wedged in his back pockets, Brett ambled around the store. The two bronze horses were still there on the upper shelf, galloping side by side over the rings of Saturn in the dimensional poster behind. Daring the ahead, their heads turned slightly to each other, their wind-hungry manes jagging into the bottomless, seashell white. He flicked his gaze to the numeric minutes that actually switched forward inside the antique table clock below, then stepped on and glanced over the sailboat models down the shelf. He turned to stand in the middle of the floor and brought up his mail. Beside the new portfolio alert, he skimmed through the mass thank-you note from his mother and stepfather to all who had joined them for his stepfather's "heart-brimming" retirement party. He deleted it and idled over his mother's prior message beneath it. "Where are you at with your trip? Please let us know dear," she wrote, and signed for all four in the family. He looked out the storefront and felt his day-old shave.

"Eighty here, and two twenty here"—Vitaly clacked the second metal piece down as Brett turned to him. "Plus minus point one grams." He slid the two pieces forward and, silent, watched him pick them up. "You know, I could probably match what you're trading these for even after tax," he said, and looked up at him over his glasses. "If it was a large quantity."

Brett slowed his hand inside his jacket. "How large?"

"Large."

He shifted his weight on the other leg. "That's interesting… 'Cause I'm actually thinking of staying longer."

"Oh… How much longer?"

He swayed his head slightly. "Longer."

Vitaly smiled. "Well, there you go. No sweat cutting little strips and squares."

His chuckle led him to a severe cough, then he bulged his paunch over the edge of the case again. Toying with his corded glasses over the chest, he turned his naked, milky-blue eyes to the streetlight. "So there's this jewelry center in Tencun. The bid is sweet but the logistics are a drag, so it's got to be quantity." He glimpsed the ceiling corner and turned to him. "I'd be the escrow agent and you'd pay the Commons sales tax here just the same."

"Huh. What kind of bid?"

"It works out to about twenty percent above the quote. Which is pegged to the industrial quote here." He took his voice down another notch. "Which their government can't enforce, and you get the street price."

"But, it's all in recorded transactions."

"It is. Though they're rumored to have missed the physical count here and there," he said, and edged back. "But we're all good from this end."

"Wow…" Brett murmured. "How safe is it?"

Vitaly stared out anew. "As safe as you want to keep it." He glanced back at him, when the rowdy group entered the store. Frowning, he tapped his fingers on the case top and shifted his weight. "Let me see what these little punks want."

"Yeah, sure." Turning with him, Brett nudged his chin at the nearest gadgets on display. "'Cause I was starting to wonder if you actually sell any of this stuff or—"

"Hahaha!"

———

Hefting a plump duffle bag on her shoulder, Susan walked to the visitor carport at the outer end of the hotel drop-off. Brett drove his beaming rental against the empty one-way loop and lowered his window at the curb, beside her.

"Nice car!"—he leaned his head out the window, wheeling to a stop.

She peeked his way, then turned her head fully as the rear hatch of her car slid open. "Brett? Look at you!"

Grinning, he rested his elbow on the door and nodded. "Told you we'd make it."

She rolled her eyes with her smile and dropped the bag inside the car.

"One way or another," he added. "Still moving?"

"Just some leftovers," she said, rubbing her hands slowly, and tossed her hair back over the white knit. "We moved Wednesday."

"Yeah, I was wondering. So you're all checked out then."

"Yeah."

"Good…"

"You?"

"I'm still looking." He paused for a cab squeezing by on his other side. "How's Tara? I was thinking to take her out tomorrow. Or Sunday."

She hemmed, hugging herself against the new rush of the wind.

"We said three mornings a week."

"I know but, you can't just tell me the day before, you know?"

He shook his head. "I was being flexible," he uttered plainly, and sliced the air down with his hand. "I said tomorrow or Sunday."

She exhaled and glanced away. "Father all of a sudden…"

He hastened to wheel the car closer to the curb to make room for the shuttle coming down, then creased his brows at her up close. "Father what?"

Pulling back, she whisked her hand through and put her shades on. "Whatever. I'll call you tonight."

"Yeah. Do so!"

"And I'd like to get my share of that physical, before we see anything else like this"—she nodded at his car. "Do I just go to the bank?"

He looked at her as she waited motionless behind the black shades with her hair whipping over, then he turned to the dashboard warning. "Well, I meant to talk to you about that," he said, and tilted his head out the window again. "This is for everyone's benefit, okay? I found this deal to cash out."

"That's all right, I can keep mine the way it is."

"Susan, just listen, we're talking a huge difference. I didn't even think you wouldn't do it, so I kind of committed to it."

"You can't be serious."

"It was a no-brainer!"

She stepped closer. "Brett, I want my share just the way it is, you understand?"

"Oh, this is just stupid." Shaking his head, he grabbed the steering wheel. "Fine, have your share. I'll take mine out, so you can just leave yours there, or whatever."

"Thank you! And the key is the same?" she added quickly as he began pivoting the car.

"Yes. Oh, I had to get a temporary pass." He paused for her to call her set. "Bank chick zero one. One word."

She turned her shades at him. "What?"

"One word," he said, and darted around the drop off to the garage entry.

———

The markets had taken a breather overnight, and so had the metals. He slurped the hot latte and put the large mug back on the side of the table, then shrank off the charts, plugged the set back in his wristband, and grabbed his bacon roll. He chewed slowly, looking down the shell over the terrace railing and the sparse pedestrians.

Downstairs, he kept to the sidewalk for a long block, by the stone sidewalls and their taintless ochre begging for a touch, before stepping onto the street belt. When he walked off it and to the other side, he watched himself approaching in the building glazing. He switched the small suitcase to the other hand and unzipped his shirt a palm below the neck before entering the bank.

Ethel sat at her desk behind the courtesy counter, a coworker at her side. They looked up at him.

"Hey Ethel," he said from a few steps away before they could say anything and he nodded at the other woman, who looked at Ethel in turn. "Just checking on my stuff"—he smiled at her quiet greeting and walked by toward the safes' room. He glanced at the back of the sole other user and laid the suitcase below his box column, then unlocked the door and, with both hands, he heaved the bag out and placed it next to the case quietly. He carried them to the side counter, pressed them close together, and began rushing the thumb-sized bars from the bag on top of the sweater in the case, the metal ringing dull under his fingers as he counted again.

He shoved the lighter bag back in the safe box and then rolled the suitcase behind him to the bank lobby. Ethel was at her desk, still side by side with her colleague. He walked closer. "Training day?"

They smiled. "Yes!"

"Ah"—he leaned back theatrically. He pointed at his suitcase. "Too late for this customer."

"Oh, you're leaving, sir?" Ethel said.

"Well, if this is what it takes." He grinned. "C'mon, it's definitely Brett now."

She blushed, coiling her hair around her ear, as the other woman pasted on a smile and looked at them both in turns.

"Later!" He held up his open hand and walked out. The suitcase hummed smoothly under its weight on the sleek pavement, as he picked up the pace. He weaved through the busier next block and brought the case in front of him, then crossed to the belt and frowned lightly with the curving street frontage as the south end of the shell came into view.

# 14

The two silhouettes rushed behind the lucent office partition, one chasing the other. "Sir, wait! Mr. Falco!..."

Brett jabbed the office door fully open and walked in, with the distressed receptionist holding his hands out helpless behind him. "So how exactly does this work, Clarens?" he charged, bracing his fists on the desk. "You snatch my money, snatch my partner, and now you're screwing me too?"

As more heads turned to look in from out on the floor, Clarens rose from his chair and exhaled. He nodded to the receptionist and looked at Brett. "Calm down, take a seat."

"Don't fuckin' tell me to calm down"—Brett jarred the desk under his fist. "Tell me this is not happening!"

"Look, it's not that bad, considering—"

"It's not that bad?" He hung over the desk, jaws clutching under the flawless shave.

An arm's length away, Clarens looked into his throbbing blue eyes, then stepped slowly around the desk. As Brett swiveled his head to watch him, Clarens nodded again at the wary receptionist and swung the door closed as the receptionist backed out of the room. "There's no need for this," he said to Brett. "I'm on your side. Please, take a seat."

Without budging, Brett watched him return to the desk.

"Look, we knew they would scrutinize everything."

"It's a freakin' roundabout on an empty road!" he struck the desk again saying.

"Well, four of them. And I know"—Clarens raised his hand to halt him—"but that debate goes nowhere."

"Are you still saying we won't appeal this?"

He shrugged. "Any infraction like these speeding tickets automatically resets the process. But really, until this probation expires, the two visits per year give us a lot of stay."

"No fuckin' kidding!"

Snorting, Brett let his head down and looked over the matrix of documents on the desk, pausing on the paper sketch pad at the end. "Three years..."

"I'm sorry. I'll see if we can have any money refunded."

He wried his face at him, then looked back down and shook his head. "Can I stay past the two weeks left?" He looked over and, as Clarens pressed his lips silent, he snorted again, always resting on his fists. Under the downlights, the spry bristles of his hair meshed over the short part line. He straightened up and turned away. "Take care of the kid."

"Of course. Be in touch anytime—" Clarens stalled as Brett stabbed his finger at him. Brett lowered his finger slowly. "I owe her."

The door struck the full-open stop under his thrust as he walked out.

Clarens watched his silhouette melt into the opposite wall, then remained standing by the chair, fingers tapping the headrest lightly. He glanced back at the faces out on the floor, then stepped aside to grab his jacket from the ottoman and put it on slowly.

The receptionist rushed in the doorway. "I'm sorry, I couldn't stop him."

Stepping his way, Clarens checked his pockets and peeked back over the desk. "Don't worry... Can we move my meetings to tomorrow?"

As the receptionist whizzed through his scheduler, Clarens walked by him and out. He kept his eyes just below the sightline down the aisle, which stayed empty, except for the young staffer who passed a smile while crossing through. And for the ever louder treble in the back of his ears. He almost made the end turn when the different pitch nicked in. He picked up the call.

"Hey, did Lynden give you the news?" his sister said.

"Yes."

"Told you to hold out." She voiced her smile through. "We should take the offer."

"Uhh… probably. Let me call you from my car," he said, with the elevators port clearing in sight. "There's this other news I meant to give you."


He went to the afternoon class instead, where he was still early, but he picked a station at the rear of the vacant room anyway. Ruffles and chairs rolled in slowly around him. With the buzzing class, he turned to his board to lay out his charcoal and ink bottles for the technique du jour. Near the end of the hour, he had filled a third sheet with the classic still life on display, the pears and mangos and bananas spilling bolder out of the wooden rectangular bowl. He rotated the drawing upside down. He widened the curves to the edge of the paper and left alone the little basket atop, as if it overlooked the emerging waves and slopes below, then poured the entire ink bottle in the working jar to brush olive green over. He stared out anew, then twitched back, knocking the jar and ink tray which spilled down the board and in his lap and to a puddle on the floor. In the ensuing silence, he bent to pick up the containers, then grabbed the handful of paper napkins that showed up before his face.

"They used to call this the consummate artist," the teacher said, to the mirth of the class, as Clarens patted his color-soiled trousers next to the green tones of the drawing. He turned closer. "I have aprons to cover up if you want one."

Out in the street, Clarens pinged the car, but came to a

stop and checked for the nearest spa instead, which mapped a block away. He looked down his gray apron, then crossed the street to the narrow sidewalk behind the line of parked cars and walked the block. In the unstaffed lobby, he stepped to the clothing display and flipped through the samples of active wear. The sweatpants were all flimsy.

The side door opened and a suited technician glanced him down. "'Bout time. I'm ready for that extra pair of hands, whenever you can," he said, and left the door open for a hesitant Clarens to follow him down the corridor and inside the single guest room being serviced. "If I were you I'd snap in a whole new slab, but…" he added, and set off the telescoping stand to lower the white ceiling alcove, revealing the intestinal machinery of pipes and wires and housings in the dark space above. They went up with the stand, instead, and, per his instructions, Clarens reached high inside the machinery for the cold, black pipe stub. He twisted it while the technician disconnected the module from the other end and let it down slowly with him. He gazed on from the floor as the technician flicked and lit his handhelds through the ceiling cutout, until the man paused to look down at him and nodded.

He picked up a pair of sweatpants from the lobby dispenser and checked into a single room. He undressed and tossed the apron and trousers in the disposal, then his all-dyed shorts too. In the shower, he reeled and leaned helpless into the wall, scrabbling for the surround rail to anchor himself as the floor turned reddish brown around his feet, then green, then gray, all streaming into the drain.


Susan lay in the chaise longue in the bay window, taking a call. With the roll of drawings under his arm, he gently clicked the apartment door closed and swapped the art case back to his free hand. The contents rattled inside, just above the low music volume, to which she glanced over and lifted her finger.

"Sorry, I got to go," she said to her caller. "I know, I can't believe it either. Talk soon." She rose and sprang bare footed to him in her tank top and capris. "My friend, she's so excited." She pecked him on the cheek. "Almost as much as I am." She smiled as bright as her white top and turned to tiptoe toward the kitchen while pulling her hair into a loose bun. "These slow remakes sort of grew on me"—she flicked her hand through the air with the tune and looked over the shoulder. "Hope you haven't had dinner yet."

He pitched the roll against the wall by the island, where the seating corner was all set for two, side salads and an opened wine bottle included. "Wait, you actually cooked again?"

Mitts on her hands, she pulled the oven drawer open. "I love cooking. Besides…" She laid the baking tray on the counter tile. "What's a housewife supposed to do?"

He chuckled quiet with her, as she took a smaller platter out to bring it over and place it between their plates, two stuffed cream-laced crepes on it. She rested her hands on her waist and smiled. Her eyes turned gleaming. "I still can't believe I'm here."

They hugged.

She sniffed on his shoulder as he edged back, then loosened her arms and put the mitts on the upper counter. "So sorry again about today, by the way."

He turned to sit down. "Don't worry. He's entitled to be upset."

"Yeah but, it's not like it's your fault." She remained standing, frowning slightly. "What exactly did he say?"

"Well, he pressed for the appeal, then seemed to come to terms with it. And he told me to take care of Tara."

"He told you to take care of Tara…?"

"Yes. He insisted."

"Gosh, what is it with him now? I mean…" She shook her head and sat down, then dinged the tableware quietly as she served herself. She rolled her eyes and pointed at her ear while rising again. "You should eat," she mouthed to him before taking the call. "Hey!... I was going to... She just called me!" she upped her tone while stepping away.

She was still ambling back and forth in the bay glazing when he pushed his empty plate aside and moved on to the last greens in the bowl. He sipped the pure cab and looked her way again, with the new acoustic strings touching the air. She had left the window shading off. She raised her head and fluttered her fingers over with a smile, then turned around to look out, her contour pasted within the vivid lights of the top stories across the street, her neckline slanting over the twinkles of the downtown, all framed together in the bay's elongated opening, at the front end of a gallery that slipped closer, accelerating, indefinitely closing in.

He switched his eyes to the shuffle of the unwinding roll and watched the drawings fan out on the floor. He stacked them together and carried them to his bedroom's niche worktop, then checked over the room while changing. He hung his sleeping shirt in the closet and flipped the comforter flat on the bed, then nudged the lighthouse sculpture against the wall on the console table before moving to the bathroom. Back in the quiet corridor, he stopped to listen to Tara's snoring. He stepped to the door and eased his head in. She appeared to have rolled to the side of the bed, into the duckling cuddler that dimmed over the dark sideboard.

Susan had almost finished her meal too. "Family..." She shrugged, a twitch in the corner of her lips, before rising to put her dishes away. She returned with the baking tray and smiled to his jesting sigh, then ran the knife back and forth through the large apple pie.

He feathered a smile "We better find you a job or I'll have to go swimming every day here."

"Haha! No, it's all good stuff." She served herself too and licked her finger. "But you're right."

He relished the first bite and poured more wine. "Not that

you need to do anything," he added.

"You're kidding? I totally need to."

"I mean, if you didn't find something you liked doing."

She stilled the forked piece at her mouth. "So you like my pie..."

He looked at her, then both bowed laughing over their plates with their mouths full.

She coughed hard to clear her throat, reddened down to her tank top, and drank. "Here and now, I can do anything," she said, recovering. "Huh… I never thought I could contemplate that again."

"Why is that?"

She shrugged. "I've been told precisely what to do for eighteen years straight." She rushed a smile, then tilted her head, a few hairs coming loose off her bun. "Or that's just me. I need to run my own thing and put heart in what I do," she added, and met his eyes. "You know?"

"Right," he murmured, and dinged the silver fork through his remaining pie.

She rose with her empty plate and tweaked her top down over her capris as she weaved around the counter to the dishwasher. "But first things first, we're looking at another school tomorrow, just to compare," she said, and returned to pick up the tray. "I'll jump in the shower. See you in the morning."

———

Three of the four spots were close together and almost in a line, or a very shallow arc. The fourth one was quite a bit higher and with no visible relation to them, other than for the same light sprinkles staining the wall around it. His back against the bed's headboard across the room, Brett drank up and then crumpled the beer can in his hand, a moment before the bed shook under his pitching thrust. The new spot was still high. He turned his head to look toward the entryway and, a minute into it, he dragged his legs to the side of the bed and rose, then thumped the floor on his way to the bathroom. He looked down at the toilet and burped as he went.

He braced his hand on the dim wall and scrunched his eyes as the fridge door lit up under his other hand. He plucked the new can's spout out on the way to the window and tossed his head back to drink, then tracked the few car lights down the hotel's backstreets below.

He stepped to the nightstand, put the can down, and lay back in bed.

His open mouth dry, he woke up with the incoming voice call. He knocked the can off the nightstand while pushing himself higher and prompted his set for more information, but not even the caller's location came up. "Hello?"

"Hi, is this Brett?"

"Who's calling?"

"I'm sorry, is this too late?" the woman said.

He blinked wide and sat up on the edge of the bed, his foot in the beer puddle. "No, no. This is he."

"Hi, I'm a friend of Jana. She mentioned you're looking for something more long-term."

"Jana… Oh yeah, I am." He stood up to pat his feet on his shirt lying on the floor. "So… what do you do? I mean, how old are you?"

She took a moment. "Listen, I think I fit the picture from my end. What we need to do is to see if you're ready for a commitment. Seven hundred would make it work."

"I'm sorry?"

"Your contribution would be seven hundred thousand."

He let his foot down, eyes flitting over the wall. "That's a pretty crazy amount."

"I put myself on the line. There are people who offer five times as much."

"Yeah but, it's not like any kingpin's going to make it in

anytime soon."

"Leave a message at this number if you'd like. If I haven't changed my mind."

"Wait—"

She didn't.

He stared at the silent number in his palm, then across the room. The other bed pillow had landed in balance over the armchair headrest somehow, as if counterweighed by the empty can on the short overhang. He twitched up and called the lights brighter, mopped the beer spill with his shirt, then fed all the empty beer cans into the waste receptacle. He lobbed the pillow back on the bed, reached for the wood glue bottle inside the store bag, then grabbed the broken chair leg to drip glue between the splinters and drove the leg into the other splintered end below the chair's seat. Glue seeped out the joint cracks as he let the chair down. He crouched lower on his elbow and wiped the glue with one finger on each side of the leg and watched closely for any more seepage while rubbing the sticky fingers in his palm. He rolled onto his back abruptly to free up his other hand and began fiddling through his graph.

"This cannot be... This cannot be!"

# 15

"**O**rion Clearway."

Springing up on his feet, Brett returned the glance of the staffer across the tearoom and stepped away to take the call. "Yes. Don please," he muttered, and threw his workout bag on his shoulder while crossing the hotel foyer.

"He's still in a meeting, but I told him you—"

"That's all right, you can interrupt him now."

"Uhh… I'm sorry, I can't. Is this about your account transfer?" the live spokesman added quickly on the same, measured voice.

With the front doors closing behind him, Brett squinted at the clouds, then let his head down and exhaled. "Yes, it's about my account transfer," he uttered plainly. "Why, have you not, released it?" he yelled the last words, then hastened past the bystanders in the drop-off and toward the small green.

"I can explain."

"Explain what? You're holding up my money! You're not returning my calls!"

"Mr. Falco, do you want me to explain?"

He stopped by the pedestal fountain and combed his fingers back through his hair. "Go ahead."

"We notified everyone when Transcontinental opted out of the universal, and all our clearing is on hold until—"

"I specified either currency."

"Well, we have a bit of a liquidity gap due to the exchange

rate."

"Liquidity gap? Okay, listen carefully." He moved on and brought the image up. "If I don't see my account released by five your time, at five oh one I'll be filing a claim with the DFI that will cause you a real liquidity gap. Do you understand?"

Beside the slow-revolving stars emblem, the spokesman nudged a shrug and reiterated his stance.

"Five p.m. Don't try me. Don't freakin' try me!" Brett yelled him over, when the stars grew over the entire graph in his hand and the call went silent.

He tossed his bag onto the bench aside with a curse and, lips crimping, he began treading the stone pavers around the square grass patch. He stopped after a full lap. The lone fountain sprang a stub of water atop its small center cone and caught it back in the round basin below, like a replica of a street fountain in the old world. The sound of the thin water falling came through clear. The surrounding hedge stood neat and quiet behind it, all but barring the neighboring plaza noise and boulevard building tops. He did another lap. The aged corner shrub looked exotic with its upright, tortuous branches, clipped flat an arm's length above the sightline. He turned to a call coming from the hotel entryway.

"Sir, is this your brunch?" the tearoom staffer said, tilting out the open doors with the plastic box in one hand.

Meeting him at halfway to take possession of the box, Brett caught his glance. "Really sorry…"

He watched the staffer rush back in, then turned around and lifted the box lid. The leftover fragment rolled down and came apart against the rim of the box, with a trace of ham stuck on the pastry crust. He huffed and dropped the box in the refuse barrel then stood by as the disposal chewed it up. He stared down the remaining onlookers in the drop-off, then went back to pick up his workout bag and walked down the empty passageway along the plaza.

Under the swaying barbell, he blew out his burning cheeks but couldn't heave it any higher. He screamed and let it back onto the side supports, then breathed deeply, fixating on the ceiling rails.

He heaved again to rise from the bench, to the open hand in front of his eyes. He grasped it. "Hey, thanks."

His gym buddy pulled him up to sitting. "Was curling over there and heard you"—he gestured with his bare arms, which looked ever bulkier next to his slender body.

Elbows weighing sapless on his knees, Brett raised his eyes at him. "Still here, huh?" He stood up and grabbed his towel. "How come I've never seen you at the hotel?"

He grinned. "Actually, I help out here."

"You work here?

"Here and downtown." He swung his wobbling triceps out. "In the Jefferson."

"Geez man…" Brett cracked a smile with a measuring glance. He stood just as tall, unless that was because of the new-looking sneaks, with the light bruise under the cheekbone pushing into the close shave. "How much are they paying? Sorry, never mind"—he flashed his hand open as the man passed a chuckle, and walked around the bench.

"You?" the man asked. "Still hangin'?"

"Actually…" He threw his towel on his shoulder and stepped backward between the idle machines, then waved short while turning away. "I'm leaving in the morning."

———

"Clarens! Did you just get engaged or something?"

"The man would never lose a case…" the other colleague said and snickered as the two came to a stop before Clarens in the aisle crossing.

Clarens smiled. "Yes! I just didn't get a chance to tell

everyone."

"No, you didn't!"

Through the hearty laughs, his colleague landed a pat on his shoulder. "We'll have to throw you a party, buddy! You're in next week? Thursday?" He grinned as they moved on. "Hey, congrats! Really!"

He gave them a thumbs up and turned the wide corner, then slowed his steps again by the quiet meeting rooms. From cracked open, Talbot's door swung out slowly with the knock of his finger.

"Clarens!"

He advanced to the guest chair and held his hand out, as Talbot frowned a tad in his stock dark-gray suit from across the desk. "I'm sorry. I can't do it." He sighed. "I mean, especially now."

Talbot swiveled his chair to look out. "All right."

"And I'm sorry about the episode."

He steepled his fingers, brows ever low. "Don't worry about that. Nothing beats nature."

Clarens smiled and glimpsed the floor. "You're upset."

"I'm not ecstatic. But I'm not upset."

He slipped his hands in his trousers pockets and looked out through the gap between the adjacent high-rises. "In a way, I was hoping you'd be." He turned, as Talbot crossed his legs with his looming foot jiggling past the desk corner. "You said something a little while ago that just stayed with me," he continued, taking his gaze up the wall. "Something like… life gives if you want to take, and takes away otherwise." He looked back at him, but then steered away from the piercing eyes. "I'm just thinking that I've been doing law for a while. I'm thinking of trying something different."

"Different…"

"Quite different."

As they looked at each other, the glimmer in Talbot's eyes waned. He put both feet down and reached in his desk drawer, then rose just as slowly. He approached in stilting steps and took a sip from the little square bottle in his hand as he stood beside Clarens, who turned with him to look out again. He brought the bottle low to offer him what looked like bourbon, which Clarens declined, then he slipped it in his pocket and swayed closer to the window, pointing out.

"See that little, square brick-veneered building there? Just outside Jefferson... It used to be a furniture center. Resin printouts, wood imports, and things. I worked there nights my first year in law school, then the owner wanted me to stay but... He was this worldly guy, always sharp, always tanned. God knows where he'd get that from, 'cause he wasn't there often, then one day he'd check in and make a few sales happen out of thin air and bust your balls to keep up," he went on, popping his ankles with a heel rise. "Then he'd grin at you and push his open hand forward by his hip like this, then roll it into a fist and pull it back like this, and throw that life-gives-or-takes esotericism at you that would just wedge between your brain folds for weeks." He reached in his pocket and took another sip, then rolled his lips aloud. The frontage of the two-story building swapped the muddy-gray for a light-brown, before another cloud raced over. "So when would this be?" he added.

"Well, as soon as it won't be a problem for you, Tal."

He twitched a smile in the shade of his brows and patted him while turning around.

"I know, that's just antithetical," Clarens quipped, following him through the middle of the room.

Talbot poured a glass of water on the side table on his way to his desk. "Good luck to you, Clarens," he said, energized, and held the water in his mouth before swallowing. He picked a mint and sat at his desk, then bent forward to thrust his chair closer and raised an earnest face. "Check here first if you run out of cash."

Out the door, the same quiet corridor drifted through the

ending lunch-hour lull. The meeting room's armchairs ticked by with his soundless steps, then, past the rose-mallow oval, the humming moved in and a couple of figures blurred through the floating crescent-shaped workstations on the open floor. He stopped and rested his hand on the first workstation's limpid cornice, peering out. On the high wall across the floor, the physical artwork hung in the flooding light, one large frame after another. "Is that a new Diebenkorn?"

Inside the crescent, his young colleague rose to look at the picture too. "I don't know. It's always there whenever I'm in," she said, turning to him.

"It is, huh…"

He looked at her and smiled, then at the ones behind her. He raised his hand, wordless, then tapped the cornice and walked on. Between the grayed-out rooms down the aisle, daylight beamed silk through his half-open door and through the ceiling's apex onto the soffits above. He squinted as he walked in but left the window tint unchanged. He turned west with the restless clouds and took Susan's call.

"You can't be serious. I was just looking that way."

"And I thought I hired a serious attorney." She laughed brightly. "Hey, can you meet me downstairs at four?"

"Four, huh..." He raised his eyes over the fringe of her casting. "Enough time to count the streets to there."

————

The race sound came through the opening door as Vitaly pulled the hand truck out. He maneuvered it behind the showcase, then grabbed the bag to drag it to the counter.

Brett rushed his hands under it to help him haul it over. "Sorry again, Vit."

"Not a problem," Vitaly wheezed out then bobbed his reddened face at the open bag. "Let's make sure it's all good," he said, and checked his set. "We have… forty-one, then you cancelled out twelve, so that leaves twenty-nine kilos. Less the nonrefundable, which you can cover any way you want."

"Which was..."

"Fifteen hundred." As Brett paused, he shrugged. "I got everyone rolling at the other end."

Brett leveled the stacks inside the bag and raked his fingers through the minted bars from one side to the other.

Watching, Vitaly inched closer over the counter. "By the way, when we called it safe, it goes both ways."

Brett glimpsed his pore-sprinkled face. "Of course," he muttered back, and ran his fingers through the bag once more to pick a bar. "Who'd give a rat's ass about a guy from the FSA reporting tax evasion in Tencun anyway?"

They chortled loud, Vitaly's eyes sinking into the burly cheeks, as Brett nipped the white metal out of its sleeve to hand it over.

"Still a mess over there, huh?" Vitaly asked.

"Yep."

"Going straight back?"

"Yep," Brett said, head slanted at the assayer's readings that Vitaly turned toward him, then slipped the bar back in the bag "Wanna come? I know a town or two up for sale."

"Tempting," Vitaly chuckled. "How far from that trouble state?"

"Which one?"

He burst again, then his laugh curbed into the wheezing cough as he watched Brett make ten-bar stacks starting at his end of the bag. "Chances are you'll be back with a fresh memorial minting before I can look up the map," he snickered, as Brett held off his smile and whispered the counting louder. With the race commentary coming alive, he brought the feed over in his palm, the colorful cars piling up in a scintillating cloud of dust. "The bully will never change, you people," he griped. "It's in the Constitution!"

Side by side, Clarens and Susan watched Brett walk off the street belt with a smiling Tara riding his shoulders high. He ran a few steps closer and spun around, to her rare shriek, then grabbed her and spun once more, her legs circling the air. She wobbled laughing in his hands as he let her stand, while he too reeled sideways to find his balance.

"I'll call you every few days just the same, okay?" he said, sweeping her forehead, and held her hand. "You stay with Mommy now. And Clarens here will take care of you too"—he nudged his head at him and straightened up. His deep-blue fitted jacket circled his bare neck low under the tapered hair. He pulled a thin smile and led the girl over to Susan, then nodded at Clarens and shook his hand firmly. "Thanks for coming. Sorry again for the office snafu."

Clarens dismissed it with a sway of the head. "No problem at all. And"—he rushed to check his set—"I have that reimbursement for you..."

Brett seized his forearm, his eyes clear, and nodded. "It's all good, thank you." He let go and stepped back. "And thanks for everything."

"Sure," Clarens said, returning Susan's glance. "So, heading straight back?"

"Yeah. Back to Baires, then flying from there."

"Well." He smiled, "In six months you can fly right in."

Without looking over, Brett turned to Tara and tipped her on her nose, then hung his thumbs off his pockets just as brisk.

They all swung their heads to the threesome that buzzed out of the wellness venue behind, then watched them stride down the sidewalk.

"Well, will see you later then." Brett clasped his hands, then nodded a bye back at Clarens and turned to Susan.

She leaned forward for the one-arm hug. "Take care Brett."

He smiled at Tara once more and ruffled her hair, then walked away.

"Brett!" Susan shouted.

He turned his head.

"Drive safe!"

He pointed back with his finger as they laughed, then walked on to vanish inside the garage hub.

Feeling the girl's braid, Susan stared down the wide street before suddenly turning to Clarens to rest her temple on his shoulder. He brought his arm around to stroke her back.

"I'm sorry, I just—"

"Of course." He looked down at Tara. "It's fine. Mommy's fine."

Susan raised her head and picked her up to kiss her soundly on the cheek. "It's all fine my sweetheart!"—she hugged her and stamped her with a second kiss. She swung her side to side and sniffled between the giggles. "We can walk back with you if you want," she said over her shoulder.

He looked around. "I think I'm done for the day."

"Really? Great!"

He mirrored her smile, then looked straight up. Beyond the glazing's sheen, an amber hue aired the outskirts of the passing cloud. "Feel like going for a drive?"


The wind had waned, at least on this side of the valley. It still swayed the tops of the rusty beeches back and forth, as the trees shielded the farmhouse from the road and open hillside below. Although they looked rather like engulfing the grounds in flames, the way they wavered in the late sun setting between the ridges to the west.

On the weathered aluminum bench under the porch, Susan turned to peek at the car in the courtyard, then cuddled back against him. "So you'll be staying home every day then?" As he looked at her long, she chuckled. "Just thinking if you need it quiet, till you figure things out."

He looked out west again. "Unreal…"

She echoed him.

"You miss your parents' house?"

"Don't know. I miss this."

He turned around to look up the house wall behind them, then unwound slowly and rolled his eyes down the ceiling of the porch. "I should be buying this place, really."

She stared her slight smile at him and chuckled again. His reaction absent, she sat up to turn entirely toward him, hair jumbled beside the wisp of frown in her eyes.

"It could be a nice project," he said. "Weekend house, less than half hour from the city… The greenhouse could be fixed too," he added, pointing that way with his thumb. As she kept mum, he rested his arm on the back of the bench. "I'm sorry, too much for one day."

"No, but… can you afford all this?"

"I can. I thought you might like it too."

She looked away and tossed her hair back. She turned her head to him, eyes glowing, then brought her leg over to sit on his knees and hold his face between her palms. "I do!" She kissed him as he held his hand on her waist. "You're a little crazy, you know that?"

She slanted her head through the new kiss and propped her hand on the rounded top of the bench as he let himself slide down. He slipped his hand under her coat and up the side of her warm body, then pushed her shirt up slowly. She shivered as he felt her naked waist, then grasped his hand to hold it in place. "Sorry…" she whispered, barely lifting her mouth from his.

"Absolutely…"

She let her mouth back down one more time, then raised her head, her teeth bright between her reddened, smiling lips. "I'll get there."

A flock of sparrows took off as they walked out from

under the porch, then they waded through the weeds that pierced the courtyard's pavement on their way to the car. Tara was still asleep. They sat in quietly and he swiveled the car around, then slowed briefly to crane his head for a last peek at the house. Down the wide-curving driveway, stones ground under the wheels through the brushing of the virile grass straws.

A few lights twinkled already in the shaded side of the valley and then more came into view as they made the turn on the access road.

He glanced at her in between the sightings. "It's like some fairy-tale place."

She smiled, against the auburn hillside. "I know."

They turned on the newly paved road, toward Chesterhills proper. A light shone out the east gable of the neighboring farmhouse too, over the showpiece tractor in the driveway turnaround, and the greenhouse came into view from behind, all glowing.

"So they are farming…"

# 16

5:51 a.m. Brett turned on his back and blinked in the hazy dark. He stretched and filled his lungs, then let it all out and flipped the quilt aside to rise on the edge of the bed. It looked like a cloudy dawn. He canceled his 5:55 alarm, called the sidelights on, and walked by the two upright suitcases to the bathroom. It was just past six when he rolled the luggage down the corridor and pinged his car out of the hotel garage.

The boulevard was quiet, except for the fast-laboring arms of the cleaning trucks working the sidewalks block after block. Even the large corner deli was still closed, or just lifeless. The pole lights turned off just as he veered on the expressway ramp, and the above seemed brighter now, going east. Within the rising downtown ahead, the shining shells looked like crawling giant creatures that would never sleep.

The Jefferson was almost as lifeless inside, however. A few early risers rode the street belts, but it took several rides until he found a full-service café open. He walked in and straight to the sleek dispenser that covered half of the front wall. Scanning down the breakfast menu, he tapped on: omelet roll, three eggs, bacon fill, gouda fill, bacon side plate, wheat toast, avocado half, times two. He skipped to the side items for two apricot jams, butter, and two more toasts before stepping to the drinks bay. Slipping the loaded tray off the machine's shelf, he peeked over the steaming food at the seating area. Two people sat alone at the opposite ends of the tall, linear space. He stepped to a table in the middle and dragged his chair out, when one of them appeared to look his way. He glanced over.

"Brett, right?" The balding man smiled, barely, or rather looked to be frowning under the stuffy brows.

"T!" Brett brightened up, as T raised his hand from his graph to pass it at the chair aside. He walked over. "Cheers."

"Club night?"

"Haha! Long day ahead, rather. Leaving…"

"Ah."

"You?"

"Me?" T nudged his empty tray away. "It's the only decent twenty-four-hours near my office."

"Boy, you must either love your job or hate it," Brett said, forking his first piece of bacon.

T wiggled his cup in small circles, looking inside. "I recall you being on the love side, Brett," he said and sipped quickly as Brett chuckled. "Asset management, right?"

"Great memory, T."

"Tough times, huh?"

Mouth full, Brett swayed his head side to side. "You know…" He chewed. "Up or down, the crowd's chasing the same game. Money is always there to be made."

T stayed his eyes on him, then turned to his graph. "Sounds like you're not just good with the ladies."

"Right… These days you could turn that on its head."

He shrank his graph to a stub over his pen set-holder and took a last sip, then rose and patted him on the shoulder. "Family?"

"Yeah."

"As long as the kid is happy."

"Yeah. She's adopted so…" Brett twirled his head to him. "Did I talk that much?"

T jested a smile, then peered in his hand. "Here's my number… And perhaps I should have yours," he said, to Brett casting his business data over also, "in case you can make me some money on the back of your crowd." He twitched another smile over and slipped his pen inside his jacket, then looked out as he carried his broad-shouldered self and his unremarkable suit away. "Safe trip!"

Brett filled his mouth with the last piece of roll and picked up his latte to wash it down. None of the showrooms across the street had shutters over them. Nor did the lobbies on the side street. Just the pavement-born glazing, hardly visible, if not for the typical upper slant turning the glass back into the base building stone, and glaring with the day's lightening above. By the time he was done with the jam toasts the clothing showroom had turned live. The story-high model walked down the sidewalk and back and turned to flatten again into the front glazing, then looked patiently up and down the street. She wore white rubber gloves, and her sun cap was fitted with ear flaps.

Another tray rattled aside. Brett went back to the dispenser and tapped it for one more bacon serving and a wheat toast. Three outlets opened within seconds of each other, at 7:00 a.m. It was definitely overcast.


With Ayland twenty minutes behind him, another satellite town sprouted on the right side of the freeway. The sight was just as tidy, though more contained, in the bulks of uncommonly large trees defying the steppe around, glass and metal dazzling in between them, and with the slender exit ramp unwinding toward it like a bridge to a treasure island in an ocean of moss. It was the last one for a while. The motors hissed on at the high end but all smooth, and the charge was almost full. He breezed by two more cars, then eased his eyebrows.

Sunrays pierced through momentarily, as the border proximity showed up in the drive-path tag for the first time, at fifty something kilometers away, with Tencun reading a little farther from there. He looked at the bag on the passenger seat, then back at the road, head tight against the backrest. Cars zoomed over and sideways through another, larger town, but thinned out just as quickly. Some quarter-hour later, signs started flashing overhead. With another bow of the freeway past the crusty hillock, the customs compound loomed low at the end of the stretch ahead.

Only one car was in front of him and it cleared the scanner quickly. He fixed on the onboard instructions as he wheeled in.

"Proceed to the right," the new prompt flashed over when the car was out of the machine.

Neither one of the two officers looked familiar inside the special inspection facility. The one forward pointed to the high table, then crossed his hands and watched him lay out all the bullion bars. He passed his palm slowly over them, seemingly checking his eyeset. "You have receipts for the rest?"

"Yes"—Brett switched to his set.

Once he let Brett zip the bag closed, the officer brought him his handgun on hold, the magazine tied with the same orange strap onto the outside of the grip. "You cannot load it until you're past the struck-through Commons sign," he said, then iterated. "Have a nice day."

In the car, Brett wheeled by the monolithic glass wall and back to the main lane. A long line of cars waited on the way in, beyond the buildings in the divider. The view on the right side opened up with a green strip, where a row of armored vehicles peeked through the tall back hedge, before the compound's perimeter wall butted into the road shoulder. Past the short passageway, a few windowless, blocky structures flanked the merging lanes, then the sign flashed by. He slowed again through the small checkpoint across the border, although the auto-drive was not prompted for and the lights turned green before he could stop. Someone looked his way from behind the tinted window of the rugged steel cabin so he waved, but to no effect. Farther down, shining vending trailers lined the near side of the graveled parking lot. In red and white, the biggest read "Lamb Grill," next to the "Scrap buy/sell" one. Aside, the lone shrubs looked largely unfit to contain the unforgiving wind. The car's wheels gritted over the road as if the gravel had spilled over, but then it turned out that the regular pavement had just ended. He drove half a kilometer down before pulling over beside another cluster of shrubs. Once he loaded the gun, he reached inside the suitcase on the rear seat to pull his vest out. He turned it inside out on his lap and then reached inside the bag next to him for the first bar and shoved it into the vest's top left slot.

Tencun came up slowly and seemed to never end. In the tepid afternoon, everyone might just have been on wheels and wings and about the freeway, if the four aging concrete lanes crawling along the suburban sprawl could be called as such. That being the sole resemblance to the early morning drive-through three months prior. From the westbound bridge over the railway, black roofs and a core of low-rises staked out the old town far to the right. To the left, stripes of glass beamed in the muzzy sun like a green-era power plant, from what looked like a modern residential outgrowth that had jumped the freeway to terrace up the wide hillside. He called the music on low and cued through the latest dyno titles, then stroked the steering wheel along and just kept the car in the surface crawl. Once across the last overpass, the left lane picked up, although it wasn't until long minutes and unruly fringes thereafter when he could move up to speed. As on the way in, an out-of-scale farewell sign startled glitter through the air. It read a little over six hundred kilometers to Baires.

He turned the music off. The grays were yet to break over the flatlands ahead, with only a sheer sunray touching down on the imaginary line of the freeway. Another chain of vending trailers shone on the other side, but he didn't look.

Soon, he no longer steered around the potholes, either. Even hitting the larger, tire-carving ones sounded like no more than a dull rap behind the rear window. If that. He stayed his hands on the wheel as he fixated on the dashboard and raised his eyes a little when a truck zoomed by honking in the right lane. Having come to a stop, he looked in the rear viewer and steered to the left onto the open divider, clonking the car over the rocks and brush. He aired it to cross to the opposite lanes, looked right, and drove onto the pavement, slowly.

———————

The plastic treads squeaked under the thin burgundy runner as Brett went back downstairs, to the equally narrow motel lobby. The owner came out to the metal-girded window above the wall shelf.

Brett nodded. "I'll take it."

"You take? Very good." The owner reached down inside his cell. "I need ID and"—he raised his jaded face—"how you pay?"

"Oh, I need to pay now? You take unis?"

"No, no."

"Right. Uhh…" Brett held his thumb and index up, slightly apart. "Is there a place around where I can exchange… physical?"

"Brilla," the owner said. "Brilla exchange. This way"—he stuck his hand out his window. "Three round you take right, then go long main road, close to freeway. You will see," he added with the same swishy accent while retreating inside the cell.

The two-story building was hard to miss, if only for its Commons-style round-cornered glazing, a fine bronze and maroon signage dithering through it. And for the number of cars in the lot. Past the entry guards the inside was unlike the facade, garish and dated, a large room molded in the same pale resins seen in the motel and elsewhere, while the two salespeople appeared to work the long line expeditiously.

"Have you exchanged with us before, sir?" Brett was asked on his turn, in nearly flawless English.

"No, I haven't."

She took another moment to peer at the platinum bar and back at her graph. "Any cancelations?"

"Ah, maybe."

"There you are." She smiled curtly and asked him to cast the full ID over and look in the scanner.

Back outside, he tagged his new currency entry and jolted his vest higher on his shoulders, then detoured to the deli across the road before returning to sit in his car and bite a chunk off the steaming panini. Queuing to drive in and out of the parking lot, most of the cars looked new, even the utility ones. To the right, a top-winged red Maab remained unattended, until a man wandered around it and by the driver door. He looked in his mid-thirties and sported a deep cap and a days-old stubble. Then the rest of the family of four showed up. Brett returned to his panini and looked away. On the other side of the windshield, the freeway reemerged far out between two rooftops, a thin gray line pointing south.

He turned left on the main road and drove behind the first lane traffic, jogging his eyes between the road and the disparate buildings alongside. Most looked like pick-up outlets, with large drive-in openings into the ad-laden facades and no pedestrian presence. Two women walked out of the hair salon lost in an unfinished little plaza in between. The men's next door appeared not to have opened yet, though. He pulled in the charge station of the next block and rolled the car to the source, beside the only other car charging. The driver glanced back at him. Over the white collar, his graying goatee looked just trimmed. Once he left, Brett watched his own charge hit full and chime off, then rolled farther onto one of the service pads. As the prongs latched into the car's socket, he lowered his window and waved short at the station's operator in the high booth. He waved one more time for the man to come down and cautiously approach the car.

"Hi there!" Brett smiled out the window and waited for him to step closer. "I need to get to the Commons."

The operator pointed with his hand. "Freeway."

"Right but... is there another way? I need someone to take me there," Brett said, then looked to meet his eyes and nodded. "I'm paying."

Hunched in his oversized outfit, the operator looked at him from under his tired eyelids. He dragged his feet back, turning away. "No, no. Freeway."


When he stopped again in the small court of the motel, the street was just as quiet. The spotty metal warehouse across looked shuttered down for good. Two youngsters kicked a ball for a laugh through the large body-razor ad in front of the corner drug station.

The owner actually cracked a smile seeing him walk in. "You come back!" He looked down inside his cell. "One day?"

"Maybe two."

"You pay me every day, ok?"

Brett glanced over the five-digit payment figure and sent it off, then grabbed his suitcases and heaved them up the constricted stairs to his second-floor room. Ten minutes later he returned and cleared his throat, an elbow on the wall shelf. Through the open door in the cell's corner, the owner frowned over and approached.

"Sorry, I meant to ask you," Brett said, and hemmed to eye him anew.

Pulled neatly over his stocky chest, the owner's fine-thread sweater split open just low enough below his neck to reveal a small diamond-cross pendant, as he nudged his chin up.

Brett switched to his set. "What would be a traditional pub around here? I just can't tell from this…"

"In old town. This way, two blocks make left, then three or four blocks. You will see."

"Oh, so not far." He straightened up and pointed to the outside. "Is the parking safe?"

"Safe, safe," the owner nodded, lifting the muzzle of what looked like a large capacity rifle beside him. "But you should take car."

The shiny aluminum doors rushed sideways and three more men walked in, guffawing their way by in their work suits to the other side of the bar. At the front end, the silent drinker shook his head slightly over his gin, but not differently than he had done it through the past ten minutes. The ones seated at the idle tables erupted briefly over a saved shot on goal in the soccer game, which they then replayed from several ball-borne views against the murky rear of the room.

Brett turned back to his beer.

"No see like this in Commons, ehh?" the bartender asked with a grin.

"No, not much." Brett smiled, then drank. "You go there often?"

The bartender raised two fingers. "I go two times."

"That's it? On the freeway or…"

"Hahaha!" He left only his forefinger up. "'Scuz me," he said, and moved away to serve the blue-lipped young woman who had come up to the bar. She seemed to have ordered for everyone seated at her table, which took a while to fill. Once he slipped the last drink on the marble-like counter, the bartender crossed his arms and watched the game too. He looked a fit mid-forties, his back-combed walnut hair coiling rich above the neck.

Brett raised his glass. "Another Var here also."

"Oh, yes!"

He watched him pluck the can's spout, then looked over the foam as he insisted on pouring. "Thanks. Actually, is there another way other than the freeway?" he added before sipping.

"To Commons?"

"Yeah. Like backroads or something."

"No, I don't know."

"'Cause I forgot something there, and I can't put up with this border stuff again," he said, swaying his head toward the outside, to which the bartender halted.

"Maybe your friend can bring for you," he snickered, flicking his gaze at the lone drinker at the end of the counter, and leaned closer. "Commons developer, in Tencun," he muttered emphatically, then laughed as he lingered in front of Brett. "What you forget?"

"Oh, something personal." Brett raised his eyes at him. "I just need someone to take me there."

"Hmm... I ask." He watched Brett sip again. "I hear some people go."

"Oh yeah?"

"But..." He braced both hands on the counter and glanced at the sportscast while tilting closer. "Cost money."

"Goes without saying." As the bartender stared on at him, Brett rolled his lips in and out dry and nodded. "It's not a problem, I'm saying."

"No, I understand, I understand... You alone?"

"Yeah, just me."

A new order must have been called in as the bartender waved at the work-suited men. He then shouted at the young woman seated at the near table and jerked his chin at the bar. As she rose, a grimace scrunching her decorated lips, he turned back to Brett and lowered his voice again. "You tell how I find you, maybe I find somebody. If you want"—he shrugged.

"Sure, here's my number"—Brett thumbed his ringset on. "It's a neosat."

"Neosat?" The bartender rushed a grin. "You are police?"

"What?" Brett smiled, then looked back down. "No, it's from.... But here, take the motel number."

The bartender took longer to check his graph over his wide, leather wristband, then raised his head at the soccer game's new climactic play. Brett nudged his half-full glass away and rose to sidestep out between the bar stools, as the bartender returned his bye with another grin, hair curls ever stiff behind his neck.

Down the bar he nodded at the Commoner man, who appeared to look his way, or was just picked by the vim in the room, then he walked out the shiny doors to under the canopy. Staff at the restaurant a few doors down laid yellow cloth on the sidewalk tables, while several more holosigns now dressed up the less-than-impeccable buildings' plaster across the street, drawing the eye deeper into the old town. He stepped around the car before the pub's flags-printed window and sat in to sidle it back into the street.


It stayed cloudy through dusk. He dropped the snack pack on the table and then his vest on the flimsy armchair in the corner, which skidded back under the thump. He felt his shoulders while rotating his arms slowly one by one. Out the window, purple electric flyers spurted out the top of the warehouse one block down and petered out over the surrounding lifeless roofs, while the sub-hearing vibe made it all the way in through the glazing as he stepped closer.

He turned around. The room looked smaller in the bright-yellow, uncozy ceiling light. He reached inside his belt for the handgun and laid it on the nightstand, then stepped to the fittingly small bathroom. A black beetle came to a stop on the brim of the basin as the light came on, then raced around it. It lost grip and skipped down as he let the warm water run over his hands, then spiraled in and clung to the stained rim of the drain as he washed his face. He sank in the rich, citric scent of the towel and rubbed his eyelids down, then exhaled in the mirror. He returned to the bed and lay down, turned the light lower, and brought both pillows under his head, eyes wide.

He browsed his set for the immigration objects, then for the supporting items, and brought up the "Brett—family Christmas" titles. He skipped to the late '80s and let the staged footage run. Between the carols, he held his quiet smile beside his lively stepbrothers, as his mother and stepfather called the grandparents in front of the tree too. He zoomed in. He wore the black and green racing watch on the classic wristband. He skipped on to the following year, then to the middle-school graduation, when he flicked the graph off, lips knitted to a line. He searched through the air anew, shaking his head.

"I can't… I can't let you do this to me."


He snored off as he cracked his eyes open, less than an hour later. The door buzz sounded clear the second time and, in the wall display, the bartender smiled, pointing into his hand. Brett jumped to his feet and blinked tight a few times, looking around. He slipped the gun under the pillow then straightened his shirt down as he stepped to the door to open it head wide. Grinning in the middle of the corridor, in his same maroon jersey, the bartender pointed to his graph again. "Maybe you're lucky my friend!"

"Hey, what's up?" Brett smiled and peered at the tiny picture.

"I find this guy," the bartender said and turned his hand at him while coming forward, then stuck a handgun into his chest. "Maybe we go inside."

He pushed him back and the door open with his elbow to walk in, then kicked it closed with his heel. Eyes dilated above the open mouth, he looked around and circled the gun's muzzle at him. "Turn. Slow." He dabbed him over his belt and jiggled the gun up. "Warrants."

"I don't have any," Brett muttered.

"We do this easy, pretty boy. Or not easy."

"I don't have any physical warrants, I'm not from the Commons."

"Where the fuck you from?"

"Free States."

"From Free States?" He threw a vicious kick in Brett's leg to nearly knock him down. "How pay to go to border?"

"By transfer," Brett groaned. "I opened an account."

"Not be stupid with me!" the bartender snarled and, as Brett felt his calf, he flashed the side of the pistol's magazine at him. "No electrics," he whispered, eyes bulging wider and glanced his hand. "Show me." He peeped around again as Brett plucked his set bead off the ring and touched the back open to reveal the keyless inside. "Show me account," he hissed, and sidestepped around the bed. "No call!"

"Look." Brett swallowed, though his voice rasped just as dry. "I can make an instant transfer for you and we'll just—"

With the gun pointing higher at him, the bartender dashed his other hand through the nightstand drawer, then under the pillow. "Ooh, pretty boy has toy…" Grinning, he pointed both guns at him and returned, as Brett turned to his set and paused blank before swiping his forearm over his eyes to start over. The bartender prompted him to move back and craned his head at the account figures beaming over the table.

"Three six five thousand… from Brilla." He looked at him. "Brilla my friend?" He shoved Brett's pistol inside his belt and rushed backward to the entryway to snatch the suitcases and thrust them rolling on the floor. "Open! On the bed!" He kicked them into Brett's hands, then appeared to check his set, with a woman's moaning sounding through. Moments later, he raked his hand through the pile of clothes, shoes, and underwear on the bed, whipped a couple of shirts up in the air, then pulled the empty suitcases over and tapped the walls with the gun's muzzle before throwing them on the floor. He cursed and raked his hand through again, picked up the toiletries purse and jerked it open upside down. The two bars glistened in the downlight as they fell on the bed. He picked them up and tweezed one out of its sleeve to a full white shine, as his grin returned, then he zapped Brett in the face with the back of his hand.

"Never good to lie." He slipped the bars in his pocket as Brett braced his hand on the armchair, nose blood staining the floor.

"I thought you said it was my lucky day," Brett muttered, pinching his nose, and nudged the slanting chair back upright in the room's corner.

"Lucky nobody find you first. Or maybe you're dead"— the bartender snickered, flicking his gaze between him and the chair behind him. He jiggled the gun's barrel sideways, moving closer, then pointed it at Brett's head to make him pull back against the wall. Eyes on him, he reached for the vest and tried to lift it, when the chair overturned and the vest dropped on the floor with a thud. Clenching his jaws, Brett let his bloodied hand down. The nightclub's vibes throbbed and seesawed straight through the wall. Steady with his gun, the bartender crouched and grabbed the vest to drag it away and tug it on the bed. He frowned between glimpsing down to push his fingers in one of the slots and draw a bar out.

"Pretty boy..." He laid it aside and reached in for another. "Pretty boy!" Then another. A purple vein crossed down the middle of his forehead as he stifled his chuckles. He checked his set, rose abruptly, and shoved the loose bars in his pocket, then struggled to put the vest on, swapping the gun between his hands under Brett's eyes. "Car code"—he jerked his chin out, and whisked Brett's set off the table.

Brett kept mum.

"Maybe we put first one in leg."

He wiped the blood off his upper lip. "Freeland zero one…" he mumbled.

"Freeland zero one. You are patriot! But don't like borders, ehh?" the bartender said and stepped in front of the window, then scanned the motel parking below while tipping his finger through the set's graph. He aimed the gun at Brett's head again. "No start."

Brett looked over the floor. "It's in manual override."

The bartender tried the car one more time, then grinned and turned away from the window. His neck frizzes brushed over the vest with his raised shoulder as he reached inside his belt for Brett's gun, then his eyebrows jumped high. "Thank you my friend. I save your life."

"What…"

Brett fell on his back as the first bullet discharged in his chest. The second one pierced in without a sound.

# 17

Out of the apartment, Clarens lifted Tara up to fly her next to Susan inside the elevator. "Green light?" He led her finger to the shimmering stripe, then let her down and turned his smile to Susan.

He changed direction as they walked out onto the garage floor. "Let's take this one here"—he pointed to the opposite tier of cars. As Susan slowed, disoriented, to look his way, he called the larger vehicle out from the middle of the tier. It lit up with the doors sliding over the gleaming rooftop, and he reached in to pull the protective wrap off the rear seats.

"Wow! What is this?"

"I thought I might need it out there." He crumpled the wrap into a ball and threw it inside the empty, sizable cargo compartment as she gasped a smile. "And that you should drive the other one whenever you want," he added with a nod at the tier across the aisle.

She smiled and gazed in turn at both cars.

Squatting beside Tara, he raised the vehicle body to the upper limit, then lowered it all the way to resting on the floor and ran the surround lights. "She's happy to see you!" He stroked her and stepped behind Susan to the driver's door. "What do you think?"

She shook her head and got in too, then configured the child's seat and swiveled forward as they drove out of the garage.

He peered at the dashboard graph as they steered slowly behind the passing car on the street. "One of those things that you never see yourself doing, until a few days before doing it."

"One?"

They laughed.

He looked out with the car's turns, then glanced in the viewer at Tara, who stared out her window. "I remember going to preschool," he said louder, "and learning great new things. And playing a lot too."

Tara looked toward his seat and stayed quiet. "I like to play," she then said.

"You can play, you can learn things, anything."

"I like to play first."

He nudged his head up and down to glance at her anew till finding his words. "Playing is fun. Learning… keeps the fun coming. Together they're the best fun you can have."

As she kept mum he looked at Susan, who smirked a smile. He shrugged a smile back as they steered onto the main road.

Susan reached over to Tara. "And it's so much fun to play *with* your new friends, remember?"

As she turned forward, he worked his hand through the mapping. "So what was better about this place in the end?"

"Don't know, they were easy to take her straight in the second year. And we had already left that deposit."


Beyond the closing door of the classroom, Tara stood by the teacher, who leaned down to guide her to the nearest group of children stretching foam shapes. She let the teacher lead her away and swung her ponytail and pink scrunchie around to look back. From out in the hallway, Susan waved again and blinked her watery eyes.

The registrar smiled at her and Clarens. "She's in good hands."

"She's so sweet," Susan sighed, as they all turned to weave by the remaining parents and bumbling classrooms down the hallway.

The registrar returned to her floating file before her chest. "So, as far as your changes... You can have two primary guardians, and then you need to update anyone else every month."

"Ah..."

"Or we can call for your authorization at the time," she added, and fixed a smile as they came to a stop in the now silent foyer.

Susan looked at Clarens, then back at her. "Well, can we make him the primary then? We're engaged."

"Sure. I'd just need the release from... Mr. Falco."

Clarens rushed to send it over. "It's a blanket release, and there's the biomark... I love your front botanies by the way," he added with a tip of the head.

"You should see the skating ring in the back," Susan said. "And the pool, and the gymnasium."

"Oh yes, our kids are having the best fun," the registrar boasted while reaching through the document, then raised her head confused as Susan and Clarens laughed. She chuckled with them under the echoes of the ceiling-wide skylight, then sent her confirmation over before saying good-bye.

Susan coiled her arm around his as they crossed the foyer. She thinned her lips in a happy smile as he looked at her. They strolled on quiet to the garage passageway.

"It's funny you said that, in the car," she mused. "Part of me has always been like... hoarding the fun away, for the future."

"Well...you know my thoughts on that."

She laughed.

As they drove off, the school building flashed bright through the dwarf sidewalk trees, then passed out of sight with the row of townhouses sweeping in. A group of joggers crossed through the first intersection to the sidewalk on the park side. He let his sight follow their punchy purples and blues as the car rolled again, and the sumptuous trees lining the sidewalk inside the park grounds.

"I've never seen this side of the park," he said. "Must have been planted at the very beginning."

She turned her head. "Looks like beech. Definitely over a hundred years old."

He eased a smile. "You know trees too?"

She grabbed his hand to hold it on the console and tossed her hair back, beyond her dashing eyes. "For some reason you can't believe you're stuck with a woodsy girl."

"You know, you're absolutely right." He squeezed her hand lightly, then let go to reach for the drive path as they turned onto the boulevard. "I almost forgot, I'm dropping you off first."

Hand lying weightless on the console, she turned to follow the tall buildings' frontage gliding by. Through the second block, she glanced over again. "So, if the deal goes through, when would you start renovating?"

"Well, right away. Why?"

"I was just thinking. If I could do more of my share of things, with that or anything."

He peered over.

"I just…" She shrugged, staring at the car lanes ahead. "I know it's a bit early and all, but I'd feel more like… part of it," she said, and slipped him a smile. "I'm a hoarder, right?"

He exhaled. "Well, you can buy my old car," he said, to which she burst laughing, relieved, and he smiled along. "And the work that farmhouse needs… you'll earn your share want it or not."

With her laugh, the corners of her eyes tipped under the wisps of hair that weaved beside her cheeks once more. Beyond, the eastern connector ramp climbed higher above ground, over the expressway that cut away through the midtown and crossed under two more bridges, before meandering around the far end of the park.

She regrouped, then both looked quietly down the descending road.

"If it makes you feel better I could gladly share the project," he said. "But do you have that kind of money?"

"What's the asking?"

"Two hundred and forty-nine thousand."

She repeated the number under her breath. "Oh yeah, I can do even half that."

He gazed over. "Woodsy?"

He laughed with her as they reached the ground again, where they began marking the blocks of the limestone-clad apartment buildings. It looked just as warm outside in the breaking sun. They veered seamlessly onto the placid midmorning streets, while the trim facades faded in and out with the sunlight's bursts and angles. Past the last corner, he edged forward in his seat to glimpse their building's third floor in the middle of the block, and smiled to himself. The shading of the bay window was off indeed, and the top frame of the deck chair flashed through. He steered to override the garage entry and drop her off at the sidewalk instead, as she opted for a walk to the corner food station.

She leaned over for a frugal kiss. "So I'll just take the other car to pick her up?"

"All yours."

She smiled under her wildly fluttering hair as she stepped out of the car, then he watched her spring away. He turned to the dashboard and let his lips firm up slowly. He stretched his drive path to detour through Brookdale.

———

The burning stripe of light dashed the lip of the table, then cut up to the framed landscape picture on the wall. Below, the tip of the armchair leg stuck up in the air over the rumpled cloth on the bed corner. Brett lifted his head, to an instant scream, then rolled slowly onto his side, feeling his chest for the two nine-millimeter pins. Eyes crimped shut, he pulled the pins out and threw them away against the baseboard, then rolled farther to prop his knee on the floor and left arm on the bed and brought himself up to standing.

The police took half an hour to show up. One of the plainclothes detectives seized the pins and began to uncover fingerprints while the other took his statement, then went over to question the motel owner standing in the doorway, who raised his voice and gesticulated widely.

The detective returned, his head hanging to one side, and looked at Brett. "Not much we can do. Sorry."

Wide-eyed, Brett dropped his hand from feeling his chest and shook his head. "No, you can't be kidding with this."

"Sorry, we cannot do no more now. Nobody died."

"But he robbed me at gunpoint, for a ton of money! And you know who he is!"—he shot up, and pointed at the owner. "He let him in!"

"No, no, he… was held up," the detective muttered under the thick mustache, then shrugged. "You make money proof and we check for them, but"—he wagged his hand twice at the window— "they go far."

"Oh, no, no, no, you've got to do something. I'll pay you. Both!" Brett swung at the second detective. "I'll pay you for an entire month!"

Rucking his lips, the detective tipped his head the other way to look at the owner, who approached.

"Please! He took everything I have!" Brett went on, voice jarring. "Everything I fuckin' have! You've got to help me find—"

"My friend!" the owner prompted, then paused before Brett's quivering brows. "They cannot do nothing. They take you to border if you want," he added, "or you call somebody."

As Brett zigzagged his eyes between them, the detective reached inside his wrist to nip out a set and held it forth. "From Tencun City." He turned and put it on the table before Brett could find his words, then nodded and walked toward his colleague waiting aside.

"Wait, you can't be serious"—Brett leaped in front of them on the way to the door. "You can't do this! Who's your boss? I'm going there right now."

They brushed by him and out to the corridor. "Tencun police," the detective said with a weary glance. "Is in set."

From gaping speechless as they reached the stair, Brett turned abruptly back toward the room, but only to stoop low, face contorted in pain. Feeling his chest, he wobbled closer as the owner watched him from outside the open door.

He passed him without looking. "Where's the city hall?"

"My friend..."

"Where's the city hall?" he shouted, scrambling through the jumble of clothes on the bed.

"You go to Brilla, but stop to big round with statue and make left," the owner said.

"Left at the statue," Brett mumbled while shoving his arms through the new shirt's sleeves, then zipped up as he strode back to the door. He swung back around to pick the set bead from the table. "Can I borrow your car?" He looked at the owner, who remained quiet. "No? No worries." He slammed the door shut and breezed by, only to turn to him again. "Uhh... I don't have my code anymore. You'll be here, right?" he said, to the owner's nod, then leaped down the corridor and dove down the stair in thumping steps.

"My friend!"—the owner rushed after him and flipped his hands out as Brett turned his head. "How you pay?"

––––––––

Past the corner lamppost, his shadow thawed into the dark

sidewalk alongside the warehouse wall. He held his breath as the ribbed metal gapped for a small, weeds-covered access door in the middle of the block, then raised his eyes when he'd crossed the shade line of the end corner. The large ad beamed brightly off its side pole, always with body essentials. He wiped his forehead hard and crossed the street to the dim motel courtyard.

The owner came out to the musical chime and stood expressionless in his girded window.

Brett stepped closer and looked lower aside. "They said they'll send it to all the police units and put out a notice," he uttered on a scant voice, then frowned down as he swallowed.

"That is nothing, my friend."

"I know. Do you have some water please?"

The owner brought a cup of water from the backroom, then spread his hands apart on the inside shelf and watched him gulp down.

Brett put the cup down and nudged it to the middle of the shelf. "Listen, I can't pay you right now, but you can charge me double till I sort this out."

"No, no," the owner said, swaying his head, then pointed out the window. "You call somebody in Commons, they send you money."

"I can't right now, it's… complicated. I need a few days," Brett said, then, as the owner shrugged, he upped his tone. "Hey, you've got to help me out a little after what happened!"

"Help?"—the owner bent forward. He slapped his hands on the shelf and looked aside to mutter his swishy words. "Why me to help everybody? Go to church for help!" he roared, jiggling his pendant cross at him, then let his hand drop just as rash on the counter. "Who help me fix chair and floor?" He gestured wide. "Last week they broke sink, before they broke elevator. Nobody help me, never!"

Brett stayed quiet. "I can fix the chair."

Under his deep frown, the owner exhaled. "What you

know to do?"—he poked his chin up.

"I'm an investments adviser. I can make you money right now in your trading account, I can advise you on your allocations, I can—"

"What you know to do? Can you work?" He mimicked driving a tool against the wall.

"Uhh... I could. It depends."

He shook his head and looked away, breathing out long. He grabbed the cup and knocked it down in place. "I have house, half hour from city, in forest. You stay there," he said, then circled the cup with his finger. "Cut trees around."

# 18

The building inspector drove away, beyond the mighty boulder at the driveway turn. Clarens turned to Lynden, who kept making his notes in the property report, then turned further around to the car. He sat on the bumper ledge and pulled the high rubber boots on, then began unloading the tools and making trips to lay them down on the farmhouse porch. He returned to carefully pull out the flat broom and the shovel, their shipping mold still on.

"Seeing is believing," Lynden said, grinning as he approached. "You were supposed to migrate to the moon!"

Clarens smiled and went back to the porch. "Anything else to sign off?"

"No, we're all good." Lynden followed him slowly. "Hey guy, congratulations!"

Stooping over the array of tools, Clarens swiveled halfway. "Thanks. Guy!" He straightened up to shake hands.

Lynden didn't let go, his eyes glowing up. "Come here"— he tugged Clarens close for a hug and patted him hard. He pulled back. "I can't believe you dumped me just like that!"

They chortled loud through the new rush of wind.

Clarens turned back around to find a place for the tool case. "How's everything there?"

"Oh, you know. Talbot… My chances of moving up now are about zero."

"Come on. And the side work?"

"Pffh… Lame fart. If only I could get more clients like this one here."

Taking the jab in the shoulder, he tromped in his boots down the porch steps and to the car. "Well, I still owe you that dinner, for my mother's house," he said, and heaved the grass trimmer out. "How is next Tuesday after swimming?"

"Uhh… I'll let you know." Beside him again, Lynden stuck his hands in his pockets and measured the car from rear to front and over. "What does it do, five hundred kilowatts?"

"Something like that."

"Airfloat?"

"Four minutes."

As Lynden remained absorbed, Clarens moved around him and powered up the trimmer. "But I can see a flashy one over there," he added with a peek at Lynden's car across the courtyard.

"Yeah, got a bump in the old one. Was time anyway."

"Bump?"

"Yeah. No biggie."

With the machine's guide glimmering in his graph, Clarens began picking reference points around the courtyard. "Was that…" he picked another point, saying, as Lynden panned around with him, "when you tried the manual drive or something?"

Lynden turned with an instant grin. "Guy, you're going funny now too?" He aimed a jab at his belly. "Can't go funny. Can't go funny on me!"—he kept jabbing him, then laughed and landed another pat on his back. "All right, got to go. Later, farm man!" he shouted, walking away as Clarens recovered.

"Lyn!" Clarens stopped him before reaching the car. "Never asked… Did you close that apartment deal too?" he said, watching the machine roaming toward the first tuft of grass, as Lynden stood blank. "You know, Heslin's."

"Oh, yep. Long gone. You know Heslin, when she wants something," Lynden said, and turned nimbly around. "Got to go or Gwyn's going to kill me!" He sat in the car, but only to swing his feet back out on the bottom rail and wipe his shoes with a tissue. He peeked at the trimmer, which labored on a second tuft shooting tall through the pavement. "Beef it up skimpy, or you won't see these shoes back down here. Hahaha! Say hi to Susan!"—he waved while driving off.

Smile lasting on his face, Clarens shook his head and watched him disappear beyond the boulder, then turned to the quiet humming in the yard. From deep inside the car, the deutzia flashed its scattered whites over. He rushed to it and dragged the large pot out, then wedged his face through the leaves to see his way up the porch steps and laid the pot in place by the guardrail. The hose pack was next but none of the outlets ran water, so he emptied most of his bottle into the pot and drank the rest, then reached in his pocket for the chrome, physical key and stepped to the front door. Beside the scorched blue paint, the key gritted its way into the door lock and eventually clonked it, retracting all bolts up and down. He left the door latched on full open, then the airlock door too, and advanced over the worn flooring pattern to the middle of the two-story-high space. On the wall below the mezzanine railing, the manuscript-fashioned print "Original Fee" hung in its dusty frame next to the same small-size panel carving of "Home Free Home" in cherry wood. He raised his gaze higher to the ceiling that curved wide under the semi-cylindrical roof. Butted end-to-end between the transversal nervures, the four skylights slotted the surface with mute daylight. He pivoted slowly on his soles and lowered his sight to squint at the bright outside through the front door. He stepped out on the porch, unpacked the cleaner, and followed the machine back in.

———

Rotten from the inside out, the barkless log felt heavy

nonetheless. Brett jolted it up a second time to bring its end higher over a fallen limb, then made a back step and reached for the chainsaw on the ground. Legs apart, he wobbled as he straightened up and brought the saw forward with both hands. He nudged his feet in place, depressed the trigger, and bent to the trunk anew.

After the third cut the remaining log rolled off the limb as he sneezed loud through the moldy dust.

"Hello there, my friend!"

He staggered around to the voice and wiped his brow with his forearm.

A foot up on a stump and resting his elbow on his knee, the man stared at him. "Hard, ehh?"—he nodded as Brett frowned. "You drive a Yuejin Skybird?"

His accent was rather light, and so was his build, except for the veins-crossed robust hand hanging down his polyester pants, while half of his elongated face stayed in the shade of his sun cap.

Brett put the saw down. "Who's asking?"

The man didn't budge, only tilting his cap's flap higher on his head. "My name is Ricky. I printed a part for them." Perhaps in his forties, he watched Brett move closer, his small eyes twinkling blue against the light tan. He must have just shaved.

"For whom?"

"The dealer. The barman sold them your car."

Brett stilled. "Really..." He wiped his hand on the dry side of his shirt and held it forth. "Brett."

Ricky put his foot down and straightened for a fleeting handshake.

"When?" Brett added.

"Two weeks ago. After he cleaned you up."

"How do you know all this?"

Ricky turned his head to look around, pausing over the two-window cabin and its single-slope roof. "Why jump the border my friend?" he said, and brought his sight back around to Brett, who, in turn, didn't answer. He jogged his head to the side. "Have more metal over there?"

"Some."

"How much?"

"I can pay half a kilo to whomever can take me over and back," Brett said, just as stilled. "Same day."

Ricky looked away again. "Why the Baires number?"

"That's where I bought the car. It so happened."

He lifted his cap to pull it back on tight, gray strands topping the thick, weaving black hair over his sideburns and ears. "I might do it for one kilo, depending."

"One kilo!"

He glanced at Brett, then turned around slowly. "Excella custom parts. If you want to find me," he said and cleared his throat for a sound spit, then walked away between the two log stacks toward his car. Whether for his walk or light weight, no limbs cracked under his feet.

Brett stepped around the stump and after him. "Hey..." He caught up with him on the gravel patch before the cabin, where Ricky looked over his shoulder. "How do I know you'd stick to your word?"

"How do I know you got the metal my friend?"

As they stopped, he exhaled and glanced away. "Look. I just got screwed big. I need a guarantee."

Ricky pushed his head forth and sneered.

"I do have the metal. I just need to get there. I can pay some in unis right now."

Renewing his sneer, he glanced over the sparse woods and cabin and spit again, then ran his knuckles over his lips. "Why jump the border my friend?"

Brett stared back. "I'm not from there. My daughter is there with her mother. I need to get her back."

"Back... You mean kidnap?"

"She'll come with me."

"Two people now. Stick to your word, ehh?"

"She's a small child."

"What else?"

"That's it."

Ricky worked his jaws, as if munching on something behind his closed lips. "Two kilos."

"That's insane!" Brett bristled, then saw him turn to his car. "So what's the guarantee?"

Without responding, Ricky sat in and swirled the car in place, then lowered the window and poked his head out. "Somebody guarantees to take you to Commons and back, he's either a slime or another fool." Wheels scraping the top gravel for grip, he drove off.

Brett watched the dust tail rise over the narrow dirt road and dissipate through the trees. He walked around the wreck of the utility trailer to the cabin, where he grabbed the water jug from the flat stone beside the door. He lifted it with both hands to his mouth and drank. The large beech shed gold over the gravel patch. Above the waving crown, it looked like it was staying dry.

He returned to the halved log and stood before it, measuring it with his eyes. He picked up the saw and made another cut, then rolled the log away with his foot, when he lost his balance and fell. He rose and dusted off, wiped his forearm on his shirt to a stripe of blood, then felt his wristband for the set bead.

Between the police and motel call threads, he picked the motel. "Hi, it's Brett, at the cabin."

"Yes."

"So I'm pretty much done. Do you think you could get me that neosat set on Monday?"

"Ehh... you cut behind the house, to big stone?"

"No. You haven't said that."

The owner turned his image on and curved his hand in the air. "To big stone. I come Thursday."

"You said Monday."

"Thursday, Thursday."

———

The two crewmen snapped the headboard on, then unpacked the mattress sleeve to lay it flat over the bed frame. From opposite sides, they began pumping the foam in.

"Which one's next?" one of them asked once the mattress was shaped up.

"The guest bedroom, over here," Clarens said, and he and Susan led them out of the room and across the mezzanine floor.

They watched the crewmen snap the second bed frame in place, then swayed out to the open floor.

She pivoted around and smiled. "Looks good, all clean." She stepped to the top of the stairs to look up and down the double-story room. "This is actually a great space!"

"Isn't it? In fact, I was thinking," he said, following her down the U-shaped stair, "that wall there could come down to open up that entire side also."

"Can you do that?"

"I don't know." He went around the stair to the sidewall, tapping it over, then made a step through the doorless opening into the adjacent space and sandwiched the wall between his hands. "Perhaps you put a post here or something. But imagine…" He grabbed the folding chair from the other side of the empty room, plunked it down next to her, then laid his hands on her shoulders gently to sit her down and leaned beside her cheek. "You're here, looking out. South… window, window. West… window, window"—he pointed around the room.

"Nice!" She crossed her legs. "Can I have my coffee now?" She turned to him for the laugh, then rose. "Actually, is the kitchen usable?"

"Well, we have water."

Back around the stair, they stopped just inside the kitchen in the northwest quarter and looked over the wide, concrete-replica counters leading to the open eating area at the other end.

"Gosh, you could feed the village from here," she said, and walked farther in with a swoosh of her work pants. "What if you just reconditioned it, like retro…"

"Sure, if you're okay with that." He watched her peek inside the first cabinet. "I didn't touch the cabinets, though."

"Okay, so I'll start here."

He returned to the mezzanine, just as the delivery crewmen walked out of the second bedroom and left. He pulled the remaining paint cartridges out of the carton and laid them next to the ones on the floor sheet, then squatted closer to line them up carefully by color swatch. "Oh, forgot about you…" He swiveled around to drag the supplies bag closer and reached for the new loudspeaker at the bottom. He snapped it out of its foam and placed it on top of the cleaner case by the stair landing, then powered it on and called up Sunshine Machine on his set. He looked down over the railing as the first song kicked in.

Susan didn't take long. "Are you kidding me? Woohooo!"

He smiled and returned to the paints, grabbed the spectacles, and stepped to the empty third bedroom. His back to the corner, he put the spectacles on and began calling out the swatches.


The second album had just started playing when she showed up and leaned against the door frame. "Wow!"

"Too bright?" he said, while clawing the paint-stained cartridge out of the handle mount.

"No, I like it." Sleeves rolled up, she rested her hand on her hip, but quickly stepped out backward and to the adjacent bedroom door. "I see, this one's more purplish. Oh, I so love the cherry wood…" As he followed her, she went in to feel the glazed finish of the new bed's headboard and looked around. "Actually, what else is there to do to the upstairs?"

"The other bathroom, then perhaps replacing these floors, though they still heat well…" Wiping his fingers on his cloth, he looked over the mezzanine floor and shrugged.

"So we could stay over now."

"I guess."

"We could… even move in."

"I guess we could."

"Seriously?" She smiled and ambled closer to cross her arms behind his neck. "Coolest thing." She kissed him, then her lips curved over her beaming teeth. "I could bake you a pie, for when you'd come back in all sweaty from fixing that barn…"

He held his smile off, hands on her waist, as they edged left and right with the slow tune. "I could be your… devout accessory for when you'd come out to care for the flowers."

"I could… fill your hot tub for when you'd call it a day."

They chuckled with another sway, then he eased his gaze from her eyes and to the locks coming free from her bun. "I could review the schedule while in the tub, then brief you on the state of the settlement later at night."

She puffed softly as he lowered his sight again. Facing the shadeless window, her pupils all but disappeared, leaving the sea of green to spill onto the porcelain shores around. She swayed on, a little slower. "I might be done waiting by then," she murmured.

He slowed to a standstill and, before his words could come out, he felt the silk of her lips over his and her hand moving up the back of his head to push it closer. She pressed warm against his chest as they tasted deeper in. His hand slipping down her hips inside the nylon of her work pants didn't meet any resistance, just another grapple of the lips.

"I've been offline for a while," she whispered in between.
"I'm fully aware of that."

She jiggled her shoes off her feet and rustled out of the pants while bringing her hand down the side of his body as they moved toward the bed. She crawled higher on her back under him, shirt stretching over her thighs, and hardly let go of his lips. "Any way to turn down the shading?"

"Not in a hundred-year-old window," he mumbled back. He rested on one elbow and ran his other hand under her shirt to release her bra. "But we can do this..." He let her arch to help him bring the bra out, then rose on his knees and tied it in a blindfold around his head, before leaning to her again. "To me you're a fantasy either way."

She held his face between her palms. "Come here." She brought his lips over hers. "Where have you been this hundred years?"

————

Slanting his head with his ear facing down, Clarens dropped his heel on the floor one more time, but the thump still didn't make it through the restaurant chatter. He nudged his chair away from the table and peeked under as he lifted his heel to pound it down. The table rattled loud, and several diners turned heads. He flipped his hand upright and pressed his lips while glancing around, then nudged his chair back close. "I think we're right above it," he said to Susan, who tittered blush over her plate.

Covering her mouth with the back of her hand, she looked at him from under her crimpled eyebrows, unable to stop. He laughed under his breath too.

"So..." she struggled to speak, "y-you jumped from up there"—she pointed at the mezzanine's projecting floor slab—"t-to here?"—she stamped the floor under the table, which didn't help at all.

215

Between the snorts, he raised his head slowly. She had dropped hers all the way down, with her reddened forehead propped on her wrist and twitching. She grabbed the napkin and held it over her mouth, then looked up too, in tears, when the waiter showed up.

"You've ordered anything else?" he said, stacking the empty plates.

She patted her mouth, clearing her voice. "You're kidding? You still have food back there?"

He spared a smile and worked his magic over the born-again table.

She looked at Clarens. "You know, I wouldn't mind a ginger tea after all that."

He copied her, then watched the waiter hustle away in front of his carrier.

She rested her elbows on the table and leaned closer. "This was a great idea."

He nodded while looking around. "I wish they kept the pool, but..."

"So, what did you do after? Hang dry?"

"Lynden had an extra pair of pants. He must have planned it," he said, as the carrier returned, and let her grab her cup first from the opening tray. "And then this girl found a blow-dryer, I think."

She hummed a smile over the steaming brim.

"No, nothing like that!"—he chuckled. He looked over the tables at the vintage spa building across the street. "I was rather... fatuous back then. The hair-in-the-eyes kid who'd only dance the smart songs. And expect the best-looking girl to come over and introduce herself."

"Huh..." She rested her chin on her hand. "I always wondered about that kid."

"Why do I think you never stood the chance?"

"Haha! I actually had trouble liking anyone. I was too... determined. They had me play with the boys' hockey team."

He paused sipping, then sighed. "I feel better now."

She stifled her laugh at the turning of more curious heads. She leaned closer over the table to continue, her neck smooth from the diamond-studded earlobe to the barely visible lace inside the slack V-neck shirt of his that she was now wearing. Her tongue stroked lightly against the even edges of her teeth, which sparkled with another laugh, to her nose creasing under the fine upturns of her brows and her chest jolting as she pulled back against the chair, before she leaned forward again to bring her cup to her mouth and slay him with her eyes.

The road began curving with the terraced townhouses up the shallow hillside, then the outer side cleared up abruptly as they reached the top.

He pulled over in the widened shoulder and pivoted the car perpendicular to the road, toward the open view.

Susan rose in her seat. "What's this?"

"I just stop by every now and then. Wrote some of my better closing arguments here," he quipped, looking over the structures below.

Gray and quiet, the metal-clad buildings below scattered the techno sight all the way to the row of mid-rises on the next hillside out.

He ran his hand over the dashboard. "When these plants came up it was just naked, wind-battered land around here."

"Huh. What's with you and the old buildings?"

He returned her smile and looked back out. "It makes everything else seem more real, that's all."

"Like, the new things?"

"Things, people."

She slipped her hand around his and bumped it gently on the console. "I *am* real." As he remained silent, she turned her head to him and squeezed his hand twice. "Am I not real?"

He chuckled. "I didn't mean it that way."

"What did you mean then?"

"Nothing. It's all in my head."

"Tell me"—she squeezed his hand again.

He swayed his smile away from hers and breathed long. "I used to think that things, people, events, didn't really exist, per se. That they were only… meanings."

She frowned lightly. "Like in solipsism?"

"A little. It's just that the world made better sense that way." He turned his hand under hers. "But that's changing."

"So now… I exist?"

He laughed. "Now you exist."

Another car pulled over and swiveled the same way toward the open view, only meters apart. As the couple inside glanced over, Clarens looked the other way. Atop the first townhouse in the renewed terrace down the road, the arrow of the ornamental weather station wiggled in the wind, even though the stretch of clouds beyond appeared to drift in a different direction. A jet had just hit the contrail zone farther above, in the sheer blue.

He felt her new hand grip.

"I'd need real clothes before I pick her up."

# 19

Brett twitched his shoulders at the bang, then he and Ricky rose from behind the log stack to watch the young tree fall through the fine drizzle. "Wow… Okay," he muttered, then pointed to the thick, rubbery bracelet in Ricky's hand. "So what if something happens to one of us and can't enter the code?"

Ricky joggled the bracelet and clasped his hand over it. "I lose a hand for twenty kilos but not for two, ehh?" He glared over.

"No, I meant to either one."

"Then next day, bang!… So you chop your hand off before that"—he dropped his knifed other hand on his wrist.

"Hmm."

"Still want it?"

Brett picked the bracelet from his hand and examined it closely. He tapped on its input nub with his finger until the digits lit up. "Can we order new ones, sealed?"

"There's no override, my friend. All bio. But, if you pay…"

"Yeah, I'd like to do that." He returned the bracelet and kept his hand extended to him. "Deal."

Ricky grasped it firm, ever frowning under his all-weather cap. "Better be platinum."

They turned to walk around the next stack of logs and down to the car.

"When can we go?" Brett asked.

"I make the plan and tell you, ehh? Maybe two, three weeks."

"Three weeks?" He stopped and, sleeves rolled up, he propped his fists on his waist and looked away. The drizzle had picked up against the dark underneath of the woods. He swiped the back of his hand under his nose and moved on.

"Where do you go when finished here?"

"Don't know. He mentioned having me dig for a fence." He wiped the new cold drip off as Ricky stared into the corner of his eye.

"You come work for me," Ricky said. "I give you food and room, ehh? In the city."

By the time he brought his two suitcases out the door, puddles had mushroomed in the mud before the cabin. He squinted through the raindrops and leaped from one higher spot to another toward the gravel turnaround, where he rapped the rear window of the car with his elbow. He cleared the lifting door and dropped his suitcases in the littered cargo compartment, then rushed around and sat in, holding his feet out to thoroughly knock the mud off his shoes before allowing the door to slide closed.

"Thanks," he said to Ricky's scowling look, then rubbed his hands dry on his jeans as they drove off and down the murky road. "Any chance we can pass by the motel? I'd like to tell him in person."

"Forget that my friend," Ricky muttered. "You have bigger things to worry about."

Out of the woody patch, they climbed hard along the streaming brooklet, then up the rocky stretch to the paved ridge road. Ricky floored the power pedal, with the wheels skipping on the residual mud, and they were soon flying over the potholes. The road stayed mostly empty, as the wide, sterile foothills snailed by.

He tossed his chin at Brett. "You came together all the way, and now you're here with nothing, and she's there with your daughter and another man?"

"Pretty much."

"Fuckin' women, ehh?"

He drew in loud through his nose a couple of times, then took his cap off, lowered the window, and stuck his head out to spit. The gush of fresh air displaced the fatty odor inside the car for the next several minutes. Beside the belt bag, a pair of binoculars rattled dull on the scratch-laden dashboard with every road bump. Above it, the outskirts of Tencun sprawled into view as the road wound around the lone hillock on the right.

Brett glanced over. "You never told me. How did you know it was me?"

Ricky held course, just snorting in again. "How did you break your right spoiler twice in a month?"

Brett fixated him. "Was it you sending that part over to Ayland?" Without an answer, he turned to the road too. "Don't know, perhaps on the freeway turn..." he said, and grasped the side handle as they veered hastily to pass another car in the gathering traffic. "Is that why your English is this good?"

"No, my father." Laying his cap on his lap, Ricky let a car zip the other way, then spit out before the next one honked by. "Fuck off!"—he dashed his hand up in the air, glaring in the rear viewer, then put his cap back on. "That much he did."

The line of cars and trucks thickened with little notice, while the road stayed its same one narrow lane each way.

Between the incoming vehicles, Ricky began weaving around the slower ones in front, then passed a couple of competing cars also. Whenever they didn't give him the room back in the lane, he just stayed over the stamped divider in the middle, forcing the others sideways to a hair-raising few fingers in between. He growled a curse at the honks and open-window yells every here and there, while Brett hung on tight to the side handle, planted in his seat. When one incoming truck didn't give way, Ricky slowed down over the line while pushing right again, which forced both the truck and the shuttle being passed to come to a hard stop, as did the traffic behind them. Angrily gesticulating, the truck driver lifted his door just past the rear of the car. Ricky lifted his too, sprang out of his seat without saying a word, and squeezed in fast sidesteps between the car and the truck to reach the driver, who then pulled back in and drove off, honking away. Ricky returned and, ever silent, zoomed the car at full power past the shuttle and to the tail of the traffic out in front, where they began weaving anew.

Between the jolts, Brett regrouped and sketched a smile. "Living in the fast lane, huh?"

They veered back into the lane just in time to make the right turn on the splitting road, then Ricky switched to auto-drive. He rested his elbow on the door mold and rolled his other hand out open by his hip. "Life gives you if you want to take it, and takes it if you don't," he said loud, pulling his hand back into a fist. "That's the other thing I got from him," he muttered, then swished indistinctly through his teeth. He frowned over as Brett kept staring at him.

"Right…"

They slowed through the emerging, sparse neighborhood, then split again and bumped through several more turns onto the listless, quiet streets. The rain hadn't made it here yet, but drops began beading up the windshield as soon as they came to a stop.

"Coming down early this year," he said at the sky, and reversed the car against the sliding black gate, in spite of the cars in the courtyard being backed up all the way to behind it.

He hopped out.

Brett pulled himself out too and felt his upper arm while peeking around. The blocky houses made for mismatched frontages on both sides of the street, in one and two stories of beige or light green and set back at varying depths behind metal fences and puny shrubs. He released his arm, to which a German shepherd barked zealously through the sliver opening in the fence panels across the street.

"Ehh!" Ricky scowled over from under the rear door of the car, then nudged his head toward his courtyard.

Brett grabbed the suitcases and followed him in, bouncing the luggage along the narrow path between the tandem row of cars and the one-story plastered house on the other side.

Past the corner into the backyard, Ricky stopped and bumped his chin at the cases. "Put them down. I show you the work." He turned to the house and held both hands forth to frame the unfinished enclosure of the rear deck. "I give this to the house," he said, then put a knee down and flipped two fingers at Brett, who knelt beside him. He craned his head lower to look at the open underneath of the deck and pointed into it with his hand. "You put insulation between joists and close it up. Like this. Then we dig for more footings."

Slanting his head close to the ground, Brett blinked with the raindrops and peered into the half-meter-high crawl space. From behind the perimeter ledge, two orange strips of insulation faded away within the deep space between the resin joists toward the obscure foundation wall of the house.

"Ground is dry," Ricky added. "Maybe you see rats but"— he flexed his hand open—"you take gloves."

He rose and ducked in his collar, then cued him to move on.

Brett followed him to the small shed shoved against the fence, near the opposite corner of the house. He stood in the doorway, the trite odors gushing by, as Ricky stepped inside the single, unpainted room, grabbed the quilt that lay halfway on the floor, and tossed it back on the frameless, spotted mattress.

"I had a helper stay here but..." Ricky said, driving the

mattress into the corner with his boot. "I bring you sheets." He turned around and bumped the two chairs to under the small metal table, then stepped to the sink and stared in, growling a few words. He opened the cabinet door below. "Cleaner, if you want"—he pointed in, then rapped the door closed and stepped on. "Hot plate here, fridge in the house." He turned to him abruptly. "You come in?"

"Yes." Brett stepped forward and placed the suitcases back to back between the footprints in the middle of the floor, as Ricky went to the door. "Hey, Ricky…"

Ricky turned and lifted his chin, raindrops skewing gray behind him.

"Two weeks."

He grasped the doorknob and fired his eyes over the room from under his cap. "Maybe three," he said, and cleared his throat to spit out in the rain, then nodded before shutting the door.

———

Just as vocal, the second flock of geese passed over in staggered geometry against the breaking skies. Clarens lowered his gaze back to the easel. The gabled end of the barn arched tall and bold on the left of the house, past the glass hub spanning the short gap in between. Turned on its side, the barreled roof of the house ran long above the meager brush before it, like a truncated vintage fuselage, if not for the porch notching a step under it at the other end. Adding in the three equally-sized upper windows brought back in the human scale and period undertones.

He held the easel through the breeze and squinted over its edge at the real roofline across the backyard. He wisped the tip of the pencil over the sheet for a thin, upright rectangle, from the middle window to above the tapered ridge. It looked like a chimney. He made it twice as wide, then reinforced the new roofline beside it, just before a voice call tinkled in.

"Oh, was going to leave a message," his sister rushed. "Not watching it live?"

"What? Oh, it was today..."

"You forgot your lunar finals? What did she do to you?" She laughed. "Hey, so, any chance you can see Mom this weekend instead? I know, but I'm swamped."

"I guess I could. But next weekend is Tara's birthday."

"Oh, yes. We'll try to drive over afterwards."

"You promised."

"Yes, but we're just"—she puffed. "By the way, is she all immunized?"

He paused the pencil over the jagged tree crown. "She is. I can put it in writing."

"Sorry, but you hear of all these things out there. Anyway," she added slowly, "the other thing I wanted to ask you was... about Mom's fund. We actually could invest our share separately."

"You guys... Didn't we get a windfall sale already?"

"I'll make my monthly payments just the same. C'mon, have I ever not done my part?"

He turned his head to the feeble knocks coming from the house, where Susan waved her hand in the window, then beckoned him until he held his palm up high. "I don't know."

"You don't know?"

"About the fund. Although you had committed to make Tara's party."

"How is that comparable?"

He sighed and dropped the pencil in the bottom tray, then swiveled his stool out toward the ambered hills and rose. "In the same sense of being consistent. In fact it surprises me, since you've always advocated family."

She paused. "You won't split the fund because I won't make your friend's daughter's party?"

"That's not what I—"

"When was the last time *you* came over?"

"True, but I was by myself. And I never asked for anything."

"Precisely!" she flared, then huffed and stayed silent before ending the call.

He began folding the easel, shaking his head slightly in the new rush of the wind, then watched his steps back toward the house from one grass patch to another over the moist ground.

When he opened the hub's inner door, the pastry trails raced to his nostrils, rich and fruity. He pitched his gear against the wall beside the coatroom and took off his jacket on the way to the kitchen, where Susan stooped over the counter. He peeked over her shoulder as she worked the cutting wheel through the pears topping of the large, counter-deep pie. "You can't be serious…"

She carried the new slice to the empty second plate. "Just an experiment."

"That's simply not credible."

She rolled another laugh as he walked out. "Hey, where's your drawing?"

"That… really was just an experiment," he shouted on the way back to the coatroom.

"C'mon, be fair!"

He returned with the easel and placed it in the eating nook beside the table, then poured his cup of tea and sat next to her.

She stretched her neck forward and pointed her fork at the thin rectangle rising above the roofline. "Is that there?"

"No. I was thinking of adding something."

"For real? Like what?"

He peered through the steam weaves and slurped, then felt the cup in his hand. "You know the small bedroom upstairs, in the middle? Perhaps there's a way to open up the roof there and build this… glass cube above it"—he passed his other hand at the ceiling. "Like a sunroom, or vista room, where you could go and look over all this farmland around," he continued, circling his hand over the table, "and the valley, the sunsets, the storms, the clear nights, everything. You could read there, work out there, sunbathe there…" He stopped as she restrained a smile, and smiled too.

She choked lightly and reached for her cup. "Awesome! How are you going to do it?"

"No idea." He laughed with her, then ate the first piece of pie. "My… this is good."

"Isn't it? I love that oven," she said, and looked down the kitchen counter. "I'll do two pans for Tara's birthday."

He ate silent for the next minute, peeking with her at the drawing in between. He clacked the fork down into the bottom crust and glanced over. "I need to pass by the apartment. Shall I get her?"

———

Through the gateway into the school foyer, Clarens looked around the striding adults in front of him to spot the pickup room. Inside the doughnut-shaped glazing, preschoolers shrieked about, tagging one another and the virtual domestic animals on the lime-green floor. He leaped aside to avoid the halted young man who crouched to embrace his diving boy, then stopped inside the opened doors and kept scanning the room. The purple scrunchie flashed through the animated heads, then reemerged on Tara's chestnut ponytail as she stayed squatted with another quiet girl to fondle the parading fowl. He funneled his hands to call her louder a second time, to which she turned and looked long at his waving. She reached for her backpack and ambled closer with her hands hanging down, glancing up through her bangs.

He smiled and ruffled her hair gently, when a woman's voice rushed from over his shoulder.

"Advance apologies! Do you mind casting your full IDs?" the school staffer asked, then ran her hand over Tara's bracelet.

"Thank you, Mr. Mann. Hers just hadn't read well."

"Sure," he returned the smile. "How's she getting on?"

"Good! She's catching up."

He grabbed Tara's hand and squeezed out through the parties back to the foyer, then looked down at her as they crossed silently toward the garage gateway. "Had fun today?"

She bobbed her head and hooked her thumb off the backpack's shoulder strap.

In the car, he slipped a close smile while checking the rear seat molding snug around her, then glimpsed her in the viewer as they wheeled out of the garage. "So, did you roller skate again?"

"Yes."

"With your friends?"

"No... Where is Mommy?"

"She's at home, waiting for you," he lifted his tone, then paused with the car halted at the joggers' crossing. "Music on? Tara?"

She grabbed her backpack and laid it on her lap, then crossed her hands over it and turned her head against the seat's side-rest to look out her window, slowly bumping the seat with her heel.

Beneath the unfolding boulevard frontage, he glimpsed the viewer again. "I saw the geese today. Did you see them?" he said, to no avail. "Any up there right now?"

She rolled her eyes to the car roof, to which he pivoted his seat around and looked across the sky too.

"Oh, is that a... No." He kept turning, slowly. "You know, when I was little I would watch for them to fly over my backyard. Like these big arrows in the sky"—he drew his hand in long lines under the roof. "And I wondered what they pointed at. So I would walk that way, and they've always helped me find something." Having come full circle, he held off his smile as her gaze fixed on the back of his head. "One time I found my old doggie that had got stuck in the bushes.

Another time I found… a spot of soft purple moss, just like your scrunchie there," he said, ensuring her eyes stayed on him. "But then I thought that, together with friends, I could see more arrows and find more things. Imagine that!"

She took a moment. "What things?"

"Oh, so many things, I even forgot."

She rolled her eyes at the above again. Large and light-hazel in the filtering daylight, still without a trace of green.

"But when we get home we can look for the geese together if you want."

As she brightened up a wisp, he smiled to himself and turned to the road, where they glided high on the eastern connector. He scouted the cityscape from the apex of the bridge. The far beyond had turned a shade lower, although all in the clear now. He tipped the new path point in. "In fact, let's do it now."

The east city's generous flat lots and single homes slipped by behind the molting street shrubs, as he rolled to a stop in front of the white, two-story house. The shaded south-facing room looked unlit behind the glass, and the garage below appeared empty, by the abundant daylight from the other side reflecting through and out the top window. In the entry alcove, the green trowel jutted a few fingers over the rosewood planter's brim.

He stepped out of the car and helped Tara out too, then walked with her down the sidewalk to the side of the lot and turned onto the lawn, walking in slowly by the juniper hedge.

"This was my backyard… The pool room… And I just remembered finding a yellow zep one day too, when I was floating on my back in there," he said, turning his sight between the sky and the gray vaulted glazing. "We were home early, with a couple of school friends each. My dad was still at the High Court in Norpen back then, I think." Ignoring the business call chinking through, he stopped and looked over the neighboring rooftops as her hand edged inside his for a grip. "I saw the arrow through the glass, then the tiny zep, then watched it going bigger and bigger until it was in our backyard and we all screamed. My mom was already out to get us the ears of corn. A little charred, wood-fire roasted, so good... She had called it over. Or it happened to be there for us, I thought."

She tugged his hand down. He turned to the lights that flashed alongside the house, as the call came through again.

The private guard summoned them to retreat to the sidewalk. "Her ID doesn't read well," the live operator added. "Please wait for a patrol scan."

Back at the car, he sat her in and leaned on the side of the open door, arms crossed as they waited.

"I'm hungry."

He looked at her and smiled long. "Of course."

He called for the nearest snack, then they both watched the small zep sway down in the balmy wind.

They munched quietly on the warm fish sticks as he stared at the leaves stroking the front lawn.

"Daddy Clarens, the geese!"—she threw her finger up.

He squinted at the distant flock as she kept prompting him for words.

# 20

His mother held Susan's hand in her own and swept her face with her peering light-blue eyes. She tilted her head and brought her other hand up to feel Susan's cheek, prompting the caretaker to leap closer from behind. She looked at Clarens aside, then back at Susan, who both kept smiling. A few stray hairs hung long off her back-combed snowy hair, cutting through the mist of the rainforest indoors setting beyond. Her eyes gleamed even larger as she looked at him again.

"You're happy." She attempted a smile, her eyebrows laboring between scowl and wonderment under the wrinkle-ridden forehead. She turned, then they all did so to walk on with her, though she only made a few steps to the first bench where she reached for the armrest. The caretaker rushed his hand under her elbow for support, but she only paused to look at it and slap it, and strived to sit by herself.

"She's getting tired," the caretaker mouthed to Clarens and Susan, then froze his smile on as she looked up.

Clarens squatted to her and held her hand gently between his palms. "I'll see you later, Mom." Beside him, Susan smiled and leaned forward too, with Tara gripping her arm from a little behind.

She peered long at all of them one more time, then thinned her lips in a resolute smile and withdrew her hand, before looking aside somewhere, over the facility's lush gardens.

"I like her a lot. She's so expressive," Susan said, as they walked through the jasmine court toward the visitor's exit.

He kept his sight on the trellis at the end-turn, his head high. "She's always been quite... associative," he said. "Which we've always dismissed as esoteric perceptionism, but she's never been deterred." He turned to her hum. "You know, drizzly morning meets the... tone of the first caller, meets the... ripeness of the mangos, meets the color of the tea mug. That sort of thing." They halted to narrowly miss another resident crossing their way in his self-drive transporter. "And she's always got the right cues somehow."

She grabbed his hand tight as they stepped into the main foyer, although he didn't turn. "It's great to have her around."

He blinked a few times and squinted into the daylight flooding the top of the ceiling dome. He looked over. "You talked to your father?"

"Yeah, for five minutes." She shrugged, then slowed for Tara to dip her finger in the waterfall beside the garage hub. "C'mon sweetie, we get to go to the toy house now!" She glimpsed her set to call her car out while the girl hopped closer. "We're passing by the party outlet to check out the actual props," she added for him. "You think that slider would fit in the main room?"

"That... we might want to downsize. It looks like it's going to be just Lynden and Gwyn."

"Oh, your other friend couldn't make it either?"

He pursed his lips with his head shake, to which she paused walking, with Tara prodding her in the thigh.

"Well, she gets the singing at school... And we'll make it fun anyhow!"

"Absolutely!"—he reached Tara for a tickle, then checked his set too. "In fact, I'll run this errand also, before I meet that architect," he said as Susan pecked his cheek, then he raised his head as the two of them sprang toward the blinking carport.

She glanced a smile over. "Don't forget my greenhouse!"


The fruity scent spurred the entryway, although the store was nearly empty otherwise. Of people, that was. He craned his head looking around and over the freestanding showcases and clusters of vintage effects as he circled the floor to the sound of the sportscast in the background. The film displays, printed posters, and art reproductions were all crammed together on a single wall section, floor to ceiling. He browsed through the array in his graph, then rolled his eyes up to scan the wall one more time.

Parting voices loudened from across the store, then the doors chimed behind just as the storekeeper cleared his throat and approached.

"That's an original. I can do five fifty, beautiful as it is," he said, a witty smile lifting his locks-sided, brawny cheeks.

Clarens returned the smile as they both turned to the subject oil painting in the middle of the wall. "Why is that?"

"Well, look at it, it's different. The frame is different, the medium is different, the epoch is different," the storekeeper said. "It throws off my collection!" His healthy paunch hung low inside the orange shirt as he bent to grab the framed poster that stood out of place on the floor. "It just got in and already knocked out this guy here…" he wheezed, then swung his gray hair around with a chuckle.

Glancing around, Clarens renewed his smile. "I thought you'd support diversity."

"Haha! I go with harmony!" Pitching the ousted poster against the wall on another shelf, the storekeeper passed his hand over the exhibits. "But I can be convinced otherwise."

Clarens joined his chuckling, then, arms crossed over his chest, he slanted his head at the first painting once more. "All right, I'll take it."

"Splendid." Once he kicked the small stepladder to under the painting, the keeper unhooked it carefully and turned in place with it. "This one out... this one in"—he swapped it with the poster on the shelf. "How did you find me anyway?"

"You know, I always wanted to see your antiques firsthand. I used to work nearby," Clarens said, pointing at the outside. As the storekeeper laid the painting on the low showcase and left, he stooped over to examine it closely. He strayed to the mix of jewelry and gadgets inside the glass case and paused over a tiny, sailboat-shaped pendant.

Having returned with the large, flat box, the storekeeper tipped his puffy finger on the glass. "White gold, both necklace and pendant. Bio tracking."

"Can I see it?"

———

"Ricky!... Ricky!"

As the woman crouched to look under the deck, Brett, lying flat on his back, raised his head higher and hit a protruding screw in the board above. He held off his cursing and turned the lamp away from beaming in his face, then raised his head slowly.

"Is Ricky here?"

"I don't know," he rasped, then cleared his voice. "You checked the workshop?"

"The workshop?" Her head disappeared above the deck ledge, briefly.

He dragged the lamp out of the way, then grasped the two joists left and right and wormed on the ground toward the edge of the deck. He cleared the end ledger to daylight as she looked down at him, then rolled to one side and pushed himself up on his feet.

She smiled in the corner of her mouth. "So you're the prisoner."

He took his second glove off and glanced over while dusting off. "I guess."

She held her half fist forward. "I'm Vivian." Her sprightly voice and eyes countered her overstated fragrance and wear, an all-black and rather unwarranted bodysuit under the flashy beige jacket and matching boots. "Ricky's my cousin."

"Brett." He touched knuckles with her. "Nice meeting you."

"Likewise. Oh!" She pointed to his forehead. "You're hurt."

"What? Oh, just now," he said, feeling his forehead, then took his knit cap off to feel his head higher and looked at the blood stain on his finger. "Got plenty of those," he smiled saying and ruffled his hair, as she pulled a tissue from her pocket and reached over before he could add anything.

"Let me wipe it, it's my fault," she said while carefully patting the wound, her blackened eyelashes under his uneasy gaze. She appeared to wear an eyeset and, by the few wrinkles, she wasn't all that young, though not unattractive.

"All right, thanks." Switching his eyes from side to side past her, he pressed the tissue down until she let go, then whisked his hand back through his hair. "Let's check the workshop."

She kept up with his stride across the backyard, toward the long metal shed. "You're from the FSA, ehh?" She chuckled. "The prisoner from the Free States."

He eased a smile over. "You're so right." He stopped before the black and orange car imprint on the shed's door and dinged the sheet metal. "Ricky!"

"I never met someone from your country, actually," she continued.

"Really." He cracked the tall sliding door open. "Must be because we're hiding under the decks." He let her giggle and stuck his head in through the opening to call Ricky again. With the shady interior unanimated around the two dismantled car chassis, he pulled out. "He might be in the back, but he made a point to not bother him there. Perhaps you can."

"No, if he didn't hear you." She dismissed it with a lax pass of the hand and looked out toward the front gate. "Can you do, how do you say, a touch-up? Because somebody scratched my car right in front of my office"—she zipped her ring-laden finger through the air.

"I don't, I'm sorry."

"I'm a notary," she added quickly. "Assistant. And translator."

He nodded and closed the door, then turned to step back toward the house with her.

She sighed loud and pointed at the gate again. "Because I'm going to this party tonight and I didn't want this scratch on my car. You know?"

"Right. I'm sorry I can't help." He pressed his lips.

"I know, I know." She left her hand hanging toward him, with a new sigh. "Everybody will be there. And they look at you. You know?"

"Right…" As they slowed before the deck, he glanced at the packing clouds. "But you shouldn't notice it by then."

"You think so?"—she turned her head swiftly, then laid her hand on his arm. "You know what? You should come with me and everybody will look at you instead when we get out of the car!" she perked up saying, her accent unwinding a little, then giggled short and turned entirely toward him, raising both arms to redo her side bun of hair. "It's a good party."

"Uhh, don't know. By the time I finish here I'll be kind of tired, so…"

"So you do like it under the deck, ehh?" She smiled under her caramel eyes. "Come on. I'll show you some real Tencun people. I'll buy you a drink."

Sweeping his sight over the yard, he felt his days-old beard and couldn't hold off his smile, then looked at her and exhaled. "You would have to, actually."

The low ball bounced between his hands as the two red helmets broke through the block. He ran to the side and made the throw from nearly on the line, then reeled through the crowd, and the camping chairs, and the swinging doors, and plunged under the cafeteria table between the two rows of shiny acrylic boots. They helped him rise, then she let him hold her hand and walked with him down the hall's stories-tall colonnade to the orange Maab inside his father's paddock. Her hair strewed a plume of gold over the sunny Thirty-Second Avenue cafes and bike racks and construction dust curtains and holograms, then turned into the orange of the car and many shades darker and her eyes turned deep green with her new smile, before the hard tackle from his other side knocked him down in the patchy grass. On the snap of the ball he ran with it and spun out of the boy's grasp, fended off the next two lunging for him, and kept running into the cheering crowd. His hand in the air too, his coach rather frowned and beckoned him to the sideline. "Your father!..."

On skidding sideways off the track and hitting the uneven ground, the car took off swirling in the air over the berm and over the taxiing planes. His father stroked him on the head and swiveled back to the dashboard to make the road turn himself. He wore the white and blue, linen short-sleeves. In the passenger seat under the nautilus umbrella, his mother tilted low the other way. "Slow down!" her words reverberated. "*You* broke the zipper!" his father voiced over. "*You* wanted carry-ons!" she argued, and lay lower into the door mold, and so did his father to the other side, while the freeway widened ahead and he skimmed on the soggy surface and reeled back into running, with the coach pitching whistles from the sideline and running along with him, whistling on.

Brett called off the alarm and rose to sitting, then on his feet and folded the protective foil, soiled face in, over the bed. He tipped the second suitcase on the floor and reached through the tangled clothes, settling for the navy overshirt. He laid it on the clean side of the bed, then flattened it top down under his palm. He gulped two beef pasties from the open pack on the table and took his work clothes off, then yawned long and began stretching his torso side to side.

His arm around his girlfriend's neck and gesturing with his bottle in his other hand, the man shouted over the dance tune. "If free state, why they not let them go?"

"They need their tax money," Brett shouted back from across the booth.

"But it's free state."

"It used to be. But the government got in debt again."

The man looked at another friend two seats down, who, seemingly as confused, bent over the table. "So they pay debt and they go."

Brett smiled and drank. "They say it's not their debt," he shouted as everyone stared at him, if only to follow his English. "They say it's the central government and the big parties who kept borrowing to pay off their voters. Same old."

The two looked at each other again. "You stay in Tencun, free to do anything!" the one guarding his girlfriend said, and as everyone laughed, he raised his bottle. "Government not do anything!"

Amid the erupting guffaws, everyone raised their bottles above the under-lit table and roared. "Tencun! Tencun!" Heads craned over from the adjacent green and yellow booths and joined the deafening chorus, which then picked up on the dance floor also.

Hot-faced, Vivian returned and huddled against Brett at the end of the bench. "What's going on?" she beamed asking, grabbing her vanilla punch.

"No idea," he shrugged, and kept pumping his fist in the

air like the rest of the crowd.

As the music reemerged, she swayed her body sideways with the twining vibes. "Let's dance this one."

"I'm wasted, I'm sorry."

"Come on! The last one."

"Seriously. I wouldn't mind you taking me home actually."

She stilled. "Sure. I can take you home."

She slipped around the table corner and leaned over to talk to her friends seated across the booth as he pulled himself out. The word "prisoner" seemed to come up a few times, then the laughs instantly turned into a new roaring. "Prisoner! Prisoner!"

He raised his hand and let his head down with a smile while Vivian joined him to leave, then pumped his fist lightly above his shoulder as they walked away, with her peeking back for a few more yaps and giggles.

Despite the chilly breeze, she fanned her silver-laced top over her chest on the way to the car. "That was fun!"

"Oh, it was awesome."

"I told you. You should stay here, they'll make you mayor," she cheered as they got in, and turned to toss her jacket on the rear seat. She swiveled back a little to face him and propped her hands on her waist, ever mirthful. "You're a good dancer."

"Ah... A thing or two came back to me," he said, swaying his head to look out and then back at her, by which time she had already lunged over to press her lips against his. "Vivian... wait..." He grabbed her waist, pulling his head back slowly. "Wait."

She gazed into his eyes.

"You're an awesome girl but... I'm not in for this."

"You don't like me?"

"I do, I do. I just have so much on my mind right now, you know?"

She dropped back in her seat and turned to the steering wheel. "I'm sorry, I drank too much."

"You're okay?"

"Yes." She blinked quickly, then passed a smile. "I'm okay."

She called out the address and cued the large, luxury car to drive off. She recovered somewhat past the first roundabout and began playing city guide again, then called out another destination to detour through her favorite, rather opulent neighborhood on the west hillside, where she also happened to live. They descended the hill and crossed back under the freeway to the city proper, then Tencun-by-night turned dimmer as they headed north, and the potholes mushroomed with the smaller streets. She grabbed the steering wheel and rose higher in her seat to weave through the black spots under the headlights, which hardly spared the car but did bring back her giggles.

"Thanks, I owe you one," Brett said as they pulled in front of Ricky's gate.

She shrugged a smile. "If you say so." She kept her hands high on the wheel, her neckline bleached in the lone lamppost light.

"Come here…" He opened his arms and leaned over for a hug. She felt warm. He stroked her back and drew his cheek back against hers slowly, when she jolted with a shriek at the hard rapping on the window. He yanked his head around to see Ricky frowning at them from behind the glass.

The moment they stepped out, Vivian and Ricky lashed out and strode toward each other, which only brought up the fervor in the German shepherd across the street.

Brett rushed between them. "Hey, hey!"

Jaws clenched, Ricky turned to him. "We talk inside"— he twitched his head at the gate. Turning back to Vivian, he picked it up again with her. Her eyes all but popping in his face, she dashed the back of her hand through the air and pulled back, then hastened to the open car door.

"G'night Vivian!" Brett called, to which she flashed her hand above the windshield before jumping in to zoom away.

He walked inside the courtyard and waited for Ricky, who watched the sliding door close fully before turning. "What was all that about?"

Glancing at the neighbors' windows, Ricky treaded the gravel toward him with his hand out to prod him toward the backyard.

"Hey, no need for that, okay?"

"I thought you were a man," he grumbled, lip pushing up. "And you're fucking the first bitch who drives by?"

"She's your cousin for God's sake! She wanted company. We didn't do any—"

"I told you to stay low," he cut him off, as they stopped in the darkness behind the house corner. "I don't do this work to have a woman fuck it up, ehh?"

"What work? Where's the plan?" Brett raised his chin at him. "You told me we'd talk about the plan."

Halted, Ricky twinkled his eyes through. "What work? Come." He prodded him into walking on. "I show you what work."

He strode with him toward the workshop, where he yanked one of the sliding doors half open. As the lights came on, he nearly clipped Brett's elbow sliding the door closed behind him, then strode on around the first car to the covered one in front of it. He grasped the end of the loose nylon sheet and hustled it over to the other side. "This work."

Brett moved closer, gazing at the skeletal mix of wire harnesses, open seats, and the resin-like chassis lying low between the four oversized wheels. The front cargo hatch and one wing were in place, albeit of different colors, while various body parts lay scattered around against the clutter lining the workshop walls. "What is this?"

"The car," Ricky said, and clamped down a hanging harness on the passenger side. He rose and dusted off his hands, frowning. "How do you want to cross over? Push stroller?" As Brett snorted, he arched his leg over a stack of tools to

241

find the next clear spot on the floor and turned to look the car over. "Four fifty kilowatts, half-meter lift, two-minute float, six-minute body."

"Wow." Brett propped his hands on his waist, eyes fleeting over the vehicle. "Six-minute body?"

Without answering, Ricky turned to reach for the ruffled cover on the floor and threw one end over the top frame of the car.

Brett helped him pull it over. "So when are we talking about the plan?"

Ricky sucked in loud, then worked his jaws and headed for the door. "When are you gonna know about your daughter?"

"A week from now."

"A week, we talk."

"C'mon..."

Hand on the door handle, he glared over the shoulder, jaws still working. Close up under the pendant light, red vessels engulfed the deep blue of his set-free eyes, while Brett's alcohol-tinged breath traced good company through the stillness in between. He cleared his nasal passages again and stepped out to spit beside the door, then locked it behind Brett, glanced his set, and walked away toward the house. "Women, ehh?"

# 21

"**R**eally sorry guy. Will do something soon," Lynden said, and pushed his finger forth from the graph. "Deal?"

Once he palmed off the call, Clarens looked down the driveway at Susan and Tara, who had already reached the house-number post at the road and looped the first balloon's ribbon around it. He squeezed his lips and walked on.

Raising the "BIG 4" party-sign in place, Susan glanced over. "What happened?"

He shook his head a tad and mouthed, "Not coming."

She gasped quiet over the child's head, who turned to squint up at him. "Why?" Susan said, slipping the sign's velvet ribbon around the post too.

"I don't know. Gwyn thinks she might have passed some bug on to the kids."

She sighed and fluffed the double bow, then bent to Tara for a long hug. She wiggled the balloon's ribbon stemming up from her hands. "This one too, sweetheart?"

Her curls mingling with the furry collar of her coat, Tara raised her gaze to the wind-hiking balloon. "I keep this one," she said, and toddled around with it.

Susan warmed her hands at her mouth, then, lips pursing, she examined the decorated post. She turned to him. "What do we do?"

They stepped behind Tara, up the driveway. From Susan's quiet sigh, he turned to the ashen grays over the glimpsing ridge of the barn, when they both started at the dog's barking behind, turning around.

"Such pretty balloons!" a woman called from the road, over the spurred barking.

Her male companion summoned the black Labrador back and rushed after it as the dog, tail wagging, kept jouncing in hesitant steps onto the driveway. He restrained it by the collar, while the woman walked closer and extended her hand to Susan.

"Hi! I'm Fay"—she smiled brightly, the creases around her cheeks in contrast with the fitted, youthful wear. "And this is my husband Noren," she said and pointed to her age-alike partner, then farther out. "The neighbors, on the corner."

"The renovated farm? Great to meet you, finally!" Susan said and introduced herself, as did Clarens, then she reached behind her. "And my daughter Tara…"

"The birthday girl?" Fay cheered at Tara, pointing at the post, as the girl remained fixated on the restive, tongue-hanging dog next to its master.

As Susan echoed her cheer and stroked Tara to bring her forward, the balloon's ribbon slipped out of the girl's hand and glided away with the breeze. The dog bolted from Noren's hand to chase it up the driveway in high leaps and barks, with a screaming Tara running after them both, to everyone's laugh.

"Forgive him, he's got border collie," Noren quipped, and sprang agile after the dog, which, meanwhile, had clutched its jaws around the end of the ribbon and trotted, its white paws flashing, back toward him. He pulled the ribbon out of its teeth and handed it to Tara, now beside them. She held it still in front of the hyper-breathing lab, then released it to the side, to which the foursome chase restarted.

"Hahaha! Oh, it's my favorite mix," Susan said.

"Is it?"

"I grew up with two collie mutts. And two younger sisters."

Fay chuckled. "Forgive me but… where is your accent

from?"

"I'm from the Alliance. South Kewan."

"Ah! My great grandmother was from Kewan!"

"You're kidding!" As Fay switched between her and Clarens, Susan stroked his arm. "He's from here," she added, to Fay's understated "Oh," when they turned to the girl's loud shriek.

Cheeks radiating and with the dog springing alongside her under Noren's watch, Tara held on to the balloon and dashed to Susan for cover.

"Tell you what." Susan tottered on her feet. "Why don't you come in for a slice of pie? She'd love it."

"Well," Fay waffled, "we have the horticulture class at four…"

"Oh, Susan can show you all that," Clarens said, and pointed backward with his thumb. "And the melon bouncer's for the rest of us."

They laughed, then Fay turned to Susan as they all walked up the driveway. "You're in the business?"

"Yes. Mostly flowers," Susan said, smiling.

"'Cause we're trying to get started with our greenhouse. In flowers, we think."

She looked back at her and both let out a chuckle. She bent to Tara, who stayed focused on taunting the dog, and kissed her loudly on her cheek. "Well, let's start with the pie!"


The last present was the same popular scooter character, only in yellow. He sent it to the printer at half-scale, then deleted all the apologetic party replies. He browsed through his contacts list slowly, with the graph dimmed down and the floor texture beyond crisping through.

He raised his head and felt the bottom of the cup. Beside the nook's tall window, the strip of beach blurred through the fast-rising steam. In the equally colorless twilight outside, the two shrubs now whipped the purlins of the roofless greenhouse in short, gusty swings.

The light came on, then Susan's chypre wisped through the ginger steam as she slanted her head over his shoulder from behind. "She fell asleep right off. This turned out great."

"Pure providence."

"You wouldn't know…" As he tried to turn his head to her she kept hers in the way and added quickly, "I couldn't believe you bouncing in there."

"Neither could I."

She poured her cup and rested next to him against the end of the counter, facing the painting.

He sipped with her. "Will this be too much here every day?"

"Uhh, let me see… Awesome lake where you take me last-minute on our first trip," she mused, leaning on him with a glance. "Beach where we sit next to each other in swimsuits…" she swayed the other way, saying. "Pier where you dive off that barge like… you're waterborne, to save Tara, and then tousle your hair and go like… *Pretty good exit I thought*," she mimicked a deeper voice, to his chuckle. She shrugged against his shoulder. "Not too much for me."

"Well, technically, half of that beach is under water now, and the pier was rebuilt. And, you see those villas in the background?"—he pointed to the side of the painting, "It looks like it's just before they started bringing up the dome, which was only twenty years after this farm was built, so essentially—"

"Shh…" Her finger on his lips, she turned his head slowly toward her. "Essentially," she whispered, and kissed him, "it all makes real sense."

She held his hand and stepped backward with him through the kitchen, then sipped again under her smiling eyes before leading him out to the main room.

He reached back to find the counter's end under his cup.

"Not the bouncer again."

She stifled her laughter, reddening her cheeks, then climbed the first two steps of the stair and paused to touch lips anew. "I was thinking… You may stay over more often if you want."

———

"Two thousand one hundred fifty-sev—"

"Yes, I know, I see it!" Brett cut in. "I'm telling you it should be in the order of three zeroes attached to that," he said, and crushed the bead-bodied spider crawling down the joist, next to the account register beaming off his wristband.

"I don't know, sir. This is all we received."

"Listen. I've been on hold for twenty minutes. I pay a ludicrous rate for your time. You can't tell me you don't know!"

"Just a minute," the live representative said, then his image morphed into the logo.

Brett grabbed the truncated shovel and turned on his side to continue digging in short, grinding hits. He scraped the bottom of the shallow hole to gather the dirt and scoop it out, but the end of the handle hit the joist above and most of the dirt fell back in. He tossed the shovel and held his breath in the rising dust while fixating on the slowly pivoting logo.

"We show the amount as insurance payout for an intermediary called Orion Clearway, which went insolvent," the rep said, his bust back on. "That might explain why it's smaller than the transfer you anticipated," he continued, with the same utter lack of intonation, other than his voice waning away. "You might be entitled to other recoveries and…"

Brett laid his wrist down slowly over his chest. It went up and down with his breathing through the new silence. The screw above completely missed the joist, and the next one down cracked the plastic at an angle to come out just as needle sharp in shining alloy. He felt the ground for the lamp and switched it off, too, ever staring at the pitch-dark underside of the deck. Some of the framing grid began showing again with the scarce daylight making its way in.

The squeak of the gate broke through. He switched the lamp back on, then held his head raised with his hand to look down the joists. The fast steps treaded the gravel around the house corner and stopped abruptly.

"Not hard to find you!" Vivian giggled, face upside down, her loose hair touching the ground below the side of the deck.

"Hey..." he let a smile out. "What's up?"

She lowered a shallow container below the end ledge. "You like quiche?" She felt the underside of the container with her other hand. "From the oven."

He dug his heels in the ground to begin worming out of the crawl space. Outside, he wobbled onto his feet and smirked awkward at the container.

She kept smiling. "I thought you liked it, at the party."

"I do. It's just that…" He pitched his thumb at the house. "You talked to Ricky?"

"I don't need to talk to Ricky. Is he here?"

"I haven't seen him."

"Good. Let's eat!" she said and brushed by him to head toward the shed in her white, calf-high boots, a veil of fragrance behind. "This is where he keeps you, ehh?"

"Yes but... Vivian!"

He dusted off and followed her as she didn't turn. She walked in and swiveled in the middle of the room to look around, then smiled at him in the doorway. "Not too bad."

"Vivian, Ricky made it sound like—"

"You're afraid of Ricky?" She stepped closer, holding the container like a tray over her shoulder and with her other hand propped on her waist, and lifted her finger before her sobered face. "Because he cannot lift a finger at me. He owes big money to my father." She propped her hand back on her waist and crooked her lips in a new smile. "You have plates, prisoner?"

Brett snorted and eased a smile back, then stepped in and
to the sink cabinet. "One here..." He picked the reusable
plate from the drainer, then cleared the table of crumbs and
leftover flatware. "I can eat from the box. I'll be right back,"
he added, grabbing a T-shirt from the chair.

"Change here, I turn this way," she glanced over to say,
while laying the container on the table.

Turning the other way, he removed his sweater. "So what
does your father do?"

"He's a businessman. All kinds of business, with the city."
She snapped the plastic open. "Mmm! Zucchini, mushrooms,
onions, bacon, ricotta, olives, red peppers... Oh, look at you!"

"What?" Pulling his undershirt up over his head, Brett
twisted his naked torso to look at her, as she gazed at his back
with a spatula in her hand. "You were supposed to slice that
thing!" he said, smiling, and swapped the shirt with the new
one, but she kept staring and moved closer.

"What happened?" She extended her arm to touch his lat
with her fingertips. "You've been fighting?"

He shook his head and pulled his new shirt down. "You
guys are really gutsy, you know that?" He grabbed his sweater
and turned around to her. "No, I ran into a few stumps and
stuff, and then the screws in there."

"Oh. What is gutsy?"

"Gutsy? Like, lively."

"Oh." Her eyes swept down his chest before rolling back
up to search for his. "You like it that I came back?"

He exhaled. "I actually do. I'm glad you came."

She coiled her arms around his neck and kissed him, the
spatula tinking onto the floor. He let go of the sweater and
laid a light hand on her waist, then stared through her hair at
the paintless wall spot by the sink, then lower, before closing
his eyes.

———

"Hey, it's me."

"Brett?"

"Sorry I have no image. My feed just died on me."

"What's this number?" Susan livened up. "Where are you?"

"I'm actually in Tencun."

"Wha-at? You're kidding!"

"No, I just thought I'd see what it's like. Like you said."

She rolled another laugh. "So it's not bad then."

"Actually, no. Depends." His back against the workshop's ribbed wall, he ungrounded a new stone with the tip of his shoe. "Hey, is Tara there?"

"She's still at school. We actually had her party on Saturday."

"Oh… I'll call later then."

"Yeah, I'll pick her up in two hours. But how are things with you?" she upped her voice again. "I thought you'd have called by now."

"Yeah, had a glitch or two." He kicked the stone to rolling through the high weeds and to under the door-less car wreck. "Goes fast, huh?"

"Yeah."

"What school is it, by the way?"

"Same one. Where we signed her up. Wait," she rushed as someone called her in the background. "Can you hold?"

"Let's talk when I get this image on. Just tell her happy birthday and… that I love her and stuff."

"I will. You take care of yourself!"

"Yeah, you too," he said, and hung up. He shifted his weight, his sweatshirt catching against the corroded wall panel, and moved on to the next stone.


Clarens stepped around the stairs to the middle of the main room and called her again.

"I'm here!"—she appeared at the mezzanine handrail above. She smiled and nudged her head to the side. "Sorry, master planning my office."

"In that business attire?"

As she laughed and pulled back, he whiskered a smile and raised the art utensils case in his hand. "I'm going to the city and I could pick up that desk for you, unless you want to print it."

"That would be great! Oh, wait." She checked her set. "What was that code again, for the pendant?"

"Skiff."

"That's right. There she is!"


Off the moist tip of the brush, the ochre raced through the paper's pores and to the penciled contour to bring the boulder alive, then the glimpse of wall at the end of the driveway followed in gray. He cleaned the brush in the water jar and peeked at the front of the classroom, where the teacher returned the good-bye of one of the few remaining students and ambled closer in his dark purple pants.

"So, what did you want to ask me?" he said from a few steps away. "Look at that!" he added quickly, and scanned Clarens's drawing as he turned around the board at his side. He looked at him, then switched back and forth to the brush in his hand. "It's the one!"

Clarens chuckled. "I love the technique, but..." He reached for the roll of drawings pitched against the station leg. "What I wanted to ask you was if you happen to know an architect," he continued, unrolling the drawings over the board. "For my house." He weighed down the end of the top sheet with the aquarelles tray and eased back in his chair, as the teacher scanned over the barn and farmhouse in the lead-pencil drawing.

Glancing a light smirk over, the teacher rolled the sheet

aside to reveal the house's interior view in the drawing beneath. He remained silent as he went through the three other drawings in the stack, his ponytail brushing his collar back and forth. "Rather idyllic stuff here Clarens." He smiled between his red sideburns and placed the tray back down. "Were you not an attorney?"

"Yes, I was."

"You *were*... Well, I *was* an architect."

Clarens looked at him, hardly suppressing his smile.

Unreacting, the teacher continued. "Why *do* you need one?"

"Well, I talked to two so far, but I didn't seem to get my vision across."

"No, why do you need one?"

As they looked at each other again, Clarens let out his chuckle. "You're serious. You were an architect?"

"In my ex-life."

He nodded at the drawings. "Interested?"

The teacher scratched his sideburn. "Not only am I completely disinterested but, between constraining you to aesthetics of real quality—of mine that is—and blowing through your budget, and keeping tight tabs on contractors till you'd have to start practicing law again for your own sake," he said, slowly rotating his head back toward Clarens, "you'd become a very, very melancholic man."

He stepped beside the board as Clarens chuckled on, then smiled and slipped his hands in his pockets. "What you need is a builder," he continued, bumping the flat bronze clasp of his pants against the edge of the board. "You have the vision, you can draw, go for it. This is simple residential stuff."

Musing, Clarens tipped the brush handle onto his chin. "So, you left architecture for the art class, if you don't mind me asking?"

"If you're asking why," the teacher said, and slowed his bumping to look out the glazed side of the room, "I like it better numb." He recollected quickly. "But how about *you*?"

Clarens looked out too. "I… could never get de-numbed."

The teacher laughed while turning to nod at the last students leaving. He then struck the farmhouse in the top drawing with his finger. "Give it a try!" he upped his voice saying, and turned away. "Draw what you want to see there every day, when you drive back home, when you snooze under that porch. Go inside, feel the walls, make them soft, make them concrete, make them clear, make them something, and with a reason why," he went on, swinging his extended hand as he returned to the front of the classroom. "Tone it down, or you'll grow bored of it in no time, and go broke even sooner. Think where you put your weights, your shirts, your significant others, where you charm your guests, where you groom your dogs. Bring the snow, the rain, the pests. Build it as if you'll live five hundred years." Having reached his desk, he grabbed his weathered leather bag and pivoted around with a grin. He raised his hand to poke his finger at the drawing board in front of Clarens, who remained arrested, chin propped on his brush. "What have I said, four months?" He held his hand high while walking out. "You're close!"

Clarens rushed a "Thanks!" to the empty door opening, then turned to stare out anew. From the metal-clad building rear that filled the view, he neared his focus to the muntin of the glazing frame, then arched higher along the backlit ceiling grooves to the opposite wall, sheen with art exhibits. He panned back across the stations and to his board. He rolled closer to put the brush down and pick up the pencil instead, then stilled to examine the airy jut in the farmhouse's roofline.

# 22

"What is that?"

"A stair."

"Around the bedroom?"

"It runs with the cutout in the ceiling, to the glass room," Clarens said over the sketchpad, then paused his pen to look at Susan standing next to his chair. "Good morning."

She bent over her frothy mocha for a peck on the cheek. "You should come with me to Fay and Noren's today," she said, walking on to the kitchen counter. "You've got to see what they've done to that barn."

"Oh, really?" He checked his empty cup, then picked up sketching. "Next time perhaps. How are you getting on?"

"Great! We'll farm out of their greenhouse till I can get ours going," she spoke up while clanging the pans into the dishwasher intake. "Can't believe the nurseries here. I could so do it for half the price." She stopped the loading. "What was that?"

He turned his head with her. A truck horn sounded off as if from closer than the road. He rose and followed her to the main room and the porch-side window as a trailer-hauling truck turned wide in the courtyard.

She swiveled to him, brows high. "You brought your furniture?"

He shook his head and stepped close to grab her hand and walk her to the coatroom. "The last proofs came through from the Alliance last Friday," he said to her long face and reached in for her jacket. He held it out for her to slowly turn and slip into it and smiled. "Congratulations. You're now a Commons resident."

Her jaw dropped. "You're kidding me. Are you kidding me!" She rumpled his sweater in her fists, then tugged him close to give him a suffocating kiss. She let go and laughed, before covering her mouth with the back of her hand under the watering eyes, then threw her arms around his neck to kiss him once more.

"And you can register your own business now," he said, hands out, as she came back down on her heels and cheered, when the honking went off again.

She wiped the corners of her eyes. "So what is that?"

He reached in for his jacket too, grabbed her hand, and led her to the front door. "It just called for a gift…"

In front of the porch, the truck operator stepped down from his cabin. "Glad you're here, 'cause I couldn't leave him with nobody," he shouted while heading to the rear of the trailer, and unlatched the gate.

Susan stepped down the porch steps toward him as he peeped inside the lowering gate. She glanced unsettled back at Clarens, then came to a stop behind the trailer, her gaze delving into the enlarging, shaded opening. "No…"

As if the snorting and manure odor could leave any doubts, the lone horse came into view, anxious and bucking its head against the side railings to look back from facing the other way at the front end of the trailer. Babbling his soothing cues, the caretaker walked in and beside the animal, then removed the crossbars and began to back it up as Susan stepped close to the ramp.

Radiant, she turned to Clarens behind her. "This is crazy."

He shrugged. "It all started with you riding, after all."

She leaned her head back to chuckle, then swung to the dark-brown horse backing out. "Oh my God."

"Snowleaf"—the caretaker patted the horse's shoulder when they were both on the ground. "Six-year-old quarter, smart and funny. All trained but I can learn more," he said, then stroked the leaf-like white pattern on its chest. "Call me Leaf."

Susan felt the idling horse's neck. "Leaf." She ran her arm under it, cheek up close, to stroke it on the other side. "Oh my God."

Keeping an eye on them, the caretaker tied the horse's lead line to the ramp railing and stepped alongside the trailer. "And I have my own saddle here somewhere…" he went on, reaching in the side storage. He pulled the saddle out and held it against his belly, looking at Clarens and Susan in turns. "Where do you want it?"

Susan looked at Clarens, then back at him. "Here"—she tapped Leaf's back.

"All right." He smiled and stepped to the other side of the horse to lay the saddle on.

Minutes later, he led it in a slow gait around the courtyard with her in the saddle. On the second full circle she asked him to unhook the line, to which he looked for Clarens's nod and complied. As she nudged her knees higher in her cream jeans and clucked to the horse, he stepped back next to Clarens and threw a tipping smile over, then crossed his arms over his chest too and watched her trot the horse away. He turned. "You want to show me where I set up that stall?"

When Clarens returned from the barn, Susan was cantering Leaf around the very limit of the courtyard, hitting the pavement loud. Her hair bun gone, she sped up while approaching and cheered by him over Leaf's neck, then slowed to turn around and pat the horse's back behind her. "Come with me!"

He stood still and stared at her figure, and at her beaming face within the weaves of black. Which shifted sideways as the horse zigzagged and snorted restless in the middle of the yard, and as the leaves shimmered amber and rust in the steady breeze across the tall beeches behind.

She ran her hair off her face. "Clarens!"

"Yes!"

"Come with me!"

———

The blanket wrapped around her, Vivian grasped it below her naked back and slipped out of the bed to tiptoe to the table. Glimpsing through the folds, her thighs rubbed against each other down to her knee pits and then the legs diverged slightly, or less so with the aid of the ankle bracelet.

"Don't look. I haven't worked out this week!" She giggled without turning and reached inside her white tote on the table.

"What? No..." Brett said, pulling his hand out from under his head, then grabbed his wristband from the makeshift heater-box nightstand and graphed up his set. "Just browsing." He relayed the graph larger above the end of the bed and went through the news, where he picked the front object in the Tensana header: "FSA—the healing begins."

She turned to the voice-over and watched over her shoulder as he skipped through the bland layover of suburban settings, maps, and talking political figures. "They don't split anymore?" she asked.

"No. For now."

"That's good, ehh?"

"Good for some," Brett muttered, "who use the others..."

"Like me," she smiled saying and bit off the pastry roll, then tiptoed back to the bed with the full pack of rolls over two hanging napkins.

He smiled and shook his head, as she laid the pack on his chest to slip under the sheets again.

She pointed at the pastries—"Vanilla almond, coconut choco, mozzarella"—then ate her roll and licked her powdery lips.

He pushed himself higher against the pillow and gobbled a whole cheese roll before her pleased eyes, then reached inside the nightstand for a beer can.

"Brett…" She ran her finger slowly down his arm. "Come work for my father. He pays way better and everything. You know, till you get your money back," she said, and looked up at him. "Or till whenever you want."

Her auburn locks curled over the golden necklace to below her bare shoulder, which poked soft up in the air. She blushed a shade as he didn't answer, and felt just as warm beneath the blanket.

He rose a notch higher and turned his head away to drink. "That's too nice Vivian, but it's not that simple."

"Why not?" She turned closer above his chest. "He needs a smart accountant, somebody he can trust. He could get you an apartment in the hills, I'm sure."

"How can he trust me?"

"Believe me, I know my town," she said, switching her tone.

He looked at her, before turning quiet to the news display.

"He also does business in Baires. We can go there sometimes," she continued. "He'll do anything for me."

He switched to the sports. "You have any siblings?" he mumbled, sweeping down the football scores.

She rested her chin on his arm. "No. You?"

"No. I mean, two stepbrothers. My parents split when I was a kid." With his eyes on the replaying highlights, he swung his hand out to reach for his beer can, then rotated it slowly before his face. "Sometimes I feel like… adopted," he added, and drank.

"Adopted?"

He frowned and turned back to the game.

She raised her chin and picked up another roll, then began following the game too, munching over her napkin. She jolted as thudding knocks shook the door.

"Brett!... Brett!" Ricky yelled with the pounding, while Brett slipped in his pants and grabbed his shirt on his way to the door. The moment he unlocked it, Ricky burst in and to the middle of the room, the alcohol odor behind him. He stooped forward and wobbled slightly as he speared his finger at Vivian in bed, then the yelling began, with Brett jumping in between them. She poked her finger back at him and at the door, screaming along, with the bed sheet up to her chin in her other hand and her back against the wall, as he attempted another step forward, though he ran into Brett's extended arm.

"Ricky! Too much, man!" Brett shouted, then nodded at the door. "Please go."

Quieted, Ricky looked down the barring arm, then swiveled his head slowly to look at him. "Put your hand down, boy," he grumbled, still wobbling.

"It's better that you leave," Brett nodded again, to Ricky sneering.

"Or what? Boy plays throwball?"

Without waiting for an answer he punched him hard in the stomach, to which Brett heaved and bent low, then aimed a second punch at his face but wide enough for Brett to dodge it, as Vivian screamed on. He almost fell on the bed with his momentum if not for Brett's tackle, then wrestled him in the middle of the floor and jabbed another elbow and a right fist into his abdomen before they took the table down with them. On top, Brett raised his fist to punch him but held it in the air above Ricky's palpitating eyelids.

Vivian jumped in the bed. "What are you doing? Hit him!"

"He's gone."

"He's dead?"

"No." Rising slowly, Brett kept his eyes on him, as Ricky began snoring through his open mouth next to the overturned table. "He banged his head pretty hard."

Cursing a few more swishy words, she dragged the sheets down from the bed with her to leap closer and picked the custard-squirting roll from the flattened pastry box on the floor to throw it at the motionless body.

"Hey, hey"—he grabbed her shoulder to hold her back. "Want to wake him up?"

She let herself be pulled back and unwound slowly. She turned to him big-eyed. "Come with me. Why stay in this hole?"

He opened his mouth, but only to breathe in, and looked down at Ricky, who had rolled his head to one side, then at her again. He grasped her shoulders above the rumpled bed sheet. "I can't. Not right now." He let his hands down. "You should go."

"Okay," she whispered. She raised on her toes to kiss him, then gathered her clothes from around the bed. A minute later she was in her bodysuit and cherry fur jacket, and sprang back to him as he lifted the table back upright. She wrapped her arms around him from behind and dabbed her lips on his cheek, then picked up her tote and glowed on her way to the door. "I'll call you."

By the time he'd scraped the last food spots off the floor, the flap of the pastry pack cracked beyond use. Ricky snored off abruptly and choked, then turned coughing on his side and the snoring picked up again. Hands on his waist, Brett watched him for a moment longer. He crouched and heaved him upright from under his arms, then staggered as he grabbed his arm to bring it over his own neck while bracing his left arm around him. Ricky slit his eyes open and groaned as they wobbled across the floor, then they almost collapsed while backing away from the swinging door. He firmed up a little in the cool air of the yard, on the way to the house's back steps.

Shoulder resting against the door, Brett tried the knob. "Unlock it," he said through his short breath.

"Ehh?" Ricky lifted his head slowly, then somehow

thumbed the right code in his palm.

Slamming the door open, they stumbled in. The air was as stale as the motley decor of boxes and furnishings, or almost. Brett kicked the obstructing tool case aside, then the two crates of ground-beef cans on his way to the single, oversized armchair, which he dropped Ricky in.

He caught his breath and ran his fingers back through his hair while looking around the cluttered room and kitchen alcove. He turned to Ricky once more. "Ricky... Ricky! Is the car ready?" He leaned closer. "When are we gonna leave?"

Dragging his feet closer to the chair, Ricky tried to sit higher. He groaned with his eyes shut and rotated his head to the other side of the sullied, floral upholstery. "I make the plan..." he mumbled.

"We made the plan. I told you everything. Bank, school, every fuckin' thing!"

He turned his head slowly and cracked his eyes open. "I make it perfect. They don't take me in no more." He stayed his sight on Brett's face briefly, then his eyelids weighed back down. "Perfect..."

———

With his palms united and arms wedging forward precisely between the two shadowy bands, Clarens then split the wedge outward and pushed the water back but, just like every other time, the bands remained equally spread apart and the space in between stayed inaccessible. He thrust up and broke above the water to fill his lungs then dove again, to which the bands wavered with the upper lane dividers, before reversing to their silent straightness under his breast strokes just above the bottom of the pool. At the wall turn, he glanced at whom appeared to be Lynden standing on the pool coping, and rose to the surface.

"Hey guy, where's Susan?"

Clarens removed his goggles, a smile in the corner of the mouth. "Is that why you finally showed up?" As Lynden stabbed his finger at him, he grabbed the lane divider and wiped the water off his face. "She'll begin next time. She's gone to see an outlet for rent."

"An outlet for rent?"

"I thought I told you. She's starting a nursery business."

Head slanted, Lynden kept stabbing his finger his way. "The girl's a kicker!" Chortling, he pulled his goggles over his head, then his belly quivered on above his slick black jams as he shook his slippers off. "If she needs an agent I can have Heslin write a referral," he said and snickered. "No, she's not pissed anymore."

Clarens hung on to the divider. "How do you know?"

"Gwyn…" Lynden shrugged, then brought his goggles over his eyes and jumped in with a large splash. He hardly went under, and grinned when his head poked above the water. "Lesson one: stay afloat!"

Past the end of the crowded counter, the free-form stair climbed wide off the barroom floor and then split into two narrow flights that swung to the opposite sides of the mezzanine landing.

"Now he's looking for financial planners to add to the realty group," Lynden griped on. "Whatever got to him."

"To whom?"

"Talbot! Guy, are you listening?"

"Sorry." Clarens switched back to him and reached for his ale. "I never really noticed that stair there."

"What?" Lynden turned around, hand always on his stein. "It's been there forever."

"Yes but, if you can make abstraction of that splitting flight behind it"—Clarens traced the stair with his finger—"you see how it narrows a little as it rotates? It's like pulling you up," he added, zipping his finger higher. "It's modifying the time frame, essentially."

Lynden swiveled back and brought the beer to his mouth. "Guy..."

Clarens managed a sip before a former colleague cheered at him on arrival, with two others following him through the bystanders.

Grinning, the colleague stepped closer and patted him on the shoulder. "How's farming?" he said, to their chuckling, and moved on to bump Lynden's fist too.

"She gives him horseback riding lessons," Lynden jested, to which they burst louder. "Seriously!"

As the first two grabbed stools, the third one took his turn to pat Clarens while holding his other hand low for a shake. "I want to thank you once more for the work you've done these past ten years to keep our clients happy," he nodded straight-faced, saying, "all of which, along with your office and assistant, have now been passed on to me." He chortled with Lynden as Clarens snorted amused, then he added, "Hey, you're not getting your old man's cabinet?"

"Uhh.... I will. I just didn't get the chance yet."

"So Clarens," another cut in, "starting up your own or something?"

"Not really"—Clarens shook his head. "At least not for a while."

"So then, what do you do?"

"Well," he drawled, when Lynden threw his arm around his neck and clucked, bumping his hanging fist in the air.

"Hahaha!..."

Widening his smile through the guffaws, Clarens turned to reach for his glass as the newcomers' orders arrived. More of the firm's employees showed up shortly, while the entire place clattered up with the after-hours upscale crowd. Drinking in small sips, he turned his head left and right to the flying jokes and gossip and threw in a question every now and then, which seemed to slow the laughter, if only for the moment. The garlic yams came fast and tangy, and fast they disappeared, but they did call for another round of beers. He grabbed his new quince ale and slipped off his chair. "I'll check out that mezz," he said to Lynden, nudging his head at the stair. "Coming?"

His face ruddy from his side chat, Lynden blanked. "What? No," he said, and turned back to the bar counter as Clarens walked away, but quickly turned again to shout over his shoulder, "More yams?"

"Sure. Just order."

He poked his finger at him and grinned, then turned swiftly back around.

Stuck against the wall by the second exit, the stair was conspicuously empty. Clarens stepped on, then felt the meandering satiny handrail on the way up. The mezzanine was empty too, and small, although the handful of mahogany tables and burgundy-upholstered chairs made for a cozy spot. He advanced on the open floor, then turned and inched backward through the chairs to look at the distancing stair. He laid his glass down on the last table behind him, then dragged the few chairs in front of him to the side to clear the path toward the curving stair's landing, which remained partially obstructed by the two tables in between, however. He stacked the chairs and dragged the tables out of the way to the back of the floor, where he stilled to look across the cleared floor, then he stepped sideways to change his point of view. Skirting along the higher ceiling, the clerestory crossed over the stair's pathway below and, fittingly, returned in a wide loop above the split, rounded landing. He snapped the view.

He moved on to the middle of the floor and shuffled in small steps to pivot around. On the full turn he stayed his sight on the pub staffer, who stared as he slowly climbed up the last step onto the landing.

Clarens smiled. "Sorry. I'll put them back."

"Not a problem..." the young man stumbled saying, and

walked off promptly to the private door across the floor.

With the seating back in place, Clarens grabbed his glass and went to the edge of the floor. He let his head tilt back with the drink. The shell lights sparkled out the clerestory above, off the glass cladding, against the indigo backdrop farther out. Below the handrail, the moving heads filled the floor from one tall sidewall to the other. His chair was still there, engulfed in the swarming.

# 23

The builder peered at the house, tracking the roof contour with his pointer, then lowered his head over the flat drawing in his graph and stretched it larger. As the clouds thinned out under the sun, he stepped farther back in the shade of the overhanging shrub with Clarens on his side. "So are these true dividers? Or decorative, over a solid glass cupola?"

"Oh, can it be cast solid in that size and shape?"

"It can," he pondered, "at a cost. Plus the reinforcing for the weight and AC booster. But you've got no joints, no worries."

Musing, Clarens looked out. "I'm thinking of true dividers, rather," he said, and extended his arm at the barn. "Like in that old apex window under the barn roof, with the three panes. I'd like to use the same spacing and relate to that. I mean…" He tilted his head. "The contrast with a clear cupola would be interesting too, although," he wavered once more, "I'd prefer staying with the original aesthetics. And I'd like to be able to open the panels all around, not just the top. It brings you closer to the outside I think." He edged his hand higher in the air. "You're climbing around the room, then up in there… then you're out there." He looked at the builder. "If that makes sense."

The builder removed his gaze from Clarens's slanted hand. "Yes." Clearing his voice, he annotated the drawing. "Then, what I suggest is that we make this a separate item also, and see if we can get started with something else before May," he said, then raised his head to speak up. "I'm sure we can build a prime residence here for you and Mrs. Mann," he slowed his last words saying as he turned fully toward Susan, who walked closer from the greenhouse behind.

"Connelly," she beamed. "Susan." In fitted jeans and a soil-stained shirt loose under her open, flapping vest, she took off her work gloves to hold her hand forth. Once the builder introduced himself, she pointed back to the decayed greenhouse. "And you can start with that!"

The builder laughed, taking quick turns to look at the greenhouse and Clarens, as she walked away.

"Kidding!" She pirouetted on the grating silt. "I'm in for anything he wants." She tipped her head at Clarens and then, a few unhurried steps farther on, she turned again and walked backward. "Still coming for a ride?" she shouted, before heading toward the house door.

Clarens looked at the builder. "You're sure you want to do this?" He passed a smile, to the builder's chuckling relief, then turned toward the greenhouse with him. "I guess that's one thing ready for the redux."


The trail narrowed through the gathering woods, then dried up into a rocky ditch as they began to descend. When it flattened again, the field glimpsed a grassy green through the thinning young trunks, ashore the lake that shimmered farther out.

"Which is an option," Clarens continued, one hand behind him on the extended cantle, the other wrapped around Susan, riding the horse with him, "and you'd see two columns instead of the low soffit, which makes the pool room more of a separate space."

She halted the horse and jumped off.

"Wait, it was my turn."

"I know." She grabbed the reins and led Leaf onto the meadow, where she turned to give him the reins, shoved his feet tighter in the stirrups and, before he could question it, she smooched the air and tapped the horse's hip.

Not to fall on his back as the horse took off, he squeezed it between his legs and so cued him into a full canter. He recovered and pulled the reins to slow it down and, as they turned along the water's edge, he glanced shaken back at her.

Laughing, she walked to the middle of the field. "You're doing great!"

He trotted Leaf around under her watch several times, then followed her instructions with a short canter across the field, between the lake and the woods. When he trotted it back he tried to hold it to a neat stop beside her, which turned out being too abrupt and caused him to jolt forward and his foot to slip off the stirrup. Clawing the saddle for grip, he slid off the horse to a crooked landing and, with nothing else to hold onto, he lost his balance and fell on his back.

She rushed to him. "Are you okay?" She knelt and leaned over him, her head against the cottony clouds.

He felt his lower back. "I think so…" He brought his hand under his head and exhaled, then smiled.

She brightened up and sat against him, bracing her arm on the ground on his other side. "Your grand finale there, huh?"

He shrugged. "Professional trait."

She chuckled and leaned lower to kiss him. Snorting, Leaf sounded like walking off. He laid his hand on her waist and cracked his eyes open to look straight up through her ruffled hair.

She slipped her hand inside his padded jacket. "Hey mister, how's dreaming?"

"Never been better."

"That can quickly get outdated."

He puffed and pressed his hand gently over hers, then brought them together to over his chest and kissed her. "Not sure it can." He looked toward the lake as she laid her head quiet on his shoulder. "See that glacier on the other side?" he murmured. "Right now, it would all melt in here."

Without budging, she grasped his shirt tight under his hand.

Wading through the shallow water, Leaf craned its neck low to drink anew, before moving on. They kept watching it cross over the host of flickering waves, Susan soon lying alongside him on the grass.

An icy droplet darted his cheek. A couple more did so as he squinted straight up, tracing the falling up to the small, darker cloud, which soon strayed away. She twitched below his shoulder when he raised her collar, as if coming out of snoozing, then her eyelashes tipped open in the corner of her eye but she kept quiet, as he returned his hand on her side.

"About... thirty-two years ago, we were here in Kierwoods one day," he said slowly, "a little lower down the lake shore. It must have also been in the fall. My father was watching his fishing rod and was resting still against a tree like that one there, and he saw this small hare move in really close. He managed to throw his net over it and brought it to us to pet it for a minute." He looked higher over the treetops. "The beat in that creature, through the fur and the net and all... It felt like it was plugged straight into raw life somewhere."

A dozen meters away, Leaf grazed diligently, reins looping low. The tan horn-bag beaconed on his back with the clouds' short-lived clearing.

"If that makes any sense," he added.

She bent her leg up slowly against his leg. "Am I a hare now?" she mumbled.

The horse nearly started at their laughter. She rose halfway to sitting, rubbed the grass off her hands, then lowered her collar and combed her hair back in a few long strokes. "At one point my dad would take me hunting every week, and he would rarely manage a clean shot. So yeah, I know what you mean."

He watched her tie her hair back in a low bun.

She looked over her shoulder at him. "Shall we snack? We have to head back soon." She turned her head and whistled sharp before he could rise.

———

Elbows forward on the table, Tara rolled her eyes up somewhere. "And then I did roller skating too."

"You did!" Brett perked up, while tuning his set to block out the bed's white-leather headboard behind him. "Remember when you and Daddy skated there together?"

"Uhh... Tuesday!"

He smiled. "And what else did you do today?"

As she rubbed her eye with her knuckles, Susan moved in from aside and fondled her over her bangs. "We're done I think," she said to Brett. "Wow! Amazing view you have there! What's with the dresser?"

"That... was left over," he said, twisting in the armchair toward the purple oval chest of drawers below the panoramic window, then stayed turned that way to look far out over the leaden city outskirts. It was getting dark early.

She broke, saying, "So now you're staying there till—"

"Actually, I got to go too," he interrupted her as the door downstairs slammed shut.

"Oh, I thought— Is everything okay Brett?"

"Sorry, got to go," he said, and hung up as Vivian treaded the last steps up with the familiar, striped packaging in her hand.

She scrunched her smiling lips and stepped close to flip the top of the flat package open and pass the steaming quiche under his chin. "Ehh?"

"Nice."

"What would I do without this deli!" she said, crossing the

plushy-carpeted floor to the dining area on the other side of the flat. She glanced over. "Who was that?"

He looked back outside. "What? Oh, Ricky."

"What does he want now?"

Quiet for a few more seconds, he rose abruptly and reached for his sweater beside the bed. "I can't stay. I've got to go finish something."

"Now? Brett..."

He zipped up and, head down, grabbed his jacket and rushed to the stair. "I'm sorry. I've got to go."

"Brett!"

Thumping down the steps behind him, she caught up with him downstairs as he slipped his second shoe on. "Brett! Why are you afraid of him?" she shrilled. "My father can send the police over!"

Hand on the doorknob, he turned his head to her.

Her brows wrinkled up high above her wet eyes as her lower lip quivered. "I don't understand!"

He exhaled. "I'm sorry. I can't right now."

He turned and walked out, to her bursting through the open door, "But why?"

He braced his hands atop the locked gate and jumped on it to flip over it, then hastened down the sidewalk and pulled his jacket on. He kept his sight on the peachy pavement tiles and their bas-reliefs of pastoral scenes, hands shoved in his pockets and exhaling deeply with every few steps.

Two streets down, the pavement changed to narrower, concrete slabs, then the striped joints disappeared also, and filler patches or just gravel mixed in. All of the same gray as the unfinished house walls sliding by and the fine drizzle taking hold. He pulled his hood over his head, shoved his hands back in, and peered at the nearing street corner. The street sign was missing, and the next one didn't read like anything familiar, but he strode on down the hill.

The blows kept coming, until his stepfather stuck his hand in between them to stop the fight. He bent close to examine his cheek, then grabbed his gloved hands in the large towel to wipe them, as his stepbrother started punching him again. When his hands were released they hung down heavy, but he did heave them up beside his face and peeped over the ring ropes, at the stair out of the basement, where his stepfather walked his mother away. She looked back over his embracing arm, before his second stepbrother came around from his other side and the blows intensified. They called his name loud in between.

As Brett twitched his head back, he hit the wall and slit his eyes open. He braced his elbow on the floor to sit higher against the wall, knocking an empty beer can rolling, just as the door opened wide. The backyard light beamed through the pairs of legs walking in, then Ricky switched the room light on in front of two other men. Pointing at Brett, he stepped aside to let them come forward, then glared at him. "You tell them you're free."

Brett swiped the back of his hand over his squinting eyes and struggled to rise. While one of the two men appeared to examine the door lock, the other stepped in slowly and looked around. He kicked the lone can to send it rolling from the middle of the floor back toward the ones littered next to Brett. "You," he nodded at him. "Come with us."

"What? Where?"

"More good place," the man said, when Ricky held his hands out and switched languages to query him in a raised voice. The man swished a curt reply and turned his head back to Brett, poking his chin at the suitcases beside the bed. "You take things. Now."

By the time Brett rubbed his eyes again, Ricky had downed his companion by the door and dashed his arm through to strike the man's gun-pulling hand. As the bullet sparked off the floor, he landed a lightning-fast punch in his face to fell him too, over the jarring cans, narrowly missing Brett who wobbled up onto his feet. Brett gazed at the moaning, slow-turning man, then back at Ricky, who picked up the handgun from the floor, set it in the man's hand, and clasped it over to shoot him in the neck.

"What are you doing?" Brett stumbled, hands up.

Ignoring him, Ricky tugged the inert arm toward the man creeping by the door to put a bullet in him also.

"What the hell is going on?" Brett yelled, as Ricky leaped to the door and stuck his head out briefly before shutting it closed.

"Your fuckin' bitch called the police, that's what's going on," he growled through his teeth, to Brett reeling to the sink to throw up.

He choked under Ricky's hand splashing cold water on his face and pulled back.

Ricky slapped him. "Get your things. One suitcase"—he raised his finger.

He made runs between the bed and the table as Brett scrambled through his belongings, then muttered the time a couple of times, stopped abruptly, and rolled one detective's body on its back with his foot to pump the heart, then the arm up and down. He clasped the gun over the deadened hand to zip another bullet in the neck of each twitching body as an awed Brett peeked on, then he snapped Brett's suitcase closed and pushed him with it to the door.

The outside looked just as eerie through the breath-condensing air. The rain was gone, but the saturated ground slushed under their rushing steps across the backyard to the corner of the house. Ricky switched off the driveway light, while the street lamppost shone on to twinkle in his bulging eyes.

"Time to roll. To the car"—he nodded at the garage, then called up his set to reverse the end car from the driveway row and park it in the street.

Brett sat still in the shaded passenger seat as the new round of voices neared and car doors chimed open from the end of the outlet's parking lot. He peeked out the opposite window at the leaving car. In the new silence, the sliver of yellow light cut through the packed cargo space behind him and crossed over the film-wrapped dashboard.

Fast steps creaked on the sandy pavement, then Ricky opened the rear passenger door and hung what looked like a dark-gray business outfit off the ceiling hook. He went around the car and sat in. "Like it?" he muttered.

Brett turned to glance at the outfit in its clear plastic sleeve, as they drove off. "Real nice," he muttered back, and felt the middle of his forehead. "Where to now?"

"North."

"But you haven't found a crossing."

"I will find a crossing," Ricky said, then snorted and shook his head. He clasped his hands on the steering wheel and veered hard on the dimming main road. Speeding up, he cleared his throat and lowered his window for the spit. "You still want your kid back? Ehh? Wanna leave this fuckin' place?"—he glared over. "'Cause I need my metal now!" he roared, weaving around another car, and jabbed his fist low over the console. "Ehh? Still want it?"

Brett frowned back at him, quiet. "I fuckin' want it."

———

The laser cut lower through the concrete block, but it switched off again as the machine's head swayed outside the margins. Rather irked, the showroom operator reseated the strap on Clarens's shoulder, then checked his grip on the machine's front and back handles. Clarens tipped the machine's head onto the block and ran his finger through the graph to lock the cut line over the physical mark anew, but he lost it when the sectional depth and guides all lit up.

"Like this"—the operator flicked the line over. "It snaps." He then gripped the gun alongside Clarens and helped him cut down the concrete block clean. He picked up the off-cut and weighed it in his hand. "Is this for home use?"

Removing his mask, Clarens smiled. "I haven't happened to touch one of these before, if that was the question."

Attempting a smile in return, the operator took the machine from his hands and docked it back in its powered stand. "It will happen, it will happen… Can always make it happen," he drawled and switched the display into demo mode, as Clarens stepped back onto the soft flooring strip. He wheeled the stand in line with the other machines and walked back toward the front of the showroom, but turned his head as Clarens didn't follow.

Keeping the apron on, Clarens weighed the trial block in his hand, then checked his set and skipped through his tasking matrix. "So I can take that one now. And also need a rotary and a class-5 printer."

In the garage, he left the laser-cutter case on the dolly and pushed the picture frames aside to make room in the car's rear bay. He slid the case in slowly, staying clear of the basket of anemones on the other side. All stooped in, he lingered over the flood of blue petals. Through the grassy scent, the ribbon sheered around the dainty, hand-fashioned "Susan's Darlings" tag.


The movie was playing quietly at half-size over the end of the bed, although his mother had fallen asleep. He nodded at the nurse behind him, who turned and left the room, then he stepped around the bed to place the flower basket on the sideboard by the window.

He turned to the bed. She lay long under the purplish comforter, with her hands crossed below the middle of her chest and her chin dropping with the open mouth. Her untied, glittering-white hair split almost symmetrically beside her face to run down onto the deeper purple of the pillow.

He slowly dragged one of the armchairs closer to the bed and then sat and watched the movie for a minute, then just looked that way. He turned the sound volume to barely audible and looked at her again. He reached for the small sketchpad and clutch-pencil in his chest pocket and began honing over the stairs in the front-page sketch.

Next time he heard anything, it was the private ring in his ear.

"For God's sake Clarens, I called three times!"

Blinking hard, he sat up in the chair and gawked at his palm and his scowling sister. "Sorry, I fell asleep," he uttered low and glanced aside at his mother who, still sleeping, had turned on her side.

"You fell asleep? You mean you blanked out?" his sister railed, as he felt his ear and rose. "You were supposed to confirm!"

He stepped to the entry vestibule. "I fell asleep. I was early, I lay back, and fell asleep."

"They don't even let you sleep there."

"It just happened," he spelled out. "It could also happen if you spent time with her for more than fifteen minutes, all right?"

"Oh, oh"—she dropped her head back—"so neither that just happened."

He stopped. "What?"

"It's not genuine. You didn't *want* it to happen."

Bending inside the wall turn, he firmed his tone. "I'm here, it happened, I meant it that way."

"Oh, just spare me your meanings and stuff." Seemingly in the driver seat of her car, she looked over her shoulder.

276

"Stop it! We're going back!" she yelled over the background shrills, then turned her scowl forward again. "You ruined my afternoon, that's what happened. That actually, objectively, happened. Unlike much ever in your... evasive reality."

He stayed bent down after she hung up, then straightened and turned around slowly to stare out over the room. The pole lights beamed in the dusky sky above the rear gardens, with the room's interior scattered over the mirroring glass in between. In staggered, pale shapes, the back-wall light gradient just discernable left of the middle, his contour bounding it on one side.

The reddish tag drew his stare to the anemones basket below. He stepped to the chair and crouched to pick the sketchpad and pencil from the floor, then leaned closer to the bed. She barely snored, but her hair glittered on.

# 24

Wedging the bottom branches apart, Ricky brought the binoculars to his eyes with the other hand as Brett crawled closer behind the skimpy brush. His chin and nose struck out below the fitted camouflage cap, which managed to compress his hair down to only the virile ends spilling over his collar. He swept wide and paused briefly over the grounds across the dry creek on the far right, then swept all the way to the left, just as steady. "This works," he muttered, a trace of steam leaving his mouth, then handed the binoculars to Brett and nudged his chin to the right while holding the branches still. "Between the big rocks. Slow."

The north-facing slope was as rocky as all others, albeit the crevice that climbed it at an angle between the two larger boulders rendered it less steep. Beyond, the shrubs darkened into what looked like the fringe of a forest. "But the band is crossing uphill," Brett said, sweeping back.

"The band does nothing, just shows you the border. The heads are in the rocks, trees, sky, every fuckin' where," Ricky said, and let the branches unwind, then, rolling to his other side, he groped his genitals at the sky with a grunt. "Wait here," he added and wormed backward on his belly down from the small ridge, then rose to squatting steps to reach the gear.

He picked up the captive hare and seemed to tweak the snare loose as he tossed the startled animal away from the backpack, then reached in, when the hare took off. He lunged after it toward the ridge, then leaped back to grab his rifle and, as it raced down the creek bed, he fired a shot slightly beside it, which made it change direction toward the border marking. A quiet monotone sounded when it crossed the band, for a mere couple of seconds. Grunting anew, he stood up in full view to aim at the runaway hare and took it out with a single shot, as Brett lay put behind the brush, then, ducking inside his high collar and with his face deep in the shade of the cap, he walked over the ridge. A minute later, the border warning went off as he crossed over, this time intensifying while Ricky advanced to search for the game. He turned around unrushed and, head ever down, he held the animal up in display while walking back to this side of the border, to which the sound ceased.

"Can shit and they watch your hole, ehh?" he said when back behind the ridge, then spit and tossed the hare by the loosened trap.

Brett stepped closer, snug in his neoprene jacket, and watched him dust off. He nodded at the twitching animal. "Can you just…"

"What?" Ricky frowned, then crouched to it to slit its throat, wiped the blade clean on his pants and clicked it in to drop it back in his thigh pocket. He cupped his hands at his mouth and rubbed them together slowly as he scanned the humpy grounds along the border creek. He glanced right across it as he turned to look the other way. He put his gloves on, threw the backpack in Brett's arms, then snatched the dripping hare in the trap's noose and brought his rifle over the shoulder. "One more. This way."

————

With the flames twiddling before his eyes, Brett tore through the tough meat and worked his jaws slowly.

Beside him, Ricky bent forward on his folding stool to pitch a couple more sticks in the fire, then moved the grill out of the smoke column and poured more wine over the leftover animal quarters. He took another bite off his piece, then munched with his elbows on his knees and looked over. "Good?"

Brett pushed his chin out to help the meat lump get down his throat. "Yeah, a little hard. Just never had fox before."

Reds and yellows dancing in his eyes, Ricky worked on his hind bone. "Be hard to be free, ehh?"

Brett nodded at the grill. "Apparently not always."

Ricky snorted, then rose and took a few steps away, opposite from the tents. His back to the fire, he began urinating. "So what do you do when you go to your country, my friend?"

Brett stared at his cap between the hunched shoulders, then back at the flames. "Don't know. Straighten up a few accounts, take care of my daughter," he said, squinting through the shifting smoke. "Then I might just lie low somewhere and get fuckin' numb."

Ricky turned around. "You and me…" he lagged his words, hand inside his open fly, "we can't get no numb, my friend." He wiped on his pants as he plodded back toward his stool and picked up his knife. "You just get what's yours to get," he said, slicing the shiny blade through the dark meat.

"I'm just saying. To get out of that goody politics bullshit," Brett griped, and tossed the cartilage-laden bone in the fire. He turned his head to Ricky who, munching on, looked at him impassive. "You know, to somewhere where you get what you get and are who you are."

Ricky staked another carving off the grill with the tip of the knife and, a grin on his half-shaded face, he stuck it under Brett's nose. "Free."

Brett pulled the steaming piece off the blade. "Right." He joggled it between his blackened fingertips and took the shredding bite. He watched Ricky stoke the fire. "How did they get you the second time? In the Commons."

"Some fucker turned me in."

"Huh… Trying again?"

"No, fuck this." He peeked around. "Let them stay in their fuckin' glass. I know better place." He pulled the grill aside to spill more wine over the remaining carcass. "People don't make the place, nature makes the place," he said through the smoke, then brought the bottle to his mouth and looked over. "Ehh?" He guzzled as Brett didn't respond, then swiped his sleeve over his mouth and held the bottle out to him with a firm hand, to which Brett reached for his cup beside the chair and held it under the bottle. He tutted and hit the rim with the bottleneck as he filled the cup to a messy spill, then thrust his head back to empty the bottle in his mouth. As he tossed it on the ground, he kept looking up. Brett did too. The smoke went almost straight up now, hazing grays into the pitch-black sky. Another spark flit up with it but it quickly dulled into ash and glided down to the side, a little slower than the brighter flake that came down from much higher. They watched a few more snowflakes fall.

Ricky graphed up his wristset and frowned over the glimmering weather aerial, then rose and hastened toward the car under the shrubs. "We leave in the morning."

Brett wiped his greasy fingers hard and tossed the crumpled napkin in the fire. He twitched with the sudden shiver as he stood up, then let his arms unwind slowly. "I'll shave then—"

"No!" Ricky said over his shoulder, then turned to the lifting cargo door. "Before we leave."

————

Eyes shut, Clarens arched his neck back and pressed the top of his head into the cushioned bed headboard, then let his lungs deplete. He felt the silk of Susan's nightgown weigh down with her breast on his chest, then her lips on his, for a glimpse of the secret land of promise, under the sea of slow-weaving, scented, dark strands. She rolled lazy back next to him as he opened his eyes, then pulled the slack quilt over and reached for his hand under it.

He turned to her slitting eyes and eased a smile too. The 7:40 time digits behind her read out of sync with the look of dawn outside, even if overcast. A soft square of daylight left the top of the window to fade onto the obscure ceiling.

"I was thinking," he said, bringing his free hand up. "If this was the ceiling in the other bedroom, and you cut an opening along this side and half of that side, for the stair… What if you made another cutout along the other side?"—he pointed around, then ran his thumb and index, closely spaced apart, on an arc through the air. "Just a sliver opening, to counterbalance the one for the stair, and get the light from the cupola down that wall too." He paused his hand as his gaze circled the ceiling still. "Then imagine the upstairs, with glass all around, and the floor detached from all three walls… It sort of makes it float." He turned his head to her. "Don't you think?"

From staring past his hand at the lightening window, she switched to the ceiling and murmured a "hmm." She pushed back the wisps of hair crossing her face and removed her other hand from his to feel his arm. "You know best. You've drawn it so many times," she said, and flipped the quilt over to rise and pluck her nightgown down. "I have to get going. I have this presentation, so I'll take Tara to the school bus."

"Me too. The builder's here in half an hour." He rose on his side of the bed and watched her tiptoe to the bathroom. "I told him about the countertop."

"Great," she said quietly, hair swaying as she glanced a smile over.


The two workers carried the first bundle of downspouts

over to lay it next to the new gutters at the base of the porch, then went back to the truck.

The builder bent to the spouts and slashed the wrapping on the three-meter-long side with his pocket cutter, then held down the rolling spouts. He grabbed the one by Clarens's boot and lifted one end up, turning it in his hands until the stamping came atop. "Exact replica," he boasted, leaning shoulder to shoulder with him, and pointed to the lower marking. "Titanium."

"Ayland Metals, 2120," Clarens read slowly. "Nice!" He stepped back to let the workers lay down another bundle. "Now, if we only had the time," he said and squinted up through the ever-thriving snowflakes, when the barn door rolled open.

Driving by, Susan waved her hand short. He did too, then watched her speed down the driveway.

"Nah, just that late May flurry," the builder said, glancing across the sky, then put the spout back down. "So you've decided on the sky room?"

"Almost. But, something else… Over here."

Boots strapped over his calves, Clarens treaded the whitening ground toward the west side of the house then turned and made a few steps backward, away from the round-gabled façade. He took his gloves off and reached in his jacket for the folded sketch, with the builder back on his side. "Those two windows"—he pointed at the wall under the porch extension, then at the drawing. "If we had only one large one and removed the wall in the middle… For this," he added, turning all around to the row of silvery beeches and the view beyond them out west.

Taking turns between the view and the sketch, the builder considered. "Well, I can price it. Moment frame all around, vintage plating…" He smiled briskly. "But this would be a spring job."

"Absolutely." Clarens handed him the folded paper and

rubbed his hands together before his mouth. "I'm ready for the spring."

They chuckled and walked back to the roofing crew, who had already aligned the scaffolding tripods in place. They all watched the legs self-level and the telescoping arms branch out, when Clarens turned aside to take Susan's call.

"You're all right? Where?"


The wipers hustled on as he almost flew the car over the last road top, before slowing for the turn. Midway through it, his old car lay slanted off the road with its underneath pinned atop a flat boulder and the front wheel free in the air, at the end of the still visible skidding path.

He pulled over and jumped out, as Susan opened the passenger door and held onto the frame to climb out of the car. She looked down as they walked toward each other, then glimpsed him with tearful eyes and landed her face on his shoulder. "I'm sorry!"

He stroked her back with the long hug. "First snow. Just leave it on auto."

"No…" she sobbed, quivering in his arms. "I'm sorry I left like that."

"It's nothing. I understand."

She sniffled, then bumped her damp bun into his chin as she turned the other way. "It's just that … Maybe I'm touchy on this, but I felt like you weren't there. You know? All the restoration, the sky room, the old pictures." She turned her face back into his shoulder. "I'm sorry, it's just my silly anxieties."

He raised his head and looked over the roadside berm. The valley behind was no more, or just a long shade crossing slowly through the soft, particulated matter. "No, you're right. I should've put that dome painting somewhere else."

"No, no, I like it." She pulled her head back to look at him, then rocked him gently. "I just want you there too."

As he felt his eyes moisten, he stroked her back higher to bring her on his shoulder anew. Turned this way, her laden eyelashes dripped warm inside his neck, while flakes melted into her hair strands below his cheek. "I'm trying," he said. "The project… is the one thing I can get a grip on. And it wouldn't make sense without you."

She tried to raise her head but he didn't let her. She firmed her arms around him. "I'm so sorry."

They swayed slightly back and forth, snow building on their shoulders. A car sailed by, side jets twirling the snow, then picked up as he nodded at the driver.

He eased back and pulled his gloves out of his pocket. "Take my car. Perhaps you can still make it."

"You're sure?"

"Absolutely. I'll get a tow back."

She kissed him, then her lashes blurred again around the sparkling green. She pulled back with a trembling smile, then hustled in small steps down the berm to the new car. "Can I keep it to pick up Tara too?" she shouted from inside the open door.

He raised his hand high, then watched her drive away till the dimming red strip disappeared beyond the next road turn.

———

Having boxed up the camping pad, Ricky shoved it under the brush and ripped two branches off to shuffle them over the exposed end. He rushed to the fire pit and hurled the blackened stones away, then ripped a larger limb and to smudge the wet ash into the snow with it. He scattered it in pieces and dusted off while striding toward the car, where Brett zipped up his one-piece outfit to under his chin before settling in next to him.

He reached for the metal case inside the console and

flipped the top open, then jiggled the two rubber bracelets out of their molded slots. He handed one to Brett and darted a glance over, then latched the other one onto his right wrist. Brett did the same, then pivoted his seat outward too and tapped the bracelet's input pad, pausing between each digit registration. He stilled until Ricky finished entering his own code, when the two bracelets beeped and clicked locked at the same time.

Raised high, the car rocked and jolted over the unmarked terrain. Ricky kept switching his eyes between the topographic mapping under the windshield and the intensifying snowfall outside, swishing a curse every time they went over larger brush or something hard clunked the underside of the car. Ten minutes into it they slowed down and made the sharp turn south, then pulled behind the first mound when they were half a kilometer from the border mark.

Ricky brought up the weather overlay, where the heavier snowfall looked just about to move in. They pulled the scan-block masks over their heads and waited fixed. Brett glimpsed the time, then his unperturbed, substituted face in the inside viewer.

In another twenty minutes everything but the shallow ridge a few hundred meters out had disappeared, while a coat of sleet covered the car hood. "Perfect..." Ricky murmured, and powered up to drive abruptly out in the open.

The car rocked and jolted again, only much harder, as they headed for the lower end of the ridge. They steered wide around it and dived into the brook descending to the other side, wheels bumping the jutting rocks as the air-float couldn't keep up, then flew between the large boulders on the opposite slope up. The border warning pierced sharp through the rattles and rushing blood. Pushing just as hard, Ricky flicked the chronometer on. His hands kept wriggling left and right with the steering as they reached the new plateau and switched back to traction. He pulled his mask off and tossed it over his shoulder. His back tight against the seat, Brett followed suit, then stretched his arm behind him to turn the dummy off and tug it down from the bench to behind his seat. The wipers kept working the windshield clear, as futile as that seemed through the dense downfall, albeit the mapping did show the road closing in. Forty seconds in, the ditch came early but, jets on and bouncing hard off the other rim, the vehicle managed to land on its wheels and Ricky skidded a turn onto the narrow two lanes. He maxed the power once more and lowered the car down through another skid-limit turn, glancing in the rear viewer. "It starts to fuckin' stick."

No jet or wheel tracks showed on either way, or the sleet was too wet to tell, until they hit the junction and several patterns mixed in. At eighty-two seconds they slowed abruptly, just as the highway grayed fuzzy into view, and jounced the car off the road into the woods. Ricky cut off the mains and jumped out, pulled the sweeper out of the rear trunk, and, ever glancing at the skies, sprinted to the road to feather out the car trail backward into the woods. He leaped around the car, as Brett struggled to pull the scan scrambler over it, and snatched the remaining corner of the fabric to yank it over the rear bumper and to the ground.

"Down!" he whispered loud and rolled under the car, butting shoulders with Brett below the mud-dripping center beam. He silenced his breathing and inched aside on his back, then eased his head out the side of the car. He eased back in and turned his eye corner to Brett, nudging his chin up. They stemmed their breathing mist.

The brown drip seemed to fall every two seconds. Under the nylon outfit, the wet ground didn't feel cold or hard, although his back arched up a little. He dragged out the knotted, poking wood from under him. The ground didn't feel cold still. Just the hissing loudened inside his ears.

Ricky gave it another three minutes, then crept aside to peep up again. He moved a little farther, before jabbing him and rolling out from under the car.

He flung the cover over to expose the rear hatch, then let Brett fold it up as he knelt to deploy the first jack. Moments later, he clacked the last of the new wheels on its hub, while Brett heaved the removed oversized wheels inside the car. Bent backward and crimpling his face red, Ricky brought the last one to the opposite rear passenger door and crammed it into the empty quarter in line with the other three.

"Body!" he ordered while slapping the fake bench back on, to which Brett rushed the car body parts out and began placing them by their mark around the car.

Catching his breath, he squinted through the cottoned tree crowns as Ricky depleted the power-wash tank over the car, then watched him swap the parts, just as manic and sure-handed. He leaped at his menacing glance and raced around the car again to collect the old scattered parts, then strove to fit them all back in the case.

Having gummed and sprayed the last joint flush to the new body, Ricky tossed his steaming tools in the trunk and bumped him aside to stamp and shatter the parts inside the case. "Get in the fuckin' suit!" Glancing at the clouds, he tugged his protective outfit down from over his spotless business wear alongside Brett, shoved them both in, and tossed the case in the trunk too.

Out of the woods, Brett toggled his sight between the empty road and Ricky feathering their trail into the sleet on the shoulder, then drove off the moment he jumped back in on the rear bench, keeping the car on the whitening tracks. He peeked down as Ricky reached inside the center console to pull out a long-barreled handgun, then frowned in the viewer at him. "Is that a firearm?"

Ricky snapped the magazine back in and checked the safety. "As I said," he sneered and lay down below the bench. "They don't take me in again."

"But what did we—"

"Drive!"

Brett grasped the wheel over. Through the double turn the road began to descend toward the highway. The speed read seventy, but he didn't seem to get much closer.

"Car…" he muttered, and kept the course as a vehicle approached in the opposite lane. The single passenger of the plain four-seater barely glanced over.

Under the light traffic on the highway aqueduct, the ramps looked quiet. He crossed under and veered left on the ramp, although the frail shadow above appeared to stay with him. He sped up smoothly to merge behind the first passing car and switched to auto-drive. A long few seconds through it, the drone moved on to the next row of cars, before suddenly flying off with two police vehicles that flashed by the opposite way. He whisked his hand back through his hair, picked the inner corners of his eyes, then felt the neck of his jacket around, all neat. The wrapping gone, the dashboard and front seats looked impeccable. He loosened his zipper a jot.

From the fast lane, the front end of another car pushed slowly through the whirling flakes in the side of the viewer. He played the recorded call over the dashboard and talked over Tara's smile as the car inched by, then glimpsed the rear of the distancing police vehicle. When the next one went by, the flurry had lightened up, though the midmorning traffic sprouted through the Ayland suburbs.

# 25

Shoulders even, Brett spared a nod and walked by the attendant toward the safes area. Number fifty-two sharpened up below the hair-thin gridline in the middle of the nearing wall. He looked down to input the passphrase in his palm. Access was denied. He raced his fingers through the dial again as he slowed before the box, but the bank's field still didn't allow him in. "Bitch…" He fixated the pinhead red light, then turned around and walked back to the courtesy counter to ask for Ethel.

The attendant rose slowly from his desk. "Ethel… We don't have an Ethel here, sir. Can I assist you?"

Brett glanced at the riverbed wall across the lobby. "Ethel. Thirty-something, short brown hair."

Gawking, the young man shook his head. "Perhaps before I started." He drooped slightly as he held his hands together low over his starchy teal jacket. "I can ask the manager."

Brett idled, then shifted his weight. "It's just that she knew the drill," he said, tapping the counter, and pulled a smile. "Triple-digit environment, huh? Have one of those enablers handy?" he added quickly, nipping his set off the wristband, then pulled his sleeve over the blinking rubber bracelet and brought his hands over the counter. "You know…" He tipped the set's aperture open under the attendant's eyes and clawed the tiny pin out. "For my access key."

"Oh, yes," the attendant said, and reached for the lower

shelf. "I also need your ID on, sir."

"That too, of course," Brett waffled as the attendant stared blank from across the counter, then tapped the slab again. "You know what, I don't even need this now"—he pinned the key back in the set, nodding a smile. "Thanks though!"

He glimpsed the shadows behind the partition wall as he turned, then pushed his bag strap higher on his shoulder and walked stark to the front doors.

Out of the elevator, he glanced over the garage floor, now full. He mapped the car's spot and strode down the self-drive aisle, scowling at the floor flashers.

A small brown leaf stuck to the rear bumper of the car. He flicked it off in passing and got in. He held the bag on his lap and didn't turn to the rustling behind, then felt Ricky's breath on the side of his neck.

"Show me."

He kept looking out. "We'll get it. She changed the passphrase."

The breathing stopped, then the blow shuddered the back of the seat. "My friend…"

"I said we'll get it!" he said over his shoulder. "Plan B!"

"No, we get her first!"

"How are we gonna get her first, huh?"

They halted, only breathing faster.

Brett glanced at the time, then wiped the drops of sweat off his hairline. "It's only eleven. We should go there."

Under the scarce, whitened branches, a few cars colored the sides of the street. Brett pulled over on the park side, then sat still and watched the school's garage entrance a hundred meters down on the other side. The yellow cleaner wiped the front courtyard in slow passes from side to side, the glossy pavement steaming dry behind it. No one went in or out the front doors, other than the staffer who checked on the machine's progress, then swept out a fleck of sleet from the airlock. One car pulled in the drop-off but didn't stop, and drove out to turn into the garage entryway instead, like all others.

"Wasn't that a Hanjing?" Ricky muttered.

"It's dark green. Unless she bought her own car."

"Call her."

Brett locked his jaws and turned his head to the empty passenger seat. From the corner of his eye, he glimpsed Ricky lying low on the back bench. He looked out the windshield again, grasped the steering wheel, and pulled out of the street parking spot. He wheeled past the front court and to the garage, where he stopped under the glass canopy of the gateway. The light remained red and a young woman's face beamed before the dashboard. "I'm sorry, I can't read your ID. Please ensure it is on."

He smiled back. "It's updating, just had surgery. But I should be on your list there."

It took a moment for a live figure to glitter over. "The garage is for authorized guardians, sir. Would you like me to authorize you with the primary guardian at this time?"

"Uhh… no, I'll talk to her. I'm too early anyway," he said, and tipped his lax hand up while swiveling the car around. Back outside, he drove away and made a left turn on the quiet side street around the school grounds.

Ricky rose up close behind his seat. "Now we call her."

"To do what? Chitchat? We follow the plan."

"We don't wait here with no metal, ehh!"

Head turned away from his grumbling, Brett scanned the rear of the two-story school building, which ended in a tilted glass wall overlooking the playgrounds. The busy skating track snaked through it, though all enclosed now in clear, square tubing and yellow-dotted with access doors in between the

292

connecting segments. He slowed further to sweep over the track, all the way to the point where it wound out tangent to the fence near the end of the yard. He made a right turn on the next street, opposite from the school, where he U-turned and pulled over, then dimmed the windows a shade and reached for the binoculars. The shrieks and shouts came alive through the lenses, and his heart throbbed closer yet. The children looked to all be of kindergarten age, though, if not older.

Ushered by the same two school staffers, a new group swapped in every ten minutes, the fourth one now. He blinked hard a few times, then pressed the binocular's rims against his eyebrows anew. Two boys raced through the turn, with the first one bumping into a slower one in front of them and knocking down all three, then a couple of girls added to the merry pileup from behind. Ruby of laughter, they crawled against the tube wall and let the rest flow by in a busy line of colors, helmets, and fluttering hair. He picked on the long curls flashing by, then ticked his sight to the next ones, rather blond and wavy however, when Ricky held the binoculars down from his eyes. Wiping his greasy forehead, he glanced at the time and looked aside over the passenger seat. "This one or the next. Must be."

Ricky let go with a jerk of the hand and rustled low again. Lenses back to his eyes, Brett searched on. The children had spread apart somewhat, in pairs and threesomes, with some alone in between. The two boys came wobbling round again, heading a row of slower red-helmeted children. Coiling over one's neck, the brown hair looked too short, but the boat scrunchie was there, under the brim of the helmet, flashing pink. His eyes blurred, an instant before he put the binoculars down and slid the door open. "She's there."

He stepped out of the car and crossed the street, then walked by the light metal fencing, glimpsing her as she went around the far side of the track. He slowed to time meeting her where the track touched upon the sidewalk, stretched his arm through the horizontal fence bars, and, smiling, he rapped the tube's glass a few times as she skated by. She jolted and almost fell, then tottered back with her hands tapping the tubing inside. He stuck his finger at the near access door until she understood and stepped out.

"Daddy?"

"Angel!" He reached through the bars one more time to feel her shoulder, then her arm down. "I'll see you in a bit," he said, slipping the little sticker under her school bracelet. "But don't tell anything to Mommy. Promise?"

He turned her around with a pat on her buttocks and jabbed the flimsy door shut, then walked on. He twitched his knit hat and zipped his jacket slowly over his suit, then crossed the street to stroll toward the park. He paced up to circle the block instead, then rushed on the back street to the car, where Ricky tracked Tara on his set.

"Drive!"

They zagged through the small neighborhood to come out at the far end of the park and pulled over, but drove right off again as the tracker moved into the school garage. It traveled out in the street just as the school came into sight over the car roofs ahead. They switched to the passing lane and drove by the tracking, steel-blue vehicle.

"It's her."

"Some fuckin' car," Ricky muttered, turning his head in the window corner. Now in his sporty vest, he pulled his cap on as Brett sped ahead.

They turned sharp on the second side street and pulled over for Ricky to jump out and go jog in place a few meters from the quiet street corner as Brett stepped out too. Ricky let another car go by, then leaped to cross the street diagonally as Susan came to a stop. He looked for traffic the other way and slipped, tagging the front of the car before falling on his knees, then stayed there feeling his lower back as Susan rushed out to him. He put a foot on the ground and his arm tight around her neck to rise, eyes blazing, as they struggled to the sidewalk and Brett walked around the other side of her car. Behind the new steering wheel, Brett slid the door closed on the bypassing line of cars.

"Daddy!"

He tried a smile and turned to Tara in the backseat. Stroking her knee, he glanced down the side street where Ricky pulled Susan into his car, his arm still around her neck. He breathed in, switched to manual override, and cast Susan's ID off his set.

"Where is Mommy?"

"She's coming. In the other car."


Water dripping down his nose, he straightened up above the sink to wipe his face and then his hands before his stern reflection in the mirror, when he received the call. He tossed the cloth and rushed to the end toilet stall, feeling his earlobe.

"She left. Check image, ehh."

He sat and brought up the feed in his palm. In the front and back surround views, Susan stepped out of the elevator and crossed the busy garage hub toward the street-exiting doors. It looked like the front feed-pin lay on the left side of her chest, over the wide-collared beige coat. She quivered her chin, flicking her eyes from one side to another, above the bruise on her cheek. She walked onto the main floor of the shell. The image changed hues and jolted along, although he did recognize the jewelry outlet display, then the Sargent Bank sign closing in.

"Nothing stupid, or she's gone," Ricky hissed over.

She nodded and brought her hand to her mouth, about to burst, then kept her head low while walking in and to the safe deposit boxes. She stopped and checked her set in the middle of the empty room. In the lobby behind her, the attendant escorted a stooping silhouette all the way to the side office door, then returned slowly to his desk and looked her way. She stepped closer to the wall grid, holding her finger out as she searched over the boxes, then checked her set again. The young man swung by his desk without sitting and closed in. "Just sit…" Brett muttered, then coughed dry as steps squeaked inside the restroom and into the next stall, with the door clicking shut.

Susan swung around to the attendant, who had offered to help. "Yes. Number fifty-two."

"Fifty-two…" He led her to the box, then stepped away as stiff and quiet while she dithered her fingers in her palm in front of the closed door, but then turned back around. "Fifty-two. We placed a block on it earlier today, actually."

She swung to him, her hair flying over the view, and smiled just as startled. "What?"

Brett brought his fist to his forehead and slipped to the edge of the toilet seat. "Fuck, fuck, fuck," he whispered, as Ricky cursed in his ear. "Should be fine," he scrambled to type in, by which time the attendant had led Susan to the partition wall in the lobby and through the opening to the first office enclosure on the other side where, at a wide desk, the manager raised her head.

Coughing another expletive, Brett rose and stepped out of the stall, his sight on the curly-blond figure in his hand. He palmed her as the security staffer stared at him from his open stall door, crimped his lips in the mirror, then rushed to rinse his hands and walked out onto the garage floor.

"He's in training, I apologize," he heard the manager say as the audio went on. "This won't take a minute, but I'll need you to consent to this new bio-ray…"

He brought his graph back up as he approached the car. On the edge of the armchair, Susan clasped her hands in her lap, eyes flitting over the manager's desk. Inside the car, Tara had fallen asleep, though the game was still playing. He sat in the front seat and watched on. Susan just gazed now.

"Can I see this?" she asked, reaching for the half-oval glass pot that somehow rested its rounded bottom in a single point on the desk.

"Of course. Beautiful, isn't it?"

"Yes..." She held the small pot before her, flashing the view as she ran her hand over it. "It is." The pot's flat top was closed except for an orifice allowing the stem of the miniature plant to grow out, while inside the clear glass, its roots were entirely visible within the transparent granular material. She felt the rim around once more, slowing her finger over one point, when a tear appeared to cross her cheek. Behind the steering wheel, Brett pressed his fist against his forehead anew. She almost dropped the pot as she rushed to wipe her tear, before setting it back on the desk.

"Are you all right?"

"Yes," she uttered low, her chin beginning to quiver as the manager fixed on her.

"Are you sure?"

She twitched at Ricky's yell and brought her hand to her earlobe, then stood up and tossed her hair back while the manager came around the desk. "Yes, just..." She pulled her lips into a terse smile. "Is it done?"

Tall and pale against the rich pink of her lips, the manager beamed over the feed-pin. "All done. You need help out with your contents, Ms. Connelly?"

"Oh no, thank you," Susan said, and stepped ahead of her out of the enclosure. "Thank you so much!" She threw another smile over her shoulder and hastened across the lobby floor, as the blond curls blurred motionless in the wall opening behind for a moment longer.

Minutes later, she turned the street corner around the deli terrace with the indistinct black bag low in her hand. A late luncher turned his head to measure her down, then, with the swarming in the garage hub all gone, she rushed to the self-drive elevators.

"C3664," Ricky instructed.

"I want to talk to my daughter."

"You talk, you talk. When I say."

Three levels under, she walked out on the empty floor and to the pedestrian aisle. At the first branching, she stumbled and tossed her head left and right at the signage array.

"Six, left."

As she rushed on, the fading elevator doors slid open again behind her and a golden tuft fluttered atop the thin silhouette, which quickly moved to the side aisle.

"Slow..." Ricky said. "She followed you!"

"What? Who followed me?"

"Bitch! What was that bowl? What did you fuckin' tell her?"

Panicked, she hunched down. "I didn't—"

"Kid is gone!"

She burst, her voice crumbling. "I didn't tell her anything! Please! You saw me!"

"She didn't tell anything," Brett typed in. "Stop!"

"Shut up! Walk slow," Ricky said, then popped up on Brett's graph, teeth gritting. "You go to her now!"

"What? To do what?"

"Now!"

Brett looked over his shoulder. Tara had sunk her cheek into the side-rest. He lowered the volume further and reset the game, then slipped out of the car and raced to the elevator.

Out on the C-three level he kept tracking Susan and craning his head over the car roofs while switching aisles. He let his head down to whisper again, "To do what?" He spotted her past the two parking tiers in sector five ahead, then glanced around the garage as he closed in on her. Between the columns and the few moving cars, he glimpsed the blond at the end of the next tier over. "To do what?" he prompted once more under his breath.

"You kiss her and I come get you."

"What?"

"Go!" Ricky yelled.

"I can't do that!"

"Go!"

His footsteps lighter with each breath, he crossed through the cars to the pedestrian aisle in the middle of the tier. A trace of chypre lingered behind her ruffled, waving dark hair. He quickened his last steps.

"You turn and kiss him," Ricky voiced-over the feed.

She slowed to a stop. "What?" She turned, her reddened eyes growing wide. "Brett?"

"Susan, I didn't—"

"Kiss! Fuckin' kiss!"

He caught her in his arms as she wobbled and kissed her, with the bag thumping the floor. He wrapped his arms around her trembling body, her tears salty on his lips. He turned slightly with her and peeked through her hair at the garage behind, where the bank manager had stopped at the far end of the tier and looked elsewhere before walking away. On the side aisle, Ricky drove by and pulled into the nearest empty spot. Pressing the front feed-pins between their chests, Brett grasped Susan's shoulders and pulled his head back. "Do what he says," he whispered before she could utter anything, "or this dick will take Tara and might kill us both."

Eyes flooded, she choked. "Wh-what are you doing here?"

Holding her arm, he reached down for the bag and walked her to the car. He glanced over by the opening door, his eyes wetting too, then nudged her in.

His front seat swiveled inward, Ricky grabbed the bag from Brett's hand and dropped it on his lap next to the muffled pistol in his other hand. He brought out a platinum bar and ran his pocket assayer over it, as Susan, straining backward on the makeshift bench, held her boots tightly together over the straws of tape littering the car floor. His hand chinked the bars inside the bag as he counted, ever switching between her and Brett. His frown deepened. "One kilo two hundred.

Where's my fuckin' metal?"

Brett reached in the bag too and whisked his hand through the bars. He looked at Susan. "He told you two kilos."

She shrugged, her cheeks going pale inside the rumpled collar. "That's all I have left."

He extended his hand to barely hold off Ricky. "Where's the rest?"

"I sold it. I bought a farm."

"You bought what?"

She bumped her head against the back of the bench as Ricky roared and dashed the pistol to her face, to which Brett intervened again and Ricky switched the gun between them.

"Put the gun down! Just put the gun down!" Brett squinted, hand at his temple, till Ricky lowered the gun a notch, then he turned to Susan, jolting her out of her crying. "Susan! What about what I left for Tara?"

She turned her distraught face slowly. "I cashed out and invested it. He gave me a good price"—she shivered with her words.

"Whom did you sell it to? When?"

"To the dealer you told me about. Over a month ago."

He turned to Ricky. "It's not far. Some must still be there, most likely."

Ricky fired his eyes over at him, then at Susan, then at him again and twitched the gun's muzzle at her hands. "Hold 'er." As Brett complied, he laid the gun on his lap and grabbed the tape roll. She sobbed, shaking anew as he taped her mouth, then he ran the tape around her head and over her mouth again, below the begging eyes.

Brett let go as her fingers barely ticked under the tape. "Tara will be fine. I promise," he said, when Ricky pushed her down her on her side. "Hey! Can you just—"

Ricky shoved the bag in his arms and grappled her legs to tape them up. "Go wait in your fuckin' car."

He struck the elevator cabin wall and clenched his jaws while feeling his knuckles over. He swung to the doors and checked on Tara as "Level B-five" sounded off. She seemed to have cracked her eyes open, now turned toward the window, although still leaning quiet in the corner of the seat.

"Where is Mommy?" she said when he reached the car and helped her out.

He held her hand as they walked away. "Mommy… went to get a few things. Maybe she's coming with us on the road trip."

"Yay! And Daddy Clarens too?"

"Uhh… I don't know. He's busy I think." He switched aisles back toward the elevators. "But let's get you a good snack first!"

As she hopped along, he nudged his head the other way to mutter into Ricky's feed. "Meet you at B-one in thirty. I need to get her a sleep drink, don't trust the other crap." He dropped the volume over the yelling reply, then kept on working his fingers through the tiny map in his graph. "Let me in you piece of shi…"

Rushing out on the hub floor, he snatched her with one arm and headed to the public access point, where the shell guide beamed up. He held her to one side and bent over to mutter into the guide. "Child sleep drink."

"Not available," the guide returned below the search query, to which he then tried "child sleep candy", then "child sleep pill." He felt his forehead as the map stayed inanimate.

"Can I help, sir?"

He turned to the voice. It was the same security staffer, now clearly revealing his eyeset in a slight blue. He pulled a courtesy smile while glancing at the query, then at Tara hanging in Brett's arm.

"Just learning. Thanks, though"—Brett smiled back, bringing Tara around. As the staffer bobbed and backed off, he lifted Tara over the guide and flew his hand through the shell's mapping, pointing aloud for her the first few venues catching his eye. He ruffled her hair and stepped out in the street. "Make that D-one, D-one," he spelled for Ricky as he turned the corner.

"You call Mommy? "Tara said.

"No, a friend. I think he's coming too."

She showed her small, gapping teeth through the pinkish smile as she pushed against his chest. He rolled his lips in tight in a smile of his own, then strayed from her eyes and ran her bangs back under his palm. He stopped and skipped his sight from one building to another under the shell. He paused over the next garage hub across the street, then raced that way.

"Bi-work fitness," he called into the access point inside and watched the gym's downtown location twinkle up, near the boulevard side. He opened it up. His wooer was there on his working day. He called him, to his awe. "Listen," he cut through his new question, "I need a huge favor."

———

With each back and forth stroke of the brush, the varnish spread new life over the sanded walnut. Two tiny air bubbles in it, the thicker trail drifted lower down the side of the pear-shaped handrail, but Clarens stroked it over before it could sin. He aimed backward with his foot for the next step down, dipped the brush anew, then brought the riches over the wood and glanced at the new handrail shine up the stairway and along the edge of the mezzanine. The slow milonga's piano dropped into the background at the honk of the truck. He ducked his head to peek out the window under the porch eave and waved at the builder in the front seat as the truck left the courtyard. When he reached the lower landing of the stair, he checked the time, pitched the brush inside the can slot, and sat on the step to review his mail. Atop the array, Susan's old message blushed small. He played it again. "Made the meeting here… So sorry. You will understand…" she typed in, her eyebrows creasing slightly. Clearing her throat, she brought her palm to her lips, where the message froze on the close-up.

He picked up his teacup from the higher tread and, his whiskered smile on, he walked to the kitchen for a bergamot refill. Out by the greenhouse, sleet glossed over the yellows on the lower branches of the beech tree, still. He called her back once more, but she didn't pick up. "Hey, barefoot farmer here"—he smiled in—"wondering when you girls plan to get back. No rush, just to know if you come swimming tonight." He flashed his hand open, then thrust forward from the edge of the counter, but idled his sight on the nook wall. Next to the window, the early Dome Lake painting hung large in the meager daylight. He went to it and lifted it off the hook. He tried out two new spots for it along the way to the dining area, where he eventually swapped it with the sheep farm picture on the wall surrounding the house core and facing out toward the windows. He grasped the sides of the frame to let it down on the new hook. Up close, the pier railing, bright pennants and shirts, peachy round faces, all vanished into the paintbrush strokes. With two steps back and the westerly light casting over, the small foaming waves rapped the sand and the blithe voices filled the boundless room.

He rushed to the kitchen, where the teacup was still warm, then back to the lower stair landing in the main room. He had varnished the remaining handrail down to the floor post when the call came through. From the car service. His car was repaired and ready for auto-delivery to the village parking on the main road, or by truck all the way to the farm first thing in the morning. He confirmed the morning option, then twitched up the dripping brush that he had stilled in his hand. It had not dripped anywhere on the stair, and the lone drop had instead fallen inside the rim of his cup by the step riser, with the amber dot growing over the remaining tea. "Thank you," he murmured, and then finished off the rounded end of the rail. He walked up the stair to the mezzanine to feel the handrail's fine grit along the span to the side wall. It was ready for the second coat. Now at twenty past three o'clock. He stared over the soft shadows on the floor below, then turned the milonga down.

# 26

"The one in the corner," Brett mumbled, shoulder to shoulder with Ricky on the descending escalator. "I could knock on the door after he closes, at seven. My kid's set till—"

"We wait for no seven," Ricky said, as they stepped onto the lower level of the shell. He kept his hands in his pockets and his head slightly down as they approached the dead end of the street, scouring the corner storefront from under his overhanging brows. He snatched the bag from Brett and hung it on his shoulder while slipping his gun in it.

"For God's sake. Just don't pull it out in the store, remember?"

Inside was its usual quiet. Two youngsters gazed at the collection of wood boat models, the background sportscast played on. A step ahead of Ricky, Brett crossed toward the back of the store, where he cleared his throat.

Munching on something, Vitaly came out from behind the armoires and brightened up. "Must be a darn good store!" He chuckled, wiping his hand down the side of his paunch.

Sparing a smile back, Brett touched knuckles with him. "Hey Vit."

"My friend, traveled the world and back?"

"Well... yes and no," he said, as Ricky stepped up and placed the bag on the counter between them.

Under Vitaly's watch, Ricky split the bag open, creased the sides halfway down, then slipped his hand under the grip of the pistol at the bottom of the bag, the muffled barrel toward Vitaly and his finger on the trigger. He glared at him and nudged his head to the side. "Tell kids to leave. And nothing stupid, ehh."

Vitaly looked at him, then at Brett, then back at him and chuckled, stooping closer over the bag. "Is this a real Beretta?"

Before he could touch it, Ricky pulled the gun's slide and let it snap back, then held the ejected round in his palm and pushed the bag against Vitaly's belly. "Close the fuckin' store."

The redness in his cheeks gone, Vitaly looked at Brett, who stayed tight-lipped and looked down. He ran the closing call and uttered a shriveled "Tomorrow" to the insistent youngsters, then choked but complied to make the inviting gesture toward the backroom and led Ricky and Brett over.

The first safe was stuffed with small bags of period eyewear and phones, sports medals, and silvery necklaces. Prompted by a hard blow to his spleen, he opened the second safe in the opposite wall panel, then wobbled back and grasped the desk corner to keep standing, heaving loud.

Ricky switched his gun to his other hand and ransacked the shelves of the safe to litter more of the same small valuables onto the floor. A thumb-sized flat piece skipped out of its wrap, shining off-white. Eyes on Vitaly, he knelt to dash his hand through the trinkets, but did not uncover any more bars. He stood up and stepped to him, working his lips tight. "Where is it?"

"That's all I have, I swea—"

With another jab to the spleen he felled him, groaning, to his knees, then withdrew his foot to let Vitaly's saliva drip onto the floor instead. As Brett grabbed Vitaly under his arms to lift him back on his feet, he pointed the gun at them. "Where's my fuckin' metal?" he lashed out, and zipped a bullet into the desk.

Brett struggled to keep the shivering Vitaly upright. "Vit, the bullion from Susan Connelly, about a month ago… Where is it?"

Vitaly gaped at him.

"Long story. He's not kidding."

"A-at the bank."

With Ricky one close step behind, they walked off the street belt and crossed toward the bank entrance. The inside looked unattended and the doors were locked, now at ten past four, and Vitaly declined the after-hour's assistance at the sign-in, the front end of the bag pointed into his back. They walked in, then by the lifeless, floating counter on the way to the safe deposit boxes.

Bobbing his sweaty forehead down, Vitaly fingered the passphrase in his palm on a new try. They edged backward in their same awkward formation so he could drag the seemingly heavy case out of the box, then they walked to the wall shelf where he unlocked it. Ricky pricked him to step aside and, right hand always in his shoulder bag, he lifted the lid of the case and peeked in, then brought a minted bar up to his eyes and sneered. He put it back in and raked his hand through the bullion, which chinked full. He clacked the lid back closed, rested his bag next to the case on the shelf, then gritted his teeth as he heaved the case into the bag with his free arm.

"Whoa, whoa"—Brett frowned—"it's like ten kilos in there!"

"Shut up"—Ricky glared, then snarled at him as Brett didn't back down. Pistol atop the case, he jolted the bag onto his shoulder and poked his chin out. "Go!"

They walked back toward the lobby, when a voice broke above the quiet street droning, from somewhere behind the partition wall. As the silhouette closed in behind the translucent resin, Ricky grasped Brett's arm to shove him into Vitaly and prod them both into a U-turn, then into stooping over the convenience shelf. He scuffed the outside of the bag with his free hand and mumbled numbers as the steps rapped closer on the floor.

"Yes, I'm sure… In his bay window, tanning," the woman added and paused again, seemingly on a call. She lowered her voice abruptly as she walked into the safes area behind them, but she didn't sound any less familiar. "Yes, from my apartment, back then. Is that the point?"

Brett peeped back at her over Vitaly's shoulder.

Ricky had also recognized the bank manager. "One bank in your whole fuckin' Taj Mahal, ehh?" he hissed at Vitaly, scuffing the bag over.

"I don't know, I could check the live log," she continued, slowing her steps in front of the wall grid, and paused with the thin buzz of a safe's door opening, at which Ricky prompted Vitaly and Brett to leave again.

"Yes, it's empty," she said. "Wait. Tell him that it just looked like something he should know."

At the buzz of the door closing, Brett glanced back and frowned as the number fifty-two read clear. "She can't do that!" he muttered as she turned around and he turned his head also to keep walking, but her steps behind slowed to a stop.

Ricky slowed the three of them too, with only Vitaly wheezing through the silence, and brought his head between them from behind. "You move, you die," he whispered to Vitaly's ear, then he sounded like stepping back and running the bag's zipper.

"Do I know you?" the manager's voice skipped a little.

"Shut up and smile," Ricky muttered, "or I put one in your bony face."

Brett grasped his forehead, searching between the floor lines. Next to him, Vitaly's wheezing grew unbearably loud. "Walk," he heard Ricky say, and turned his head again over his shoulder, enough to glimpse the manager's stunned look.

She looked back at Ricky as her voice dried to a rasp, and

she swallowed to speak. "You know that... security will be here in a minute—"

"Shake my hand"—Ricky skimped a smile. Swapping hands inside the bag, he switched it to his left shoulder. "Or they find a dead bitch. Now."

"Please. It's a fire gun," Vitaly shuddered saying.

"What are you doing..." Brett murmured.

"Everybody shut the fuck up," Ricky said, accent swishing in. "Look at me." He stared into her eyes for eyesets. "Point finger to street. The other way. Walk."

The tape creasing in his febrile hands, Brett ran it one more time around the bank manager's ankles and let the trainer's new call go unanswered in his ear.

Ricky watched restive from the passenger seat, when he pitched forward to snatch the tape roll from Brett's hand, pinched the end of the tape between his teeth, and unrolled an arm's length of slack to loop it hard around her calves too with one hand. She fell against Susan, wailing anew.

"Break the law again bitch?" He sneered, grabbing her by her curls, and straightened her up to run a layer over her taped lips and all around the back of her head. "Even hostage they drive you crazy," he grumbled, and tossed the roll below Brett's seat. "Drive to the other car. We take fat man only."

"But—"

"Drive!" he thudded, then cleared his throat and lifted the door enough to shell his spit out. "They'll find them."

He wiped his mouth and tapped the pistol's barrel on his lap as Brett drove out of the parking space. Taped up and eyes bulging, the manager and Susan struggled to sit upright shoulder to shoulder on the rear bench, with Vitaly on Susan's other side snorting heavy and fixating on the floor.

Both spaces next to Susan's car were taken. Brett pulled into one of the side-by-side spaces in the parking tier behind and jumped out to walk over. "Big, big favor," he said hurriedly when the trainer picked up his return call. "Meet me at B-one instead, in five." He wheeled the car into the aisle behind the exiting cars, then pulled next to Ricky's car.

Behind the dark window, Ricky sliced his hand down over his forearm as he voiced over, "No waiting."

Brett turned to the pedestrian aisle and strode to the elevators. He gushed out into the livened hub. Through the step raps and shuffle, Tara's crying steered him to the waiting area across the floor, where the trainer held her hand trying to talk to her.

He raised his head with a theatrical sigh. "Finally! I made friends with more uniforms I've ever dreamed of here," he quipped, nudging his head at the opaque enclosure in the corner.

"What?"

"I just told them she's my boyfriend's material." He smiled as Brett lifted Tara in his arms. "For once."

Queasy, Brett glanced around and started walking away. "Listen, I owe you. Got to go."

"Wait"—the trainer hustled after him. "You're all right guy?"

"Yeah, you know…" Brett threw over his shoulder, nearing the elevator. "Wife stuff"—he winced from the cabin, as the trainer's face brightened outside the closing doors.

"Call me."

"Will do."

With Tara in one arm, he checked for Ricky's live ping as they zoomed to two levels under, where the sole other self-driver stepped out, then he dashed his finger through the fifth level band.

"Are we going on the road trip now?" Tara asked.

"We are." He pushed the bangs from over her eyes, then fixed on the doors. "We're going on the road trip now."

From the end of the parking tier, he spotted the car door

sliding over its rooftop, then Susan's car door lifting higher next to it. Ricky's cap tipped beside the bank manager's blond locks for mere seconds before both ducked under the rooftops again. He slowed and switched Tara to his other arm, glancing over as Ricky moved Susan to her own car also, then raced again as the door closed down. A twinge bolting through his body, he held Tara tighter against his shoulder as they closed in. "Another friend is coming too," he said to her, and swallowed down his rough throat. "We're playing a game. Who stays quiet the longest, wins." He turned between the cars and slipped her in on the bench as Vitaly goggled over jittery from the other end. He moved her next to him in her harness over the middle spare wheel and clinched it on, then flicked his front feed-pin off while pulling back out as Ricky scanned her for signal. "I'll get Dodo," he patted her knee, but Ricky jerked his seat further around.

"Get the fuck in and drive!"

He bent to glare back at him. "It won't take thirty seconds, please…"

He rushed around Susan's car where, inside, she lay on her side on the floor with her face pressed into the bank manager's back, amid the scattered ringsets and bracelets. They both paused their writhing at the light coming through the open door, and he knelt to grasp her by the shoulders and hold her face to face with him. Behind the tangled hairs her reddened eyes went wide, as his moistened instantly too, and she started jolting and moaning wild, with the other woman following suit on the floor. "Listen!" he mouthed, reaching in his pocket for the torn medal envelope from the pawn store, and brought it to her face. "Track Tara, to the border. Don't tell anyone or he—" He slashed his hand through the air and slipped the piece of paper with the tracking number in her pocket as her moaning slowed, then whispered before the tape on her mouth, "We can still make it. Come with me." Her eyes startled, she burst into muffled howls, when he laid her back down, tore the tape around her wrists halfway through, then grabbed Tara's duck playmate and rushed back.

"They'd fallen on it!" he griped at Ricky's roaring, then landed the plush toy in Tara's lap and felt her hand and under her bracelet while grabbing the steering wheel with his other hand.

Fixating him, Ricky seized Brett's lost feed-pin between his fingernails, then watched him tip it back on as they wheeled behind the exiting cars down the aisle. He lay lower in his seat, ever turned in, with his right hand under the hem of his jacket.

"Daddy," Tara mumbled, "he is not nice."

Brett stayed quiet, breaking away from the first hoister line to merge into the next one. "Just pretending. It's part of the game," he said. He glanced over his shoulder and crossed his lips with his finger. "Remember?"

He steered away from the slowly rising decks of the second hoister as well, then the garage login waned off the dashboard as he drifted the car toward the nearly empty self-drive exit. He picked up speed, but the light turned red for the merging lane into the tunnel. He wiped his hand on his pants, then clasped it back on the steering wheel, with Vitaly's loud snorting behind his ears.

"Is Mommy coming?" Tara whispered.

Another car caught up with them in the rear viewer, a burgundy city zoomer, then one other, when the light turned green and they sped into the tunnel traffic.

Ricky scrutinized the rear viewer as they merged into the main tunnel toward the expressway. He nudged the bullion bag out with his feet and swiveled around toward Vitaly, then sniggered and reached over to tap him on the cheek. "Don't die on me, ehh?"

"Is Mommy coming?"

"Give her the pill," he muttered to Brett.

Tight-lipped, Brett kept scouring the road ahead. "That, I

won't do," he muttered back, then said to her, "She's coming, she's behind us. Give Dodo something to eat."

She strove to rise in her harness to look out the back window and asked for her again, to which Ricky lunged at Vitaly and rasped the tape off his mouth.

He speared his finger at him as this one gasped for air. "Keep her busy, or we put it back."

She turned as Vitaly caught his breath and dithered a smile at her. "You win," she said, and watched him gasp again, as they reached daylight.

Brett toggled back to the rear viewer. In another five seconds the navy blue car came out of the dark end of the tunnel, then veered onto the west ramp for the expressway, also. He nudged his chin at the viewer. "Blue car, from the garage stop."

Ricky bolted at it. "They picked up my face..." he gritted, then his nose and upper lip trembled with his native curse.

Brett sped up slightly. "Or mine," he murmured, shifting lanes, which the other car also did behind them.

He glimpsed the interior viewer. Tara picked fish and greens through the toy's graph for her duck. Vitaly paused talking to her and raised his frantic eyes at him.

———

The car was in the same spot in section B-one of the Jefferson shell garage. He tried Susan again, without a live answer.

He traced the rail and touched up the few thirsty spots on his way back upstairs, then walked to the empty middle bedroom. He switched the vintage blinds closed and edged backward into the room corner, arms crossed over the stained sweater as he examined the contour of the luminescent tape around the dark ceiling. He repositioned the stepladder to the opposite corner to peel down the tape on the adjoining sides, then moved around and began reshaping the mockup of the ceiling cutout closer to perimeter.

He fixed his collar and palmed his hair back, and called the school. "This might sound odd," he said with a smile, "but I can't remember when we picked up my partner's daughter today, please. Tara Connelly."

Once she verified Clarens's information, the administrator took a moment offline. "We show Ms. Connelly picked her up at one oh five."

"At one oh five…"

"Yes, one oh five."

"All right. Thank you."

"Sir?" she added. "Weren't you together?"

"We… are, yes."

"Today."

"At school? No."

"Because we show that a man familiar to your daughter reached to her through the playground fence just before dismissal." Without his reply, she continued. "We ask that custodians refrain from doing that and just wait in the foyer."

"Oh. All right."

"Do you want us to investigate? Sir?"

"Uhh… I'll call you back if needed. Thanks again."

He looked away from the hanging stretch of tape and stepped down to amble out of the room, then around the rocking pony and the fern throw that draped the back of the sofa on the mezzanine floor. He set his empty cup down with a gentle knock on the kitchen counter as the lights gleamed up. Between the two graying windows, the bare nook wall looked just as indistinct. He crouched to the sheep farm picture resting against the wall, then took the time to hang it all-level before returning to his spot at the end of the counter. He didn't move again until a call came through.

"Lyn, greetings."

"I know guy, my bad. Been super busy," Lynden shook his

head saying, in his office chair. "What's with the dark? Power out in the woods?" He chuckled, though Clarens just looked left and right and called up the lights.

"No, just… stepped in here for a snack."

"Chef's not home, huh?"

"Not yet. What's up?"

"Guy, listen. None of my business. I mean, not that it's not my business too, for my bud, right?"—he grinned, then pinched his lips just as abruptly and turned his palms upright. "Just passing on the message," he said, and sighed. "Heslin saw Susan earlier today with some dude. Making out."

Clarens didn't budge, just dropping his sight line a little.

"She says she came over kind of agitated and emptied her bank safe, and then left with him or something," Lynden continued, peeking down too. "Sorry guy. She says she only mentioned it, you know, for your protection."

A long moment into it, Clarens slanted his head. "They've never met…"

"She scoped her from her apartment. Back then."

"Ah." He let his sight drift back down. "How's she doing?"

"Who, Heslin? Great, great, she says."

"Good." He straightened up and walked toward the unlit hallway. "Lyn, can we keep this low-key you think?"

"Hey, it's me." Lynden laid his hands on his chest. "Absolutely."

In the west wing, a haze of daylight clung to the dining area's loaded wall. He replayed Susan's message in his palm. "Made the meeting here... So sorry. You will understand..." He made it larger in the midair. She did seem to twitch her lips in a smile just before bringing her hand over, too quickly to tell. He went around the house core and back upstairs, searching through the thick gray-brown. The middle room was much darker, with the marking tape now a silver sheen around the ceiling. He picked the loose end from up on the stepladder and tried a few points before pressing it down to close the new contour. The mezzanine light now beamed through the door, which he nudged to only a palm open, then he brought the lone chair against the wall, sat down, and leaned his head back as a tear crossed below his temple. He raised his eyes higher, through the indigo inside the silver line.

The feeble chime nicked the darkness. He scrunched his eyes at the glitter in his hand: "Tara's pendant on." He murmured the set's prompt, then sat up and flicked through the mapping. The tracking point pulsed on through the high grounds northwest of Ayland. He checked his car, which tracked far behind, although out of the downtown now. "She wouldn't..." He rose and zoomed in while walking out of the room, though only ghost-imaging came through the overcast skies, then the pendant signal disappeared. It returned within seconds, disappeared again, then came back to stay on.

He called the emergency system. His log remained unconfirmed, a live operator coming on instead.

"Sir, this is the fourth time in four months that this child is being reported missing," she said. "Are you sure?"

"Well, I'm not, but that is the point."

"Are you reasonably sure that her device is current, and that it's in her possession, and that she's not under someone's authorized care, sir?"

"No, I'm not, but— You know, I can probably try one more time."

"Let us know immediately if in any doubt."

He stilled through the new silence, then looked down, felt his thin slacks, and swung his head toward the bedroom door. He rushed downstairs instead, two steps at a time, pulled his boots on, then burst out to the barn hub, gloves and jacket in one hand and the flashlight jouncing in his pocket.

Ears up, Leaf was watching the door already as the lights came on. It snorted short while he rushed closer and zipped his jacket on. "Leaf boy…" He felt its forehead down, and slid the stall gate open. "You and I, huh?" He flattened the underlayment on its back, fastened the saddle on, and pulled the horse out the main barn door.

It was dry, the scattered whites now firming into ice. He switched his set to his wristband and pulled his gloves on, then mounted Leaf on a second try. He leaned to pat it on the shoulder as it snorted out a plume over the dusky western skies, then cued it into trotting down the driveway and brought up the glistening map in his palm. The two points pulsed on, the first one approaching Kierwoods.

————

Tara's giggle broke through. "I didn't know that!" As Brett looked in the interior viewer, she stayed turned toward Vitaly and looked down her nose at her pendant to push the sail back low into the tiny boat's hull. "And… like this?"

"I—I like it better the other way," Vitaly babbled.

"Like… this?"

"Yes, th-this way it looks like sailing."

She giggled again and nipped the mast in and out once more.

"Shut up!" Ricky thudded over his shoulder, to her twitching back in her harness and Brett seizing his arm.

Biting his lip, Brett glanced ahead to veer around another car. "Her father's still around."

Ricky jerked his arm off his grasp, glaring, and swung his head back again. "Maybe I shut your mouth, fat man," he said, and returned to scrutinizing the rear viewer.

Brett reached back to feel Tara's knees. "I'm sorry. He's… not happy."

"Why?"

He wiped his forehead with the back of his hand and flicked his eyes between the viewer and the freeway. "Because we're late."

Ricky swayed his frown left and right over the shrinking lanes behind. "It dropped back. Move to auto lane."

As Brett complied, the girl turned to Vitaly and his fretting smile.

"You are happy," she said, and appeared to pick at the tape around his legs, then mirrored him and brought her knees together and hands behind her.

The blue car dropped farther back and moved over from the fast lane to let another car pass, then it veered beyond the row of light posts on the splitting freeway.

Ricky swiveled his seat in once more and lurched at Vitaly to poke him in the belly, extracting a couple of gasps. "Happy, happy! You'll be free, ehh?" he said and sniggered over Tara's brimming giggles. "No worry, insurance pays. I send you pictures"—he pinched Vitaly's cheek, ignoring her hush, and slapped him lightly. "And big medal, ehh?" He turned his grin to Brett, who stayed taut, then he peeked at the mapping. "You're a good man. Everybody is a good man. You're a good man, I'm a good man, Brett is a good man, that man is a good man," he bumped his chin at the outside saying, ever scouting the surroundings. "But…" He rolled his fist out into a hand and back, eyes on Vitaly again, then raised his finger sober. "I keep my word. I keep my word." He paused, but not to the new hush, and twirled back around, as Brett had already zoomed into the rear viewer.

Having shifted behind the cars in the middle, the passing car reemerged in the left lane and approached fast. It was a police vehicle. It slowed at just over fifty meters behind and began trailing them.

In the whizzing new silence, Tara began bouncing her feet against the wheel under her, keener and keener. "Daddy, when is Mommy coming?" she said, then didn't wait long to ask again.

"Shut up!" Ricky roared, then at Brett too.

As the child began to cry, the graph started flashing bright blue over the center of the dashboard along with the voice prompting to pull over. Ricky gripped the pistol in his lap and plucked off the muffler, then scuffled inside the console and shoved the gun's magazines in his pockets. He whisked the receiver off and stretched the mapping over instead, following it through with the gun's muzzle. He poked his chin at the windshield. "Go!"

They sped up, the blue lights beaming into the rear viewer. Brett pressed the steering wheel to stiffen his arms, but that didn't stem the shivers. He thrust his arm back to check on Tara's harness. Her crying had withered out. "Two exits"— Ricky held his fingers up at him, his voice not quite matching the strained mouth and riot in his eyes. They weaved widely through the slowing cars in front, the police vehicle keeping the same distance behind, as if they hauled it along on a tight chain. The new exit sign shone by, with less than two kilometers left to the next one: "Kierwoods County Preserve." Ricky descended his hand through the mapping hills to land it with a tremor on the dashboard. "Faster..." he mouthed, eyebrows creasing to new depths. The car responded without delay, but the high-pitch whistling persisted, even when he maxed the brakes to squeeze by the ramp divider. Swaying back and forth between the map and the outside, Ricky crooked his hand into the lower right corner of the windshield. They merged skidding onto the crossing road and rammed the side of the car into the passing vehicle, which honked loud— shrieking loud—to which the whistling stopped and Tara's crying flooded his ears anew.

He worked the wheel fast to recover as Ricky roared "Drive! Drive!" in his ear and the police car, having flown over, turned to fly back toward them over the narrowing two-way road, flashing on. "Where to?" he yelled back at him.

"Fuckin' drive! Three ks!"

They swerved around the landing vehicle and managed to

pull away a little on the first straight, then the lights behind closed in fast as the now empty, dark road started winding uphill, with Vitaly fallen on the floor and groaning over Tara's crying at each turn. Ricky slammed the blinding rear viewer off and craned his neck over the dashboard to look up and curse at the police vehicle, which flew narrowly over with its wings deployed. The car jolted under the first stun beam, but the motors didn't stop. Through another screeching turn, Ricky stuck his arm out and fired a quick series at the police vehicle, which suddenly dropped behind.

"Right, right!"—he stabbed his other hand at the right corner of the windshield once more.

Skidding onto the gravelly parking pad, they scraped against the small shelter and made the turn onto the side trail, which then narrowed through the flashing-blue boulders and shrubs. Ricky worked the controls to raise the car, as they hardly slowed, but the float system was gone. Between the jolts and sweat drops, Brett glimpsed Tara in the interior viewer, as she trembled, calling for Mommy. He blinked quickly to contain the flooding in his eyes, when a low boulder cut into the trail. They bounced on two wheels, then razed several shrubs before bouncing high again and flipping over twice, then one more time to come to a slanted stop.

He raised his head slowly as Ricky cursed. Tara was screaming but appeared to be fine in her harness, while the police vehicle had landed on the trail a stone's throw away, beaming two spotlights on them through the cloud of dust. The car's power was on, but they must have landed onto some thick brush since the wheels didn't find any grip. He let his shoulders down. "How stupid…"

Blocked by Vitaly wedged into the space behind him, Ricky kept jerking his seat around as the loudspeaker outside sounded off crisp.

"Get out of the car, one at a time, with your hands over your head! One at a time or you will get impaired!"

As the message repeated, he dragged Vitaly out on his feet and, staying glued behind him, brought the gun to his head. "You get out!" he roared back, his steam fleeting in the freezing air, then aimed and shattered one spotlight with one shot, to both Vitaly and Tara screaming. "All of you!" He took out the second light too, then squinted into the new beam casting from above and yanked Vitaly along to find shelter against the tilting car. "Get the fuck out now! I got two more in here!" he thundered, and fired his gun into the ground, or Vitaly's foot, as Vitaly shrilled his lungs out.

Hunching tighter over Tara, Brett peeped out the rear window. Two officers appeared to step out of the ever-flashing police vehicle and duck behind the open doors.

"Don't shoot!" one shouted over Vitaly's howls. "Let everyone go and you're free to go."

Sniggering into Vitaly's jumbled hair, Ricky stepped on his foot, to more pain "Move out now! Throw guns here." He didn't stop. "Guns!"

The officers stood out slowly and threw their guns between the cars, as he switched between them and the spotlight hovering above. He thrust his arm up to aim at it and fired a deafening series. When Brett raised his head again, twilight fringed atop the black woods, with the spotlight gone and gunpowder smoke hitting his nostrils. Ever shielded behind Vitaly, Ricky hobbled out to the two guns as the drone snapped branches, crashing in the woods beyond. He shattered a flashing light yelling another curse and briefly let go of Vitaly to hurl the guns away, then hobbled backward with him to the car and grabbed the bag from beside Brett. "To the other car. Move!"

With Tara in one arm, Brett climbed down to the ground, then the four of them advanced toward the police car. A step behind them, Ricky took turns pointing his pistol around as the two mute officers moved away from their vehicle, when a new set of headlights flashed through from down the trail.

No car was coming from either side of the narrow, unlit road, so Clarens squeezed Leaf into trotting across. They cantered again on the continuing, gravelly trail, which began rolling shallow with the terrain. A park trail marking appeared to hang on the larger shrub ahead, and indeed the colors shone in the flashlight beam. It was still the green trail, just like his mapping showed, but it led northwest and away from the yellow trail where Tara's tracker had stopped. He pocketed the flashlight to grab the rein back and steered Leaf off the trail and into the patch of woods aside. He lunged to the horse's neck to pass under the overreaching branch, then stroked it below its alerted ears as it moved on rustling through the frosted leaves. He tipped the graph off to a dot inside his sleeve and blinked wide to bring his eyes to reading into the new darkness. "And suddenly, three hundred years back. Or four. Which probably never existed…" he murmured over the cadenced rustle. "Yet, they're a given. As far as change is a given." He dropped one rein and reached for the light again. Pearly white, a stretch of sleet wedged out between the spreading shrubs. It crackled under Leaf's hooves as he let it follow it along. "How come I never change, Leaf? Does anyone? Does she?" He twitched his shoulders up with the cold shiver. "Perhaps you do all exist after all." He looked up and pulled the reins as a silent flyer passed low across the dim sky to disappear with a distant thump. He stayed turned that way, while Leaf kept snorting and fretting sideways. "But, if she exists… she wouldn't change this way, would she?"

He turned the horse back onto the white stretch and tapped it into trotting. However faint, the next pop didn't sound like the crackling under its hooves. He stretched his arm to let the map glimmer out again, with less than five hundred meters spanning to the tracker. The ghosting showed two cars and several moving bodies, while his own car had left the road and was closing in from the south. He switched his eyes to the dark ahead, although unable to discern even the branch that grazed his face. Thrown off balance, he dropped the reins to try to grasp the edge of the saddle while his foot slipped through the stirrup too, and he fell awkward on the ground. The horse dragged him on, then responded to his call and stopped. He felt the back of his head, then jiggled his hanging foot slowly out of the stirrup and rolled over to kneel, scooping the ice from inside the neck and back of his jacket. He rose and stroked Leaf up close on his nose, then rummaged through the sleet and low brush for the missing flashlight under the glimmer of his graph. He gave up on it and climbed back in the saddle. The white faded out once they were in the open and then they trotted on dry ground, only minding the large boulders on the way, till the shrubs picked up again. At eighty meters away.

A man's voice scraped through. Low over Leaf's neck, he glanced back at the mapping. His car had stopped near the other two. It looked like he was headed to somewhere in the middle, if he went around the left side of the rocky knoll in between. He did and, coming out, he peeked past the slope of the knoll, as Susan stood in the headlights of his car with two policemen and their vehicle on her other side.

"Susan?"

As Leaf pushed on, hooves clonking atop the slanted rock, Brett, Tara, and two other men came into view also, but too briefly before the pain tore through his shoulder with the bang. He couldn't grasp the saddle. In fact his fingers hardly tried this time and he just fell backward off the startled horse, foot still hooked in the stirrup. He hit the rock hard and, past another blow, didn't hear Susan scream anymore.


Ricky turned his gun on the officer who had lurched

forward, as Susan ran after the horse and Tara twirled out of Brett's arms to run between them, after her. With Brett lunging at him, Ricky missed the officer and scored the dirt instead. He dropped the gun as they both hit the ground along with Vitaly, but he was the first one to recoil on his knees and jabbed Brett with a hard fist in his face. "No drunk no more, boy!" he jeered and clicked his knife out to spear it at Brett's neck and make the rushing officers halt again. Ever moaning, Vitaly wobbled up on his feet, and Ricky leaped behind him to hold his knife at his throat instead. Peeking left and right in the new car lights, he felt the ground around with his feet but didn't find his pistol.

"Tara!" Brett called, struggling to rise.

Ricky dropped Vitaly to pick up the bag and pitched the glistening blade at one officer. "You fool," he growled at Brett, and landed a violent kick in his guts which made him coil back down, choking. He was sprinting to Susan's car when Brett could raise his head again, while the fallen officer grasped his thigh in pain and his partner hustled a rifle out of their vehicle. He turned and aimed, but held his shot as Ricky shoved the bank manager's face in the car's window.

"Go! Shoot the bitch!" his yelling came out the opposite, open door. He kept yelling it and mopping her taped-over mouth across the glass to take shelter behind her. He clung to her blond hair as she slipped out through the opening door and as the officer slinked in, until he managed to power up and take off, whirling up gravel and thick dust.

"Tara!" Brett coughed a shout, feeling his abdomen as he rose. "Susan!" He ran by the officer, who had rushed back to his colleague. Ignoring his prompting to stop, he crossed the trail to run after the girl. Two drones whizzed the other way. A scant light twinkled from afar.


"Clarens…" the voice called his name again. A woman's

voice, closer this time, but still an echo behind the drowning white, which looked like long, glittering hair, equally split between right and left, when the voice became more youthful with the blinding light. He couldn't blink, or turn, or lift his hand to cover his eyes. He tried again but, other than for the heat enfolding the back of his head, he stayed inert. The light moved to the lower right, under the wide, glowing eyes. Green-glowing eyes. Susan's eyes.

"Clarens!" she screamed, tears flowing and hands tight on his temples. "Stay with me! Clarens!" She dashed her gaze over his body, then at the crying girl beside her, then out somewhere, then back to him and pulled her hand up to scream into the light inside it, before smudging the tears down her cheek, and the blood, beneath the black wisps of hair.

He succeeded edging his hand higher to touch her arm. "Hey…"

She grabbed it tight. "Yes! They're coming, they're coming!"

He eased the corner of his mouth. "Pretty good exit, I'd think."

"What? What…?"

She screamed his name again, but not as loud, and appeared to bring the light back onto his face. Her wisps mingled into the deep indigo above.

# 27

The nurse rapped Brett's arm rapidly with his finger, only higher up. "Feeling anything?"

"No."

He administered another dose, just below the shoulder, then winced slightly as he glanced at Brett's bandaged nose and the bruises and scratches on his body, and nodded at the two police staff standing by.

The nearer staffer stepped to the cart beside Brett's bed and checked the steel diaphragm that wrapped tight around Brett's forearm, where the arm entered the safe container. She made a few steps back, and so did the other, then she began operating the robot inside the container from her graph, while Brett breathed deeply and looked the other way. A minute later, she stepped close again to release the diaphragm and slide the cart and the container down his bracelet-free hand.

"Thank you"—he exhaled, eyelids halfway down.

"Sir, are you…" the other police staffer said, slowing to read off his set, "Luis Nicolai Thomassef of Tencun City, Belines? Or"—he looked in his other hand—"Brett Daniel Falco of Kewan, the FSA?"

"No, that was…" Brett swayed his head to the side, then spoke up. "I'm Brett."

The staffer took turns between looking at him and at his second set. "The detective will be here in forty-five minutes," he added, and opened the door to help his colleague out of the room with the explosive disposal equipment.

Brett rose higher in bed. "Is it possible to see them, please?" he said to him, while the nurse returned to pierce the post-anesthetic impulse in his arm.

The staffer looked away to query his unit and nodded curt, then waited for the nurse to help Brett put his shirt back on. Out on the corridor, two officers walked him several doors down, to where one of them knocked and went in, then they both stayed a few steps behind as Brett advanced into the deep room. Looking out at the lights in the hospital courtyard, Susan didn't turn. In the bed beside her chair, Tara snored over the mint edge of the quilt.

"Susan…"

He stepped closer. Dry-eyed, she kept staring out and remained mute, only bringing the crumpled tissue to her reddened nose once. He stood by the end of the bed and turned his head to look out too, then brought his tingling arm to his chest with his other hand to cross arms.

A nurse entered the room. "Ms. Connelly?"

As she approached, Susan turned her bruised cheek slowly.

"Would you like to spend the night here or at your place? Someone would stay with you there as well."

She nodded and looked down at Tara.

"At your place, ma'am?"

She nodded silent again and rose, then slipped her hands under the quilt to grapple Tara in her arms and lift her gently over her shoulder. She gathered the hanging quilt under her and stepped around Brett, who followed her to the door.

"Just to the lobby," he murmured to the officers, who then shadowed him down the corridor.

The lobby of the emergency ward was inanimate, with a handful of people waiting. Standing in the wide aisle by the seating recess, the blond bank manager spoke to a man and another woman. Brett lowered his head to feel his nose as he walked on, when the woman turned her head this way and looked at Susan. The manager stopped talking and she and the man turned their heads too. As the leading nurse passed them by, the woman stepped forward, gaze fixed on Susan.

"You know, it takes more than a bosom to be a woman," she said stern, as Susan lifted her eyes at her. "If you people could ever understand."

"Hey, she had nothing to do with it," Brett crossed.

The woman switched her large blue eyes to him and stared him down, as Susan moved on, then she turned to the blond and her male companion. "Let's go, I'm tired," she brushed by the man, saying, and walked down the aisle.

Brett looked at the man again, who had been the manager's same companion when he had run into them both several months earlier, in the garage accident.

As the three of them glanced at one another, the other woman turned and stepped aside to let the nurse and Susan walk by. "Heslin dear, we'll see you tomorrow."

Brett stopped at the officer's prompt and called Susan, but she didn't react. He curbed his step forward as she walked out the sliding doors, while the officer watched him steadily.

From the other side, Heslin's companion spoke loud. "Hey there, sorry about that…"

Brett glanced at him, looked out the glazing, then back at him.

"If you need a good attorney"—the man nodded and pressed his lips—"I'm in the business, with Ketner and Baum." Next to him, Heslin turned slightly to grimace a smile under the large bandage on her cheek, her other arm hanging in a restrainer below the chest. As Brett glimpsed out resigned once more, the man reached inside his jacket. "Here's my office. Call me in the morning," he said, flipping the physical token between his fingers and handed it to Brett. "It's important that you don't say anything without your attorney," he added, swaying away, as the other woman turned in the doorway to him.

"Lynden!"

Through the icy rain, the little bird darted into the evergreen bush before the window, then stuck its tiny brown head out just as another gust ruffled the bush to the core. It flew out and to the top of the window where, centimeters out in the rough, it fluttered its wings against the wet glazing without finding any ledge or shelter, and then darted away. Brett lowered his sight through the hasting grays again. His eyes mirrored faint in the glass, above the close shave. The state flag hologram shimmered large atop the pole in the building's drop-off, surpassing the elements.

He turned at the hiss of the opening door, as the attorney raised his head over his work on the table.

"Mr. Falco." The detective paused next to his colleague to look over, then nodded at the table. "Let's sit."

Brett pulled out a chair slowly, across from him. On his side, the attorney rested his elbows on the table and nodded a tight smile over.

Once he adjusted his graph to his liking, the detective peered through it for a long minute, shoulders stooping below the short-trimmed white beard. "June nineteen… Sorry it took this long," he said to the attorney. "Trying to get anything from the Tencun PD is like trying to get a sandbox from the moon"—he passed a smile at his colleague. "Or Saturn, rather," he added, and glanced at Brett too before backtracking to his material. He poked his finger through the graph and switched to the attorney again. "Any additions to this?"

Palms out, the attorney shuffled brisk in his chair.

"All right, just a couple of things," the detective said, then began to skim through, nudging his head left and right and mumbling to bridge sentences over. "Then, they say, you've sold the bar at the main exchange… where you had previously attempted to sell a large quantity, from here in Ayland, through an intermediary named Vitaly Penske, which we knew… at which time you were traced down by the acquaintance of the now fugitive Ricky Durand, who was a regular at the exchange, in the course of his auto parts business with several body shops around Ayland, etcetera. And who," he picked up lower down, "being tipped of your substantial holdings in Ayland, and of your location after the motel robbery, and appropriation of your car… coerced you into physical captivity on his premises… as evidenced on your body and noted by the two officers alerted by the fugitive's cousin Vivian Durand, and who attempted to liberate you, on May fourth, 8:20 p.m." He paused a little longer, then looked at Brett. "So, he knew of two or nine kilos?"

His back straight in the fitted sky-blue sweater, Brett edged a shrug. "I don't know. I only mentioned my remaining two kilos."

"Right, right… Did Mr. Penske offer you a better quote than the official quote, such as a so-called street price?"

"That," the attorney broke in, "is in the recorded transaction."

"Right, of course," the detective said, and returned to reading. "The other thing was… Have you assisted Mr. Ketner with anything at all? Other than with meeting your… counterparts," he said to Brett, raising his hand to hold off the attorney. "Such as with speculation in debt markets, or anything?"

"No."

He rasped another "Right," then coughed to clear his throat and looked out the window. "Talk of time for fieldwork," he threw at his colleague, who murmured a "hmm" and looked out too. He switched to Brett. "Why didn't you mention she's not your natural child, by the way?"

"That was not required," the attorney said.

"Remarkable nonetheless"—the detective kept his nimble

sight on Brett.

With the attorney's stare in the corner of his eye, Brett looked a tad lower, then outside, always staid. The sleet fell down thick, now whipping against the glass, which blurred up some. "I vowed not to tell. For her own good. I just stuck to that," he said, then his view remained blurry through the silence.

The detective appeared to stoop back down and mumbled on under his beard. When he paused next, he sat higher in his chair. "Mr. Falco." He firmed his voice "Have you considered living with your ex-wife and adopted child again?"

The attorney held his hand over the table. "Honestly, detective, we've gone through that so many times—"

"The reason we're asking," the detective said, retracting his graph, "is to know if you need accommodation when you leave the facility. Since your funds might remain unrecovered." He pocketed the large, standalone set and met Brett's searching eyes, then rose along with his colleague. "Mr. Falco, we're sorry for what you went through. You're free to go"—he nodded as Brett rose slowly too. "And I speak for the department to iterate our thanks for saving the life of Officer Darst." His hand extended, he waited for Brett to grasp it, then turned to his younger colleague, who spoke up.

"Should you still consider it, Mr. Falco, we may recommend to the Foreign Office to reinstate your multiple-entries program. We would expect a response by the end of the day," he said and shook Brett's hand too, as the attorney patted Brett on the shoulder.

"Nice perk!"

Brett turned to him and finally squeezed a smile, brows wrinkled and eyes blurring anew, and leaned over for a pound hug. He let go, shaking his head. Having stopped in the same spot in the middle of the room to watch him, the two detectives nodded and left. He laced his hands on his head and looked up, then laughed short at the attorney's mimicked dance move, who then left too.

He rested his hands on his waist and looked across the room, then stepped to the window. The film of warm air stroked his face in front of the large, immaculate surface. A tad farther, the ice pellets dashed across it, always wild.

———

The shutter lifted to let another car roll inside the drop-off, then the plainclothes driver strode across the lobby and rapped away toward the backrooms. Brett looked down at the new message that came in. "Heslin here, untaped!" she wrote next to her beaming shot. She congratulated him for the clearance and offered to trade a flight to the Alliance for the "street smarts" of a local, as she was stuck with a spare ticket. He thumbed to the trainer's last message and froze it on the opening, a street view of the narrow apartment building. "Thanks man," he replied. "I'll let you know."

He glanced at the time, then watched the new foot traffic that crossed the lobby and out. Clear through the drop-off's glass walls, the cars drove out and away on the empty access road. He slid to the edge of the bench and let his head down, bringing his hands over his temples and tight over the ears. He pressed tighter against the rumbling inside and rested his elbows on his knees. He raised his head slowly and exhaled. He edged back, braced his hands beside his thighs on the bench, and pushed himself up thirty more times.

The green Hanjing slowed down before the blocky sculpture at the main road and turned this way. He rose and threw his bag on his shoulder, then walked out to the drop-off pad as the rear shutter lifted for Susan to drive in.

He bent to the opening car door. "Hey."

She glimpsed him, while Tara bounced her furry boots in the backseat.

They drove out and back to the main road, to make the

same left turn.

He looked at her. "How was the drive?"

Dotted with shrunken molds of snow, the roadside was dry. A row of leafless trees looked brittle under the ashen beyond, with minus two degrees showing over the dashboard indeed, above Susan's side-stained coffee cup.

"We take Daddy Clarens now?"

"Tara…" Susan glanced a frown at her in the viewer. "I told you. He went somewhere else."

Tara kept kicking the edge of the seat. "But where?... Why he likes it better somewhere else?"

"Tara. Why don't you play a game? Playdate? Train of Friends?"

She called up the car command and Tara's game of choice, as they reached the freeway ramp. She tipped the auto-drive up to yellow and let her hand hang low on the steering wheel, though never taking her eyes off the next car ahead.

He passed another glance. "Thanks again…"

"Don't." Her chin then pushed out slightly with the quiet words. "I'll never forgive you."

He exhaled and turned his head to his end of the windshield. "Shall I?"

She hit the brakes and glared over, as cars weaved around from behind them and he raised his hands.

They picked up speed again.

The freeway flow gained some through the city outskirts. Below the shooting downtown, the nearest shell lay out bright, its lights on already. It stayed distant however, as they merged south onto the outer ring, then it slipped out of sight when they veered wide onto the new freeway ramp, westbound.

"When are you getting your insurance money?" she said.

"Don't know. As soon as they reset my ID, then liquidate whatever's left. A few weeks, a month?" He looked at her but she kept frowning out. He turned to the windshield again. "I might have a job lead."

She sighed quiet and looked the other way. Her low hair knot brushed back over her crisp ivory collar. "You have a month," she said. "Just don't talk to the neighbors. We're running a business."

The signs flashed by fewer and fewer, and the freeway narrowed down to three lanes. They filmed along the rounded hedge divider to the nimble sounds from the backseat. Buffered in cypress, a one-story eatery went by, then the steppe cleared up all the way to the string of hills rucking the horizon.

"Or I could help around the house," he said. "You know, down some trees, clear the barn." He wisped a smile over, then turned back weary and felt the scar crossing his nose. "What did he have in mind there?"

She let the steering wheel slip slowly through her fingers with the car shifting to the first lane. She dropped her sight over the car hood briefly. "I don't really know."

The exit marker glittered up. They slowed to merge onto the abruptly narrower road, where she grasped the wheel anew. A far, white peak faded in above the nearing hills.

Past a couple of barren ridges, the mossy green thickened up. And then some more into the opening valley, beyond the brightly repainted, period road sign: "Chesterhills, founded 2107." More flecks of color and glass roofs scattered over as they rolled in.

Also by Lucian Leonte
*Ne Nifiri's Far in Noetrea - A Novel and Exploration of Motives*
Versantae, 2007




About the Author

Born in 1968 in communist Romania, Lucian Leonte completed his architectural studies in 1993 in London and then lived in various places between the Pacific and rural France. Nowadays he can be spotted as the chauffeur of his family in a time-anchored New England coastal town. He authored two short films and two novels.

www.lucianleonte.net

www.ingramcontent.com/pod-product-compliance
Lightning Source LLC
Chambersburg PA
CBHW032237010726
47494CB00002B/524